To Shabana

Best wishes

Ginger Cat
Unit 140792
PO Box 7169
Poole
BH15 9EL
United Kingdom

Photo credits: Kirtling Tower, Shakespeare memorial, John Snow memorial, RSC production of *Arden of Faversham* © Alamy; Faversham Moot Horn, Faversham Charter © Faversham Town Council; *Arden of Faversham* Stationers' Register entry TSC/F/0201-Liber B © Stationers' Company of London; Shakespeare coat of arms application © College of Arms MS; Shakespeare draft grant 1, reproduced by permission of the Kings, Heralds and Pursuivants of Arms; portraits of Edward North, Ben Jonson © National Portrait Gallery; portrait of Richard Burbage © Dulwich Picture Library; title page of *Arden of Faversham* first quarto © Huntington Library; *Arden of Faversham* woodcut © Bridgeman Images; author photo © Elena Kravchenko; 80 Abbey Street, Anthony Aucher memorial plaque, excerpts from Faversham wardmote book © GD Harper; excerpts of John Stow manuscript (HARL MS 542) & Holinshed's *Chronicles* (9IOL.1947.b.164 pp1062) © GD Harper, with kind permission from the British Library Collection.

British Library Cataloguing in Publication Data. A catalogue record for this book is available from the British Library.

Email: gdharper@gdharper.com

Printed and bound in Great Britain by Clays Ltd, Elcograf S.p.A

Typeset in Caslon

ISBN 978-1-7396778-3-1

ARDEN

A NOVEL
by

GD HARPER

Arden

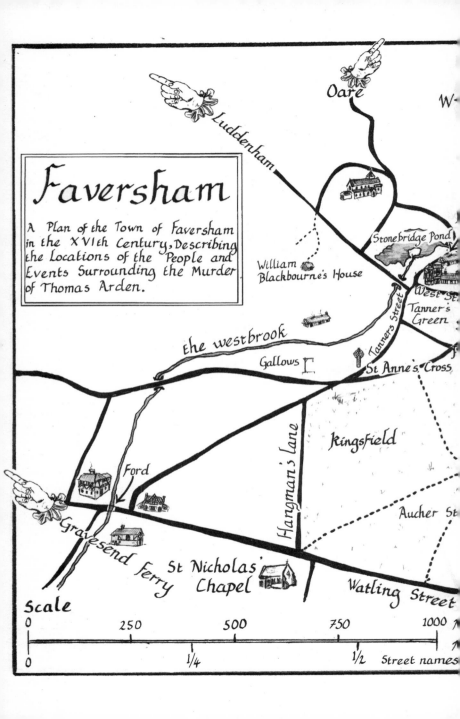

Faversham

A Plan of the Town of Faversham in the XVIth Century, Describing the Locations of the People and Events Surrounding the Murder of Thomas Arden.

Oare

W-

Luddenham

Stonebridge Pond

William Blackbourne's House

West St.

Tanner's Green

Tanner's Street

the westbrook

Gallows

St Anne's Cross

Hangman's Lane

Kingsfield

Ford

Aucher St

Gravesend Ferry

St Nicholas' Chapel

Watling Street

Scale

| 0 | 250 | 500 | 750 | 1000 |

| 0 | 1/4 | 1/2 | Street names |

E

Faversham Creek

To the Swale

Standard Quay

thorn creek

John Greene's Hop Field

Abbey Street

To John Greene's House

Great Quay

Abbey Gate (Arden's House)

Abbey (site of)

Physic Garden

Shooting Meadow

Parish Church St Mary of Charity

Guildhall

Court Street

Jail

Spring

Market Hall (Built in 1574)

Hog Cross

Deadman's Stile

Preston Street

Preston Parish Church St Catherine

Canterbury

oman Road

...e the ones in use at the time, with modern spellings

The Theatre
(1576 ~ 1597)

The Curtain
(c. 1577 ~ 1627)

...vels Office

Bedlam Hospital

Charnel House

City Walls

Bishopsgate

St Helens.
Will's lodgings 1596

St Mary Le Bow

Leadenhall Street
(John Stow's house)

St Andrew's
Undershaft

Watling Street

St Michael's Priory
(Thomas Arden's
London Lodgings)

Will's Lodgings 1599

London Bridge

To Gravesend

...lobe
(1613)

AUTHOR'S NOTE

This is a work of fiction. However, all the characters are real people and all the historical events and dates are believed to be true, with the exception of the discovery of John Greene's confession, which was invented by the author.

Some scenes have been simplified and characters omitted for dramatic purposes. Modern dating has been used throughout, treating each year as beginning 1st January rather than 24th March, as was the custom at the time of the narrative. Most dialogue and descriptions are imagined, although some are based on documents of the time. The quotes from these documents are accurate, but modern spelling and punctuation have been used and they have been edited for clarity and succinctness, without changing their intended meaning.

Shakespeare's involvement in the play *Arden of Faversham* and the consequences thereof are conjecture, although many experts now believe he is at least part-author. The details of his early years are based on what little is known about him before he became famous, with some events and dates still disputed by historians.

'Shakspere', the most common spelling of the playwright's own signature, is used throughout the novel as opposed to the modern convention of 'Shakespeare', to fit with the notion that, as Will is narrating his chapters, this is how he would pronounce and spell his name. Given that opinions vary as to the order in which Shakespeare wrote his plays, the novel follows the chronology proposed by the renowned Shakespearean expert, Harold Bloom.[1]

1 Harold Bloom, *The Invention of the Human*, Fourth Estate, 1999.

DRAMATIS PERSONÆ

FAVERSHAM AND KENT

Arden, Alice   1519 – 1551 *Wife of Thomas Arden*

Arden, Thomas   1508 – 1551 *Mayor of Faversham*

Aucher, (Sir) Anthony   1500 – 1558 *Thomas's business rival*

Blackbourne, William   *Painter and poisoner*

Black Will   ? – 1552 *Assassin*

Cole, Robert   ? – 1577 *Faversham priest*

Colwell, Agnes   *Faversham gentlewoman*

Dunkyn, Thomas   *Former mayor of Faversham*

Fowle, Adam   *Innkeeper of the Fleur de Lis*

Greene, John   ? – 1552 *Aucher's man and co-conspirator*

Marshall, William   *Faversham mayor after Thomas*

Mosby, Tom   c. 1511 – 1551 *Tailor, Alice's lover*

Pounder, Cislye   ? – 1551 *Tom Mosby's sister*

Mr Prune & Mr Cole   *London grocers*

Saunderson, Michael   ? – 1551 *Thomas's manservant, Cislye's fiancé*

Stafford, Elisabeth   ? – 1551 *Cislye's daughter, Alice's servant*

STRATFORD AND THE NORTH

Greenway, William   *Will's neighbour and London trader*

North, Lady Alice   1500 – 1560 *Mother of Alice Arden*

North, Sir Edward   1496 – 1564 *Step-father of Alice Arden*

Sadler, Hamnet   c. 1562 – 1624 *Stratford friend of Will, baker*

Shakspere, Anne   1556 – 1623 *Will's wife*

Shakspere, John   c. 1531 – 1601 *Will's father, glover and wool trader*

Shakspere, Mary   c. 1536 – 1608 *Will's mother, born Mary Arden*

Shakspere, Will   1564 – 1616 *Playwright, actor and theatre owner*

LONDON

Burbage, James   1530 – 1597 *Theatre owner*

Burbage, Richard   1567 – 1619 *Actor, son of James Burbage, Will's friend*

Greene, Robert   1558 – 1592 *Playwright, Will's jealous rival*

Jonson, Ben   1572 – 1637 *Playwright, Will's friendly rival*

Kemp, Will   c. 1560 – c. 1603 *Actor and clown, Will's friend*

Laneham, John   ? – 1591 *Leader of the Queen's Men*

Nashe, Thomas   1567 – 1593 *Playwright, Will's second collaborator*

Pope, Thomas   ? – 1601 *Actor, Will's friend*

Stow, John   1525 – 1605 *Antiquarian*

Tilney, Edmund   1563 – 1610 *Master of the Revels, official censor*

Tarlton, Dick   ? – 1588 *Member of the Queen's Men, playwright*

Watson, Thomas   1555 – 1592 *Playwright, Will's first collaborator*

Prologue
March 14th 1551

I T IS SAID there had never been a bigger crowd for a burning.

It had passed noon, and the baying throng were growing impatient. There was a huge cheer as the small group was spotted, led by the Sheriff of Canterbury, walking in front of the ox cart that carried the prisoner. Behind were the mayor of Faversham, William Marshall, and the young priest, Robert Cole. Following them were the town's twelve jurats, goodmen of Faversham who had elected Marshall to be mayor only the year before.

It was unusual for the procession to be on foot, but the sheriff had judged that the mood of the crowd was so feral that even the most docile of horses would have become agitated and unpredictable. Although it suggested a loss of dignity and status, the most prudent way to reach the site of the execution was for the dignitaries to walk alongside the cart. This they did with their heads held high, staring impassively forward as they tried to ignore the shouts and the occasional missile from the crowd. As they moved nearer to the execution pyre, the crowd became hysterical and the city's bailiff ordered twenty of his stoutest men who had been at the rear of the procession to shift forward and form two phalanxes, striking the worst offenders with their cudgels to maintain some semblance of order.

The prisoner stepped out of the ox cart and knelt to pray with Robert Cole for a few minutes in front of the stake. He helped her to her feet and moved back, granting her one small final act of dignity by allowing her to remove her own shoes, gown and petticoat, rather than having them stripped from her. Now dressed only in a simple smock, the prisoner was led to the stake and climbed onto the stool that stood in front of it. She remained composed, silent; aloof from what was unfolding around her. Chains were fastened around her body to hold her firm, then her wrists were shackled together behind the stake. The executioner pulled away the stool on which she was standing and, to a huge roar from the crowd, she was left hanging and swaying in the chains, three feet above the ground. Wood, bundled together in faggots, was pushed quickly under her and set alight. The crowd fell silent.

She remained calm, only coughing a little with the smoke, but when the flames reached her feet she lost control and cried out, struggling in her chains. Her fists clenched, her body contorted as the flames shrank the muscles of her legs and arms. The executioner called for more wood to be added, but the sheriff waved his hand, palm downwards. The flames were to take as long as possible to do their work. For over an hour she had to bear this ordeal, her voice becoming rasping and then silent as the skin tightened around her neck. Then she slumped down in the chains, unconscious, spared the agony of her last few moments on earth.

Cole had made a final blessing when the wood had been lit, and his were the only eyes not on the fire as he turned his back and moved through the crowd to seek out John

Ponet, Bishop of Rochester. The two men stood at the back, huddled in conversation. Cole became agitated, and Ponet placed a calming hand on him. A huge cheer went up from the crowd, causing the men to turn to see what had happened. A sudden gust of wind had caused the flames of the fire to roar and the flesh on the left side of the face had melted away, transforming it into a half-skull. But there had been no movement from the body, not even an unconscious involuntary spasm. A smell like roast mutton drifted over the crowd.

After two hours, the fire had achieved its objective. The executioner gave the signal to stack up the wood around the corpse so that every last fragment of flesh was destroyed in a roaring inferno.

Their rage sated, the crowd dispersed.

Chapter One
Will ~ 1586

A WEARY SIGH escaped my lips as I scraped the awl across the deerskin, marking out where to cut. I could never tell how to get the most gloves from a tanned hide, and my stitching skills were better suited to making mittens than sewing fourchettes and quirks. But that mattered little; I was a prisoner of my father's gloving business, bound to it tighter than any stitched seam. And when Anne gave birth to twins, our joy was tinged with worry. Although my father kept our financial condition to himself, I could see from his careworn face that funding a second household was out of the question – but one day soon we would have to leave the family home.

A gnawing emptiness took hold inside my belly as I smelt that Anne was preparing that evening's stew in the room next to me, no doubt with the same marrow bones she had used the night before. One of the servants was chopping the vegetables, cutting the mould off carrots and the soft parts off onions. The last of a sack of rye would provide some substance to the meal, but we would all still go to bed hungry until we could buy another. It could easily be a week, maybe more, before our bellies would feel full again. Hamnet was screaming, partly from hunger, partly because that was his way. I despaired at our wretched life.

The sickly-sweet tang of the cured hide had clung to me like a second skin as I went to work, my mind spinning as I tried to think of ways out of our woeful situation. To my horror, I had been so little concentrating on the task at hand that my scissors had slipped, ruining what had been a fine piece of deerskin. That was the last piece of prepared leather; there would be nothing else to work on until Father approved the use of the next hide. I shuddered at the thought of how great his rage would be when he discovered what I had done.

I needed to show that I had some worth in my father's eyes, and to do it now, rather than squander a fruitless afternoon. But what? Wander around town like a beggar, seeing if I could assist another glover in his trade? Too shameful. See what help I could be to Anne in the house? That wouldn't bring food to the table. I ran my fingers through a scrap of rabbit fur that I had earlier discarded, too small to be of use. That gave me an idea. I headed off to meet with Hamnet Sadler.

Hamnet was my dearest friend in Stratford, and we had named our twins after him and his wife Judith. As a baker, he rose early, and by now should have sold the last of his bread for the day and be making preparations for the next day's batch. He greeted me with a smile and I saw a single penny wheaten loaf on the shelf behind him. I picked it up and weighed it in my hand.

'It seems a little light to me, Hamnet. Does no-one want to buy the runt of the litter?'

Hamnet grabbed it from me and returned it to the shelf, shaking his head.

'Take care not to let Judith hear your jest. I was denied her favours for a month because of the burgess's diligence

6

in checking my wares. She will not take kindly to being reminded of my disgrace.'

All of us were aware what had cost poor Hamnet much embarrassment. A few weeks before, he and Stratford's fellow bakers, Richard Ange and Thomas Allen, had been fined twelve pennies each for lacking an ounce and a half in their penny wheaten loaves. It was only that all three of the town's bakers had been caught doing the same that had saved my friend's business from ruin. Some townsfolk had been outraged, but as time passed, the incident was forgotten. Not by me, though. I revelled in Hamnet's discomfort and reminded him of it at every opportunity.

He had poaching nets, which he had used to trap rabbits on Charlecote Park, Sir Thomas Lucy's estate, where rabbit and deer could be found in abundance. But poaching on the estate was a risky enterprise; Sir Thomas took a dim view of trespassers and his gamekeepers were armed with cudgels. And Anne had voiced her displeasure whenever I talked of bagging a few coney.

'Poaching is a pursuit of the lower classes,' she told me. 'We have not fallen so far as to have to resort to thievery to put food on our plate. Think of the shame if you are caught.'

Judith had been even more direct with Hamnet after his fall from grace over the wheaten loaves scandal. Though I could not get him to repeat the words she said to him, his nets had gone unused ever since. But now I was desperate. No matter what wrath I would endure on my return, I had to bring home some food for my family's table. I begged Hamnet to lend me his nets.

'You are a bold one, Will Shakspere,' he said, but he could not disguise an amused twinkle in his eye. 'I have had to endure much mocking from you these last few weeks and now you have the cheek to demand a favour.' He sighed. 'But true friends should always help each other. Take my nets when my back is turned, so I can truthfully report to Judith that I had no dealings with you on this matter. But bring a ripe coney when you return and plead in front of her for forgiveness for taking my nets without my leave.' He gave me a conspiratorial wink. 'Now please excuse me, there is something I must attend to in the storage room. You know the place of which I speak? It is next to the small cupboard where my poaching nets are stored. To keep them hidden.' He grinned at me. 'God speed, Will Shakspere. I fear you may be gone when I return.'

I grabbed the nets from the cupboard and set off for Charlecote Park at as fast a pace as I could muster. I soon found a suitable warren and prepared small bundles of twigs and dry leaves, which I placed at every rabbit hole facing into the afternoon breeze. Then I laid the nets at the four biggest holes I had left untouched and sparked my flint to light each fire in turn. The sweet smell of the burning twigs hovered in the spring morn, then tendrils of smoke snaked down into the burrows. It soon had the desired effect. Within a few moments, the first rabbit shot out, then another. In a matter of minutes, I had six plump creatures struggling in the nets and with one quick flick of my knife, each was swiftly despatched. I stamped out the fires, quickly to avoid being discovered, and headed back to Stratford feeling like a king. I returned the nets and gave the largest beast to Hamnet, playing out in front of a sceptical Judith the performance we had discussed – that I had borrowed them without permission.

As my family feasted on rabbit stew that evening, my father gave a nod of approval and I treasured the gesture. Anne's face was more difficult to read, torn as she was between pleasure at the sight of the children happy and full-bellied, and disgust at the measures I had taken. But I knew her well. Her love for her children would override her scruples at my distasteful behaviour.

And once we felt the satisfaction of a full belly, there was no going back. Hamnet's nets were put to use week after week.

There was another reason why stealing from Sir Thomas gave me such joy. My mother was born Mary Arden, and when I was a boy I heard great tales about our ancient and noble family. Our line could be traced back to before William the Conqueror, and the family had been prominent in Warwickshire affairs, residing at Park Hall, a fine country seat. At one point an Arden was even sheriff of the shire. When I was a child and Father was away on business, Mother would make wistful comments about how her branch of the family had fallen on hard times and she was now married to a penniless glover.

'But your father is a fine man and I would not swap him for any other,' she would always conclude. 'Let the other Ardens have their grand houses and rich silks. We are happy with our lot.'

I listened as Mother repeated her tales about her family to Susanna, my elder daughter. She sat open-mouthed as Mother described the Arden family as the most noble of the noble, their men the most courageous, the women the fairest in the land. As a descendant of an Arden, she told the child, I was the equal to any squire or betterman; it was only cruel fate that had dealt the blow of poverty that prevented us, the Wilmcote Ardens, from being recognised as part of the illustrious family. My heart gladdened at first when I saw the child squeal with delight at almost being a princess – as Mother would have it – and then I looked around our humble home.

'Do not fill the child's head with such nonsense,' I beseeched Mother quietly. 'She will develop airs and graces above her station, and that can only lead to a lifetime of disappointment. And never tell her of the fate that befell our noble family. Allow a child to keep her innocence.'

That fate came three years ago, on December 20th 1583, with the execution of Edward Arden, the last male heir of Park Hall and my mother's distant cousin. Edward had been arrested as a conspirator in a plot to assassinate Queen Elizabeth, and had been sent to London to be hung, drawn and quartered. He had been arrested by none other than Sir Thomas Lucy, and Mother, usually the most mild-mannered of individuals, flew into a fury every time she was reminded of this dark episode in our family history.

'My cousin was innocent,' she had told me. 'Sir Thomas chose to believe the accusations of John Sommerville, the ringleader of the plot against the Queen. His naming of Edward as a co-conspirator was the raving of a madman.'

There was indeed some truth in Mother's assertions. Only Sommerville and Edward Arden had faced the hangman's noose. Sir Thomas needed to save face for rounding up and arresting many innocent men based on the ramblings of a lunatic, and Edward Arden was the one chosen to suffer. Afterwards, all who were associated with the Park Hall Ardens came under suspicion for papist sympathies, this distrust reaching even to my mother's family's door. They took to celebrating their Catholic faith in secret and there was no more talk of Arden being a great and noble family name.

Perhaps, one day, some great man would avenge the injustices brought against the Arden name, and restore the family to its rightful place as one of the great dynasties of England. Until that day, Mother would only have her Arden fairy tales and fantasies to console her.

Chapter Two
Alice ~ 1536

ONE DAY SOON, I would meet my husband. He would not have to be a handsome man, for that would mean he was not vain. He would not have to be a passionate man, for that would mean he would not stray. But he would have to be bold and daring, someone with an adventurous spirit and an inquisitive mind, someone who would free me from my humdrum existence here in Kirtling Tower. The high point of my day was practising my scales on the virginal and having Mother patiently correct my mistakes. I wished for so much more.

A commotion from the courtyard below broke through my reverie. Peeking through the leaded panes, I saw that it wasn't the arrival of a shipment of wool or a visiting nobleman that had caused the stir, but a man I had never seen before. I heard him being announced as the new tailor, here to measure my step-father for his summer doublet. As I pushed the window open a fraction he looked up, and our eyes momentarily met. His gaze held a flicker of warmth, which I found most disquieting. I turned away from the window, embarrassed.

After what I considered a decent interval I headed downstairs, and by the time I reached the front parlour the man was measuring Sir Edward, who introduced him as Tom

Mosby. Unlike the other tradesmen who shuffled into our home, this man carried himself with a quiet dignity. His jet-black hair was tied back with a colourful ribbon, a touch that seemed really quite daring. I amused myself with the notion that someone from his station in life could have more flair about him than any of the dandified peacocks to whom I had been introduced as potential suitors. As I watched him work, a strange energy filled my soul, and when he had finished and Sir Edward's back was turned, he stole another glance in my direction, smiled and gave a little bow. I could feel my hair tickle my neck. As I brushed it away, I blushed like a child.

IT HAD BEEN MY custom to take a daily walk around the village with my maid, Betty, to receive the benefit of some wholesome air. It was a chance for us to converse with freedom, often gaiety, once we were out of earshot of my family and the other servants. After that first encounter, I decided that our next walk should be in the direction I had heard Tom Mosby's cottage to be. It was a little further than our usual walk to the River Cherwell, and Betty made no secret of her dismay that we were walking so far on such a hot day. She was a well-fleshed lass, sturdy enough to perform her chores with great efficiency, but she did not take to the heat well, and our usual chatter and gossip soon dwindled to nothing. By the time we arrived at the tailor's cottage, Betty's cheeks were flushed a crimson red, and I was already feeling pangs of guilt for forcing her to participate in such a foolish endeavour.

Tom was half-sitting on a low stone wall, next to what I took to be his cottage, and he turned when he heard the sound of our arrival. He looked startled when he recognised me, but his alarm turned to amusement when he looked over to Betty. She was in a most dishevelled state by now, streaks of sweat running down her face, her eyes bulging with the effort of fanning herself vigorously.

'Greetings, milady. May I offer you a seat in the shade?' He smiled and gestured towards a weathered bench nestled beneath the boughs of an ancient oak.

The invite had been directed at me, though clearly it was Betty who was in need of assistance. But I hesitated before replying. Conversing with a stranger, especially one of Tom's social standing, was something that would be frowned upon, which was why my maid always accompanied me when I ventured out of Kirtling Tower. But I felt I had to do something to make amends to Betty for being so cruel to her in indulging my foolish fancy. And I had to admit, there was something undeniably disarming about Tom's smile that made me want to tarry a little.

I squared my shoulders and inclined my head in a gracious nod. 'Thank you, kind sir. We would be most grateful. Betty, why don't you take a rest on that bench?'

Unbidden, Tom went into the cottage and returned with two cups of water. The man was without doubt handsome and his face, though creased by an arduous life, held a roguish charm. He wore a simple doublet and breeches, the worn leather speaking of honest labour. I declined the cup offered to me, but Betty gulped down both in an instant. Refreshed, she recovered her composure, ready to leave on my instruction.

I stepped forward to offer Tom my gloved hand.

'I am Alice Brigandine,' I said. 'You are Tom Mosby, the tailor, are you not? We met briefly when you called on my step-father at Kirtling Tower.'

'At your service,' he replied.

A long pause hung in the air. Finally, I spoke.

'I think this hot weather does not agree with Betty. Now that we have rested, we must be on our way.'

'Warm indeed, Miss Alice. My roses could use a touch more rain.' Tom gestured towards the vibrant blooms climbing the side of his cottage.

'Your roses are truly magnificent, sir.' My voice surprised me, a touch lower and huskier than usual.

A low cough broke the spell. I turned to see that Betty had stood up and had a pointed expression on her face. Now it was my cheeks that were burning. I withdrew my hand.

'Perhaps another time,' I said hurriedly. 'We must be going.'

My eyes met his, and for a moment the world seemed to fade away. Tom gave a courteous bow, and we turned and began to walk away, Betty following determinedly behind me. As we rounded a bend, I couldn't resist one last glance back. Tom was standing by his roses, an enigmatic smile playing on his lips. The encounter, brief as it was, had left a strange, exhilarating mark upon my heart.

Betty and I quickened our pace along the path back home, the setting sun painting the sky with a fiery palette. When we reached the gates of Kirtling Tower, the encounter with Tom was still playing on my mind, leaving it in delightful disarray.

'Well, milady,' Betty said, now recovered from the day's exertions. 'That was a most unexpected encounter.'

I couldn't help but let out a small, breathless laugh, relieved that she suspected nothing, believing our meeting to be one of pure chance.

'Indeed, Betty. An uncommonly handsome man, wouldn't you say?'

'Did you see the look in his eyes, milady? Like a puppy chasing a butterfly.'

I batted away her words as we walked the last few steps home. 'Nonsense, Betty. He was simply being polite.'

But Betty wasn't finished. 'Polite, perhaps,' she conceded with a sly smile, 'but I think more than that. Dare I say, he found you … pleasing.'

I swatted at Betty playfully, and a giggle escaped my lips. 'Honestly, Betty! A man from the woods would not be so forward.'

Betty's grin widened. 'Perhaps not, Mistress Alice, but a man cannot hide his thoughts. And if I am any judge' – she lowered her voice to a whisper – 'that Tom Mosby was positively smitten.'

A giddy feeling bubbled up inside me. It was a sensation I hadn't felt since I was a child, a carefree lightness that felt deliciously forbidden.

After that, I made no pretence that the purpose of our walks was to engage with Tom Mosby, and I swore Betty to silence on the matter, promising in return only to go to his cottage when the air was cool. We saw him some days but not others, and on the days when we did not meet, a shadow was cast over me.

Our exchanges always followed the conventions of polite society – comments on the weather, or some matter that affected the village or the health of one of its inhabitants – and

Betty took to sitting on the bench under the oak tree to leave us to our conversing. There was never any impropriety, and of course I never stepped over the threshold of his dwelling. One day, I placed a silver comb in my hair before I set off on my walk, as my fiery curls were most unruly that morning. It was perhaps too fine a piece to be displayed outside a formal gathering, but my antler comb was nowhere to be found. I checked my appearance in the mirror before I left; the comb was a most tasteful adornment and I persuaded myself it would not be too ostentatious to wear on a village walk.

Tom's eyes were drawn to it immediately.

'That is a most appealing comb, Miss Alice,' he said to me. 'It bestows on you such a lady-like air. It is so beautiful. As...as beautiful as you yourself.'

I should have been offended by such a forward remark, but instead I looked downwards to hide a grin.

'That is most kind of you,' I said, permitting him to see the final traces of my smile. 'My hair needed taming this morning and my silver comb was all there was to hand. I was concerned it might be unfitting for a morning walk.'

'Not unfitting at all. And I have a piece of cloth that would make a most stunning gown to complement its beauty. May I show it to you?'

It was a shocking proposition to discuss without my mother's presence. But Mother had remarked recently that I should soon have to be fitted for a new gown. This would save the tailor from making an unnecessary trip to Kirtling Tower.

Tom smiled to put me at ease. 'Stay there,' he said. 'I will bring it to you.'

He rushed inside his cottage before I had a chance to reply. I beckoned Betty to join me as he reappeared a few moments later with a bolt of velvet cloth in his arms. He laid it down on the low stone wall and began to unbutton my cloak with surprising dexterity. He was a tailor, I told myself, and so would be familiar with the fastenings of garments. He draped the velvet over my shoulder and stepped back to observe.

'I knew it,' he said, producing a mirror from his pocket. 'Look how the green brings out the lustre of your hair.' He draped my long red tresses so that they lay over the cloth, and wrinkled his brow in concentration. 'I would cut the sleeves Spanish style, a single long slash from shoulder to wrist ...' He nodded to himself. 'Where it falls open it will reveal the sleeve of your kirtle beneath. That should be in red, with embroidery on the front. Every head, milady, would turn to you, no matter how grand the occasion. What do you say, Betty? Is your mistress not so beautiful she could melt the heart of the coldest warrior?'

Betty giggled her agreement, and I had to admit to myself I had enjoyed this brief moment of indulgence. I simply shook my head, reluctant to bring it to an end.

'Sir Edward,' I said, 'would never countenance such extravagance.' I fingered the green velvet, lightly tracing the tips of my fingers over its rich smoothness. 'But thank you for your kind words, Master Mosby. Perhaps one day I will be able to call upon your services.'

I made enquiries about him from the womenfolk on my step-father's estate. Tom was eight years older than me, but his swarthy appearance made the gap in our years appear wider. He lived a carefree life, a baker's wife told me with the faintest hint of disapproval in her voice, moving from town to town as the fancy took him, unburdened by responsibilities and formalities.

I rather admired his venturesome ways. True, he was not as learned as Sir Edward and his friends, or as knowledgeable in society matters as Mother and the gentlewomen of Kirtling, but that mattered not. I decided, in the way young girls do, that he would be my secret lover, and ours would be a pure romantic love, unsullied by any temptations of the flesh. Not that I would ever tell him this, or even give the slightest hint of my true feelings for him. I embroidered a heart, with the letter 'T' in its centre, and slept with it under my pillow every night. Tom would never know of its existence.

There was, of course, no question of marriage. I would have been disinherited on the spot had such a union taken place, cast out as the wife of a jobbing tailor, the whiff of scandal and gossip following the two of us wherever we went. But my actual marriage was becoming a more pressing concern for Mother as each week passed. She herself had been married at seventeen, the same age as I was then, to John Brigandine. My father was a dashing sea captain – a good match for a country lass from a family of little standing. He died at sea when I was four, too young for me to remember him. How I wish I did! I heard tales of him capturing pirates and winning sea battles, which I was later told were stuff and nonsense, made up by Mother to beguile an impressionable daughter. But I believed them. To me, Father was a hero.

So comely a widow attracted much attention, and within the year Mother was wed again, to Edward Mirfyn, another brave adventurer who made his fortune trading with the Low

Countries. When he died within two years, Mother believed herself to be cursed, being twice widowed so young, and that no man would look at her again. But then she caught the eye of Sir Edward North, one of the great noblemen of England and a member of the King's Privy Council. With this third marriage, Mother's place in high society was secure. With the proceeds from Mother's Mirfyn inheritance, Sir Edward bought Kirtling Tower, a great country estate near Newmarket. In a few short years, Mother had gone from country maid to lady of the manor by being skilled in the art of finding the right husband. Now she yearned for me to do the same.

Fine weather was making travel on the highways less demanding, and I was to be presented to every suitable gentleman who visited in the coming weeks. And some not so suitable. When I raised the prospect of marrying a man for love, I was roundly admonished for being so foolish.

'It is said that she who marries for love without money has good nights and sorry days,' Mother said. 'And good nights do not last, whereas a life of good fortune is forever. You must dismiss these fancies from your mind, Alice. Time is moving on and we must find you a husband soon.'

I had no idea what she meant by good nights, having only heard vague whispers of what transpired between married couples when they were alone in the bedroom. That tingle of excitement when Tom's hand touched my shoulders the day he showed me the cloth ... Could that feeling last all through the night? I shook my head in disbelief.

By now, I had been formally introduced to all the sons of the local gentry, young men I had known for years, and each encounter had been more disappointing than the last.

They were all men of limited horizons, and when I showed neither curiosity about sheep farming nor enthusiasm about joining them on a hunt, their interest quickly waned and they looked elsewhere for a wife to help manage their estates. So when Sir Edward sent word that he was returning from London with a young lawyer of his acquaintance, for the first time I awaited an audience with a suitor with some interest. Lawyers were learned men, Mother told me, and a man in his profession would be well read, and might even be inclined to travel to foreign countries. That thought excited me. I had started lessons in French and Italian, and dreamed of one day visiting these far-off places and seeing sights I could not begin to imagine. This time, I made a real effort to look presentable, applying some tin ash to make my already pale skin even more fashionably pallid, and chewing on cumin seeds to ensure my breath was fresh. Mother fussed around the green ribbons until they set off my red hair nicely. As I waited for the sound of hooves to signal my suitor's arrival, my heart fluttered in nervous anticipation.

He was of a rather sober demeanour, dressed in drab clothes that did little to impress, but perhaps men with great minds did not consider trivial matters such as their appearance. Unlike my other suitors, this gentleman was not acquainted with me, so I was paraded in front of him like a prize horse in a paddock. It was humiliating. He stared at me in undisguised horror, and from the brief look she cast in my direction it was clear that not even Mother could ascertain the reason for his discomfort. After a few minutes of stilted conversation, he developed a peculiar fascination with the tapestries that hung on the walls above the wainscot. In desperation, Mother bade me play some tunes on the virginal. I was mortified, for I had only recently taken up the instrument, and in the event my playing was strewn with so many errors that it made even a man of Sir Edward's inscrutable manner wince.

When it came time for the lawyer's departure, I sat with Mother upstairs, so that we could hear his farewells to Father without being observed. After the usual courtesies, Sir Edward enquired if he would care to visit again, to partake of my company some more.

'I fear not,' the lawyer replied. 'And I apologise for imposing on your hospitality by engaging in a fruitless enterprise to be introduced to your step-daughter without first determining the balance of her humours. She is not the wife for me.'

'Balance of her humours?' Sir Edward's voice had risen a little. 'I can assure you she is as hale and hearty as any young woman you will ever meet. And she is fertile, my wife has informed me of that. You will find none better to produce you an heir.'

The man leant forward and spoke in hushed tones, and I crept as close as I dared to the edge of the landing to hear what he said.

'It is not her physical condition that troubles me, sire, it is the balance of her mind that is the concern. I have never seen a woman with such abundant red hair, which all learned men agree is a sure sign of a copious amount of phlegm in the body, which can lead to bouts of uncontrolled passion and insatiable lust. Desirable in a mistress or a courtesan perhaps, but not in a wife. You and I are gentlemen of the world, Sir Edward. We know that men can restrain their carnal desires but women cannot, and have an uncontrollable urge for the hot essence of a man, especially women in whom the phlegm humour is so dominant. Once these urges are awakened, marrying such a woman would be like marrying an untamed beast.'

Mother and I looked at each other in horror, and I fled to my room in tears. I was still sobbing into my mattress when she came in and sat on the edge of the bed.

'There is truth in what your suitor said – that in these more informed times your appearance may be off-putting to any man seeking a gentle companion for a wife; he may fear that in fulfilling his marital duties he might unlock passions in you that you cannot control.'

Her voice had the soft, almost musical quality that showed itself when she was trying to instruct me as to how to make the best out of my life. There was a brief silence, then she stood up and busied herself needlessly tidying my room before speaking again, this time in a more matter-of-fact tone.

'We can eliminate fish and fruit from your diet. That might help to balance the phlegm in your body and make the lustre of your hair less unsettling. And if that does not work, Sir Edward can look to find a widower from his own social circle, to lessen the risk that uncontrolled lust will result from your marriage.' She saw the look of horror on my face. 'Now, dear, that is not as bad as it sounds.' The softness returned. 'Many a young woman has found amiable companionship in marriage to an older man. His demands on you will be modest, if any at all, and you will find caring for him in his final years quite fulfilling.'

I told Mother I needed some air, some time alone to compose myself before I could face my step-father again after the day's humiliation. Before she had a chance to object,

I headed off on the path to Kirtling village. There was only one person I wanted to see, someone to tell me again that my hair was not unnerving but alluring, just as he had done once before. I knocked on Tom's door and entered before he had a chance to respond. He was standing in front of a basin washing, naked to the waist. I gasped an apology at my intrusion before bursting into tears.

Tom made no attempt to cover himself. Instead, he came over and embraced me. His earthy sweat was like a perfume, the scent of honest labour; it mingled with the smell of freshly chopped wood.

'Tell me again the words you spoke when you held that cloth up to my hair,' I sobbed. 'Are my locks pleasing? Do you find me beautiful? Do not think it kind to hide behind falsehoods. Tell me your true feelings.'

'Let me show you my feelings,' he replied.

I tried to relax as his face moved closer to mine. He undid the button on my shawl and let it fall to the ground. I offered no resistance as he leant forward and kissed me and ran his fingers through my hair.

'It burns like the rays of the sun,' he whispered. 'I have never seen anyone more beautiful.' He buried his head in my hair, my hated, loathsome hair, and breathed in its essence.

WE LAY TOGETHER AGAIN many times after that, and I would blush in the evenings as I sat doing my embroidery and my mind wandered to the lustful antics of the afternoon. It had been most embarrassing to have to tell Betty of these developments, but I had no choice. Tom had built a rough shelter for her at the edge of the Kirtling woods and she would wait there, doing some darning, while Tom and I ventured deeper into the forest to our secret place. My walks with Betty towards the village still had some of the carefree chatter of old, but when we returned to Kirtling Tower afterwards it was always in silence. Betty did not approve, I knew that, but she was loyal to her core and would never betray me.

Tom had chosen the woods as our meeting point not only to get away from Betty, but to avoid discovery by any villager passing by his cottage when we were inside. But this arrangement couldn't last. We had finished our lovemaking one summer evening and the birds had begun their evening chorus. Breathing in the dank musk of the forest floor enriched the glow I felt throughout my body.

'The dusk is getting earlier and the winter months will soon be upon us,' I said, turning a twig between my fingers. 'We will have no more pleasant evenings to spend time together in these woods until the spring arrives.' I gave a thin smile. 'How will I survive till then?'

Tom stood up, brushing off the dead leaves that clung to him. 'We will need to be indoors, that is for sure.' He looked around, as if he was expecting to see a cottage hidden somewhere in the woods. 'My home is too public. We need to find someone to accommodate us, someone we can trust to keep our secret.'

'I know of no such person,' I said. 'And I have already had enquiries as to why my walks with Betty now take so long. I fear that speculation may turn to suspicion, and soon we will be discovered. Sir Edward would disown me, I am sure of it.'

Tom nodded. 'My sister Cislye has a daughter, Elisabeth, who wishes to work in service. If I were to get Cislye to make an approach to Sir Edward, could you help in securing Elisabeth's appointment? It would not be unreasonable for an uncle to visit Kirtling Tower to meet with his niece. There would surely be a hiding place for us that Elisabeth could arrange.'

The plan was a good one, as it would end the awkwardness of Betty's involvement in my subterfuge and Sir Edward had already talked about adding more staff. He had fathered four children since marrying Mother, and our household was large. Elisabeth came for an interview and I stressed to Mother that, although she lacked experience, I had heard talk of her good reputation in the village and would be happy for her to be my maid, and for Betty to take on new responsibilities elsewhere in the household. There was an unused peasant hut near our family home, which had space for both mother and daughter, and I pleaded with Mother for them to live there, so that young Elisabeth would have her mother to support her as she took on her first position in service. To my delight, Mother agreed.

Cislye and Elisabeth moved in a few days later. The winter rains meant no new suitors would arrive at Kirtling Tower until the spring, and Tom and I met regularly in the peasant hut over the following months, Cislye and Elisabeth leaving to give us privacy. I came to love that hut more than Kirtling Tower itself, its earthen floor covered in river rushes and the small doorway through which we had to stoop to enter, being far cosier than the slate floors and high ceilings of Sir Edward's mansion. One small window meant the inside was almost in darkness, but we rarely left the hay-filled sacks where Cislye and Elizabeth slept.

Then disaster struck. I was taking my leave of Tom at the door when I heard a twig snap behind me.

'I knew it,' Mother said, her eyes cold, flinty. 'I have seen in your demeanour you have experienced that which you should not have, and waited for you to reveal yourself. And with my husband's tailor, in a peasant hut on our land? Disgusting.' She addressed Tom. 'I will insist my husband dispenses with your services, and your sister and niece will be banished from Kirtling Tower forthwith. You are fortunate not to be flayed for your debauchery.'

'Madam, do not reproach your daughter thus,' said Tom. 'There is no impropriety. Alice is of a habit of stopping to talk to my niece, enjoying a brief rest on her daily stroll. I happened to be visiting and she indulged me with a few moments of pleasant conversation. There is nothing untoward here, I assure you.'

I had been about to confess all, to beg Mother for mercy, but bit my tongue, hoping Tom's words would convince her. They did not.

'Do not think I can be so easily fooled, Tom Mosby. I know of your reputation as a scoundrel and a womaniser and how many virtuous maidens' hearts you have broken. I pray I have uncovered your designs on my daughter before it is too late, but I am in no doubt about your intentions. You will be on your way, sir, just as you have been sent packing before for your licentious behaviour. Leave Kirtling before the week is out.'

Tom promised that he would leave forthwith, never breathe a word of this scandal, and he implored Mother not to punish his young niece. I tried to hide my disappointment that he had agreed to leave so easily, but now Mother gave me the full glare of her attention.

'And you, my harlot of a daughter. You have disgraced yourself and your family name. I know not what Sir Edward will do to you.'

'Mother, please grant me forgiveness. And know that I will follow your instructions on whom I should marry, no matter who you choose.'

Mother waited a lifetime before she finally spoke. 'Perhaps some good can come of this. I do this to protect your good name, so your step-father does not disown you for your wanton acts. But be warned that finding a match will not be easy. Pledge you will indeed accept whomever I choose as a husband for you, and I will stay silent.'

I agreed. I had no choice.

Chapter Three
Will ~ 1586

FATHER'S GLOVING BUSINESS consisted of a ground floor shop at the front of the house on Henley Street. A sign hanging outside featured a pair of glover's compasses against a fading green background, and animal hides were hung on the inner walls. The front shop was where the two of us and our two apprentice stitchers worked, away from the outbuildings at the back where we did the stretching and drying of the hides.

Father sent me to the tannery on the edge of town to collect a doeskin he had ordered for some fine ladies' gloves. It was an errand that filled me with dread; you always know when you are close to a tanner's workshop, such is the stench from the human shit and piss in the cess pits used to turn animal skins into leather. When I saw the de-furred hides being prepared to be soaked in the yards of curing pits, an idea started to grow in my mind. Excitedly, I shared it with Father when I returned to Henley Street.

'I paid four shillings for this hide, which will be good for a score of gloves, no more, even with the most careful cutting. And at our stall on market day, we are paid but four pennies a pair for the finished article. That's less than five shillings for three days' work by ourselves and the stitchers, even with the rabbit fur lining now courtesy of Sir Thomas. If it were not for the special commissions from our gentleman customers, we would not be able to survive. I have been thinking—'

'I don't need you to tell me this,' Father said, an edge in his voice. 'But until the other glovers decide to increase their prices, we have to suffer these indignities. If you were to pay more attention to how you cut, we could get another two pairs of gloves out of a hide, but I am burdened with a son who spends his day with his head in the clouds rather than focusing on his work. That's eightpence a hide we are throwing away.'

'But what if we saved four shillings instead?' I said. 'That's the price the tanner pays the butcher, and every time I venture onto Lucy's estate I see deer everywhere, so tame they stare me in the eye as I bag their rabbit neighbours. We could swap deerskin for tanned hides and have venison a-plenty for the kitchen table. Think what a difference free hides would make. Our business would prosper and grow.'

Father frowned. 'A dangerous game, Will. If Sir Thomas's gamekeepers catch you poaching rabbits, you will have only a fine of three times the value of the bag you have on your person. Deer poaching is a different matter. You will be sent to prison, perhaps even whipped. I cannot countenance such an outcome, and not just for your sake. Think of the disgrace.'

I bowed to my father's wishes, but the idea kept gnawing away at me. I knew that it would bring even sweeter revenge against the injustices that Sir Thomas had meted out to the Ardens in the past. It was at the end of a night's drinking at the Greyhound when temptation finally got the better of me.

Anne did not approve of me squandering our few extra pennies on the inns and alehouses of the High Street, but a few months earlier I had discovered a means to have most convivial evenings with Hamnet and some others without parting with any coin, by simply penning some bawdy verse and then reciting it in return for a glass of ale. My best was this:

With too much beer, it will not stand,
Come, said the maid, give me in my hand,
She took and rolled it on her thigh,
And when she kissed it, it grew quite high.

But this was the one that was cheered the most:

And soft my fingers up her dress they rise,
Until I come to reach her thighs,
She shuts her eyes, and wiggles out her tongue.
Oh, what pretty maid can hold so long?

They were, of course, only recited when there were no womenfolk present, but it meant that I could enjoy many a drunken evening without ever putting my hand in my purse.

As we staggered out of the Greyhound after a particularly boisterous time celebrating my twenty-second birthday, Hamnet was studying the full moon just as a cloud passed in front of it, darkening all around us.

'A hunter's moon,' he observed.

I looked at him. 'Do you still have that crossbow of your father's?'

I told him my plan to rid Sir Thomas of a few deer, and said that now was the perfect opportunity.

'Judith will be asleep …' he said, his eyes gleaming.

Another cloud passed the moon. We could hear an owl in the distance.

'Come, Hamnet, put fire in your heart and brimstone in your liver. It's Charlecote tonight for us!'

Hamnet retrieved the crossbow and we headed out of town. The bravado brought on by the beer had left me now and every nerve in my body seemed like a strained harp string ready to snap, but I would not lose face by being the first to say we should turn back. As we entered the forest in Charlecote Park the darkness made finding the warren difficult, but after much stumbling and cursing, we reached the familiar clearing. Hamnet set the bow and we waited.

The first young buck we saw was perfect. No more than two years old, it would be easy to carry and would provide the softest buckskin. Hamnet brought it down with one well-aimed shot and we rushed at it with our daggers to slit its throat and finish the job. Exhausted by our labours, we sat and rested for a moment.

I never heard a sound before something crashed down on the back of my head. Falling to my knees, dazed, I saw the shadow of Hamnet running off into the woods. A second blow made stars explode around me, before all went black.

I woke to find myself in the Cage, Stratford's jail, where I was told that Sir Thomas's gamekeeper had already given sworn testimony against me, so there would be no need for a trial. It had been decided I should be held for one week, but should not receive whipping, given my good reputation and that this was my first offence. The term was doubled to two weeks when I refused to name my accomplice.

'You were two fools,' the jailer told me. 'Every man in Stratford knows that Sir Thomas has his gamekeepers on night patrol when there's a hunter's moon. No poacher with any sense would chance his luck on such a night.'

I WAS EXPECTING STRONG words when I was let out two weeks later, but Anne and my parents showed more concern than anger.

'Your poaching days are over, Will Shakspere,' my wife told me. 'A second offence, even for a single rabbit, will lead to a public flogging. Promise me you will never be so foolhardy again.'

I duly promised, and when Hamnet visited a few days later, I told him the same. He told me what he had seen that night. He said I had been slung over a mule by the gamekeeper to be brought into town and he had followed at a discreet distance, hoping to free me. But when he heard the gamekeeper address me by my name even in my senseless state, he realised there was no merit in trying. I had been identified, and would be punished even if Hamnet had been able to free me.

Our financial woes were back to where they had been before, and now it was too risky even to poach rabbit. Hamnet took me to the Greyhound to try to improve my mood. After the third ale, or maybe the fourth, my spirits had recovered and I decided to recite another of my ditties, rising unsteadily to my feet. A cheer went up from my fellow ale-drinkers which I found most gratifying, and I waved for them to hush.

'I have a new verse for you tonight,' I said. 'For I have had much free time of late to think up some words.'

> *A parliament member, a justice of peace,*
> *At home a poor scarecrow, at London an ass,*
> *If lousy is Lucy as some folks miscall it*
> *Then Lucy is lousy whatever befall it.*

I knew it to be an inconsequential piece, and rough at the edges, but it made fun of Sir Thomas's notoriously unkempt appearance and gave me pleasure entirely out of proportion to its merit. I was greeted with a loud cheer when I finished. But some of the older men were shaking their heads in disbelief. Even Hamnet, who liked a jape even more than I did, looked worried. He made me promise to recount my drunken performance to Anne when I reached home.

When I did so, my wife could hardly contain her fury.

'You have been branded a thief and a criminal, and now you have proved you are a fool to boot. What possessed you to risk Sir Thomas's ire again? For the amusement of your erstwhile friends? To show off this poetry of which you seem so proud? Why did I marry such a feckless youth?'

I hung my head. Anne's words struck home, and Father wasted no time in joining her in condemnation.

'You are indeed a fool, Will. Sir Thomas accepts that the loss of an occasional animal from his estate is the consequence of having such extensive lands. But impudence he will not tolerate. You should pray that these words would not reach his ears, because if they do, you can expect to be tied to the whipping post and given a public lashing. But I fear it is only a matter of time until he hears. You have only yourself to blame.'

They were right of course. 'What has been done, cannot be undone,' I said, sighing dejectedly. 'I have been taught some cruel lessons these last few weeks – that I need to curb my impulsive actions and to hold my wayward tongue to avoid making matters worse. When I say my prayers tonight, I will beg for a second chance, for some miracle. And if such a miracle is granted, I vow I will never again place myself in such jeopardy.' I went over and took Anne's hands in mine. 'One day, dear wife, you will have a husband you can be proud of.'

She gave me a wavering smile of support.

Little did I know that my prayers would be answered, and that chance would present me with an opportunity.

An opportunity that would change me forever.

Chapter Four

Alice ~ 1537

WHEN I HEARD I was to be introduced to Thomas Arden as a suitable bride, I breathed a sigh of relief. I had envisioned being married off, as Mother had threatened, to some gout-ridden acquaintance of Sir Edward's age, but from what I heard about Thomas he was more of a compromise for Mother than he was for me, being a mere eleven years my senior. He had started life in modest circumstances, and there were nasty rumours that his mother was a professional beggar on the streets of Norwich, but I was told he had ambition to improve his lot in life. By the time Sir Edward met him on one of his trips to London, Thomas Arden had already made a name for himself as prudent and sensible, with an eye for a deal that would make him money. And most importantly, when my step-father casually mentioned my flaming red hair, it had seemed to concern Thomas not one jot.

He visited Kirtling Tower a few weeks later. Sir Edward ushered Thomas into the drawing room for our formal audience and I wondered if it were possible for a man to be too handsome. His features were perfectly proportioned, he had a slim build, and there were no scars or deformities that could offend the eye. But there was a blandness about him; as if God had created a fine-looking gentleman, but one who had not a jot of interest about him.

I sat bolt upright in my chair, perched on the edge. Mother sat less than an arm's length away, so that she could signal if I said something untoward, or was too silent. Sir Edward announced that he had some pressing estate business to attend to and promptly left the room. This was a most inauspicious start to our discussion, signalling that my future happiness was not of great concern to him. Still, I was not going to permit this to get in the way of my making a favourable impression. I waited a few moments for Thomas to start the conversation and when it became clear that he would not, I took it upon myself.

'You have journeyed up from London to meet with us today?' I widened my eyes and blinked a few times to convey an air of charming nervousness. 'Pray tell, how was the journey?'

Mother shot me a reassuring glance. The correct etiquette would have been for Thomas to speak first, but as he showed no sign of doing so, I had avoided a prolonged, embarrassing silence.

'Uneventful,' replied Thomas. I noticed a stale odour from his breath and shuffled back in my seat. 'I left London on the Great North Route and journeyed on to Baldock. Do you know Baldock, Miss Alice?'

I shook my head and smiled to encourage him to say more.

'No matter. It is a place of little consequence. I then took the Icknield Way to Dullingham, where I spent the night, and thence to Kirtling.'

'Ah, I know of Dullingham,' I replied. 'It is but a league from here. Did you enjoy your stay there?'

'I spent the night in the inn, so saw little of the town.'

'Oh.'

There was a long pause. 'And your business keeps you in London? Do you venture to Suffolk often?'

'Not often. There is money to be made in London, so it has to be a considerable investment for me to leave such opportunities behind.'

'Well, I hope your investment proves a worthy one,' I replied. Was I being evaluated as a business opportunity rather than a wife? 'Shall we take a walk around the grounds? They are delightful at this time of year. At least then your journey will not be completely wasted.'

Mother shot me a disapproving glance and tried to make light of it. 'What a splendid idea, Alice,' she said, her voice a little louder than normal. 'The roses are magnificent at this time of year. You lead the way with Master Arden and I will follow behind. I'm sure you young people will have much to talk about.'

We began our stroll and I wondered if Thomas Arden had ever been young. I tried to make myself sound interesting and well-informed on the walk and took pains to enquire on topics that I thought would interest him – his life in London, his upbringing in Norwich and how close Kirtling Tower was to his childhood home. But I received no enquiries in return and the only topic that sparked enthusiasm from him was his merchanting in the city. By the time we completed our perambulation, I had heard all I ever wanted to hear about buying hemp and sailcloth from the Hanseatic traders of Rotterdam; the best ways to store grain to prevent rotting; and more about how to export wool than I ever thought possible.

After a torturous meal, Thomas made his excuses and left, though a room had been prepared for him to stay overnight. As we watched him ride off back to London, Mother sighed.

'Pity,' she said. 'He would have been a good match. Next time, do not be so forthright in your views, Alice, and try to show more interest in the ways of commerce. Don't forget you are more likely to marry a grocer than a lord.'

So, it was to our great astonishment that a letter arrived for Sir Edward a few days later from Thomas, asking for my hand in marriage. Mother was ecstatic, but I was concerned. Was that to be the extent of our courtship? We had found little in common to talk about. How could he feel so sure as to propose marriage after such a fleeting visit?

I felt no desire for Thomas, he stirred none of the feelings Tom Mosby had awakened in me. I will force myself to love him, I told myself. I will support him in his ambition. When we lie together – that will be when passion will enter our marriage. Passion will create affection, affection will lead to fondness and fondness will lead, in time, to a deep and everlasting bond between us. Slowly, I became infected by Mother's enthusiasm. Yes, this was how a marriage would flourish. It must be nurtured and grown, like a tender seedling that would grow into a sturdy oak. When it came time for Thomas to visit again, I awaited his arrival with eager anticipation.

I made sure I had prepared some questions on the complexities of the wool trade, to which Thomas gave the most expansive and detailed replies. The specifics of the wedding were left to me and Mother, Thomas spending most of his time at Kirtling Tower determining with my step-father the fiduciary details of our marriage. He was to become Sir Edward's man, a sponsorship that would open up new opportunities for his business career. Mother insisted that, in return, Thomas was to stand bound to Sir Edward for the sum of one thousand marks to provide me with a jointure for life of £40 a year in the event of his death. I thought this a most macabre condition of our marriage, but Mother convinced me otherwise. Early widowhood, she said, without the security of a jointure agreement could make my life very precarious indeed.

Thomas agreed to move to Kirtling to act as an agent for the Suffolk wool traders, and to use his contacts to secure the most favourable tariffs for export. Sir Edward gave us some rooms at Kirtling Tower, and it was with some excitement that I looked forward to the day of our wedding. Mother persuaded Sir Edward to consent to me having a new gown for the occasion, of the finest Suffolk wool, dyed a deep cerulean blue. I had hoped to be dressed in green velvet, but Mother informed me that such a dress would cost three pounds ten shillings, the wool dress just thirteen shillings, and Sir Edward had stated that velvet would be worn only by his blood daughters. No matter, I would make sure Thomas was the envy of every man there. On the day, he also dressed finely, in a most fetching doublet, breeches and hose, splendidly set off by his box-pleated neck ruff and sizable codpiece.

All through the wedding feast, my thoughts kept turning to the night ahead. I shamed myself by allowing memories of Tom Mosby to enter my head. Would it be the same? Or even better? Surely it had to be. We would be lying in Kirtling Tower's best bed rather than on the forest floor or a sack of hay. More comfortable for sure. We would have the night to ourselves, without the worry of being discovered. Thomas had exercised remarkable control over his desire for me and would now be able to submit to his manly urges. I could hardly contain my excitement.

We feasted on a peacock adorned with its splendid plumage and covered with a German sauce, accompanied by gilt sugar-plums and pomegranate seeds; and after the wedding procession to Kirtling Tower, we said our goodbyes to the guests and headed off to our room.

Thomas pushed open the door and stood aside to let me enter. My mouth was dry, and I concentrated on maintaining a dignified composure as I entered, my senses on high alert. The room was beautiful, festooned with flowers, scented candles on the tables either side of the giant tester bed. I breathed in the sandalwood aroma and waited for Thomas's touch. I had promised myself I would resist all temptation to take any initiative. My husband needed to feel that he was the one who first guided me through the act of love. My husband! My body quivered as I thought these words.

Thomas slumped down on the bed and began attending to his buttons and cuffs. I stood there, unsure of what to do, and wandered over to scrutinise a portrait of one of Sir Edward's ancestors on the wall, who I was sure was staring at me with thinly disguised hostility. Behind me, I could hear grunting as Thomas struggled with his clothing. Finally, I heard him stand up. I turned to meet his gaze, only to see him in his night gown, pissing into a chamber pot in the corner of the room.

He put the pot down and turned towards me.

'That was long overdue,' he said. 'And I am quite overcome by the stresses of the day.' He stifled a small belch and slid under the bedclothes.

I stood there, feeling like a fool, not knowing whether I should disrobe in front of him or if that would betray my wanton past. In the end, I took off my wedding dress and slipped into bed still wearing my smock. I waited for his embrace, for nimble fingers to caress me, but there was nothing. What was wrong? Was my smock not to his liking? I edged an inch closer to him, waiting for him to respond. Nothing. Did he find me too unsightly to kiss?

'I am exhausted from all the festivities,' he said, 'and I am sure you are too. Let us get some sleep. We can take care of our marital obligations when we are both more rested.'

He turned his back to me and I lay on mine, staring at the ceiling, my eyes wide in horror. A gentle snore filled the room.

THOMAS ATTEMPTED TO CONSUMMATE our marriage the next night, but it was a most unsatisfactory affair and he gave up at the third attempt. I felt ugly and unwanted. One time when he returned from London, I summoned the courage to touch his manhood, but nothing stirred.

'I am so weary,' he said, his voice a flat whisper. 'Let me fall into sleep after my travels.'

Another night, I decided to tempt passion into our bedroom by disrobing and standing naked in front of him, but the look of shock on his face made me quickly regret my audacity. I jumped into bed and wrapped myself in the sheets, burying my head in the pillow to stifle my tears. I lay awake for hours that night, finally realising why having a wife with such striking red hair had not troubled Thomas.

My passion was not to be feared because my life was to devoid of it.

Finally, I realised. He had wed me not from desire, but for advancement. My step-father meant more to him than I ever would.

WE HAD BEEN MARRIED for three uneventful years when, in 1540, Thomas told me that he had secured a second sponsor, one Sir Thomas Cheyne, warden of the Cinque Ports, the historic harbours of Kent and Sussex. I was delighted. Anything would be better than Kirtling Tower, where I had to play out the role of happy wife before the watchful eyes of my mother. We were to move to a town called Faversham, where Thomas would be steward of the Cheyne manor on the nearby Isle of Sheppey.

I would be moving to a strange town, where I knew not a soul, and would be leaving all that I knew behind, but at least I would not have to maintain a daily pretence.

Steward of the manor was an important post, my husband told me, and if he made a good impression, there was talk that Sir Thomas would make him the King's collector of customs.

'And there lies the potential for riches,' he told me. 'Many traders are quite unscrupulous in their dealing with customs officials. They feel that duties and levies are too high already, and are always looking for a friendly face to help them with their difficulties.'

To my horror, Thomas explained what he meant by that. He would receive what he described as *'douceurs'* to look the other way when goods arrived in port. My husband, in plain English, would be taking bribes, like a common criminal.

I persuaded Thomas to allow me to take Elisabeth with me as my servant, so there would be at least one familiar face in our new life, and for Elisabeth's mother to come too, to provide support for her daughter in a new town. I had pleaded with Mother to let Elisabeth stay on as my maid when I had been discovered with Tom Mosby, telling her it would distress me greatly that a blameless girl should be harmed by my thoughtless actions and be dismissed from service at such a young age. My mother was unconvinced, and only when I argued that by allowing Elisabeth and her mother to stay in the peasant hut we could be sure they could be relied upon not to spread gossip in the village, did I manage to convince her. And I had been proven right – there was not a breath of suspicion anywhere about what had happened between myself and Tom Mosby that summer.

I could not say that Mother was happy they would be accompanying me to Faversham, but she could say nothing without disclosing her part in concealing my past behaviour.

We all headed off a few weeks later.

Our new life would be a new start. Maybe that would fan the flames of passion in Thomas's heart.

Chapter Five
Will ~ 1587

I HAD FIRST ENCOUNTERED the Queen's Men, a troupe of actors sponsored by Queen Elizabeth herself, when my father and I delivered some gloves to the Earl of Derby in Latham, some forty leagues away. That was a most prestigious commission; Henry Stanley, the fourth Earl of Derby, was a prominent nobleman and privy councillor and Latham House a most imposing dwelling. I marvelled at its opulence. Large windows, divided by stone mullions, both let in abundant sunlight and showcased the beauty of the surrounding gardens. In the great hall, a vast room with a soaring timbered ceiling adorned with intricate plasterwork, the Queen's Men were preparing to perform their play.

We were invited to stay and attend that evening's performance. The play was called *The Spanish Tragedy,* and it was the most wonderful thing I had ever seen in my life. It told the story of the ghost of a Spanish nobleman who sought revenge on the Portuguese prince who killed him, and I was amazed at how I was transported to the Spanish court and even to the gates of Hell by the skill of the actors and the fine costumes they wore. When Earl Stanley and his entourage departed after the performance's end, I plucked up the courage to go up and speak to John Laneham, the troupe's leader.

'Sir, this has been the most marvellous evening of my life. Can I give you and your men my heartfelt thanks for such a wondrous entertainment?' I saw the look of confusion on Laneham's face as he struggled to place me in the Stanley household. My cheeks grew hot as I continued. 'Forgive me for the intrusion. I am Will Shakspere, a mere glover who finds himself staying the night at the Earl's request after travelling here with my wares from Stratford. It was a great honour to be in your presence this evening.'

'A glover, eh?' Laneham replied, giving a shaky laugh at his relief that he had not offended someone of importance. He slapped me on my arm. 'A fine trade. Have you seen one of our plays before?'

'No, this was my first.' I gestured to the script he was holding, which he had used to shout out lines the actors had forgotten during the play. 'Are these the words I heard this evening? Pray, let me cast my eyes over them so I can enjoy their beauty a second time.'

'A glover who can read? And who no doubt writes as well?'

I nodded, embarrassed.

'If you are in possession of these talents, it seems churlish not to oblige you.' Laneham handed me the sheaf of papers. 'Here you are, Master Glover. You may feast your eyes while we prepare to depart. Now I must help the others. They will not thank me for jawing when there is work to be done.'

If anything, reading the words on the page was even more magical than hearing them being performed, as I could savour and re-read every moment of the play. I had completed but a third when Laneham came over, this time with two fellow actors, whom he introduced as William Knell and John Towne.

'We have bloodied this man tonight and he seems quite enamoured by the experience,' he told the two men. He pointed to the sheaf of paper. 'Tell me, young Will, now that you've read them, what do you think of Thomas Kydd's words?'

I gave a slow, disbelieving shake of the head. 'This was written by a man of our time? I thought all plays were written by the Romans.'

'Indeed, they were,' Laneham replied, giving a wide grin. 'Plautus, Terence, Seneca – the great Roman dramatists. But now we have Master Kydd and his fine play to perform. I hope it will be the first of many.'

I talked to the three men for over an hour. Knell was their leading actor, and had played the main character in the play, the ghost of Don Andrea. Towne played the part of Horatio, his friend who sought revenge for his death. I found the conversation easy, the actors enjoying being flattered on their performance and Laneham much amused by my enthusiasm. And even more so by my astonishment to discover that Thomas Kydd was a mere six years older than I, and from a similar humble background. It stirred a curious feeling inside me, admiration tinged with jealousy.

As a clock chimed midnight, I reluctantly called a halt to our discussion.

'Gentlemen, this has been a most rewarding conversation, but I must detain you no longer. I have to rise with the cock crow on the morrow, for I have a long journey to return to Stratford. If your travels ever take you there, you can be sure I will attend your performance.' I shook each of the three men's hands in turn. 'If not, then this parting was well made. For now, I bid you good night. Whether we shall meet again, I know not. If we do, why, we shall smile.'

'Well said, Will Shakspere,' Laneham replied. 'You speak with a fine tongue. No doubt we will meet again. If our journey takes us near Stratford, you can be sure of it.'

THREE MONTHS LATER, THE Queen's Men did arrive in Stratford, two days after I committed the indiscretion of reciting the Lucy poem in the Greyhound. The fear of retribution from Sir Thomas still held my stomach in a vice, and every time I saw the anguish etched on Anne's face, my anxiety grew worse. The obvious solution would have been to leave Stratford and go into hiding for a while, but had I simply headed out of town and scraped a living wherever I went, I would soon be arrested as a vagrant. At the time of the Queen's Men's arrival my mood was so black I was tempted not to visit them, but then I decided there was no harm in being distracted from my worries for an hour or two.

I arrived at the inn where they were to perform to see the troupe in disarray. Laneham was a shadow of the booming giant of a man I had met at Latham House, sitting on a box of props with his head in his hands while the other members of the troupe sat sobbing around him. Of William Knell and John Towne there was no sign. I summoned up the courage to ask one of the other actors what was amiss.

'William Knell is dead,' he told me. 'We had been performing in Thame last night and he was killed in a drunken fight with John Towne.' The actor's hands clenched into fists. 'Dead! And all because of some stupidity over a game of cards.' His skin bunched around his eyes as he stared at me. 'I know you, don't I?' His stare dissolved and I saw his eyes water. His voice softened. 'Do you have some tale of William Knell you can tell me? Some amusing little trifle to embrace, to comfort me in this great loss?'

I shook my head. 'I met him only once, and the rest of you also, at Latham House when I was delivering some gloves to the Earl of Derby.' I rubbed my hand around my jaw. 'William Knell is gone? I cannot believe it. He was such a great man and a fine actor. How could he be visited by the fearful owl of death so soon? This is indeed a tragedy.'

At the sound of my words, John Laneham raised his head and looked over, and the smallest sparkle of energy came forth from his muddy eyes. 'Here comes our salvation, lads,' he said. 'It is Will Shakspere, the glover, is it not?' He rose and gave me an embrace. 'You showed much interest in our work when we met in Latham. Would you care to join our troupe for tonight's performance? You need say a dozen lines, no more, which can easily be learnt and recalled. What say you, Master Shakspere? Will you be on stage tonight?'

I was somewhat shocked. 'Such tragedy has befallen you here,' I said, 'yet you think only of how a play can be performed ... Should you not be mourning your loss?'

'I mourn that we are two men down,' Laneham replied, running his hands through his hair. 'William Knell dead and Towne fled. Their fates could easily have been reversed; they were both men of passion who could fly into a rage at the slightest provocation. But a songbird does not weep when a tragedy occurs, it sings away its grief. That is what we must do here. The play's the thing and tonight's performance must go ahead. But without Knell and Towne we need to act swiftly to save the show. You spoke with much passion when you saw us perform in Latham, Will the Glover. Bring that same passion to the stage tonight.'

I shook my head. 'I am not an actor and have never made any public speech. It would be too much of a humiliation for me to attempt such a thing. I could not bear the shame.'

But even as I said the words, I felt my heart flutter. I wanted Laneham to convince me.

'Tish tosh,' he said. 'We have three hours until our performance at two of the clock. All of our players know every part, and there are but a few moments where we need another actor on the stage to say a few lines. I will play Don Andrea's ghost and will be on stage for the whole play. If you forget your line, I will whisper it to you. You will find an audience most forgiving in the circumstances, and happy that a local lad has saved the day. Come, Will, there is nothing for you to fear.'

Indeed, there was not. There was a murmur of recognition when I first appeared on stage and a burst of laughter and applause when I said my first line, but that did not put me off. I marvelled at how all that I had been told about the business of theatricals happened with effortless ease, the audience blissfully unaware of all the tricks that were being used to create the illusion of reality. At one point a prop fell over, and I improvised a line to cover what had happened, and saw a surreptitious nod of approval from Laneham for my initiative. When the play finished, and I stood at the end of the line of players taking bows, a wild thought entered my mind. Was this a way out of Stratford and a chance to escape the retribution of Sir Thomas Lucy? The troupe took a bow one last time and Laneham made me step forward to take a bow on my own. A cheer went up from the townsfolk, every one of them with laughter on their faces. I looked over and saw Anne in the crowd, clapping her hands above her head. I blew her a kiss and she coyly flapped at her cheek in response.

'What happens now, for your next performance?' I asked Laneham, as I helped dismantle the stage after the crowd had left. 'Will you have to find another fool to come to the rescue in the next town you visit?' I could not help a grin spreading across my face.

Laneham chuckled. 'Why find another fool when we have one right here?' he replied, pinching me on the cheek. 'Life is an adventure, Will, and to live it to the full you have to seize the moment. We return to Thame tomorrow to bury poor William Knell and deal with the coroner's questions. Put your affairs in order and join us there tomorrow eve, and you can travel with us for eight weeks. There are four left in the troupe now, and with you we will be five. I will grant you one tenth of our takings from every show we perform – that should be sixteen shillings a show, more if we put on a private performance for a nobleman. You will return to Stratford before Michaelmas with a purse of two pounds or more. Does that not match the coin you make as a glover?'

He knew it did, and it seemed the answer to all our problems. I could escape Stratford and Sir Thomas, and ease my family's financial woes at the same time. But to leave behind Anne, when the twins were so young? That would be a cruel thing to do.

I described my plan to Anne in the clearest of terms. 'John Laneham has invited me to join his troupe on their journey down to London, winding through the shires and circling around the capital before the winter rains arrive.'

I rushed my words. 'I will be understudy to the cast of the most talented actors in the land and a player in my own right, doing whatever role Master Laneham sees fit for me, and I will return with two pounds or more. It will provide ample time for Sir Thomas Lucy's rage to subside. Let this fortuitous turn of events solve all our dilemmas.'

'Acting is the profession of wastrels and scoundrels,' Anne replied. 'You would bring shame on the name of Shakspere by being part of that world. And who will mind the glover business while you are gone? You are needed here, Will. Do not forsake your wife and children.'

'You will have one less mouth to feed and our apprentices are already able to cut leather, as well as stitch the gloves,' I said. 'Do you want to see Sir Thomas's men arrive at my door to have me flogged? Perhaps my foolishness in penning that ditty has resulted in fate giving me a way out of our financial woes. And two pounds is hardly a trifling sum to add to our family's coffers. Laneham says it could be maybe more if we perform for a lord. When have we ever had two pounds saved before?'

'Don't take me for a fool,' Anne replied. 'Two pounds will not solve all our money worries, and what if you decide this is the life for you? I would be left in Stratford to bring up three children on my own, while you indulge your fancies. Put these ridiculous ideas behind you. You have a family, Will, and with that comes responsibilities. It is time you faced up to them.'

Anne was right. My mind had become possessed by the rapture I had felt while performing on stage, the joy that had filled my heart as I spoke the words of Kydd's wondrous play. I was being selfish, and I knew it. I needed to curb my impulses and settle down to live a humble life; never put myself or my family in jeopardy again.

But at that moment, Hamnet Sadler came crashing into our home, ignoring all propriety.

'Will, Will, I have terrible news!' he cried, then noticed my wife and children. 'Anne, send the children away. They should not hear what I have to tell you.'

Anne shot me a look of horror and bundled the children out of the house, ignoring their protests. My stomach was churning, and watching Hamnet wring his hands as he waited for the three of us to be alone only heighted my anxiety. Anne closed the door and leant against it, then slid down its frame as if the energy had been sucked out of her.

Hamnet drew his mouth into a fine line before speaking. 'Richard Ange, the baker, visited Charlecote Park this morning, to make a delivery of cake and bread to Lady Alice Lucy for a society gathering this evening. When he arrived at the gates, he saw a note pinned to them. It was four lines in length, and although Richard is not sufficiently well read to know all that it said, he had seen that it finished with the words, *By Will Shakspere, Stratford.* I fear some mischiefmaker has posted your poem about Sir Thomas for the amusement of his guests when they arrive.'

'Tell me Master Ange pulled the note down before it could be read,' I said. 'Tell me that, man!'

'He did not,' Hamnet replied, his voice thickening with emotion. 'He told me that he did not know if he was being observed. He feared that if one of Sir Thomas's men had already spied the note, they would make it hard for him if he tried to hide it. He made his delivery and hurried back to tell me of his discovery. I did not waste a moment, not even to inform you of what I had learnt. I rushed off to Charlecote and found the note gone, just a scrap of paper flapping on a pin to show it had been there. Sir Thomas now knows of your insolence. We have to pray that none of his guests were the ones to tell him, otherwise his humiliation will be even greater.'

'Calamity!' Anne cried. 'Sir Thomas's men will be on their way, I am surprised they did not arrive before dear Hamnet came with this news. You are done for, Will. Sir Thomas will have you endure a dozen lashes for the offence you have caused him, fifty if he has been the subject of ridicule by his guests.' She burst into tears. 'I cannot bear the thought of that. God has ignored our prayers.'

I collapsed into a chair, a roaring sound in my ears. Closing my eyes, I lost myself in silent prayer, beseeching the Lord to show me mercy, to spare me from what surely lay ahead.

Anne was shaking my shoulders.

'Quick, Will. He will not order his men to come after you until his guests have left. You have an hour or more before that reckoning. Throw some clothes into a sack and head off to join Laneham's men in Thame. When Sir Thomas's men arrive, I will tell them you have fled, I know not where. In a week, maybe two, I will visit Charlecote Park and throw myself upon the mercy of Lady Alice and plead with her to ask her husband to excuse your actions in return for some suitable penance. She is a good woman, some say the most pious in Warwickshire with her generosity in giving alms to the poor. If anyone can convince Sir Thomas not to have you whipped, it will be she.' Anne paused and nodded to herself before continuing. 'When you reach London, visit the Bell Inn by the cathedral called St Paul's. That's where

William Greenway stays when he travels to London to trade his lambskins. I trust our neighbour – I will have him leave word there when it is safe to return.'

I stared at Anne in awestruck amazement. 'God-a-mercy, that is a plan.'

Then I hesitated. 'But what of my responsibilities here in Stratford? Your words had much wisdom to them and made me see how unthinking I had been. A man should never think to abandon his wife and family.'

'I still think it is a plan that was hatched in foolishness,' Anne replied. 'But now it is a way out of the catastrophe you have brought upon yourself. For that reason, and that alone, it has my blessing. But remember you are a family man, Will Shakspere. Although I know nothing of the world of these players, I suspect there will be many vices to tempt you in the weeks ahead. Do not get drawn into risking your purse on a game of dice and promise me you will remember your wedding vows. Swear this oath to me and you can go with my blessing.'

I got down on bended knee and swore an oath of fidelity and to avoid the vice of gambling, then rose and kissed her, my heart bursting with gratitude at her generosity of spirit. 'I will never forget this trust you have shown me today, dear Anne. You will not regret this moment.'

'Such idiocy is the price I have to pay for marrying a youth of eighteen, when I have eight years' more worldly experience to give me a more sensible view of life.' She gave a half-hearted shrug. 'Hurry to the Queen's Men this moment, and find a coldharbour tonight to break your journey to Thame. We have no connection to that town, so Sir Thomas's men will not search in that direction. And hold your tongue when you are with the players. It is well known that Queen Elizabeth uses the troupe to spread Protestant propaganda and royalist enthusiasm throughout England. Keep your Catholic sympathies to yourself and take care not to offend any nobles you meet along the way.'

I said some rushed goodbyes. Anne gave me a brave smile; Susanna tried valiantly to hold back her tears; Father was stony-faced; Mother's face was etched with worry. Only the twins seemed oblivious to my departure. I walked with Hamnet Sadler as far as the Clopton Bridge before we said our farewells.

'I am indebted to you for your intelligence about the note,' I said to him. 'And to Richard Ange, for the risk he took in informing you of it. Be sure to thank him for me. I am forever grateful to both of you.'

Hamnet shrugged off my thanks. 'It is of no consequence. And if it means that your jesting at my expense about selling under-weight penny loaves has come to an end, that is reward enough. I think you win our competition of fools.'

'Deservedly, though I take no pride in being the victor,' I replied. 'Still, I have become a man in these last few days, even if it has taken a woman to make me so. Look after Anne while I am gone, good friend. You will see a changed Will Shakspere on my return.'

And with that, I took the Oxford road south to Thame.

WE TOURED THE TOWNS and noble houses of the Midlands on our way to journey's end in Kent. Travel was uncomfortable, the lodgings were basic, and the audience could be rowdy and unpredictable, throwing rotten fruit and heckling one moment, cheering and applauding the next. Every performance was unique, but I quickly learnt what actors have in common – they all wish to be the centre of attention and seek praise for their performances. Indeed, their desire to be flattered and feted, especially by those with power and influence, was insatiable. But I was not inclined to share these characteristics. I wished to listen rather than speak, learn rather than boast, be cautious rather than reckless. I became known as Quiet Will, and that suited me well. I kept opinions to myself, absorbed gossip but did not spread it, and never, never betrayed where my sympathies lay on politics or religion. Sir Thomas Lucy had taught me one lesson, at least.

The sternest tests of my new-found self-discipline and resolve were the hedonistic scenes that followed our afternoon performances. The new friends we had made during the day came to cheer us on our way, and the beer and wine flowed freely late into the night. Many a young maiden was bedded by my fellow actors, with varying degrees of discretion, and sometimes our departures were hasty. But all of these temptations I resisted. I would take only a few sips of wine, lest my tongue be loosened and I say something I might regret. I resisted all advances from womenfolk, but if truth be told these were few and far between. I had never been blessed with a handsome visage, and my balding pate did nothing to improve my allure. But that suited me well enough. Let people think me drab and dull, with little to contribute to the merrymaking.

I had been surprised to learn that we would not be playing *The Spanish Tragedy* at every performance. There were three other plays in the Queen's Men's repertoire – *The Troublesome*

Reign of King John, by George Peele, *The True Tragedy of Richard III* by Thomas Lodge and *The Famous Victories of Henry the Fifth* by Dick Tarlton. The first two men were poets from rich families, but Tarlton was one of the troupe, the actor who played the clown parts. He was the son of a pig farmer and had worked as water carrier in London before joining the Queen's Men as an apprentice.

I set about reading the other plays, and was shocked at what I discovered. Tarlton's play was an entertaining piece, about how a riotous Prince Henry transformed into a warrior king and had a great victory at the Battle of Agincourt; but *The Troublesome Reign of King John* was, to be blunt about it, dreadful. The dialogue was wooden, the rhetoric clumsy and pretentious; it was almost painful to read. *The True Tragedy of Richard III* was somewhat better, but even that lacked the drama and excitement of *The Spanish Tragedy*. Laneham had given Tarlton the job of re-writing the plays to take into account that, with Knell and Towne gone and I as their only replacement, they had to be performed with one less actor. *The Spanish Tragedy* had been easy to do for our Stratford performance, but the other plays would be more troublesome, as they already required actors to play multiple roles. Tarlton was working on his own play and I realised that here was my chance to impress Laneham, and at the same time to have something to do in the evening when the other players were cavorting with the local townsfolk.

Tarlton was delighted to be spared the effort of restructuring all three plays, and Laneham humoured my enthusiasm with an indulgent smile.

'There is no doubting your keenness, young Will,' he said. 'Tarlton had to have his arm twisted up his back to forsake a night's drinking, and you freely volunteer for this thankless chore. Make a start on *The True Tragedy of Richard III*, I think it will be the easier to fix. But don't take too long. It is to be played the day after next.'

I worked through the night and had it finished at first light, and after a few hours of sleep I presented it to Laneham and the rest of the troupe.

'Will, this is a marvel,' Laneham said after he had finished it. 'And do not be modest with your achievement; you have improved on the original.' He called the troupe to gather round to listen to his words. 'See here – when Thomas Lodge has King Richard call for a horse in the heat of battle in Boswell Field and cry out, *"A horse, a horse, a fresh horse"*? Will's line is … *so* much stronger. And he does the same throughout the play. Who would have thought a Stratford glover had such a way with words?' He turned to me. 'Take more time with *The Troublesome Reign of King John*. It pains me to recite some of the lines in that play, but the story is a favourite with our audiences and we are frequently called upon to perform it. Let's see if you can achieve the same miracle twice.'

Dick Tarlton was very generous with his time in helping me to do so. He was a most remarkable man. After each play was finished, he would ask the audience for a subject and improvise a poem on that topic on the spot. He could dance, play musical instruments and reduce a crowd to howls of laughter at his witticisms. On the stage he played the fool, but once he stepped off it he showed how wise and learned he was.

Tarlton took it upon himself to teach me the craft of play-writing. He described the rhetorical devices of stichomythia, antithesis and alliteration that the Greeks and Romans employed to make a phrase more memorable or striking, and explained the use of iambic pentameter to furnish the lines of a play with their rhythm. A glover from Stratford and the son of an Essex pig farmer improving on lines written by the likes of Thomas Lodge, the son of a Lord Mayor of London? The more I thought about that, the more excited I became.

Once I had finished *The Troublesome Reign of King John*, I continued to work hard, memorising the lines of every play we performed, practising on the musical instruments we used until I was passable on all of them. And volunteering for every task that needed to be done to set up and take down each performance. I wanted to know everything about stagecraft, so that no aspect of the playhouse would be a mystery to me. I honed my skills in dance steps and quick costume changes, saw the ways to swell out a crowd scene, and found myself making suggestions for improvements on how we performed the plays. Laneham sometimes became exasperated by my constant questions and suggestions, but he relented when he saw how diligently I applied myself to gaining these new skills. And he was patient when I asked him to explain the economics of performing in London. A great man called James Burbage had constructed a playhouse there, he told me, in Shoreditch, just outside the city walls, and had called it 'the Theatre'. I had not heard the word before, and Laneham told me it was based on the Greek word '*théatron*', meaning a place for viewing.

It was the first building since Roman times to have been constructed in England solely for the purpose of performing plays, and Laneham said it had been a great success. Plays were performed there to over a thousand people at one time, six times a week, a different play every day, with the ground-lings paying a penny to stand, the rest of the audience two pennies for the gallery, thruppence for a seat with a cushion. It was a marvel of our time, Laneham said, costing £700 to build, but he had yet to perform there, it being for the exclusive use of Leicester's Men, Burbage's own company of actors. And now he also had another playhouse, the Curtain, a few hundred yards away. At the time, our company – along with the others in London, the Admiral's Men and Lord Strange's Men – performed in the inn yards of any hostelry outside the city walls that would host us.

I enquired why all performances had to be outside the city of London itself, and was amused to be told that the city fathers considered acting a lewd entertainment. They did not want to attract crowds of strangers inside the city, so all performances had to be outside the city walls. But Laneham's words had me thinking. The number of people attending the Theatre meant up to eight pounds was earned for every performance, a sum beyond my wildest imaginings. With four acting companies in the city, the combined takings, even with the smaller size of the other venues, would be over twenty pounds a day. Just the beginner's share of such riches would match what I earned as a glover, and if I were to be successful, I could match the earnings of a gentleman. That was the argument that might convince Anne that I should try.

By the time the tour came to an end, I considered myself to be the equal of any of the players in the mechanics of performing. They might have been more charismatic and better actors than I, more skilled in the arts of juggling and acrobatics, but I was the one who knew the most about how to get things done. When we came to the last night of the tour, in the Kent town of Faversham, my mind was made up. I wanted to be an actor, or even better, write the words that would be spoken on stage. But I could not betray the trust that Anne had placed in me. I would only lead this life if I had her blessing.

After our final play was performed, Laneham gathered the troupe together and sang my praises.

'Will Shakspere has saved our skin after that unruly night in Thame,' he told everyone. 'He is a fast learner, has an exceptional memory, and is a master at improvisation.' There were cries of 'Hear, hear!' all around. 'And so, let us drink to his health tonight, lads, for tomorrow we travel to Gravesend and catch the ferry to London to go our separate ways. Will, you can be a glover again.'

Everyone cheered, but another reality of this actor's life dawned on me. The Queen's Men would rest for a time while Laneham got his affairs in order. Some actors would come, some would go, and I was being dismissed. An actor's life was precarious as well as footloose. Still, now that I had tasted this life, I could not return to the one I knew before.

My first duty, however, was to make good my promise and return to Stratford and my family, if the message awaiting me at the Bell Inn in St Paul's told me it was safe to do so.

I prayed that when I did see Anne again, I would be able to convince her to give me permission to return to London.

London, and whatever destiny awaited me.

Chapter Six
Alice ~ 1540

FAVERSHAM TURNED OUT to be a much bigger town than I had imagined, with three hundred houses and tenements, and a town warehouse down by the quay. Ships arrived daily with hops, herring and eels from Ostend and Dunkirk, and put to sea again laden with wool. It was an important port – a navigable creek ran northward to the Swale on the Thames estuary, making Faversham the first junction of road and sea since Dover. This was an important consideration, Thomas told me, as it meant that the town enjoyed many natural advantages that could be gainfully exploited.

We found a modest place to live, but did not stay long. It turned out that Thomas had made a most profitable bargain with Sir Edward before we left Kirtling Tower. My step-father would notify Thomas when the Privy Council decided the land and property that would be put up for sale from the dissolution of the monastery at Faversham, and my husband would buy it at a most advantageous price. And finding the money to make the purchase was not a problem. Thomas was now responsible for ensuring that customs and duties had been paid by the merchants using every port between Faversham and Sandwich. The amount varied according to the size of the ship, and there were many traders and merchants who would happily provide a sweetener to ensure that the size of their vessel was underestimated.

The combination of ready cash from his appointment as controller of customs by Sir Thomas Cheyne, and the lucrative intelligence being passed to him by Sir Edward, meant that Thomas became very rich, very quickly. After a few months we moved out of our first home in Faversham and into Abbey Gate, one of the finest houses in the town.

As it had lain empty for some time, Thomas organised an event to warm the house and to cleanse it of the vagrant spirits that occupy uninhabited dwellings – and, of course, to make his mark on the town and show he was now a person of considerable wealth.

Each of the guests brought a bundle of firewood as a gift with which to build fires in all available fireplaces. All the great families of Faversham were in attendance – the Colwells, the Drylands and the Norwells, along with the town's brewer, John Castlock, and Lewis Merden, the mayor. The success of the occasion was of the greatest importance to Thomas, and he almost emptied his coffers by bringing down a cook from London to prepare the meal, but it turned out to be a most worthwhile investment. The centrepiece, a testament to the artistry of our cook, was a magnificent roasted goose with all the trimmings. Delicately carved vegetables and gilded pasties nestled around it, a feast for the eyes as much as the stomach. The chef brought with him from London candied fruits, imported spices and exotic cheeses from faraway lands, offering a taste of the world beyond our shores. Mayor Merden pronounced it the greatest feast in Faversham he could ever recall.

Thomas was caught up in the moment, engaging in an animated conversation with a town jurat tipped to be a future mayor, one Thomas Dunkyn. Their conversation became so intense that I had to gently intervene, reminding my husband to share his attention with the other guests in attendance. Only Anthony Aucher, from a great noble family who resided in the neighbouring town of Otterden, seemed unamused by the proceedings, but I was told he rarely visited Faversham so his disdain was of little consequence.

'Old money always despises new,' Thomas muttered to me when I commented on Aucher's thunderous expression.

Aucher was the only guest with whom I did not engage that evening, as he left early, without farewells. Why he had even attended, I could not fathom.

But his rudeness could not mar what was otherwise the finest evening of my marriage. The priest had given a fulsome blessing to the house and it had been a night of lively conversation, shared laughter, and the promise of a future filled with both prosperity and genuine warmth. Looking around the table at the relaxed and animated faces, I felt a surge of satisfaction. This was my destiny. The clinking of glasses and the final strains of the lute marked the end of a truly memorable evening. I knew this was a housewarming party that would not be soon forgotten.

That was the start of our efforts to make the Ardens the golden couple of Faversham. What gay evenings our efforts undoubtedly turned out to be. Laughter erupted like fireworks, witty repartee crackled in the air, and the conversation flowed as smoothly as the finest aged wine. Serious discussions among the men about the Faversham charter and the effect of the recent wool tariffs on trade were interspersed with light-hearted banter and playful teasing. Agnes Colwell had made a recent trip to Bath, and I found her descriptions of the Roman baths and the latest fashions to be found there fascinating. I countered with anecdotes told to me by the Faversham ladies not present, careful to choose stories that were both entertaining and appropriate. A supper at the Arden household was soon the most coveted invitation in all of Faversham.

I practised the art of holding a gentleman's attention at supper, and found myself being described as charming, enchanting, even captivating; all the accolades I hoped to hear from my husband, but instead spoken by others. Thomas seemed most pleased by my new-found status, and took to clasping my hand between his as a sign of his growing appreciation of me. That was the limit of his affection, however, and an unspoken agreement formed between us. I would fascinate husbands and charm wives; he would provide a wealthy and extravagant life, that we might be the envy of all.

I also took great delight in showing off our new home when Mother came to visit. She had travelled with news of my step-sisters' betrothals – Christiana to William Somerset, third Earl of Worchester, and Mary to Henry Scrope, ninth Baron of Bolton – and she had obviously prepared herself for the need to remind me again that my own marriage had been a disappointment to her. I could see a change of heart as soon as she alighted at the house.

'I am most pleased that your husband has put Sir Edward's sponsorship to good use,' she said, gazing in surprise at the size of our accommodation. 'Fortune has smiled brightly on you, with so many riches available to those who wish to assist in ridding the monasteries and abbeys of their land and possessions.'

I bridled at Mother's accusation that Thomas's success was all her husband's doing, even if I nursed a secret sympathy with the insinuation that it was somehow tarnished.

'It is an opportunity available to all, dear Mother,' I said. 'But my Thomas has the boldness and the means to take advantage of this historic chance while others hesitate and falter. He is a man of strong nerve and resolution.'

Mother lowered her chin to look down at me. 'Yes, Thomas has strong will and determination. And he is doubly fortunate in having Sir Thomas Cheyne as sponsor as well as Sir Edward. I never realised that a shipping clerk could be so well paid as to be able to pursue these great opportunities.'

Mother was perhaps more unreservedly pleased to hear of Thomas's other ascendancy. My husband was not satisfied with merely becoming wealthy; he had other ambitions in Faversham. Three years after our arrival, he was elected one of the town's twenty-four common councillors, the first step on Faversham's political ladder. His property purchases expanded beyond Faversham and he began to have dealings with other merchants and financiers who were also taking advantage of the opportunities afforded by the dissolution of the monasteries and the riches that could be grabbed for a fraction of their true value by those with the means and connections to do so.

It was then that I first started to hear more about Anthony Aucher. He was the paymaster at Dover, so was in an even more advantageous position than Thomas to receive improper inducements. But he was also a radical, who wanted religious change to go faster and further than many of the more conservative men in power felt comfortable with. Aucher had been Thomas Cromwell's man when Cromwell had been the King's chief minister, and so could have had no greater or more powerful sponsor unless it were King Henry himself. But with the demise of radicalism and Cromwell executed on the order of the King, Aucher's position in recent times had become much weaker.

Thomas rarely discussed his business affairs with me, but he did have something to say about Anthony Aucher.

'Aucher thinks himself beyond reach,' he said, 'but the heretic Thomas Cromwell was his sponsor. Now that the King has had Cromwell beheaded, Aucher would do well to keep his own counsel, to be as reluctant to express radical views as are the other Kent gentry.'

'But I've heard that the Auchers are one of the great families of Kent,' I replied, 'with a manor house that dates from the time of Edward the Second. And that Anthony Aucher is known as someone who makes enemies easily and never forgives any who cross him. He is not a man to be trifled with.'

Thomas looked uninterested in my observations, so I took the matter no further. He was as indifferent to what I said as he was to everything else in our marriage. Were it not for the constant tasks involved in running a household, and the flattering attention of Thomas's business acquaintances when they came to supper, I would have pulled out my hair and gouged my face with my nails at the empty hollow in the centre of my life. Thomas spent most evenings out with the one close friend he had made since our arrival in Faversham, Thomas Dunkyn, playing card games and drinking heavily, staggering home barely conscious. One night I plucked up the courage to place my hand on his private parts as Thomas was sleeping, performing the action I practised with Tom

Mosby when I wanted to stimulate him into renewing his affections. Thomas moved my hand away and the next night he demanded we sleep in separate rooms.

Every day, I yearned for his touch, that he might come to visit me in the gloaming, but he did not. Was this true of many men? How could I find out? No lady of my acquaintance would openly talk of such matters. But I needed to know. In the end, I decided that if anyone could tell me, it would be Agnes Colwell. She was one of the Faversham ladies' circle with whom I kept company, and she had a large brood of children, five in all, so she obviously received considerable attention from her husband. I invited her for a stroll and waited until we had left West Street and turned right at Tanner's Green. Now that the Guildhall had moved from there to Court Street, near to our home, it was a quiet part of town where there was less chance of being overheard. Her servant girl had just been wed to her childhood sweetheart, and I remarked on how happy the couple looked.

'A marriage of love,' I said to her. 'It must be wonderful for a man to be free to choose the woman of his dreams. How I envy that young couple.'

Agnes stared at me as if I were mad. 'A love marriage borders on the indecent, if you ask me,' she said. 'Working folk have hot blood and can be allowed to give in to their base instincts. But it is not something to be tolerated in polite society, where decorum and decency must be preserved. There is no place for wanton thoughts and actions amongst ladies of standing.'

I thought of my liaisons with Tom Mosby and a hot flush came across my cheeks. It was true, then. Love-making of that intensity would always be denied me.

'But God ordained marriage for the procreation of children,' I countered. 'Surely He means a husband and wife to lie together?'

'For children ... yes. And my husband is most insistent on these duties. For my part, it is but one of the burdens a wife has to endure.' She spotted two ladies coming in the opposite direction. 'Look, here are the Dryland sisters, Joan and Edith. I'm sure you know them. Let us ask them to join us on our walk.'

I decided to seek counsel from another – Tom's sister, Cislye, who had travelled with us to Faversham from Kirtling to be with her daughter. No doubt some would consider it shocking that I should discuss such intimate matters with the mother of my maid, but Cislye and I had grown close since moving to Faversham, and she now had her own dwelling on the other side of the town. Our friendship had first blossomed because she was the only person with whom I was acquainted when I began my new life in Faversham, and in due course she became a confidante. Cislye, of course, knew of my affair with her brother and must have guessed at the passions that it unlocked, that we should both have taken such risks in indulging them. Her husband had died a few years after Elisabeth was born and she had told me that none could replace him. This hinted, to me, of a marriage that was more than one of convenience.

One evening, when Thomas was away in London, I told Cislye of my despair.

'Thomas is spending more and more time in London as his commercial opportunities grow there. This has attracted much commiseration from the ladies of Faversham, that a husband should be away so often when I am not yet with child. But the truth is, I fear I may never be with child. It matters not to our marriage whether my husband is at home or away. You have no doubt heard from Elisabeth of our new sleeping arrangements in this house. We are not truly man and wife.'

'I thought as much, Miss Alice,' Cislye replied. 'There should be a bloom about you, as is common in a wife who knows herself to be loved. I can see there is not.'

I hesitated. How could I confess how truly troubled I had become? Then the words tumbled out.

'Thomas is so caught up in his desire for wealth, he quite forgets me,' I said, my voice trembling. 'He sees me as his companion, not his wife. He married me because it was expected of him to have a wife, not because he desired one. He chose me as he would choose a horse for his stable.'

'I am sure he loves you, in his way,' Cislye replied. 'And his feelings may grow over time. Be patient, my lady. I am sure all will come good in the end.'

A tear pricked my eye. 'I am not so sure,' I said. 'And having tasted passion before, it is painful to think I shall never feel it again.' I blushed and caught my breath at my indiscretion. 'Forgive me, Cislye. I have spoken more frankly than is appropriate. But we both know to whom I refer.'

'And I'm sure he feels the same way. My brother enquires after you every time I hear from him. But some things are not meant to be.'

I knew that to be true. But a month later, a miracle. Tom Mosby arrived in Faversham.

He had come for me.

Chapter Seven
Will ~ 1587

WE TRAVELLED as a group up Watling Street to the Gravesend ferry, and it was there that the members of the troupe went their separate ways. The actors heading north to their homes and families crossed the Thames to Tilbury, and those bound for London waited for the next long ferry up the river. If I were travelling straight to Stratford, I should have joined the first group, but I needed to be in London to see what message awaited me at the Bell Inn. My decision was greeted with much ribald humour.

'So Quiet Will has turned his back on his wife and children?' Tarlton laughed. 'Have our tales of the fleshpots of London proved too much of a temptation at last? You're a queer one, Will Shakspere. You resist the charms of many an innkeeper's daughter and now that our journey is over, you head to the whorehouses of London. It will not take long for you to empty your two-pound purse.'

I had never spoken to any member of the troupe about my troubles with Sir Thomas Lucy, so I endured the teasing with as much dignity as I could muster.

'I am a mere country lad who has never ventured this far south before. Why would I not want to see our great capital city? I am told the Roman road we have taken out of Faversham heads north through London and on to Stratford and the Forest of Arden. I will walk the road of history, not some muddy track through the fields of Essex.'

It was a lame excuse, but all that I could think of in the moment. In truth, though, I did have a desire to see London, a place I had heard of all my life.

I went over to John Laneham. 'Can I sit next to you on the journey to London?' I asked him. 'I visit the city, not for the reason these fellows suggest, but to see if another company of actors there might have need of my services. You mentioned the Admiral's Men, Lord Strange's Men and James Burbage's Theatre.' I wrapped my tongue around that last unusual word. 'Can you tell me whom I should call on when we arrive? Perhaps share with me your thoughts on how I can make a living on the stage?'

Laneham, for once, looked hesitant and when he spoke, his voice had a coaxing eloquence I had not heard before.

'Will, Will, give up on these fancies,' he said. 'I fear your head has been filled with false notions from listening to tales of bravado from your fellow players. An actor's life is not for you. You have seen the rewards can be fleeting and unreliable; it's a life best pursued by those with no responsibilities and who care only for themselves. You are a family man, and have proved yourself a man of character, resisting all debauchery on this tour. Go back to your wife and children in Stratford, and live a quiet, honourable life again. These would be the thoughts I would share with you.'

A great weight filled my body. 'But acting is thriving in London, you told me so yourself. The Theatre of James Burbage, his new Curtain playhouse, not to mention all the courtyards of the inns where the other companies perform. Surely one of them would give me a chance?'

Laneham hesitated again. 'Let me be honest with you, Will. You are a fine man and a great companion. And I have never seen anyone work so hard and apply themselves so diligently in assisting us to put on a performance.' He paused. A long pause. 'But you are not a great actor. Passable, yes, but not outstanding. To be paid enough to support a family living eighty miles away, you would have to be one of the London greats, the likes of Richard Cowley or Ned Alleyn. They hold the audience in the palm of their hand when they perform. You remember all your lines and can dance a jig when required. That isn't enough.'

My toes curled in embarrassment. But I steadied myself and spoke in a calm, confident voice. 'I know my failings, Master Laneham, and I know you mean well by pointing them out to me. You are right, the life of an actor would be too precarious an existence for me to consider, given my circumstances. But it is the likes of Thomas Kydd I would wish to emulate, not Cowley or Alleyn. Kydd is only a few years my senior and has already written the play you most often perform. Dick Tarlton's play is also well received and he comes from the same humble background as I. And you yourself have complimented me on the new words I have crafted for the plays we perform. That is the life I crave; writing words, not performing them. One day, perhaps, even putting on plays; not being in them. If I can scrape a living while I try to do so, who knows? One day my dreams might come true.'

Laneham gave a little shrug, then nodded slowly. 'A bold plan, certainly. The changes you made to *The Troublesome Reign of King John* were so marked, I doubt if George Peele would now recognise his own play.' He looked to the sky with more theatricality than the moment deserved, as if weighing a mighty decision. 'Let me make some introductions when we arrive in London. I will introduce you to James Burbage, to see if he has any employment.'

I thanked Laneham for his generosity and settled down to enjoy the ferry journey. We were transported in a tilt boat – four oarsmen and a steerman – and made good time up the river. As the Thames took a sharp bend to go around the Isle of Dogs, where Laneham told me the Queen kept her hunting packs, I had my first clear view of the city. Huge palls of smoke drifted skywards and already I could hear the peal of bells, even though they were a mile distant. As the river swung to the left again, London Bridge came into sight. I knew it would be on a grander scale than our own Clopton Bridge in Stratford, but nothing had prepared me for its magnificence. Twenty arches spanned the river. Everywhere I looked were hundreds of wherries of all sizes taking passengers up, down and across the river; so many, I could have crossed by stepping from one to the next. The Thames, Laneham told me, was a giant highway, coursing through the centre of the city, feeding an endless swarm of people into the narrow, crowded streets, sinews that spread across the city from its banks. I saw a group of water carriers where the river flowed fastest against the bank, queuing to fill flasks suspended from yokes above their shoulders, and thought of the hard life Dick Tarlton must have lived, doing that every day when he first arrived from Essex. I had prepared myself to be amazed at the size and scale of the city I had heard about all my life, and had always dreamed of visiting. Now I was here, it did not disappoint.

A throng of wherries surrounded the tilt boat as it docked, Laneham shouting that we had no need of their services as we were to cross London Bridge. The commotion distracted me, and so when we disembarked the boat, I was unprepared for the sight I was to behold. There, on the Great Stone Gate entrance to the bridge, were heads on pikes, some rotting and green, others barely more than skulls, warnings to anyone foolhardy enough to plan an insurrection against the crown. I walked along this diabolical parade, pausing at each one, wondering who was the man it had once been. Was the head of my mother's second cousin, Edward Arden of that noble branch of her family, still on display? It was four years since he had met his fate after being named in Sommerville's assassination attempt. If his head were on a pike, it would now be no more than a skull.

'A gruesome sight, is it not?' said Laneham. 'Take this fellow, for example.' He pointed to the half-rotted head, its eyes pecked out by the crows. 'I do not know what crime he committed, but his torture would have been so great, he would have found it a blessing when the executioner's axe fell on him.'

I retched, such was the horror. Not just at the shockingly macabre scene, but also at the fear that one day my own fate could match that of these poor souls. I had kept my lips tight shut on the road when the Queen's Men rallied support for the Protestant cause. It went against my Catholic beliefs, but Sir Thomas Lucy had taught me a valuable lesson. And the ghoulish sight before me seared that lesson into my brain.

The others said their goodbyes, Tarlton heading off to the dice houses, the rest to the nearest tavern. Laneham gave me a leather purse containing my share of the profits from the tour, with an extra crown for the work I had done on reworking the plays. We headed off to meet James Burbage, north through Eastcheap, making a small detour to the Bell Inn to find if the landlord had a message for me. He did; William Greenway had stayed there two weeks before and had told the landlord to inform me it was safe to return to Stratford. Elated, I arranged a night's accommodation and then re-joined Laneham. We passed through Bishopsgate, past Bedlam hospital for the insane in Finsbury Fields, until we came to Shoreditch, the location of both the Curtain and the Theatre. Entering the Theatre, I gazed in awe. Three galleries surrounded an open yard where a roofed wooden stage jutted out to where the groundlings would stand. Burbage was there, and he and Laneham had some business to discuss, the two men enquiring of each other which plays were doing well. I was struck by the friendliness of the exchanges. Although they were in many ways competitors, there was an easy camaraderie between them and they both seemed to wish for the other to succeed. Laneham called me over and introduced me to the great man himself. I enacted a frozen smile, conscious of my eyes blinking. I widened them to bring my nervousness under control, and the two men laughed.

'Are you sure this one has not escaped from Bedlam Hospital?' said Burbage. 'Come, Will, you are amongst friends. Laneham here tells me you were a handy man to have on tour with him, and stepped on stage at only a moment's notice when John Towne ran a dagger through poor William Knell.'

'Aye, and wrote a fine volley of words, quickly shot off, when he had to rejig our plays to be performed with one fewer actor in the cast,' Laneham added. 'Will Shakspere is a *Johannes factotum*, a jack of all trades, who would be a useful addition to any company. He bade me introduce him to you.'

'So, you fancy a life on the stage?' Burbage stroked the edge of his goatee beard. 'Tell me, where did you serve your apprenticeship?'

'On the road, with John Laneham, and the rest of his players in the Queen's Men,' I replied, my chest out, chin high. 'It is true that I had stepped into the breach to help out after the tragedy that befell William Knell. I have studied most assiduously the craft of acting and have had a fine teacher to guide me.' I gave a bow in Laneham's direction. 'Now, I have to return to my home in Stratford to sort out some family matters, but hope to return to London and join a company of actors. If the Queen's Men are still resting on my return, would such a position be available here?'

'Sadly, no,' Burbage replied, shaking his head. 'My actors are recruited from the Children of Paul's, where we choose the choirboys to play the women's parts in our plays. Their parents pay me eight pounds to have them join as apprentices, and if they show promise they spend some years learning the skills of the trade, at fourpence a day. With a fair wind they are then accepted into the company. That is a proposition I assume would not find favour with you, Will. But you seem to have impressed Laneham, and he is a hard man to please. Give me a recital. Let it be a piece of your choosing.'

I gave him Hieronimo's soliloquy from *The Spanish Tragedy*, and when I finished I waited for a reaction. Laneham looked at Burbage and shrugged. A gesture of support or apology? I could not tell.

Eventually, Burbage turned to me and gave a slow applause. 'A speech of passion, Master Shakspere, even if it lacks the technical skills to make it work on a bigger stage. Many in the crowd will not be able to see the expression on your face, so you will have to convey your feelings by gesture – strike your forehead to show shame, fold your arms as a sign of contemplation and so on. But no matter. These things can be learned, just like all fifty-nine gestures of the hand. What matters is authenticity, so the audience believe you feel the emotions you are conveying. That you have, and it cannot be taught.'

'So, there is a place for me?' I felt as if my heart might explode inside me.

'Not so fast, Will,' Burbage replied, giving Laneham an amused glance. 'I have twenty-seven men in my company, which meets all my needs. I have not asked you for a display of fencing, nor juggling, nor even acrobatics, which are but some of the skills a professional player needs to acquire, as I sense I would find them lacking in one so new to this game. Go back to Stratford, practise these arts, and one day, if you come back to London, we can talk again. But you have done John Laneham proud today. I can see why he commends you.'

I thanked Burbage profusely, telling him I would be grateful for any opportunity, however menial, and went off to my lodgings for the night, my mind a whirl of conflicting thoughts and emotions. All my instincts told me there was a way to write for the stage. Choose a meaty topic; a murder, a battle, something to satisfy the audience's bloodlust. Make myself useful to the playhouse owners and leaders of companies of actors, so that they listen to what I have written and decide if it takes their fancy. I was breathless with excitement.

Then reality sank in. I had penned nothing original other than some crude ditties to entertain my drinking companions in a Stratford inn. Yes, I had changed, some would say improved, the words written by others. But I lacked the learning and erudition to know of a suitable topic to write about. I knew nothing of Spanish noblemen or mythical Greek goddesses. The great chronicles of record, the classical works of the Greeks and Romans, were not to be found in Stratford, and without them I had no way of knowing the details of any legend I chose for my play. Terror ate away at me, the fear of failure, of suffering ridicule from an audience, above all of seeing the disappointment on my Anne's face when I returned to Stratford, broken and penniless.

I could not face such a crop of disappointments. Maybe there was something to be said for a glover's life after all.

Chapter Eight
Alice ~ 1543

LUCKILY, MY HUSBAND was out and about in Faversham, dealing with some business matters, when Tom Mosby arrived unannounced. My shock at seeing him was followed immediately by a prickling feeling that enveloped my whole body, an insatiable yearning. He had lost none of the half-tamed ferocity in his eyes, but he had shed some of the roughness that I had first noticed about him; his manner was poised now, almost dignified. But I could still sense a black fire burning within him and when he held me in his gaze it felt as though he had penetrated into my inner being.

I stammered out a greeting and asked what he was doing here.

'I came to see my sister,' he replied, gazing at me in a way I had not been looked at since marrying Thomas. 'She has told me what a fine town this is, and how there would be many opportunities for an industrious tailor to make a living. I have come to see if fortune will favour me, and was ... Well, I was hoping you would be pleased to see me.'

Cislye must have told him of the depths of my despair and I realised that I had not counselled her to do otherwise, for deep down I knew I wanted Tom to know of my anguish. Now that I saw him standing before me, in the flesh, I longed for him to become part of my life again. But for that I needed

Thomas's permission. No wife could invite someone to visit their home without their husband's consent.

'A quite extraordinary development,' I told Thomas as we played backgammon that evening. 'Elisabeth's uncle has arrived in Faversham today. Have I ever told you about Tom Mosby, my step-father's tailor in Kirtling? He has plans to establish his business here. Shall we invite him for supper as a welcome?'

Thomas raised an eyebrow at the suggestion we should dine with someone below our social standing, and surprise turned to suspicion when I pressed him to agree.

'Is there more to this fellow than meets the eye? He would be someone without refinement, would he not? Why would a lady of your standing want to have any social dealings with a man like that?'

'He was kind to me when I was younger. I think if you got to know him, you would find him a most diverting companion.'

'But has he any culture and breeding? And how could we possibly entertain the uncle of our maid? Who would wait on him? Really, Alice, this is a most absurd proposition. Permit him to visit at the rear entrance when he wishes to meet his niece, I would not be so heartless as to deny him some time with his kin, so long as it does not impinge on the good running of the household. But he is not our social equal.'

'That is most kind,' I replied, biting down on my lip as I summoned the courage to speak more. 'But I think it could be to your advantage to afford him more than that already generous dispensation.' I fiddled with the dice shaker as I chose my words carefully. 'You are now a person of high standing in the town. It is time that you had your own man, someone you can advance as your sponsors advanced you, and in return receive his loyalty and gratitude. Grant me one wish, dear husband. Interview Tom Mosby with a view to becoming his benefactor. You would enhance your reputation still further as someone who can spot the most able. You will benefit most appreciably in return.'

'There is something not quite right about this,' Thomas replied, narrowing his eyes, appraising me as he would a horse dealer, or a chapman. 'Why have you never spoken of him before? What was the reason he left Kirtling before I arrived? Why were you most insistent at having his sister and her daughter accompany us to Faversham? I am not a fool, Alice. Tell me what is going on here.'

And so, I confessed. I told him of my shameful past and how, when it was discovered, our affair had ended. I expected Thomas to be angry, even to threaten me with divorce, but to my shock he seemed unconcerned by the news that another man had lain with me before my wedding night.

'As long as this Tom Mosby does nothing to disrupt my business, I will tolerate his presence in this town,' he told me. 'And if you feel you must meet with him, then do so when his sister is present. As to whether I make him my man or not, that is a far weightier matter. I will take my measure of him, and if I find he has merit, I will consider such an undertaking in the fullness of time. There we are. Now let this be an end to the discussion.'

Thomas's words confirmed what I had already suspected. He had so little desire for me that even the presence in Faversham of another man with whom I had lain did not trouble him. Any dealings concerning patronage or commerce that he might have with Tom Mosby were far more important than what had transpired between us in the past.

My bed felt even lonelier that night.

I tried to tell myself none of this mattered. That I could have a good life, gossiping in the afternoon with the ladies of the Colwell, Dryland and Norwell families, talking about tiffanies and spangles, powders and perfumes; playing the virginal and entertaining my husband's business acquaintances in the evening; but when each night fell it brought home to me the sad reality of my life. I had everything I could ever have wished for, except love. I had forsaken my one true love and married someone whom Mother thought was the best I could do. And although that man had exceeded Mother's expectations in terms of success, he had failed with respect to his desire for me. Tom Mosby's presence in Faversham was a powder keg, waiting for a spark. And rather than shun him as an unwelcome reminder of my past, I had petitioned for him to be invited into my home. I kept telling myself that I was being foolish entertaining these notions, that I was making my husband's rejection of me all the more painful by wanting to have Tom in my life. But I couldn't help myself. I wanted to keep seeing him. Even if the parting at the end of every meeting would be more painful than the last. I wanted to deny myself, but I could not.

I MET TOM A few days later, at Cislye's house. She busied herself in the garden so I would appear chaperoned to any who saw us.

'The Faversham air agrees with you, Alice,' Tom said. We sat on two stools at the far end of the garden, out of Cislye's hearing. 'I had forgotten how beautiful you are. I built up a good trade in London after I was forced to leave Kirtling, and hesitated to give it up to move here. But seeing you again, I have no regrets.'

My husband had never told me I was beautiful and I cursed my vanity that Tom's words had gladdened my heart.

'You are most kind, Master Mosby. But I am a married woman now. Such comments are unwelcome given my new circumstances. Let me just say that my heart is lifted to be with you today. I hope we can be friends again, much as I am with your dear sister.'

There was a gleam in Tom's eye as he looked at me, as though he could see through the façade and detect my true feelings. His smile reminded me of his greeting when I visited his cottage in Kirtling, and a delicious warmth spread through my body. I looked away so he would not see the passion his presence awakened in me.

'We will have none of this "Master Mosby" and no talk of mere friendship,' he said, placing his hand under my chin to force me to look up at him. 'We had something wonderful together in Kirtling, and I travelled here in hope that we might have that again. I know that is what you desire also, Alice. Do not pretend otherwise.'

I pulled back so his hand fell to his side, and I thought of my lonely bed in Abbey Gate. Was I to spend the rest of my days abandoned, forlorn? Would I never feel a man's touch again?

'No, Tom, we cannot,' I said. 'I have sworn to be faithful, to honour and obey my husband until my dying day. To break that vow would be a sin.' Be faithful. Honour. Obey. I repeated the words in my head, over and over again. But mere words could not drive my feelings away.

'Thomas Arden does not deserve your fidelity. We can be together again and he need never know. How often is he in London? I hear he carouses late into the night at the Fleur de Lis with Thomas Dunkyn. There will be plenty of opportunities for us to be together. He will suspect nothing, know nothing.'

'He already knows about us,' I said, staring down again. 'I told him of your arrival and he immediately became suspicious. I could not hide the truth from him. I have confessed everything.'

A flash of anger passed over Tom's face, but he quickly regained composure and leant forward, raising an eyebrow as he spoke. 'That was a little foolhardy, Alice. But it proves the worthiness of my proposal. He is a powerful man in Faversham, is he not? He could have had me run out of town at a moment's notice. Not only does he reject your love, he tolerates one who does love you, and agrees to our seeing each other. He knows his shortcomings as a husband. Does that not tell you the rightness of us being together again? Say yes, Alice. I know you want to.'

Thoughts raced through my mind in a chaotic rush. What was it that Tom had said? That my husband did not deserve my fidelity ... Did Cislye tell him of the secrets I shared with her? Was that why Tom had come to Faversham? And one more question, tearing at my heart but at the same time offering a flicker of hope. Was it not Thomas who was committing the greater sin, refusing to lie with his wife as God ordained a husband should?

I did not tell Tom my concerns, nor that I thought only of him every night as I lay in bed. Instead I said again that I could not break the vows I had made on my wedding day, unless Thomas were to agree. And no husband would ever assent to such an arrangement.

'Then we shall have but a passing acquaintance for as long as I reside in Faversham,' Tom said, his face reddening as he stood up. 'And if you will not grant me what I desire, do not complain when I seek it elsewhere.' He strode over to the cottage gate. 'It is time for you to leave, Alice. This conversation has already gone on for longer than is appropriate between a man and a married woman, chaperone or no chaperone. I rue the day that I left London for Faversham with such false expectations.'

I wanted desperately to plead with him to hear my idea that Thomas might consider making him his man, an arrangement that could lead to all sorts of opportunities for advancement, but he was looking straight ahead and I could see he desired me to leave. He waved me through the gate, gave a formal little bow without catching my eye, and bade me a curt farewell.

I knew I had made the right decision, but I returned to Abbey Gate shaken and despondent.

And that unhappy conversation was not the only reason for my misery. I had taken a practical view about the less than honest guerdons my husband was using to buy his property, and prayed every Sunday that God would forgive him on Judgement Day. But when I raised my concerns, Thomas laughed them off.

'Do you think we could enjoy this fine life on the proceeds from buying and selling skeins of wool from Suffolk farmers?

The days of my working hard for a pittance are over, Alice. Untold riches can be had by those who are bold and cunning enough to grease a few wheels to make things go smoothly, and to wink at trades that go unrecorded. And there are enough greedy men who, for a small consideration, will ensure that plenty of opportunities are presented to me.'

I offered Thomas a weak smile, the most I could do to show my support. But there was another fear that was preying on my mind. Bribery and corruption were sins, but they were not a danger to our status. Thomas was becoming adept at making enemies. Not just Anthony Aucher, but many other powerful men were starting to grumble about his aggressive behaviour when it came to business. At the behest of their menfolk, first the Norwell ladies, then the Drylands, began to refuse my invitations to call. Finally, Agnes Colwell, whom I considered to be my friend, also told me that our frequent walks had to come to an end.

'Your husband has such a vulgar obsession with money,' she told me. 'It really is most unbecoming of a gentleman. He rewards those whom he favours, that is true, and for that he has many allies amongst the menfolk of the town. Forgive me for saying so, Alice, but he can be most unkind to those for whom he feels he has no further use, and he is vindictive to any who cross him. Many are saying that he is important to do business with, but not the sort of man with whom they wish to socialise. Unless he changes his ways, you may find yourself shunned by the ladies of Faversham.'

Thomas was beginning to make life in Faversham deeply unpleasant, and things came to a head as he left for some business dealings one morning.

'I have one last encumbrance to be rid of on these new church lands I have acquired before I can turn my mind to more productive matters. I have impressed certain influential men with my ideas since my election as common councillor. I need to seize the moment to inspire new initiatives in the town, so that my star will outshine that of others around me.'

'There is gossip in the town, Thomas,' I replied. 'This "encumbrance" you talk of. Is that Widow Cook and her cottage on the edge of your new estate? There is talk that you wish her ill, yet she is held in respect and affection by all who know her.'

Thomas gave an exaggerated sigh. 'It is a matter of commerce, not of the heart,' he said. 'She pays a pittance in rent for that property, yet it would be a fine dwelling for two brothers and their families, who would be glad to secure such a home and would pay well to do so.'

I began thumbing my ear, a habit I had adopted in childhood during moments of disquiet, or even anger.

'But Widow Cook is an upstanding woman, who was left only a modest inheritance when her husband was taken from her.' I spoke quietly, but could not control the tremor in my voice. 'Could you not allow her to see out her days in the place she has lived all of her married life?'

Thomas's eyes narrowed. 'I did not buy that land with a view to charity. I am already burdened with more requests for alms than I desire to fulfil.'

'But Widow Cook has done no wrong to find herself in such desperate circumstances,' I insisted, my voice rising a little. 'Will a few pounds more in annual rent really make a difference to your exchequer?'

· Thomas walked to the door to signal the discussion was at an end.

'The church land on which Widow Cook resides will not be the last of my purchases. Do I have to accommodate every lament I encounter while I try to make the most of my acquisitions? If I did, there would be little point in pursuing the opportunities that now present themselves to me. I am sorry for Widow Cook, but she must face up to the reality. I will give her to the next full moon to make new arrangements. There we are. That is more than any other landlord would agree to. Let us put thoughts of her behind us.'

I was disgusted by his words. 'How can you show no mercy to that poor woman,' I said, 'when your own mother was given succour and support in her time of need?'

That stung Thomas. 'You will never allow me to forget my upbringing and how it compares so unfavourably to your own at Kirtling Tower,' he said. 'What was yours is mine now, and you should not forget it.'

'It is not you who should feel wronged,' I replied. I felt my face redden, and raised my voice almost to a shout. 'Now that you have shown your true self in matters of business, I cannot but conclude that you considered Sir Edward North's patronage a more important part of our marriage bargain than any feelings you had for me.'

Thomas laughed. 'You should be happy that such speculation might have a grain of truth in it. Were it otherwise, I would not be so tolerant of Tom Mosby's presence in this town. But regarding Widow Cook, I do not feel my standing in the town is harmed by the idle gossip of your sewing circle. Women are always bothering themselves with emotion and notions of benevolence when it comes to matters of commerce, but their menfolk respect me for being clear-sighted and decisive in my business dealings. I might not win many plaudits for my kindness, but I get things done. And that's what people want in a town councillor. There is already talk of my attaining higher office. If that means fewer social invitations from those who have the luxury to indulge in sentimental fancies, then so be it.'

My husband would stop at nothing to achieve his ambitions. And nothing I could do would persuade him otherwise.

Chapter Nine
Will ~ 1587

I HAD A FITFUL night's sleep and rose at dawn for the long journey to Stratford. On horseback it would take two days, but to rent a gelding would cost five shillings, so I decided to save money and walk, to have as much coin as possible to give to Anne. I eschewed the romance of taking the Roman road of Watling Street for the better highway through High Wycombe and Oxford. It would still be a four-day trudge, but it would mean I had plenty of time to contemplate what I had discovered in the days and weeks I had been away from Stratford. A life in London, away from my family, only made sense if I could provide for them more fully than if I stayed a glover in Stratford. But John Laneham was right. The life of an actor was a precarious one, and if I could not be the best, the rewards would be limited.

As I walked, it became clear to me that any talent I had displayed was in the production of plays, not the acting of them. Acting meant six years of apprenticeship to learn the many skills required to become a renowned player, and in my heart I knew that even then I would never be more than a mediocre talent. But writing – that was different. Putting pen to paper to produce words that sparkled, action that gripped; that was a task that came naturally to me. Laneham did not suffer fools gladly, but even he had been impressed with my re-written lines. My transformation of *The Troublesome Reign of King John* had been universally praised, and my suggestions to simplify the performances – adapting them to run smoothly with one fewer actor and less props – well received. They would be invaluable for future performances, especially in less accommodating venues like inn yards.

But as I neared Stratford, doubts crept in. I was a man from the provinces who had not even been to university. There again, Dick Tarlton had succeeded, I told myself. And although Tarlton's play was a basic tale, it was the easiest of all of our repertoire to perform, as it was written by someone who acted on stage every afternoon and knew how to make a play work from an actor's point of view. George Peele and Thomas Lodge, the writers of other plays we performed, were poets who penned the occasional play, and one could tell that they had never set foot on a stage. If I spent some time learning more about the skills of stagecraft, I could write words equal to or better than theirs, but with the knowledge and experience of a performing player. Surely that should give me hope?

I was still undecided when I arrived back in Stratford. Crossing Clopton Bridge, I headed up Bridge Street to the welcome sight of the Shakspere home in Henley Street. I had sent no word ahead of my arrival, wishing to surprise Anne with my return, and surprise her I did; she dropped a tray of bread and, as I buried my head in her warm embrace, Susanna, Hamnet and Judith danced excitedly around us, waiting their turn.

My heart was glad, but it didn't soar. It felt heavy and sluggish as I thought of what I was to say to Anne of my plans to return to London. But first I had to find out about Sir Thomas Lucy.

'So, what has transpired since I left Stratford? I received William Greenway's message that you said it was safe to return. How can that be so?'

Anne gave a grimace. 'Lucy's men turned up at cock's crow the morning after you left, to drag you off for a whipping. I told them you had fled, deserted your wife and children, and had left no word of where you had gone or when you might return. They did not seem convinced, and threatened to take me to the ducking stool and plunge me into the Avon until I divulged your whereabouts; but Hamnet Sadler came and pleaded on my behalf, saying that we were a family of good standing. They left after pressing me to pledge that I would give you up on your return.'

I was shocked by this news. I had never considered that my actions might have placed Anne in danger, and I cursed again my four-line verse of mockery.

Anne continued. 'I waited a few days and then made a visit to Charlecote Park to request an audience with Lady Alice Lucy, taking her a pair of our finest and most supple gloves as a token of esteem. She was gracious enough to meet with me, and told me her husband had indeed flown into a fury when he read your words, which by the grace of God had been removed from the gatepost by one of his men before their guests arrived – he had at least been spared that humiliation.'

Every word was like a nail hammered into my heart.

'And what did you say to her?'

'A line you once wrote me, the morning after you returned home drunk from the Greyhound one night – "Fools are as like to husbands as pilchards are to herrings; the husband's the bigger.'" Anne was shaking her head, and she smiled for the first time. 'Lady Alice laughed, I think it may have warmed her to me. But she said there was little she could do to appease Sir Thomas's wrath, that you were guilty of *scandalum magnatum.*'

She stumbled over the Latin, but I knew what she meant.

'Slandering a nobleman? That is a serious charge, usually reserved for making a claim that a lord is disloyal to the crown or engaged in some corrupt or criminal act. Men have been hanged for it.' I bit my cheek so hard I tasted blood. 'But now you say it is safe for me to return? Did Lady Alice convince Sir Thomas to forgive me?'

'As much as she was able,' Anne replied. She bent to pick up the bread she had dropped, and I jumped to assist her. 'Lady Alice is a kind and Christian soul and I think it troubled her that you were to be punished so severely for an act of foolishness, not malice. The next day she sent word that Sir Thomas now considered you guilty of merely speaking disrespectfully to a man of authority and you were to be placed in the stocks for two days and nights.' Anne put the bread on a shelf, and turned to me, arms folded. 'There you have it, Will. That was the best I could do.'

I think I blanched a little, but the consequences could have been much worse. The following morning, I surrendered myself to Stratford's sheriff and was escorted to the town stocks on the corner of High Street and Sheep Street. My feet were placed in the large wooden hinged boards and I sat on a bench there for two days. Fortunately, the ridicule from passers-by was half-hearted, a few shouting insults and laughing at my distress, some small boys pulling off my socks and tickling my feet, and I escaped the stoning or beating that I had seen others endure. Although the stocks were a short distance from our home, Anne made sure that none of our children saw their father's disgrace. She was permitted to bring me a little soup and water, but sleep was impossible in the stocks, and the awkward position, forced immobility and inevitable filth were a torture I confess I found hard to bear. Finally, at the end of the night of the second day, my ordeal was over. I was released and headed back to Henley Street to recover.

It took me a week to pluck up the courage to tell Anne of my idea to return to London.

'These last few months have changed me, and for the better,' I said to her, once the children were down for the night. 'Not once on my travels with the Queen's Men did I say a word out of line; no indiscretions passed my lips. I spent almost three months in the company of Protestant men and never once did they detect my sympathies for the old religion. You will never see your husband disgraced because of his words again.'

'It is behind us, Will. That is all that matters.'

'Perhaps some good can come of this sorry episode,' I said, edging towards telling Anne of my plans. 'I have discovered a talent, Anne, a talent for which I have a passion. Something that could be the making of us.'

'And what, pray tell, would that be?'

'I seem able to write, Anne. In a way that arouses passion in an actor and fascination in an audience. With your blessing I should like to return to London, to work in a company of actors.'

I saw her startled reaction and took her hand. I explained how I had been charged with changing the words of the plays we performed as we had one less man in the troupe, and how the task had come easily to me. How in London thousands of city folk flocked to plays every day, and the numbers were growing; how the owner of the greatest playhouses of them all, James Burbage, had promised me a place in his company of players if I returned to London. Once there, I would see if I could write an entire play that he would agree to perform.

'It could make us our fortune, Anne. A hundred pounds a year, maybe more. And in the meantime, I would send William Greenway with a pound a month to replace the coin I would earn as a glover. What do you say?'

Anne frowned. 'Surely you need to be well educated and the son of a lord to have your words performed as a play? I have never heard of the likes of us doing such a thing.'

'Many say that the writing of plays is not a seemly profession for a gentleman, that it is more proper that they should be writers of poems and sonnets. Let me try this and see if I can succeed. And I will do everything in my power to provide for you and the children in the meantime. One pound a month to support you, more if I can afford it. You will not go hungry while I chase my dreams.'

'But the children, Will? Susanna is five, Hamnet and Judith only three. They need their father. I need their father. These last few months have been difficult for me, enduring the ridicule and suspicion that I have been abandoned by my husband. Most were sympathetic when they heard you had fled to escape a whipping. But none will understand this story, and I will be thought a fool if I agree to it.'

'It is I who is regarded as a fool. Look at my brother, Gilbert. He had set up a haberdashery in town, with lodgings overhead, by his twentieth birthday, whereas I was still a drain on my father's purse at twenty-two. Father thinks me a dreamer and a failure who wastes his time reading any book he can borrow – and writing verse. Let me prove him wrong. It pains me to think of being away from you and the children again, but it is no different to a man going to sea to make his fortune. There was much talk in the towns we travelled through of Thomas Cavendish, who had just returned to England after circling the globe, making rich men of him and his crew. Two years at sea, Anne. Think of me also making a journey to earn my fortune, but mine only a four-day march away. If there are events in Stratford that need my hasty return, you can send word with Greenway and I can be back as fast as a horse will carry me. Allow me this one chance.'

I saw the bewilderment behind her eyes at this dramatic turn of events, but she came over to embrace me.

'I am a country lass, really. I know nothing of the world you describe. I do not know if you are being wise or foolish, but I can see your heart is in this, and for that reason alone I have a belief you will succeed. Go to London, but do not forget us when you start this new life. Yes, you will need to send coin for us all to survive, but more than that, you need to keep your love for me alive. Never forget for a moment you have a wife and children here in Stratford who love you and want to see you return to make a home with them. If you can make me these two promises, you have my blessing.'

If I thought Anne's approval would settle the decision to return to London, I had reckoned without the wrath of Father.

'You are not too old for me to tan your hide to teach you the folly of your ways,' he said. 'Abandon your family and there will be no return for you. Your brother Richard is but thirteen, but he has already shown more aptitude to the business than you ever have. Were you to go, and return shamefaced, as you surely would, you would have to suffer the indignity of your younger brother instructing you on the tasks required of you in the business. That is what you will have to expect on your return.'

I knew my father well enough to know that he would not retreat from his expressed position. I informed Anne of our discussion, fully expecting she would try to dissuade me from my plans. How wrong I was.

'Do not allow your fear of your father to keep you away from your destiny,' she told me. 'If you have dreams as great as these, you owe it to yourself to pursue them. Leave your father to me; I will do all I can to placate him when you are gone. Depart on the morrow, before he puts more obstacles in your way.'

'Tomorrow, then. If leaving is to be done, it is best done quickly.'

We spent one last precious night together. At first light, I prepared to leave Stratford again. I expected the children to be devastated that I was leaving so soon, but there was a weary resignation about them. It seemed that as children will, they had already adapted to this new chapter in our lives.

I MADE THE RETURN trip to London with a combination of sadness at leaving my family behind and excitement at the new life that lay ahead. The first thing I did on reaching the city was to find somewhere to stay. Most accommodation was inside the city walls, on the basis that it was generally considered the only safe place to live. But Burbage's playhouses were outside, to the north, an area that tended to attract unsavoury characters. Few chose to live there. But for me, that was perfect. I took the cheapest lodgings I could find, in Bishopsgate Street in Shoreditch, paying a modest rent of tuppence a week, including laundry, to be near to both playhouses. Now I had to find one that wanted me.

James Burbage was clearly disconcerted to see me return so soon, and avoided my eyes when I enquired if there were any tasks I could perform to assist in the running of the Theatre.

'We have had troupes returning from all over the country in the last few days as the summer touring season comes to an end,' he told me. 'The city is awash with unemployed actors and it is to them I feel bound to give any employment.'

'But when we met two weeks ago, you said I spoke with passion and authenticity and … and you heard John Laneham's assertion that I was a trustworthy and hardworking member of his troupe.' The shock and disappointment were obvious from my stammered words. 'I believed that if I were to return to London, there would be a position for me in your playhouses, either on the stage or off it. Well, here I am. I have left behind all that I hold dear to prove myself on the London stage. I have already taken lodgings nearby. Is there nothing you can offer me?'

Burbage shook his head. 'I'm sorry, Will, if I have misled you. But I will take it upon myself to see if any of the London companies are in need of a reliable man to help them out.'

In the end, the only work that he could find for me was as a call-boy for his second playhouse, the Curtain, a few hundred yards from the Theatre. I would arrive at six in the morning and be called on to do odd jobs – stitching garments, assembling props, making repairs to the stage and building, and so on. On the morning of a performance I would give out handbills around the city. For all this I would be paid a mere four pennies and that would be the end of my working day. Once the crowds arrived and the performance started, I would be unable to do any other tasks.

This was not enough to live on, so I had the idea of presenting myself to wealthy patrons as they arrived at the playhouse, offering to mind their horses while the play was being performed. I could earn a penny a horse – and I found I could handle four at a time before they became unmanageable. The wage of a call-boy was that of a manual labourer, and horse-handling was a job a small boy could do, so it was humiliating that this was all that was available to me. And still my financial situation was dire. After paying my rent, purchasing a daily loaf of penny bread and living mainly on pease pudding – split peas soaked, boiled and mashed – I could only afford meat once a week, a hot pie that the butchers sold on London Bridge. That left me with nine shillings and sixpence a month to send to Anne. Less than half what I'd promised.

The only solution was to take on a second job as a call-boy in Burbage's other playhouse, the Theatre, starting after the play had finished and working until it was pitch dark. Working at the Curtain I had managed to prove myself diligent and hardworking, so it was easy enough to persuade Burbage to offer me a job at the Theatre when it became available. I would return to my lodgings in the last hours before dawn, drained and exhausted, only to rise by five of the clock to start all over again.

But I told myself if I were to be a horse-handler, I would be the best horse-handler in London. It took only a few weeks for my reputation as the most trusted and reliable of the handlers to be established, but it was not an accolade in which I could take great pride, my competition being boys of tender years or reprobates who could not find more lucrative employment in the city. There soon were more horses to attend to than I could handle by myself, so I recruited the most diligent and conscientious lads I could find and had them perform their duties as Shakspere's Boys, under my strict guidance. That meant I was receiving one shilling and eightpence for handling the horses, half of which I gave to the boys working on my behalf.

Now I could send the one pound a month to Anne as promised, and have five shillings and sixpence left over for beer at a ha'penny a pint, and the occasional piece of ham or pork to add to my pease pudding. It was a miserable existence, and there was never a moment to write a verse, much less a play. On Sundays, when the playhouses lay quiet, I was so exhausted I barely stirred from my room.

I allowed myself one small indulgence. When a new play was being rehearsed in the morning, I would stop work to watch the rehearsal, for which privilege I agreed a ha'penny would be deducted from my pay. I made it my purpose to be useful as I watched – finding a prop, stitching a costume, whatever it might take to bring me to the actors' attention. Thomas Pope and Will Kemp were the two who engaged with me the most. They were the leading actors of Leicester's Men, the main company to perform at the Curtain, and both were men of many talents; Pope was a comedian and acrobat and Kemp a dancer and a clown, and both were fine actors. Their performances brought home to me yet again my limitations. Certainly, I could one day aspire to deliver a line on stage with as much gusto as any other actor, but were I to be asked to sing, dance or juggle, my shortcomings would be sorely exposed.

Pope and Kemp appeared to be idiotic fools when on stage, but in reality they were sober men who took their performances seriously and were always looking for ways to do things better. With every play I watched, I thought of new lines that would greatly improve the impact of the speeches they had to deliver. Sometimes I whispered these lines to the actors during breaks in rehearsal, and more often than not I was rewarded by the thrill of hearing them said aloud on the next attempt at the scene. But not one line was uttered by me. I was Will the call-boy, Will the horse-handler. I could persuade no-one there was more I could offer.

Both men became curious as to who I was and why I was doing such menial work at the Curtain.

'Why does a man such as you do boys' work?' Pope asked me one day as he saw me taking the reins of the first horse to arrive. 'I can hear from your accent you are from a northern town. Do you not have a trade you can practise here in London?'

'My lowly station is a coarse necessity brought about by my circumstances,' I replied. 'I wish to be an actor, and one day write plays and produce them for the stage. But I have gone about this in a most unconventional manner. I have given up my trade as a glover, and I stay close to the playhouses in hope that an opportunity may soon present itself. But I am beginning to realise that this is a somewhat forlorn dream.'

Pope gave me a grim smile. 'I hate to be the one to say this to you, Will, but what you have said may be the truth. With a steady supply of well-trained choirboys from the Children of Paul's, no-one is going to hire a new actor who has a wife and family to support in another town. Even if a man with a family were foolhardy enough to accept the pay of an apprentice actor, he would soon realise that he could not earn enough and would leave the company. You may have the potential to one day be a fine actor, Will, but it would be too big a risk to give you the chance to find out.'

I went back to my lodgings, defeated and dejected by Pope's well-meaning words. He was right, and I cursed myself for not doing my sums properly before embarking on this foolish enterprise. I had given myself an impossible task. I had stopped being an artisan glover and was now earning the wage of an unskilled labourer; I had the expense of living alone in London, and was burdened by the promise of sending funds to Anne. And all because I had been carried along on the wings of hope and a half-promise made by James Burbage.

But I would not give up. I struggled on for one year, then another, but by the beginning of my third year, things had only marginally improved. Now, if one of the actors took ill, I was excused my call-boy duties and given the chance to perform on stage, rewarded with an extra penny for my efforts. And by attending so many rehearsals and borrowing the scripts when they were not in use, I became intimately familiar with every play Burbage's company performed.

And I knew the plays of the Admiral's Men too. Burbage's playhouses had a rival south of the river in Bankside, the Rose, which had been built in 1587 by Philip

Henslowe. The Admiral's Men performed there and were formidable competitors. Burbage had the better venues, but Ned Alleyn, the greatest actor of the day, was a member of the Admiral's Men and they had Kit Marlowe write their plays. But it was a friendly rivalry. Burbage's son Richard was a member of the Admiral's Men. He had wanted to make his name as an actor away from his father's patronage, and a fine one he had become, by all accounts. During a period of difficulty at the end of 1590, the Admiral's Men transferred to the Theatre, and so for a few short months, all of London's acting talent was concentrated in just two playhouses, only a few hundred yards apart. One morning, in the rehearsal of the play *Dead Man's Fortune* at the Theatre, I saw Ned Alleyn and Richard Burbage perform alongside each other, the master and his pupil.

At the beginning of 1591, the Admiral's Men moved back to the Rose. Richard Burbage stayed behind, and with his father's backing became the leader of the company. By then the company was called Lord Strange's Men, as the Earl of Leicester had died. I dreamed that eventually I'd be offered a position in the company as a full-time actor; as only by working the hours of an actor would I ever find the time to start writing my own plays. But after three long years, that chance had never come.

And then, just as I was about to give up, in June 1591 the plague struck London and red crosses started to be painted on the doors of hundreds of households. A vast charnel house was opened on Bishopsgate, opposite St Mary's priory, a few hundred paces south of the Curtain, where heaps of corpses and piles of bones were stored. Some of the corpses were stacked one on top of the other in their knotted winding sheets, others in upright rotten coffins. Lamps burned dimly in hollow and glimmering corners, and as I hurried by one evening, by cruel misfortune a coffin lid yawned wide open, filling my nostrils with a noisome stench.

Of course, the playhouses were ordered to close down. That was it. I now had to either return to Stratford, or suffer the horror of living in a plagued city and see if a glover in London would hire a stitcher and cutter. Both terrible choices, but Stratford was the one I had to settle on. And I feared that, once I returned, I would likely never leave again.

I went to say my goodbyes to the Curtain and found it deserted, save for Richard Burbage, Pope and Kemp, who were deep in discussion when I arrived. I startled them when I announced my presence, and they looked at each other in amazement.

'God-a-mercy, Will, your ears must have been burning,' Burbage said to me. 'We were discussing our plans to keep the company going by touring the provincial towns of Kent and Sussex, which are free of the plague. And your name had just been mentioned.'

He went on to explain. 'Performing in rural towns is a different matter to being on stage each night at the Curtain. As indeed you know. Our troupe has to be smaller; everything has to go with us from town to town. You deliver lines well when you step on stage as an understudy, and my father said that he once auditioned you as an actor and found you most able. John Laneham has praised your ability to overcome any problems that present themselves, and your skill at cutting scenes to make the plays simpler and shorter to fit with the time and space available to perform them. We need a man like you on our tour, and were hoping to find you before you left this plague-ridden city. And here you are.'

'M…me? Join your troupe?'

Burbage nodded. 'As travelling players, we will be fewer in number than the Lord Strange's company in London, so you will have to step on stage each night and play multiple roles, as well as being the stage-keeper and jack of all trades to help with the running of the productions. You will find the audiences less sophisticated than the ones in London, more forgiving of any inexperienced actors that perform for them, and the work of a stage-keeper will be much less onerous than here at the Curtain. We will have two other journeyman actors with us: the tireman, in charge of the wardrobe, and a carpenter. I will be the lead actor; Pope and Kemp are to dazzle with their acrobatics and jigs, and you and your two fellow journeymen will flesh out the performances by playing the other roles.' He pointed to Kemp. 'Will here will be our book-keeper and the profits of each performance will be split four ways – a quarter each for Pope, Kemp and myself, and the final quarter split evenly between you and the two others. Every man will have to pull his weight on the road, so I do not want to bring along any recent graduates of the Children of Paul's, and you have proven yourself before, with the Queen's Men. What say you, Will? Pope and Kemp tell me you did not come to London just to be in charge of our patrons' horses. Come with us and be on the stage again.'

I wanted to say yes straight away, but something made me hesitate. This was likely to be my only chance for a long time, perhaps ever, and it needed to count. I decided to risk all, and strike a hard bargain. If they said no, I had nothing to lose.

'I will say yes with pleasure,' I replied. 'But on the condition that if I prove myself to you, I be allowed to join Lord Strange's Men when we return to London. You are right, I did not come to London to be in charge of Shakspere's Boys. I want to write words for the stage and perform upon it. Give me this undertaking and I am your man.'

The three men looked at each other, no-one wanting to be the first to speak. Finally, Burbage gave a shrug and laid his hand on my shoulder.

'You have a way about you, Will Shakspere, that makes me think you have what it takes to succeed in this game. Three years as a call-boy and horse-handler to get a chance to be on the London stage? That shows determination. Join us and prove me right, and a place in Lord Strange's Men will be yours when we return to London.'

I could scarcely disguise my elation, and shook hands with him to seal the deal. Here was a chance for me to become a full-time actor without having to serve a formal apprenticeship. But as I lay in bed that night, turning over in my mind the events of the day, one truth became obvious to me. Even with this good fortune, I would be doing only the minimum I had promised Anne. To be a success, I would have to write a play, and to write a play I needed an idea for a story.

As we headed off to Kent, I prayed for inspiration. We would be travelling through the lands of smugglers and pirates, of lawlessness and rebellion. Surely there would be somewhere on my travels where I would find a tale to enthral the London crowds?

Then destiny visited me again. We arrived in the town of Faversham.

Chapter Ten
Alice ~ 1543

THE GRUMBLINGS over Thomas's treatment of Widow Cook continued for a few weeks, but despite the widow's best efforts, these protests soon faded away. It was beyond unfortunate that they did. Thomas was emboldened now that his callous behaviour had met with little sanction, and when the next obstacle to his craving for wealth and influence presented itself, he did not hesitate to use the same tactics again. But John Greene would prove to be a more formidable adversary than a helpless old woman turned out of her home.

Greene had been an indentured servant to Anthony Aucher, and last year he purchased his freedom, only to find that Thomas Arden intended to relieve him of the field of hops at the back of Faversham Abbey – a field that his family had worked for years and which they considered they owned. There was some confusion between this land and the land that Thomas had purchased following the abbey's dissolution. Simply put, this small parcel of land that Greene believed his family owned appeared actually to have belonged to Faversham Abbey. It mattered little to Thomas, being a mere fraction of the acreage he now possessed, but it mattered a great deal to John Greene. It was all that he had to make his new start in life.

So when Thomas raised the topic at a council meeting and convinced the councillors that the land was his without hearing any representation from the other side, Greene was furious and turned up at our home, armed with a cudgel. Thomas bade me despatch Elisabeth to fetch his manservant, Michael Saunderson. In the meantime, he tried to placate the intruder.

'Come now, John Greene, lay down your weapon,' he said. 'We are both reasonable men. If you have some grievance with me, we can surely sort it out without threats of violence. Allow me to pour you some wine while I hear your concerns.'

'Damn your wine!' Greene replied. 'You have cheated me out of land that is lawfully mine. That land is all that my family have and I will endure a life of penury if it is taken from us. It means nothing to you, yet you have tricked the town councillors into finding that it belongs to you.'

'I did no such thing, I assure you,' Thomas replied. 'Let me prove it to you.' He left and returned with a large piece of parchment, from which dangled a crimson seal. Thomas spread it out on the table in front of him. 'I have of late received a final grant of the land in letters patent,' he said, his voice full of bravado. 'See here, it shows the field in question lies within my boundaries.' He pointed to the words, then folded his arms. 'There you are. What you claim is your family's field is legally mine, unless you have papers to prove otherwise. Do you have such a document, John Greene?'

Greene's face reddened. 'I have no papers,' he said, his voice cracking with emotion. 'But everyone knows that field belongs to my family and I have tilled it since I was a boy. Your papers must be in error. Admit that you know so.'

'I will admit no such thing,' Thomas replied. 'It is plain to see that this land is not yours. It is included in the abbey land, which I have bought and paid for.' He stroked his chin, as if searching for an explanation, but the pretence was laboured. 'Perhaps the abbey was unaware the land did not belong to them, but no matter – the letters patent have been issued. I will not be cheated out of land I have lawfully purchased.'

I gasped as Greene swung his cudgel at Thomas, missing his head by a whisker and slamming it into the wall behind him with an explosion of dust. Greene dropped the cudgel and stood facing Thomas, his legs apart, his hands forming fists. I saw fear in my husband's eyes. Greene was much the stronger and younger man.

At that moment, Michael Saunderson arrived and grabbed Greene from behind. Greene struggled, but Michael leant back and raised him up, Greene's legs flailing helplessly in the air.

I found my voice and shouted, 'Hold him, Michael! He is gone mad. Protect us!'

Greene continued to struggle as Michael turned his head towards me. 'Are you all right, Mistress Alice? Has this brute harmed you? He better pray that he has not.'

Before I could reply, Thomas picked up the cudgel and struck Greene with it on the side of his head. 'Hold him there,' Thomas said. 'I will fetch my sword and run him through.'

Instead, Michael released his grip on Greene and let him stumble off into the night.

'I am grateful for your intervention,' Thomas said to Michael, panting from the exertion. 'But I wish you had allowed me to despatch the fellow for his impudence. Can you believe the man? A few months ago, he was handing over some paltry coin to release himself from service, and now he feels he is my equal and able to thwart my plans. I was too lenient in giving him till next quarter day to harvest his hops. I will have the field ploughed over on the morrow.'

Widow Cook's plight had taught me there was little merit in appealing to Thomas's better nature and instead I voiced more practical concerns.

'Greene may well have come here wishing harm upon us today, but he gained his freedom from Anthony Aucher, and it is well known that Aucher wishes him well with his new life. Would it not be possible to find an accommodation on this matter that does not risk again incurring Aucher's wrath?'

Thomas dismissed Michael and ushered me into the parlour.

'Aucher is a fool who has not realised that the tide has turned against him,' he said. 'Those of us who keep up to date with affairs at court know this only too well. With Thomas Cromwell gone, his head placed on a spike on London Bridge, Aucher has no great man behind him, no-one of the stature of Sir Edward North, nor the influence of Sir Thomas Cheyne.'

He paused for a moment to reflect. 'But this upstart Greene may yet provide a useful purpose. Let him go crying to Aucher. My paths are crossing with Aucher's more than I would like. Cromwell's other erstwhile supporters in Kent have had the wisdom to stay quiet, to wait and see how things transpire in the battle between the radicals and conservatives. But not Aucher. He espouses the radical cause every chance he gets, to the chagrin of many in this town. I can use his indiscretions against him and clip his wings, so that he sees Faversham is a town where he and his views are not welcome and turns to other places to seek opportunities for enrichment. His wealth is spread all over Kent; let him go elsewhere. There are ample opportunities for everyone.'

'Clip Anthony Aucher's wings?' I was aghast. 'It is you who needs to question your boldness, my husband. You have achieved great things since arriving in Faversham, but you are no match for the Aucher family. The gap between our station and theirs is far greater than that between you and Greene. Please, find a way to appease John Greene without making yourself a powerful enemy.'

But Thomas could not be persuaded, and two days later my worst fears were confirmed. With Aucher's support, John Greene had petitioned Faversham's jurats to hear an appeal regarding the sale of the land. I was convinced that Thomas would back down before the hearing took place and agree some compromise with Greene, but he was having none of it.

ON THE DAY OF the hearing, I busied myself around the house, waiting for Thomas to return and recount the details of the day's events. I saw from the swagger in his walk that things had gone well for him.

Thomas started speaking as he opened a bottle of his best wine. 'Greene made a good pass at disguising how much of a hothead he showed himself to be to us, cowering in front of the jurats as he spoke. The man has missed his profession; he should be on stage at the Shippe if he fancies himself such an actor. And he had a canny way about him, trying to tug at their heart strings, saying that, as a recently freed man, his position was precarious and that a finding against him over ownership of the land would be a most severe blow to his circumstances. The fellow would have welled up with tears and prostrated himself in front of the jurats if he thought it would have advanced his cause.'

Thomas poured himself a glass of wine. 'I must admit, he had me worried. I saw some sentimental fools looking askance at each other, wondering if they should show mercy and reverse their decision. Greene did well in his address. I expected him to be overawed by the circumstances and either gabble incoherently or fly into a rage as he did when he visited us. But he behaved with decorum and showed only respect to the jurats.' A nod. 'Yes, it was a fine performance.'

'But you have a smile in your eyes, don't you, Thomas? Tell me how you were able to better him.'

My husband tossed his hair back, then sat with exaggerated casualness and drained his glass in one quaff. I remained standing, too tense to relax.

'I did what was expected of me.' Thomas's voice was loud now, full of bluster. 'I appealed to the jurats' self-interest, pointing out that the town's coffers were being swelled by the proceeds from the dissolution of the monasteries, and that they all benefitted from the actions of men like me who dig deep into their purse to buy the land and properties that come up for sale.'

I gave an ironic smile. The way he talked, the jurats could be forgiven for believing that Thomas was making these purchases out of a civic duty to provide funds for the betterment of the community, rather than buying up assets at a beggarly rate for personal enrichment.

Thomas responded to my smile with an arrogant laugh. 'Yes, I know, Alice. What fools some men are. But that was not the main thrust of my submission to the council.'

He gave a heavy exhalation as if he could hardly contain his pride at what he had said next. 'I stood in front of the jurats, and spoke in scarcely more than a whisper, the better to invite them to listen intently. John Greene has come and addressed the members of this court as equals, I told them, when only last year he was indentured to Anthony Aucher, who has not only granted him his freedom, but promised to support him and make him his man.'

Thomas seemed to be enjoying my anguish at waiting to hear what dishonesty he had come up with. 'I raised the fact that Anthony Aucher was not present today, no doubt considering himself too grand to waste his time attending to such a trivial matter. I told the jurats that Aucher had made no secret of his radicalism, and that while this was not a crime in itself, charges of heresy were being laid against radicals throughout the land, and the authorities in London would surely not be best pleased if a man with these heretical beliefs was seen to be so openly supported by the jurats of Faversham, a town most noted for its allegiance to the King and the conservative cause. I asked that they find in my favour, not only because of the justness of my case, but also to send a message that radicals and the men who support them will not find favour here in Faversham.'

'Thomas, how could you?' I said. 'Radicalism and conservatism are matters too weighty to be used so casually to advance an argument about a mere parcel of land. You are talking about causes that attract the King's displeasure. Those who speak imprudently find their head sitting atop a spike.'

There was a sour metallic taste in my mouth as I thought about what Thomas had just done.

Thomas waved away my concerns. 'The impact of my argument was marvellous to see, as though a bolt of lightning had struck the room.' He gave an ugly laugh. 'The jurats stared at each other in horror, each hoping the next would speak out against this attempt to align them with a cause opposed by the King. But none did, and when the verdict was announced, the decision was unanimous. John Greene's family had no title to the land and Aucher had in effect been branded a radical in open court. Two birds with one stone.'

Cold fingers ran across my flesh, and my anxiety increased further when, a few days later, a messenger arrived from my step-father, Sir Edward North. He had heard the result of the hearing and was summoning Thomas to his estate to explain himself. I was relieved to see Thomas's euphoria punctured by the thought of what recriminations might lie ahead. I travelled with him to Kirtling Tower and ensured that I was doing my embroidery in the room next to where the two men met.

I could not help but hear what passed between them. I had not heard Sir Edward express such thunderous anger since I was a child.

'How dare you use the noble battle between radicalism and conservatism to score some advantage in a tawdry matter of business! It is I who suffers as a result, with questions asked as to why I have such a fool as my man. I should publicly disown you for your folly.'

'Forgive me, Sir Edward,' Thomas replied. There was a plaintive tone to his voice that I had never heard before. 'Excuse my behaviour, it was a momentary rush of blood to the head. This fellow Greene came to my house, armed and dangerous, and tried to bludgeon me to death for daring to assert my right to the land he claimed was his family's. I feared not just for my own safety, but also that of dear Alice. I had to risk life and limb to protect her.'

Lies! I cursed my husband's duplicity. It was only the intervention of brave Michael Saunderson that had prevented Greene from doing us harm. Thomas had throughout been concerned only for his safety, not mine.

'Be that as it may, it is no excuse to raise Aucher's radicalism in dealing with this matter,' Sir Edward replied. 'Aucher is no friend of mine, in fact I despise the man for his arrogant ways. But you unleash dark forces when you draw attention to those who follow that path.' As Sir Edward continued his tirade, his voice became louder. 'The King is ailing, and there is talk that after his passing the radicals will be in the ascendancy again. If that comes to pass, you had better pray that Anthony Aucher does not come seeking revenge.'

'I know little of the subtleties of court politics and am not a pious man,' Thomas replied, his voice trembling with fear. 'I see now the errors of my ways and am indebted to your good counsel regarding the damage I have done. Let me issue a public apology to Anthony Aucher and beg his forgiveness.'

'Curse your blood, Thomas Arden,' Sir Edward replied. 'I am enraged that any man of mine should have to go grovelling to that obnoxious fellow, but your stupidity has left you no choice. You have demeaned both of us by your actions. Were it not for the distress it would cause to my dear wife to have her daughter cast out from society and left without means as a result of your folly, I would disown you here and now.'

'If I pledge to do this, Sir Edward, can I count on your continued sponsorship?' Thomas was desperate now.

'For as long as it is of benefit to Alice,' Sir Edward replied.

I felt a thrill of delight as my mind raced as to how I might use Thomas's precarious position to my advantage.

'Then I remain forever grateful for your kindness and understanding,' Thomas said in turn. 'I will ensure that Alice has all that she desires. And I will never venture into the bear pit of politics again.'

The formalities of taking leave were about to be rehearsed, so I hurried from the room so that Thomas would not know that I had overheard the entire exchange. He found me in conversation with Mother, and I tried to ignore his flushed face and agitated demeanour.

I did not enquire about his exchange with Sir Edward, and Thomas did not refer to it, either then or on our journey back to Faversham. He was sullen and taciturn throughout the trip. It was only as we arrived at the edge of the town that his usual boldness started to return.

'Your step-father made a mighty show of his displeasure at my strategy to ensure that John Greene did not succeed in his appeal. It took all my powers of persuasion to convince Sir Edward that I shouldn't hand the land over to him immediately. Think what a humiliation that would have been! Instead, I have merely to make a public apology to Aucher and watch my step in future. Sir Edward seemed untroubled by the circumstances in which Greene now finds himself, so I have need to show neither humility nor contrition towards him. Thank the Lord for that. Grovelling to that vulgar man would have been a great humiliation.'

The incident had no lasting effect on Thomas, and he remained as ruthless as ever in his business dealings. If anything, he became even more corrupt in his demands for payment to allow goods to move freely to London. There was never an attempt at reconciliation with John Greene and his public apology to Anthony Aucher was met with an ominous silence.

But time and time again, my mind returned to the conversation I had overheard between Thomas and Sir Edward. My husband had only narrowly managed to hang on to his powerful sponsor, and indeed it was on my account alone that my step-father had supported him. Thomas continued to spurn me as a woman. If I were bold enough, perhaps there was a way out of my despair. If Thomas was sufficiently desperate to avoid upsetting my step-father, perhaps he would acquiesce to my spending time with Tom Mosby.

Once the idea had implanted itself in my mind, it would not go away, though I wished it would. It could only lead to trouble.

I cursed the spell that my red hair had over me.

Chapter Eleven
Will ~ 1591

THERE WAS A pleasing symmetry that the first performance of Lord Strange's Men should be on the same Faversham stage where I had last performed with John Laneham's Queen's Men. We had been delayed for a few hours at Gravesend when we disembarked from the ferry, as Burbage went off to negotiate the hire of a wagon in which the journeyman players would travel, along with the wicker chests containing props and costumes.

The wagon was uncomfortable, but less tiring than walking, and we set off flanked by Burbage, Pope and Kemp, who rode on palfreys. We arrived in Faversham late in the evening, having made good time along Watling Street. The stench of the cesspits on Tanners Street filled my nostrils, the foulness reminding me of home; tanners cure their hides in the same manner in every town.

We climbed out of the wagon and unloaded our trumpets and drums, playing them with gusto and making a mighty commotion as we turned right along West Street and headed into Market Street, just opposite the fine hall in Market Place. Burbage presented the mayor and chief magistrate with our letter of authority from Lord Strange to prove we were not beggars, then arranged for us to perform in front of them and a selected audience in the morning, so that they would grant permission for us to have a public performance in the afternoon. The Shippe had its own trestles and boards, which we set up in anticipation of such approval, and the light was failing before all was ready. Despite my excitement at what was to come, I had an early night. I wanted a clear head for my first performance.

The mayor gave his approval, and by two of the clock the yard at the Shippe was packed to overflowing. Burbage had recruited some local boys to act as gatherers, to collect the money paid for attending, customers dropping their coins through the slot in a sealed ceramic box so the boys were not tempted to slip them in their pockets. Once we were ready, one of the actors gave three flourishes of his trumpet to calm the crowd and we were off, playing *The Spanish Tragedy* to rapt attention. The audience cheered at the end, and Burbage pronounced himself satisfied with the troupe's performance, singling me out for praise for the cuts I had made to the middle act, which made the play easier to perform with only five players. He collected all the ceramic boxes and took them to a counting room he called the box office. The seals were broken, the boxes opened and the coins counted, and I was struck by how much better organised things were in this troupe compared to the Queen's Men. Our takings from the box office were fifteen shillings and seven pence, a good start to the tour. As was the custom, Burbage, as the leader of our troupe, would hand over a tenth of this to the town priest to give to the needy and the poor, but it was still a good profit for a day's labour.

The other players helped me pack up the props and costumes and we dropped them off at the inn where we were staying. As it was a fine evening, Burbage suggested that we all take a walk around the town. I was the only one who took him up on the offer. The rest of the troupe went off to the Shippe to sample the famous Faversham beer. Richard Burbage and I headed up North Street and Court Street, with the vague intention of sampling some oysters on the Thorn Creek quay before returning to our hostelry for the night.

As Court Street turned into Abbey Street, we heard a noise coming from the right, and when we went to investigate we saw a small crowd standing at the edge of a meadow. Someone pointed to the grass and the women gave astonished screams, which were met with raucous laughter from the men.

'We should not congratulate ourselves too much on today's performance,' I said as we passed the noisy group. 'It seems that the good people of this town can get as much entertainment from a blade of grass as they can from a well-performed play. What can it be that provides such an amusing diversion?'

Burbage gave me a look of astonishment. 'Will, do you not know of the Faversham murder?' I gave a puzzled shrug and he shook his head in disbelief. 'It was surely one of the most notorious crimes this century. A wife and her paramour murdered her husband, the former mayor of this town, so they could live a life of sin together. Forty years ago, it was. That is the field where the body was found, a stone's throw from the family house.' Burbage pointed to a large timber-framed building, its upper storeys jutting out over the pavement. 'There it is. Abbey Gate. Legend has it that still no grass grows where the body lay.' The crowd dispersed a little and we could see the patch of ground they had been looking at. 'There, Will, look. Clear as day. All these years later, you can still see the outline of Thomas Arden.'

'Thomas Arden? Arden, you say? That was the name of the husband who was slain?'

'Yes, by his wife, Alice. Foul temptress. And we are staying at the Fleur de Lis tonight. Our host, Adam Fowle, was the landlord when the murder took place and even played a small part in events; albeit in all innocence, I am told. I am sure he is well rehearsed at explaining the grisly details. You can hear the whole story from him.'

Suddenly, I had no desire for oysters and suggested we turn around and head back. Burbage shrugged and said he would join the others at the Shippe, and I headed for the square behind the inn to find the Fleur de Lis, where we had rooms for the night. Adam Fowle was there alone, changing a barrel of beer. It was obvious that the Shippe was more successful at attracting custom.

Fowle finished changing the barrel at his own pace and then turned to greet me. His face had the florid complexion often seen amongst publicans who sample their own wares more frequently than they ought.

'What can I get you…Master Shakspere, is it not? I heard fine things about your troupe's performance this afternoon.'

I allowed myself a flutter of excitement at such unsolicited praise, before remembering it was common for innkeepers to praise their customers, so that they might linger longer to sample their beers.

'Thank you, indeed,' I said. 'You have a good memory for names. And you are Adam Fowle, I believe? I have come from Abbey Street where I saw what seemed a most peculiar gathering in the grounds of the abbey ruins. I now know a little about the murder of Thomas Arden, but I'm told that you are the one to ask to find out more.'

Fowle gave a tired smile. 'Indeed, I am, Master Shakspere, and I'd be happy to tell you the tale.' He stood looking at me, the smile slowly fading.

I realised what was expected of me as my side of the bargain.

'I'll have a jug of ale if you would be so kind as to tell me,' I replied. 'And one for yourself, of course.'

'Indeed, sir. Well said.' Fowle poured two beers and placed them in front of us. 'Brewed by John Castlock himself. His father started brewing here over fifty years ago and his son continues the family tradition. Thomas Arden would drink this same ale at my inn almost every evening with his one true friend in the town, Thomas Dunkyn, a previous mayor. Inseparable, the two of them were, and Arden did him many favours when he too went on to become mayor. Your good health.' He took a deep draught and put down the half-empty jug. 'So, the Arden murder, then. How much do you know about the sorry tale?'

'Almost nothing,' I replied. 'This is only my second visit to Faversham.'

'Fifteen hundred and fifty-one it was, the year of the murder. I was a young man, and had been a publican for a year. Or was it two?' Fowle paused again as he contemplated the answer to his own question. 'No, it was one year. But no matter. I have lived in Faversham man and boy, and so witnessed the arrival of Thomas Arden with his comely wife, and his rise from humble collector of customs to rich and powerful town councillor. In that position he negotiated the town's charter, then went on to be elected mayor. There was a time, in the last few years of King Henry's reign, when, for a brief moment, Thomas and Alice Arden were the town's golden couple.'

'And what grisly fate befell him? Murder, you said?'

'Murdered in his own home. Done in by his wife, Alice, and Tom Mosby, her paramour; aided and abetted by their servants, a gang of accomplices and Thomas Arden's sworn enemy in the town, John Greene. Eight murderers for one victim. Can you imagine such a thing? The fools thought they would not be caught, and Mosby fled only as far as this very inn after the deed was done.' Fowle paused. 'Alice Arden, Tom Mosby and John Greene. Blast their names.'

I was surprised by the venom in his curse; that even after forty years, the innkeeper remained shocked by the crime. 'For such evil, blast their names indeed,' I replied, nodding perhaps more heavily than was appropriate.

Fowle barked a laugh. 'You seem puzzled by the strength of my words describing events from forty years ago and more. It is not the foulness of the crime that makes me speak thus of the perpetrators.' He topped up his own beer, noting that I had not yet taken another sip of mine. 'Mosby was a good customer of mine. He took a room at my inn when he arrived in Faversham, having followed Alice Arden from her family home where he had already had his way with her before her marriage to Thomas, so it was said. It was from here that he made his approaches to her again, so that he might bed her once more. And when she decided to succumb to his advances, she used me to signal her desires to him, having me deliver to Mosby a present of two silver dice she had bought for him.' He winced as if recalling a painful memory. 'Who could have thought two silver dice could cause such mischief? On the night of the killing, the fool went to his room here and fell asleep with his breeches stained with Thomas Arden's blood. And when he was arrested, he spoke that I was somehow responsible for the crime, for giving him lodgings and enticing him to go back to Alice by handing him those infernal dice as a signal of her affection, and for this I was lashed to the underbelly of a horse and taken to London to stand trial. Only the wisdom of the judge allowed me to escape the hangman's noose.'

My pulse quickened. Here it was – the story of my first play. It had everything: murder, passion, even the super-natural event I had witnessed today, along with a striking cast of characters. It was a crime that would shock even the most jaded audience.

'A wife and her paramour killing her husband to satisfy their lust, and that husband being one of the richest and most powerful men in Faversham,' I said, the pitch of my voice rising. 'It is indeed a tragedy that such a great and noble man could be brought down in such terrible circumstances.'

Fowle laughed again at my earnest indignation. 'Time is a great creator of saints. Thomas Arden is seen as the faultless innocent victim of a heinous murder today, but back in his day he was a man who made enemies easily. He was ruthless in pursuit of land and money, and cared little for those who got in his way. If truth be told, there were many in the town who did not mourn his passing.'

'And one went so far as to join the conspiracy to murder him? Who was this John Greene you spoke of?'

'Greene was Sir Anthony Aucher's man, another powerful enemy that Thomas Arden made in his pursuit of wealth and power.' Fowle sighed. 'But I have spoken enough of the terrible events of that time. There is a full account in the town's wardmote book, which you can find in the new Guildhall that opened some years ago in Market Place. If you wish to know more details, you will find them there.'

The other players returned from their drinking and the inn filled up quickly with the news that we were to give an impromptu performance to pay for our lodgings. Afterwards, I went back to my room and hastily scratched an account of all that I had heard. There was almost a surfeit of riches in the story. The very name Arden, that of my own mother's family, gave me hope that it was a sign I had been chosen to tell the tale. I burnt through half a candle writing all that I could remember of the story Fowle had told me. The play would be written as soon as I returned to London.

My life as a writer was about to begin.

Chapter Twelve

Alice ~ 1544

AFTER THE GREENE scandal had died down, Thomas finally attempted to make peace with Aucher. He offered him two inns, the George and the Garret, at a much-reduced price; the only time I could recall Thomas selling property in Faversham rather than acquiring it. Aucher was too canny to reject the deal, but any hope that it would lead to a thaw in relations – even a pause in hostilities – proved unfounded. They remained sworn enemies, battling each other for those few parcels of monastic lands that remained. And according to Thomas, Aucher was his equal in accepting dubious payments, in Aucher's case from the merchants of Dover, the port he controlled. Although the days of rich pickings from the dissolution were coming to an end, there were as many traders in Thomas's pocket as pebbles on a beach, and no doubt the same could be said of Aucher. Nevertheless, Anthony Aucher was an irritation, nothing more – even he couldn't stem the flow of riches coming my husband's way.

All the while, Thomas continued his ascendancy within the hierarchy of the town. His greatest achievement as councillor was to be paid a fee of twenty pounds to secure a new charter of incorporation for Faversham, enriching the town with new rights and privileges which had previously belonged to the abbey.

'This is a most important commission, and it will pave the way for even greater advancement,' Thomas told me when he heard the news, his face flushed with excitement. 'Once the sources of wealth from the abbey are enshrined in the charter to be for the benefit of the town, every goodman in Faversham will recognise the rewards in the grand schemes we will be able to afford. Streets will be paved, filth removed and taxes lowered. And I will be the one who will get the credit, even though all I have done is throw rocks in a stream to encourage it on a different course. The money has always been there, but before it was hidden away by the church. With a few strokes of a pen, I have conjured up new riches for the town, and no-one will begrudge me a few of those riches for myself.'

'I am very pleased for you,' I replied, flashing as warm a smile as I could manage. 'If the town will benefit from your actions, I am sure that no-one will wish to deny you an honest reward.' I put the stress on 'honest' but Thomas either didn't notice or didn't care. He left for the Fleur de Lis to celebrate with Dunkyn.

The charter was agreed by King Henry, and it did indeed bring much benefit to the town. As he predicted, Thomas now saw a rapid rise in his power and influence, as he was given the credit for the town's new-found prosperity. When Thomas Dunkyn became mayor in 1546, he made my husband a church warden, and the following year Thomas too was elected mayor of Faversham. In only eight years, arriving as an unknown merchantman from humble beginnings, my husband had become the most important man in Faversham.

But although Thomas's fortunes had risen remarkably, Aucher's had risen even higher, and nowhere more so than in the matter of the very cause for which Thomas had criticised his rival: being a strident and vocal supporter of Protestant radicalism. Thomas's attack at the council meeting had most spectacularly backfired, as the radical movement was once again in the ascendancy. With the death of King Henry VIII in 1547, the crown had passed to his son, the boy king, Edward VI. The new king's advisers longed for the return of the glory days of his father's rule, and their first act was to repeal the heresy and treason laws that had brought down Thomas Cromwell. Radicalism was now back in favour and those who had been brave enough to voice support for the cause when Henry had turned against it found themselves well rewarded. Aucher was knighted in 1547, the same year as Thomas was made church warden. My husband had done well for himself, but his success paled into insignificance when *Sir* Anthony Aucher was dubbed a knight of the realm. Thomas pretended not to care.

For my part, the shame of having to wear the mask of a loving and dutiful wife in the presence of a man I held in such low regard was nothing compared to the wretchedness I felt that I could not be with my true love, Tom Mosby. Whenever our paths briefly crossed in Faversham, I regretted my decision to reject his advances when he first arrived. But I dismissed any foolish notion of changing my mind. I was the wife of the mayor of Faversham and such was my position that any liaisons would be out of the question. I would surely be discovered if ever I sought to see Tom in secret.

However, I decided to try again to see if Tom was interested in more than a passing acquaintance. Though there would be no intimacy between us, he could still be someone with whom I could meet regularly and share my innermost thoughts and feelings. I had a gift of a pair of silver dice delivered to him by Adam Fowle, the trusted landlord of the Fleur de Lis, Faversham's finest hostelry, to signal to Tom my renewed interest, and then initiated a meeting on the pretext of discussing some tailoring needs. I promised myself I would keep the meeting friendly but formal, to make sure that he did not interpret the confiding of my unhappiness as a sign that I was hoping this would lead to further intimacies. I met him in our parlour, and made a great show of greeting him with formal niceties while Elisabeth served us tea. Once she departed, I got up and closed the door so we would not be overheard. Then I poured my heart out to Tom, telling him I felt trapped in my marriage and feared a future filled only with despair. Tom leant over and took my hand. My heart quickened.

I drew my hand away. 'Do not entice me into indiscretion, much as I am … sorely tempted,' I said. 'I cannot submit to temptation. Faversham is a small town, full of chattering tongues. I am recognised wherever I go. There would be no place here for us to set free our affections for one another. We have no choice but to accept that this is so.'

Tom grasped my hand again. 'Then let us not skulk in shadowy corners and seek fleeting moments with each other. Tell Arden your hatred for him and your feelings for me, and demand that he consents to your living the life you deserve, free from him and his intrigues.'

I shook my head. 'Thomas would never agree. I am the step-daughter of his sponsor, and through me he is connected to the high families of Kent. The loss of that status would be a humiliation he would never contemplate. And if I were to try to initiate such an action, I would be tried and convicted of adultery, shamed and shunned by society, even by my own family. That would be too great a price to bear.'

'Then let us bear it together. Confess your love for me to Sir Edward, ask him to honour your jointure and let us flee Faversham and start a new life together. Somewhere the scandal would not reach. Wessex, Cornwall, perhaps even London. Then we can display our love openly, rather than hide it like some shameful secret.'

I fingered the collar of my silk-lined cloak and my eyes lingered on Tom's humble attire. 'You speak from the heart, not the head, my dear Tom. My family would never sanction such an arrangement. There was much questioning as to whether Thomas Arden was a suitable husband when we were betrothed, and he was already a merchantman of some standing. It pains me to say it, but they would be much preju-diced against me consorting with someone plying an honest trade as a tailor. If we were to be together, it would lead to my being ostracised from my family and there would be no question of keeping my modest jointure. And we would have to live in sin, as Thomas would never consent to a divorce. We would sacrifice a great deal to have a life together.'

Tom stared off at nothing. 'You are sure that none of your family fortune would be available to you? Then that is a forfeit I could not ask you to make, dear Alice. Knowing that your husband would have for himself all the wealth that your family bestowed on you at the time of your marriage would eat away at us every day for the rest of our lives. I would not give him the satisfaction of having all that should be yours.' He pulled me close. There was steel in his eyes as he looked into mine. 'There is nothing you could do to claim what is rightfully yours? No pressure that could be put upon him to do the honourable thing?'

'None,' I replied. I buried my head in his chest.

'Then let us accept our fate, and make the best of it. If we cannot be together openly, then surely we should not deny ourselves the pleasure of being together in secret? With care and discretion, we can love each other, and the world will be none the wiser.'

'Perhaps one day.'

I pulled away from Tom and gave him a wavering smile. Feelings rose inside me and it took all my strength to resist them.

AS THE MONTHS WENT by, Thomas became so busy with the town's new charter that he never had any time or energy, even for conversation. An evening game of backgammon – even his listening to me play the virginal – became a thing of the past. My body was as the chaff of wheat, the life force inside me shrivelled and dried. I looked at myself in a mirror and saw a ghost, a shadow of who I once was. I decided to visit Faversham's healing wife, an old woman who tended a physic garden and dispensed herbs and cures for various ailments. I was desperate for whatever remedy she could prescribe.

Mistress Parker's house was located behind the abbey walls, easy to reach but away from the town's bustling market. I pushed open a warped oak door, and a wave of unfamiliar scents washed over me: earthy and pungent from dried herbs, sweet and cloying from simmering potions. On the shelves behind the old woman was an array of glass jars, filled with mysterious concoctions – powders of an unsettling green, viscous amber liquids and plump roots that were twisted and contorted like gnarled fingers.

'Come in, child,' the healing wife said to me, her voice low and soothing. 'What troubles you today?'

I explained that I had lost all the vitality of my youth, that a listlessness had come over me, and that I felt that my humours had become out of balance. I said that I had heard that potions of galingale and zedoary could provide the heat to balance my humours again, but the healing wife shook her head.

'It is your husband you need to visit, not me,' she said, looking at me with kindly eyes. 'Wives who are young, healthy and fertile need to receive their husband's attentions in the night, to open the pores of the skin and purge the body of impurities, and to promote good digestion to release the energy in the food they eat. The belly is a cauldron, and unless there is fire in it, it is not able to turn the solids into a juice we call chyle, which is transported to the liver to be turned into blood, then pumped by the heart to feed nutrients to every part of your body. The potions that you mentioned will only work if the cauldron of your belly is lit again. Your pores are closed, so you are full of impurities, and your belly has gone cold, so you are receiving little nutrition from your food. It is this that explains your jaded temper. Go back to your husband, do more to entice him, otherwise you will become an old maid ahead of your time.'

I slipped Mistress Parker a coin and left, thinking back to those times I had tried to tempt Thomas into love-making, and how ineffective and humiliating each attempt had been.

I had no choice. I had to be with Tom Mosby again, no matter what the risk. My health depended on it.

And so, it began. I went straight to Tom's cottage after leaving the healing wife and he kissed me the moment I arrived. My body responded in a way that I remembered well, my stomach tightening as I felt his embrace. I threw my head back to offer up my throat. He kissed me there, and then along the lines of my shoulders, pushing away my smock until my shoulders were bare. I waited for more, smiling at him nervously, but invitingly too. He stroked my hair, then tasted it. He gently knelt and I joined him. We kissed again and the next moment, we were lying on the floor. Tom lingered in those parts of me my husband refused to touch. Our love-making was fierce, furious and ferocious, much more intense than before. I would never be able to deny myself this again, no matter what the consequences. I was in ecstasy; I was in shame. I loved Tom; I hated myself.

It was dark when we finished, and Tom rose to light a candle. The fire had returned to my belly and the pores of my skin were glowing and open, just as had been foretold. The remedy had worked.

I SHOULD HAVE BEEN more restrained, I should have been more discreet, but I couldn't help myself. I waited for four days before I visited Tom again, worried that if I delayed any longer my pores would close and my belly go cold again. The next time was two days later. After that it was daily, and our behaviour became more wanton. It was foolish, I knew. Such frequent rendezvous would not go unnoticed.

It was only three short weeks before Thomas confronted me with his suspicions.

'Everywhere I walk in Faversham, I hear the name of Tom Mosby. I hear that I am cuckolded, that the tailor is making sport with my wife. Many tell me that you should be stripped to your underclothes and made to hold a lighted taper in church every Sunday, as all women who break the seventh commandment are made to do. I find no fault with their advice. Tell me why I should.'

My mouth fell open and I could not prevent my hand flying to my chest. I took a moment to compose myself.

'Foolish people wag their tongues when they are looking to spice up their own drab lives,' I replied, stumbling over my words. I slid my hands down my sides as I forced myself to speak calmly. 'It is petty jealousy, nothing more. Some begrudge your good fortune in rising to the top of Faversham society, others envy my happiness in being by your side and wish me harm. Ignore these malicious people and their foul words. Tom Mosby is my tailor. I step out with you on many a gay evening, and I need my dress to be the best. A visit to the tailor is but one of the many errands to be undertaken by the lady of the mayor's household. I do not bother you with such trifles, a man in your position. Ignore all the gossip and remind those who repeat it that you have the power to consign them to the stocks for their impertinence.'

But Thomas slammed his fist on the table. 'I forgave you your sins when you confessed them to me, but do not take me for a fool, Alice. Obey me as a wife must obey her husband and find another tailor. I forbid you to see Tom Mosby again.'

I meekly said I would accede to his wishes, but even as I surrendered to my husband's demands, my words sounded hollow and I knew I would be unable to honour them. I waited but a week before I visited Tom again. We agreed that if our romance was to survive, we had to be more careful and I said that I could only risk meeting when Thomas was away on business, to the port at Sandwich perhaps, or on a trip to London. That would be once a month, no more, but we had to be discreet. The thought of never seeing Tom again filled me with the utmost despair.

I HAD TO WAIT a whole five weeks before Thomas announced he would be departing for London. After he rode off, I dismissed our servants so that I could entertain Tom alone. It was a risk, but not so great a risk as being seen on my own, walking the path to Tom's lonely cottage on the outskirts of the town. I could indulge a fantasy of our being together not just for a rushed dalliance, but as a loving couple, enjoying life together.

It was a perfect day. We had lain together and there was no rush for Tom to depart. I was playing a tune on the virginal when I heard the latch of the door. I looked at Tom in horror, and saw his eyes dart around the room, looking for a means of escape. But there was no time to get away, no place to hide. My husband burst in and found us together. I let out a shriek and saw Tom backing towards the door.

'I knew it!' Thomas put a hand on the hilt of his sword. 'Did you really think me gone to London? I may be a cuckold, but I am not a fool. I have exposed your deceit and you will do penance for the sin you have committed, Alice. As for you, Tom Mosby – you will leave Faversham at first light on the morrow or it will be a flogging for you.'

'If Tom leaves Faversham, then I leave too,' I replied. 'I care not for worldly goods and high status. I will be a tailor's wife, and you can spend your evenings alone, counting your gold. That is all you care about after all.'

I waited for Tom to speak in my support, but he remained silent.

'Alice does not know her mind,' Thomas said, filling the silence. 'She makes this vow in the heat of the moment, and when the sacrifice of what she is proposing becomes real to her, she will be back in Faversham, to her fine gowns and to servants waiting on her every need.' He turned to me. 'Admit that this is true, Alice. Or this scoundrel will surely rue the day he bedded you.'

'It is you who must consider the truth,' I replied. 'Why do you protest so much? You can divorce me and cast me out, but do you want to lose Sir Edward's sponsorship? There is no passion in our marriage, and my health has been suffering as a result of your neglect. The healing wife at the physic garden has told me that without a husband's attention, my body will wither and become old before its time. If you are not minded to provide the attention any wife deserves, let me lie with Tom. As far as the world will see, I will remain your dutiful wife. Let us all be seen openly and together, then no-one will question the seemliness of my acquaintance with him.'

I could not believe I had uttered such brazen words. Both men looked shocked.

'We will speak on this, alone,' Thomas said to me. He turned to Tom. 'Leave my home immediately.'

Without even a backward glance, Tom fled the room.

Thomas and I talked no more that night, but the next day he confronted me again with his demand that Tom Mosby leave Faversham. I pleaded with him to at least consider my proposal.

'Our house is huge, much more than is needed for two people. We have rooms for guests on the upper floor that are rarely used. Grant Tom Mosby one such room and name him as your man. Do this, and I will remain by your side in public and be seen by all as your dutiful wife.' I took a deep breath. 'But deny me this and my life will not be worth living. If death is to be my lot, I will first write an avowal that the cause is your failings as a husband, then throw myself into Thorn Creek. If my present anguish does not move you, consider the impact of such an avowal on your social standing and how my step-father will react. Sir Edward has made it clear that his sponsorship of you is dependent on my being your wife. If it comes to pass that I die and you are the cause, he will surely turn against you.'

'Do not threaten me with disgrace,' Thomas replied. 'No man would contemplate what you are proposing. It is an ungodly perversion that would be the scandal of the county.'

Thomas cared less about his own feelings on the matter than how it would look. That gave me the confidence to continue.

'No-one need know. Tom Mosby's station in life has risen; he is now of the same standing as you were when you arrived here in Faversham. My affection for his sister Cislye is well known, so there are already connections between our families. The true circumstances may not escape the notice of our servants, but Michael wishes to marry Cislye and

Elisabeth is her daughter. Both of them have every reason to be discreet and to say that no shame or immorality is being practised in this house. You care not a whit for me yourself. Why will you not do as I request? If not for my health and happiness, then at least for your own self-interest. Why risk throwing everything away, your standing in the town, your bond with Sir Edward, for something you care so little about?'

Thomas's face was red now, his nostrils flaring. 'I will not be blackmailed by a whore, even if that whore is my wife. I cannot acquiesce to that brute sleeping in my house and laying his hands on you. It would be too much for any man to bear.'

'Then I will be dead before the month is out. You are shrewd and calculating, Thomas. Consider the risks, then consider the benefits. Sit in your counting room with your tally sticks and quills and enter it in your ledger as you would any other transaction. You will see there is much to commend it.'

He gave a dismissive snort. 'I would not trust Tom Mosby to hold his tongue about such an arrangement. After a night's drinking in the Fleur de Lis he would be unable to resist boasting that he is tilling the fields of Venus with my wife.'

I seized my chance. 'Tom Mosby is an honourable man and would never be so boastful about such personal matters. Let me make this promise. Should there ever be any reports that he had even hinted at the truth of our arrangement, I will banish him from my life and accept any penance you deem fit for me. I will never again make any demands on you in any way, and I will do everything in my power to ensure that you remain in Sir Edward's favour. If I make such an oath, Thomas, will you at least consider whether such an arrangement might work?' My voice choked with emotion.

Finally, Thomas relented. 'Oh, do what you must. This whole affair has already taken up too much of my time and energy. Keep your meetings to the dead of night.' He gave me a sarcastic smile. 'Is that all to your satisfaction? But before you speak to Mosby, fetch me my Bible. You will swear the oath you described, and by God I will hold you to it, if I hear that he is the source of any malicious gossip. There we are. Let that be the end of this discussion.'

I could not believe my good fortune. My life was worth living again.

Chapter Thirteen
Will ~ 1591

THE MORNING AFTER my conversation with Adam Fowle, I told the rest of the troupe I would catch them up as they left for the next destination on our tour, and I headed off to the new Guildhall in Market Place. After some persuasion, the town clerk agreed to fetch the wardmote book from the year 1551. I opened it with trembling fingers and turned to the date of the murder. There, after a series of ledger entries detailing the final fees and expenditures incurred by the town council for the previous quarter, I found what I was looking for. A note, written in the margin: *'The manner of Arden's murder.'* I could hardly contain my excitement as I read the words next to it.

THIS YEAR, the 15th day of February being Sunday, one Thomas Arden of Faversham was heinously murdered in his own parlour about seven of the clock in the night by one Tom Mosby, a tailor of London; by Alice Arden, wife of the said Thomas Arden, and by one John Greene, tailor, all inhabitants of Faversham and intent to murder the said Thomas Arden …

I took out my quill and paper and began to copy out every word of the report. Even though it was describing the events of forty years ago in an official account, I could feel the outrage in every word. I wrote furiously for over fifteen minutes, and was shocked to read the details of the arrangement that Mosby and Alice had come to with Thomas Arden.

> ...*with Alice the said Mosby did not only carnally keep in her own house here in this town, but also fed him with delicate meats and sumptuous apparel. All which things the said Thomas Arden did well know and wilfully did permit and suffered the same.*

I pondered whether this behaviour was perhaps too explicit for the London stage, whether it might incur the wrath of the puritans.

And then, after the wardmote book described Arden's killing and the various gruesome executions of the perpetrators of the murder, came the final reckoning:

> *And all the apparel that belonged to the said Alice Arden, and all the moveable goods of the foresaid Tom Mosby and John Greene, were taken, seized and forfeited to the use of the said town of Faversham. All which goods being sold amounted the sum of nine score and four pounds, ten shillings four pence, and one halfpenny.*

Such vengeance. Not only were each of the murderers despatched from this earth in the most terrible ways possible;

all of their possessions were sold to augment the coffers of the town. Every last ounce of revenge had to be extracted. The wardmote book pulsed with hatred.

I SPENT WHAT SPARE time I had on the rest of our tour of the Kent towns sketching out some ideas for lines and scenes for the play, and started work in earnest the moment I returned to London. I couldn't wait to get started. Burbage was true to his word, and as the restrictions put in place because of the plague had been lifted, I was welcomed into Lord Strange's Men as a full member of the company. In truth, it did little to improve my financial position in London. I would earn six shillings a week as an actor, but I needed to keep the Shakspere's Boys going to have the same income as before, when I had been doing the work of two call-boys. And still it was only a pound a month to Anne, when I desperately wanted it to be more.

But if I had succeeded in getting onto the stage, I was failing in my plan to write for it. I took what I had sketched out while on tour and the few lines I had written, but as I sat in my Shoreditch garret every evening, scratching away by candlelight, I knew that I was beaten. I had borrowed the Lord Strange's Men's copy of *The Spanish Tragedy* to follow what Thomas Kydd had done in structuring his play, and thought back to what Tarlton had told me about writing his. But it soon became clear to me that the problem was not structure, but content. I knew little of the details of the events leading up to the murder, and the conspirators that Adam Fowle had told me about.

I sketched out one long opening scene set in the Arden home, when Thomas becomes suspicious that Alice is having an affair with Mosby on hearing her say his name in her sleep; then a second scene where Alice and Mosby plan and execute the murder and drag Thomas's body to the patch of grass around which I saw the crowd gather in Faversham. But that was it. The play made no sense, the characters were thinly drawn and all the action took place in Abbey Street, as I did not know where else featured in the plot.

I had been defeated in my desire to become a writer. Not because I could not find a compelling story to tell; nor because I could not get on the London stage. No, I had failed for the one reason I had never considered. I did not know how to write a play.

I decided to get in touch with Dick Tarlton, to see whether a man from a humble background such as my own would be interested in collaborating on my idea. I headed over to Ludgate Hill and the Bell Savage Inn, where I knew the Queen's Men used to perform. Trestles on the cobbled courtyard suggested that it still was staging plays. But the landlord gave me sad news when I arrived. The company had never recovered from the death of William Knell, and had lost the high regard in which they were once held. They had become eclipsed by the Admiral's Men, unable to compete against the plays of Kit Marlowe and the acting of Ned Alleyn. The Queen's Men were no more.

But it was his other news that shocked me. Dick Tarlton had gambled away all his family's money and had moved back to his home town of Hanwell, west of London, where he had died two years ago. I thought of the quick-witted clown who had been so kind to me when I stepped onto the stage after leaving Stratford, the man who had shown me it was possible for someone of modest beginnings to write a play. I told the landlord that I was saddened to hear this news, that Tarlton and I had been in the Queen's Men together and that I had called to seek his help in my own ambitions to be a writer of plays.

'Then you must seek out Thomas Watson,' the landlord told me. 'He is a poet and writer, though not of plays, I believe. He drinks here most evenings, and I fancy he will return tonight before six of the clock. Come back then and I will introduce him to you. He may be of some help.'

I came back at five and Thomas Watson was already there, sipping his ale. The landlord introduced us and I took a deep breath. My fate as a writer might hang on the result of this encounter.

'God save you, Master Watson,' I said. 'Will Shakspere, at your service. The landlord has told me of your skills as a writer. I am a member of Lord Strange's Men, with a fancy to be a writer of plays, much like the departed Dick Tarlton. If I refill your ale for you, may I seek your advice?'

Watson seemed amused by my ambition and bade me join him.

'So, I am talking to the new Marlowe or the new Kydd?' he asked. 'I confess I know nothing of you. Were you at Oxford or Cambridge?'

I blushed. 'Neither. I hail from Stratford and was a glover by trade. I arrived in London three years ago to seek the opportunity to perform on stage and one day to write for it. I have been touring with Lord Strange's Men while the playhouses in London were closed. Now that the plague has receded, I am back in Shoreditch and looking to make a start on my writing.'

Watson shook his head. 'Will, you have been spared a fate that would have been worse than you can possibly imagine. I drink here most evenings with Thomas Nashe and Robert Greene. You may know them for their plays, *Summer's Last Will and Testament* and *Friar Bacon and Friar Bungay*.'

I had heard of the second, so nodded in recognition.

'They style themselves the University Wits and they include me in that company, although I do not care for the term; it smacks of self-aggrandisement. Had you told them of your ambitions, Greene would have goaded you on to fulsome expansion of your dreams and spent the next few weeks regaling his audiences with tales of the comedy of a glover's son from the provinces writing for the London stage, no doubt inventing some dreadful prose to characterise your writing.'

My heart felt like it was shrinking as I tried to come to terms with the thought that such great men could behave with such petty vindictiveness. Watson put his hand on my shoulder. 'Do not be disheartened. As long as you can read and write, whether you know Latin and Greek, whether you have or have not been to university, should not stop you writing entertainment for the many-headed monster.' He reflected for a moment. 'After all, it hasn't stopped Thomas Kydd, and he had only been to the Merchant Taylor school and progressed no further.'

My heart leapt into my mouth. 'You know Thomas Kydd yourself?' I asked. 'I have been performing in his play these last few months. It seems unreal that such a man could be, as it were, amongst us.'

Watson burst out laughing at my eagerness. 'Kydd is no great god of literature, sent to meet us lesser mortals. He is a hot head and a brute. Like a salamander, he seems to live and thrive in fire. One day someone who crosses him will come to harm from his anger.'

I wanted Watson to tell me more of these men he knew. 'And Greene and Nashe, of whom you spoke? What sort of men are they?'

'Greene is a most prolific writer who can summon a tale every few months, has a quick wit and a flair for words, but is an irresponsible fantasist who leads a rakish life and narrowly avoids scandal. Nashe is promising for his years, but makes enemies easily and seems to seek out controversy rather than avoid it. I fear they will both meet an untimely end, no matter how great their talents.'

I was becoming disquieted by all this information. The life of a writer of plays appeared to be a short one.

'And what of you, Thomas Watson?' I said. 'How would they describe you?'

'I leave it to others to characterise the man,' he replied, a modest smile making me warm to him. 'As to my aptitudes, I would call myself a poet and composer of madrigals – the music for voices from Italy that is starting to find favour again.' He leant forward and spoke in a near whisper. 'But the truth is, Will Shakspere, I too fancy myself as a writer of plays. I am pleased to talk to someone with experience of the craft of the playhouse, so I can learn how my words could be performed on stage.'

I told him what I had observed in my three years of working at the Theatre and the Curtain, and the little experience I had had as an actor with both the Queen's Men and Lord Strange's Men, then returned to the subject of the London writers.

'And what of Kit Marlowe, whom I have heard much praised?'

Watson smiled, and when he spoke again there was a soft tone to his voice. 'Ah, Kit Marlowe,' he said. 'You are well versed in the names of the London writers for a lad from the provinces, Will Shakspere.' I blushed at the compliment. 'Now there is a true genius, not a preening gadfly like Robert Greene or Thomas Nashe. Marlowe is a Cambridge man, like Robert Greene, but there the similarity ends. Greene thinks highly of himself and wants everyone else to do the same. He seeks to display an intellectual brilliance in his writing, when the truth is that his skill is in his wit, not his learning. Marlowe is the opposite. He has a great brain and knows all there is to know about everything. But when he writes, he writes for the common man, with as much violence, cruelty and bloodshed as he can cram into two hours. That's what people flock to see, and that's why every performance of his *Tamburlaine* has had crowds crushing in all through the season.' He laughed. 'That's the secret of success in this game, Will Shakspere. Save your cleverness for conversation with your peers. Give as many murders and executions as you can to your audiences.'

It seemed the right moment to tell him of the idea I had lit upon for my play.

'I think I have found such a story,' I said, taking a quick breath before I said more. 'May I share it with you?'

'Keep me in suspense no longer,' Watson replied. 'What is the story you are looking to tell?'

'The murder of Thomas Arden in the town of Faversham,' I replied.

Watson raised his eyebrows and his shoulders shook with laughter. I did not know whether to be pleased or disappointed.

'I see you recognise the crime of which I speak,' I said. 'Tell me, do you think it a suitable topic for the London stage?'

'Most certainly,' Watson replied. 'Thomas Arden was an important man in Faversham, was he not? And murdered by his wife in a crime of passion, as I recall. I wish you luck in the writing of it, Will Shakspere. And I will take great pleasure in seeing you silence those who would doubt that a glover from Stratford can pen a play, when we see it triumph.'

'I wish I shared your optimism. I was told of the tale when we visited Faversham, and I spoke with an old innkeeper who was the landlord of the inn frequented by one of the murderers. It was forty years ago, but he was able still to recall the events of that terrible night.' I sighed. 'In my foolish innocence, I thought that was all that was needed for me to write the lines that would be performed on stage. But when I sat down to do so, I found I had more questions than answers. Which brings me to the question I have been bursting to ask you, sir. What is the secret of this craft?'

Watson smiled. 'Ask yourself, why are all the plays that you know from historical times?' He raised his eyebrows waiting for me to respond, but I gave a puzzled shrug. He laughed, enjoying the chance to educate me. 'That's because every man who sits down to write a play needs to have a record of the events to begin with, so that he can add some depth and substance to bring the story to life. The chroniclers of ancient tales are the learned men on whom we rely to tell the stories of past eras today.'

I felt somewhat dismayed, but not disheartened. 'How foolish of me not to know something so simple,' I said. 'I have wasted much time and effort on a fruitless exercise. But now I know precisely what I must do. Find an ancient saga which some chronicler has already described …' I punched a fist into my hand. 'My thanks to you, sir.'

Watson chuckled. 'Do not give up on the Arden murder so easily. I think perhaps you have a guardian angel looking after you.' I looked at my companion curiously as he continued. 'I'll tell you why. You have come across a story from modern times, which has been documented in a way similar to ancient tales.' Watson seemed to enjoy the look of astonishment on my face. 'Find yourself a copy of Holinshed's *Chronicles of England, Scotland and Ireland,*' he said. 'Have you heard of this work?'

'I have,' I replied. 'But is it not a compendium of the great moments in history, the kings and noblemen who shaped the destiny of our great land since the time of King Arthur and the knights of the round table? I cannot imagine it deals with a sordid murder in a Kent provincial town.'

'That's where you are wrong,' Watson replied. 'The Arden murder features prominently in its pages. Head off to the booksellers at St Paul's and see if you can locate a copy. It will be a sound investment if you want to be an author of plays.'

I knew the area of St Paul's well, as the Bell Inn on Carter Lane was where I left and received messages from Anne from our neighbour Willian Greenway, who stayed there on his trips to London. I stood for a moment and studied the great cathedral there, some of the banners still in place from when Queen Elizabeth had visited in 1588 for thanks-giving after the defeat of the Armada. It was still missing its steeple from the lightning strike many years before. I walked over to Paternoster Row, the quarter of London where the bookselling, publishing and printing trades clustered. After half an hour of searching, I found a copy of Holinshed's *Chronicles* in Nicholas Ling's shop in Fleet Street. But the price was one pound and six shillings; it may as well have been one hundred pounds and six shillings. Even though I now had eight Shakspere's Boys at the Curtain and the Theatre, my actor's salary meant I only had thirteen shillings and sixpence left after I sent my pound to Anne each month. I could now afford a chicken mid-week, but still did not have the means or the inclination to waste money socialising with others in the evening.

Purchasing Holinshed's book would mean sending nothing for a month to my family. I could not bear to do so. I would find another way to write my play.

I sat in my lodgings, thinking not for the first time about how difficult all this had proved to be, despite my good fortune at now being one of Lord Strange's Men. As I sat staring at my solitary candle, watching the wax melt away like the vestiges of my ambition, I decided I owed it to myself to try one last time to achieve my dreams. I would convince Burbage to permit me to work for the company, as both actor and call-boy, for two months. Saving every penny of the extra job would afford me sixteen shillings, and a diet of pease porridge and no ham hock or meat pie on a Friday would mean that in these two months I would have saved enough to buy the *Chronicles* and still send money home to Anne.

It would not be easy, but I could do it.

I RETURNED TO LING'S shop in December, nervous coins jangling in my pocket. It had been more demanding than I had imagined, doing a full day's work on an empty belly and appearing on stage six afternoons a week, so I was full of trepidation as I purchased the book and returned to my lodgings to pore over its pages.

I was astonished by what I read. Not only did it contain a detailed account of the Arden murder, but chapter after chapter described the most heroic deeds of history, ancient and modern, all of which would be rich material for future plays. The story of a Scottish King, Macbeth; the mythological Leir of Britain, an elderly English monarch; the fable of the early Celtic king, Cymbeline; the stories went on and on. I even for a moment considered abandoning the Arden murder in favour of another story, but in the end I decided that I owed it to my mother's name for this to be my first play.

At first glance, Holinshed's inclusion of the Arden murder was a strange addition to the book. I had been right in my belief that it dealt mainly with the important deeds and events of our history, and the great man himself seemed a little embarrassed at including such a relatively trivial matter. My confusion lifted when I read his opening words.

The Arden murder, for the horribleness thereof, although otherwise it may seem a private matter and therefore, as it were, impertinent to this history, I have thought good to set it forth somewhat at large, having the instructions delivered to me by them that used some diligence to gather the true understanding of the circumstances.

I smiled to myself. Raphael Holinshed may have liked to see himself as the author of an important book about important events, but he was not above including some salacious material to spice things up.

As I read Holinshed's detailed account of the murder, I became more and more intrigued. The entry in the Faversham wardmote book which I had assiduously transcribed was the only official account of the murder, but here the account was much more thorough and contained information that was not in the wardmote description. Adam Fowle, for example, was mentioned frequently by Holinshed, but not once in the wardmote book. All the events leading up to the murder were described by Holinshed in great detail, and again, this was new information. Where had all this extra knowledge come from? And when he wrote, *'having the instructions delivered to me by them'*, who were the 'them' to whom Holinshed referred? Who supplied him with the extra information? Holinshed had written his account a few years ago, when only Adam Fowle was still alive of those who were around when the murder was committed, and the innkeeper had given no indication to me that he had been interviewed at length by the greatest chronicler of our time. I went back to the bookseller in St Paul's and asked if he could shed any light on this riddle.

'I do not know the others to whom Raphael Holinshed refers,' he told me, 'but I know for sure that our own John Stow had a hand in writing an account of the murder. You must surely know of that great and good man?'

I confessed that I did not, and he gave me a look suggesting his confusion that someone who had the means and motivation to purchase Holinshed's *Chronicles* could be so little versed in literature.

'John Stow is the greatest librarian of our age,' he told me. 'Renowned both as a chronicler and as a man, as he is very generous at letting others make use of the documents in his possession. And he lives but a few paces from here, in a house in Leadenhall Street, at the Algate pump. If you have an interest in his writing, seek him out. You will find him most willing to be of assistance.'

I sent a messenger requesting a meeting and was thrilled when a reply came by return, inviting me to visit the following week. I put on hold the writing of the play until we met. I had many questions about the Arden murder, and I was excited that such a great man as John Stow would grant me time to answer them for me.

What he would reveal was to change my life.

Chapter Fourteen
Alice ~ 1547

THE FIRST FEW MONTHS of Thomas's time as mayor were the happiest of my life. He would go drinking with Dunkyn at the Fleur de Lis while Tom and I played board games in the parlour and I would play the virginal for a while when my husband returned. Then our servants, Michael and Elisabeth, would be dismissed and Tom and I would retire to our bedchamber.

The only thing that vexed me was the discovery that my Tom was good friends with John Greene, the same John Greene who was Sir Anthony Aucher's man and who had come to our house intent on doing Thomas harm when he cheated Greene out of his land.

'My husband and Sir Anthony are sworn enemies,' I said to Tom when I found out. 'If you are to be known as Arden's man, you cannot consort with the man of his rival. Give up your acquaintance with Greene, for the sake of harmony in our household.'

'My acquaintance is a trivial matter, nothing more,' Tom replied. 'He took up my trade when your husband cheated him out of his family land, and we trade cloth together when it is to our mutual advantage. A group of us play cards together, and we enjoy a small wager on the outcome. It is

Kirtling Tower, where Alice lived when she met Tom Mosby and Thomas Arden

Abbey Gate, 80 Abbey Street, the Faversham home of Thomas and Alice Arden

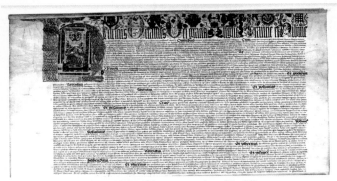

The Faversham charter negotiated by Thomas Arden in 1544 and signed by him

The Faversham moot horn which would have been blown at the start of the Arden murder trial

The author and the Faversham wardmote book

'Arden of Faversham' entry in the Stationers' Register. The asterisk and initials 'G.S.' on the left of the entry were made by the 18th-century Shakespeare expert George Steevens, who marked entries in the Register he thought were works of Shakespeare. The entry reads 'Entered for his copie under the handes of the Lord Bishop of London and the wardens The Tragedy of Arden of Faversham and Black Will'.

The hystory of a mose horrible murder commytyd at feversshame in Kente   93

John Stow's account of the Arden murder, 'The History of a Moste Horrible Murder Commytyd at Fevershame in Kente'

About this time there was at Feuersham in Kent a gentleman named Arden, most cruellie murthered and slaine by the procurement of his owne wife. The which murther, for the horriblenesse thereof, although otherwise it may seeme to be but a priuate matter, and therefore as it were impertinent to this historie, I haue thought good to set it foorth somewhat at large, hauing the instructions deliuered to me by them, that haue vsed some diligence to gather the true vnderstanding of the circumstances. This Arden was a man of a tall and comelie personage, and matched in marriage with a gentlewoman, yoong, tall, and well fauoured of shape and countenance, who chancing to fall in familiaritie with one Mosbie a tailor by occupation, a blacke swart man, seruant to the lord North, it happened this Mosbie vpon some misliking to fall out with hir: but she being desirous to be in fauour with him againe, sent him a paire of siluer dice by one Adam Foule dwelling at the Floure de lice in Feuersham.

margin: 1551 Anno Reg [.] Arden murthered.

margin: Arden described.

margin: Loue and lust.

margin: A paire of siluer dice worke much mischiefe.

The account of the murder in Holinshed's 'Chronicles', based largely on Stow's account

*The disenfranchisement of Thomas Arden on December
22nd 1550, recorded in the wardmote book*

*The entry describing the Arden murder in the wardmote book. 'The
manner of Arden's murder' is written in the margin. Note: The date of
the murder is given as February 15th 1550, as the Julian calendar in use
at the time had the new year starting on March 24th, not January 1st.*

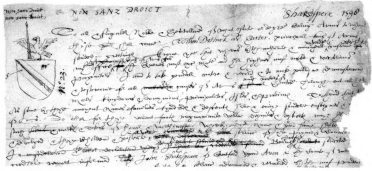

Shakespeare Coat of Arms application incorporating the Arden crest

*The strikingly similar
William Shakespeare
and John Stow
memorial statues*

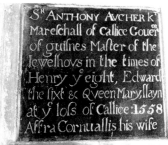

Clockwise from top left: Sir Edward North, Alice's stepfather; Sir Anthony Aucher memorial plaque; Ben Jonson; Richard Burbage

Woodcut from the 1633 quarto depicting the Arden murder

*Jenny Agutter (Alice) and Robert O'Mahoney (Mosby) in the 1982
Royal Shakespeare Company's production of 'Arden of Faversham'*

THE
LAMENTA-
BLE AND TRVE TRA-
GEDIE OF M. AR-
DEN OF FEVERSHAM
IN KENT.

Who was most wickedlye murdered, by
the meanes of his disloyall and wanton
wyfe, who for the loue she bare to one
Mosbie, hyred two desperat ruf-
fins Blackwill and Shakbag,
to kill him.

Wherin is shewed the great mal-
lice and discimulation of a wicked woman, the vnsatiable desire of filthie lust
and the shamefull end of all
murderers.

Imprinted at London for Edward
White, dwelling at the lyttle North
dore of Paules Church at
the signe of the
Gun. 1592.

✳

Title page of 'Arden of Faversham', first quarto, 1592

the only pleasure in my life, other than the happiness I have with you. Surely you would not deny this small indulgence?'

I was shocked that Tom would defend his camaraderie with one who had come to our house armed with a cudgel, and pressed the point. 'I was terrified by Greene's anger and it was only the selfless act of courage of our servant, Michael, that prevented him from attacking Thomas. I feared for my own safety as well. How can you consort with a man who has such an enmity towards us?'

Tom was not to be shifted, and so all I could do was pray that my husband did not discover what I had found out. I made Tom promise that Greene would never be invited to our house. I hoped that would suffice, and tried to put the worry out of my mind.

But I was even more concerned when Sir Anthony Aucher and Thomas clashed again. Thomas had thought the sale of the George and the Garret would end the bad blood between them, but it only made things worse. There had been two parts to the deal, the price of twenty-three pounds and more that Sir Anthony had paid at the time, and a small pension of twenty marks a year, which he had promised to pay to Thomas and myself for as long as one of us was still alive.

But to Thomas's irritation, Sir Anthony had never paid this annual stipend, and as I was named on the original contract he took me into his confidence that he was finally resorting to taking steps to get what was due to us. I advised him to desist, that twenty marks was a paltry sum and not worth opening up old wounds for, but Thomas was insistent.

'Aucher has been the bane of my life in Faversham,' he told me. 'It is not unexpected that I should have a rival for the riches that the opportunities that the dissolution of the monasteries presented, but Sir Anthony Aucher is more determined that my dealings should fail, rather than that his should succeed. Enough is enough. Twenty marks a year is what he owes us for as long as one of us shall live, and twenty marks is what he is going to pay, even if I have to petition the King himself to make him pay it. He makes a fool of me no longer.'

'But Sir Anthony is either a friend or blood relative of every magistrate in the county.' I held my arms wide, my palms up, and stared hard at him. 'How can you succeed in a court of law to press him to do your wishes? Leave him be, good husband. You do not need this paltry coin.'

'I have a plan to circumvent his influence,' Thomas replied, his voice full of bluster. He cocked his head to me and raised an eyebrow. 'He might have the courts of Kent at his beck and call, but his tentacles do not spread through the land. I will petition your step-father to ask the Privy Council to intervene and decide in my favour. Aucher will finally see that Thomas Arden is not to be trifled with.'

I tried reasoning with Thomas that the Privy Council was there to adjudicate on great matters of state, not concern itself in trifling disputes over the sale of two inns in rural Kent, but he could not be persuaded.

'Sir Edward North is a member and has much influence with the other privy councillors. Were he to intercede, I am sure he could persuade them.' He had a gleam in his eye, the inner light of confidence.

'My step-father will be difficult to persuade,' I said. 'He sees the affairs of politics and commerce to be worlds apart. You will not find it easy to convince him.'

Thomas smiled, as if he knew this was what I was going to say.

'Then it must not be I who asks him. He favours you, Alice. You will visit him and plead that he intercedes.'

I opened my mouth to object, but he cut me down with a barked command. 'I tolerate your liaisons with Tom Mosby more than would any man in England. I care not how you wish to spend your nights with him, but at any time I could have you both arrested for adultery. At the very least you would be publicly shamed for your crime and cast out into the world. Without a penny to your name, I might add.'

He saw the fear on my face, and his voice softened. Not, I felt, with sympathy, but with guileful purpose. 'But I have no desire for you to be punished. I have accepted this peculiar state of affairs and have asked for nothing in return. Until now. Go to your step-father and convince him to have the Privy Council involve itself. Let that be the price you pay for sharing Mosby's bed.'

I had no choice. I could have argued that Thomas had allowed our arrangement purely for his own self-interest, to ensure that nothing should upset his relationship with Sir Edward, but it would achieve nothing.

Thomas made one final condition – that this pact be kept secret between us and told not even to my Tom, so that no disturbance should be caused within the household. I readily agreed and swore an oath to that effect. My Tom did not need to know the sacrifices I had to make to have his love.

IT WAS STRANGE TO be back in Kirtling Tower, stranger still to visit without Thomas. It reminded me of when I was a little girl, when my existence was carefree and I knew nothing of the vagaries of the adult world.

Mother gave me a wary greeting when I arrived. I had written saying it had been too long since we last saw each other, but I also requested an audience with Sir Edward to discuss a business matter that Thomas wanted to raise with him. It was most unlike Thomas to allow another to represent him in matters of commerce, and Mother was astute enough to know something was afoot. But there was no mention of it on my arrival. We sat in the drawing room, and I asked a servant to bring me a glass of sack wine. Mother looked shocked that I should ask for such a strong brew, and in the middle of the day, but I did not care. I needed something to steady my nerves

I gulped down the wine as I batted away Mother's gentle questioning about how I was faring in Faversham, and her probing as to whether there was anything untoward in my marriage as I still was without child. Despite myself, I felt a flicker of pride as I described Thomas's ascendance through the political ranks of the town, his achievements in securing Faversham's charter and his elevation to mayor.

'There is talk of Thomas being knighted, perhaps even taking a country seat now that he can afford one. Can you imagine, Mother? Thomas and Sir Edward one day sitting on the Privy Council together, our husbands equal in the eyes of the King. Wouldn't that be a wonderful thing?'

Mother smiled, and I finally felt I had achieved some worth in her eyes.

Then I was told Sir Edward was ready to receive me. I rose, and glanced in a mirror to adjust the ruff sitting on my gown. As I walked along the long oak-panelled corridor to his library, I was suddenly struck by the thought that this would be the first time in my life I would be alone in his presence. I gave a timid knock at the door and entered when I heard a muffled response. Sir Edward rose to greet me. My step-father was studied in all his moves, but his mind was sharp and he was quick in conversation. He looked at me warily. He too had guessed that I had an ulterior motive for my visit.

'God save you, Sir Edward, and may He grant you a good and long life,' I said, greeting him fully and formally.

'Good morrow,' he replied, and beckoned me to take a seat.

I sat down and tried not to fidget. 'Thank you for taking the time to see me, Sir Edward. Thomas sends his best wishes and asks me to raise some small matter with you. I hope you will not object if I outline the details to you on his behalf.'

I should have made some innocuous pleasantries, but I could not wait to get to the point of our meeting. My mouth was dry and my head was spinning. The sack wine had not been a good idea.

Fortunately, my forthrightness seemed to have intrigued him. 'Not at all, dear Alice. Tell me, what is it that I can do for Thomas?'

I suppressed a desire to flee the room, steadied myself and forced myself to talk in a bright and self-possessed manner. 'Thomas's ascendancy in Faversham is most remarkable, and he is held in high acclaim by all and sundry. But in business matters, things have been less fortunate. He has a great rival in Sir Anthony Aucher, who has become adept at thwarting

Thomas's commercial dealings. Sir Anthony seems somehow aware of all that Thomas is planning, and either by bribery, disinformation or other despicable means, has recently ensured that none of Thomas's plans have come to fruition.'

Sir Edward gave a rueful chuckle. 'I am afraid your husband has only himself to blame. I do not wish to speak of matters I discussed man-to-man in private, but Thomas was most foolhardy to try to use Sir Anthony's radical sympathies against him in that squabble with the tailor Greene. I dislike Sir Anthony as much as Thomas does, but I cannot blame the man for trying to ruin your husband.'

I gave a humble nod to show my acknowledgement of his wise words.

'Nonetheless, Thomas feels that if he could send some signal to Sir Anthony that he has powerful friends who can be mobilised against him – that he is a rival not easily defeated – it might persuade Sir Anthony to desist in his attacks. When Thomas made his attack on Sir Anthony's radicalism and then realised the folly of his actions, he sold some property to him at a most advantageous price as recompense. But the halimote court clerk recorded only part of the agreement that was reached in the court records – the capital sum for the purchase – neglecting to include the annual stipend that Sir Anthony agreed to pay to Thomas and myself, which was also part of the deal. The correspondence between Sir Anthony and Thomas makes it clear that this was what was agreed and it should have been easy to obtain a judgement to correct the clerk's mistake. But Sir Anthony has thwarted every attempt to do so, demonstrating the influence he has over the Kent courts now that he is back in favour – knighted, indeed. Truth and righteousness are on our side, but that matters not. I have the documents here. If you would be so good as to read them you will see the merit of our case.'

Sir Edward took the documents from me and perused them carefully, his bushy eyebrows shooting up and down like a pair of dancing caterpillars as he read each page in turn. When he finished, he returned them to me.

'Your husband is right, Alice. There is no doubt as to what Sir Anthony has agreed. That scoundrel will get away with anything, if he can ensure evidence like this is ignored. But what would Thomas have me do? I am not inclined to challenge Sir Anthony in law. Even I, a privy councillor, do not fancy my chances in the Kent courts where he has such influence.'

'It is as a member of the Privy Council that Thomas asks for your assistance. Ask the Privy Council to investigate, as Thomas has told me they do when instances of potential injustice are brought to their attention. When they consider the facts, they will surely find in Thomas's favour. It would be a most public reprimand for Sir Anthony, and show him my husband is not to be trifled with. Otherwise, Thomas fears he will be ruined by Sir Anthony's vendetta.'

I was expecting Sir Edward to be shocked by this proposal, but instead he gave one of his chuckles.

'The Privy Council deals with great matters of state. Involving itself in a dispute concerning a payment of twenty marks a year would be like killing an ant with a cannon.' He ran his fingers slowly through his beard. 'But I would like to see Sir Anthony humbled. Since receiving his knighthood, the fellow has become insufferable and I would enjoy his discomfort at being ordered by the Privy Council to make amends to your husband. Let me see what I can do. But tell Thomas to be wary. Sir Anthony can fly into the most murderous rages. If the Privy Council finds in Thomas's favour, he would be well advised to look to his safety. But if he is willing to take that risk, then I am happy to have some sport in assisting him. Tell your husband I will do my best.'

Thomas was delighted when I gave him the news, and it was a great turning point in his dealings with Tom. He was openly a member of our household now. Yes, there was some gossip from the townsfolk, but none dared confront Thomas about it.

The Privy Council sent a request to Sir Anthony, asking if he was prepared to honour the commitment to pay the twenty marks a year to Thomas and myself. To nobody's surprise, Sir Anthony responded that he was not, and sent a letter to the lords of the council making the case that, as the stipend was not part of the official record, it would not be honoured.

The Privy Council sent one of their own clerks, a Mr Ashehurst, to Faversham to decide whether Sir Anthony's objections had merit, writing to Thomas in his capacity as mayor to grant Ashehurst access to the evidence of the case. Thomas, as mayor, was charged with assisting the arbitrator of his own case as plaintiff, and so it was no surprise that Ashehurst came to the conclusion that a twenty-mark stipend had been agreed. When this was ratified by the Privy Council, it became official. Sir Anthony would have to pay twenty marks a year, for as long as either Thomas or I were alive.

I can only imagine the fury that the great man must have felt about these developments, because when my Tom found out, he himself was filled with a most unexpected rage.

'You went to see your step-father on an errand for your husband to turn the Privy Council against Sir Anthony Aucher, and you did not have the decency to tell me?' he shouted, his voice a guttural roar. 'We should have no secrets between us, Alice. Do you not trust me with your confidences?'

I was taken aback by his reaction. 'This was purely a commercial matter between two vindictive rivals,' I said. 'I did not see why it would be of consequence to you. You take an interest in my husband's affairs, that is true. But when Thomas asked for the utmost secrecy on this matter, I gave him my word that I would honour his request. I did not know it would upset you so much.'

Tom calmed down a little. 'It is not the quarrel between Thomas and Sir Anthony that I care about. As you say, that is of no consequence to me.' His voice turned into an inveigling whisper. 'But we share intimacies, Alice. You were gone for a week on what you said was merely a family visit, a social call on your mother and her family. And now I find you deceived me, that you didn't trust me enough to tell me the truth. That's what hurts me the most.'

'It was not a matter of trust. I gave Thomas my word and did not want to break it. But no matter, dear Tom. I have learnt my lesson. Whatever the consequences, there will never again be any secrets between us.'

Tom smiled at this. A smile of forgiveness, I thought. But there was a look in his eyes that suggested something else. A glint of victory.

Unsettled, I leant over and kissed him, to put the matter behind us.

Chapter Fifteen
Will ~ 1591

I COULD NOT BELIEVE the generosity John Stow showed me when I visited him. For such a great man to help me, an unknown actor from an obscure provincial town with dreams of writing for the stage, was more than I could ever have imagined. I was impressed with him from the moment we met, when I discerned him to be a man of inexhaustible energy and encyclopaedic knowledge. He was tall, lean, with small clear eyes and a pleasant, cheerful demeanour, and I had heard it said he claimed never to have written anything for malice, fear or favour, nor to seek his own particular gain or vain glory. He only cared to write truth; a man of integrity as well as intelligence.

I was, however, surprised by the modestness of his residence in Leadenhall Street, a ten-minute walk east from my lodgings. I had not expected his home to be a palace, but I had assumed that a man of his status and reputation would live in a house that would impress. Instead, the humble dwelling he shared with his wife was made comfortable only by the care and attention bestowed upon it. Book presses filled the room, and every one must have been full, as piles of books were stacked on every desk and table. Despite the size of his library, it was apparent from his humble home that John Stow was not a man of great wealth.

He smiled when I mentioned that I had read the account of the Arden murder in Holinshed's *Chronicles* and that I had been told it was based on his own manuscript. He reached up to a shelf and brought out some sheaves of paper. Although to an outside observer everything looked disorganised and chaotic, it seemed John Stow knew the location of every pamphlet, book or scrap of writing he possessed.

He blew the dust off the pages and laid them out on the table in front of us.

'Yes,' he said, with a twinkle in his eye, 'I think you will find some similarities. I am honoured that Raphael Holinshed should have included a few of my words in his own account.' He leant over and without hesitation plucked a volume of Holinshed's *Chronicles* from the bookshelf behind me and opened it at the start of the description of the Arden murder for me to compare the two accounts.

'A few words' was a massive understatement. Stow's document, entitled *The History of a Moste Horrible Murder Commytyd at Fevershame in Kente*, outlined the events leading up to the murder, including Alice Arden's dalliances with Mosby and her husband's collusion in that shameful disorder. And when I looked at the copy of *Chronicles*, I saw that Holinshed had included Stow's account almost word for word.

'Why, sir, the rascal has replicated almost every sentence. I have read my copy of *Chronicles* and have seen no attribution to you, or your telling of the Arden murder. Have you confronted him regarding this disrespect? I am shocked that so highly regarded a scholar should act in this way.'

Stow gave an airy wave to the books around him. 'What is the point of learning if it is not to be shared with others?

My door is always open to my good friend, Raphael, and to any others who wish to peruse the contents of my library.'

I winced as he said this. Had I known, I might have saved myself one pound and six shillings.

Stow continued. 'He has borrowed many of the books in my collection to augment the contents of his great works, and I have sought neither reward nor recognition from him. Knowing that my life's work is being put to good use is satisfaction enough for me. He did me a great honour to use my own laboured account of the Arden murder to publish a description of the crime. Now my words will live forever – as will, hopefully, the ones in my own published works.'

'That is my dream also,' I said. 'To write, to entertain and to be remembered. At least that was the fantasy that set me on the road to London from my home in Stratford, where I have left behind my wife and children. I care for them by sending the little coin I can spare from working as a jobbing actor with Lord Strange's Men. But if the truth be known, my hopes and dreams are being dashed by two cruel realities. The London stage is not a place where it is easy to earn a good living; and the task of writing an engaging play is more demanding than I could ever have imagined. You have published two chronicles in your own name, I understand. I tell you, sir, I am mighty impressed.'

Stow gave the comfortable laugh of one who was at ease with the man he had become. 'My writing calls for curiosity and inquisitiveness, determination and tenacity, to discover and tell the truth. Admirable traits, I am sure. But the words of Kydd and Marlowe show gifts of a higher order – imagination, creativity, the ability to take a leap into the unknown. If that is the task you have taken on for yourself,

Will Shakspere, it is I who applaud you for your boldness. I am an historian, a chronicler. Much as I admire the great authors of our day, I could never emulate them. My passion to tell the truth is my barrier to writing words of fiction.'

'And my barrier to writing fiction is not knowing the words of truth that lie behind the story,' I replied. 'We make a fine pair, the two of us.'

We laughed as if we were old friends. I picked up Stow's Arden manuscript and studied it. Although most of it was present in Holinshed's *Chronicles*, some was not. And certainly, there was far more than I had read in the Faversham wardmote book. The descriptions around the events of the murder itself would make a play in their own right: a full cast of characters; several botched attempts at murder before they finally succeeded; swift retribution to the guilty in the aftermath. My head was reeling with all that was written.

But one thing was troubling me.

'This is a most comprehensive and compelling account of these horrible events in Faversham,' I said, my finger tracing the words as I read them for a second time. 'But when I was in Faversham and heard of this murder, I consulted the wardmote book to see what details I could ascertain. There was but the most perfunctory description of events and the punishments handed down. How did you come to write such a detailed account?'

For a moment, John Stow's geniality deserted him and he shifted uncomfortably in his seat. 'It is true that these are not my own recollections,' he replied. 'Indeed, for that matter, I have never even visited Faversham. To write my account of the murder I had to rely on Robert Cole of Bow.'

'And who might he be?'

'A priest, a good man, who was a young cleric with no parish of his own when by chance he was in Faversham at the time of Alice Arden's trial. He attended the proceedings and wrote a full account of what was described. I came across his description of the murder when I purchased the books of the publisher Reginald Wolfe when that great man died in 1573, and found an unpublished manuscript called *A Cruel Murder Done in Kent*. It piqued my interest and I made enquiries as to who was the man who wrote it and where he could be found.' Stow spoke in hushed, excitable tones. 'Imagine my surprise when I discovered that he was the rector of the Church of St Mary le Bow, near Watling Street, a short walk from here.' Stow pointed out the window. 'I called and introduced myself to him, and he told me of how he came to write his account. He knew none of the conspirators before the murder, but attended the trial and prayed with Alice Arden and John Greene afterwards and on the eve of their executions. Yes, a fine man. When he died of the plague the year after I met him, he was sorely missed.

'Cole is gone?' I could not hide my disappointment. 'Then I fear that Adam Fowle is the only one left who was living in Faversham during those grim days. It was he who gave me my first account of the murder.'

'The innkeeper?' Stow looked surprised. 'You have talked to someone who was there at the time, and knew all the key players?' At this, he produced a bottle of wine from a cabinet behind him. 'Stay a little longer, Will Shakspere. I would be keen to know more of what you discovered. What sort of woman was Alice Arden?'

'I know nothing of Alice Arden, other than that which I can surmise from her vile actions. Adam Fowle was an old man when I met him, and tired easily when pressed on the details of the murder, so I learnt little from him. But this Robert Cole sounds like an honourable man. What can you tell me of him?'

'That he was a decent and upright man of God, who spent many years, both in London and abroad, bringing comfort to people imprisoned for their religious beliefs. A dangerous calling in those turbulent times. I wrote the manuscript you have in your hands based on my conversations with him and his papers, which I had in my possession. And I gave him full credit at the end of the story. Just here, you see?' Stow pointed to the end of his manuscript.

> *Vide exactores et certiorum personarum et locorum in quibus perierunt descriptiones quod a magistro Roberto Colo de Bow petere licet.*

'I'll translate for you. *See the charges and descriptions of the various persons and places where they were put to death, which may be had of Master Robert Cole of Bow.*'

I bridled a little at his assumption. 'Thank you for that, Master Stow, but I am well versed in Latin. Not all men from the provinces are uneducated.'

Stow gave a booming laugh. 'Well said, Master Shakspere. It is right that I should be taken to task for my preconceptions, as I have suffered the same from others. I was the son of a tallow-maker, never even went to grammar school. I was a tailor by trade, and gave up that worthy profession at the age of forty to devote my life to learning and researching English history.' He gave a rueful smile. 'And I have been penniless ever since as a result. I constantly rail against the prejudices of those better educated and more high-born than I and so it is right and proper that you should bring me to task for my own failings. I apologise to you, good sir.' He stood up and gave a short bow.

It was my turn to be surprised. I had not imagined that a man of John Stow's standing would not have had a university education.

'Let us drink a toast to the health of the great John Stow. I feel giddy that I have met such a learned gentleman who is less schooled than I. To my mind that makes you a better man than these University Wits. To the university of life!' I raised my glass to him.

'The university of life,' Stow echoed. 'It is the best of schools. Robert Cole is a good example of its students and he was a man I much admired. And I suspect that, as a man of religion, he had to keep his true sympathies hidden. His passion for championing those who were imprisoned for their religion made me think his calling was more towards the old religion. He was a good man, even if his sympathies lay with Rome.'

Stow fixed me a stare as he said this and I felt he was probing me, watching for my response. If he was hinting at being of the Catholic faith, I should do the same.

'It was not long ago that that religion was the orthodoxy in this land,' I said, my voice barely more than a whisper. 'Who knows, one day it might be so again. It is not for the likes of us to raise questions on these matters.'

There we had it. That was as far as two men of recent acquaintance dared test each other on such a sensitive matter. But the exchange had served its purpose. I felt a kinship with John Stow. We were two outsiders in both class and religion, battling to create a presence and a legacy in a society dismissive of who we were and hostile to our beliefs. One of us at the beginning of his life's journey, the other nearing its end.

'Robert Cole must have had the keenest of minds to possess this degree of recollection,' I murmured, looking again at Stow's manuscript. 'Do you by chance have his papers for me to peruse?'

Suddenly, Stow's mood changed. 'Sir, I do not have endless generosity. I will allow you to take my manuscript to aid you in your attempts to write a great play, but I cannot have you denude my collection more than that. Is that satisfactory to you?'

'M-most satisfactory,' I replied. 'Please be assured that I meant no disrespect with my request. You have been more than generous. I apologise sincerely if I offended you.'

Stow regained his composure. 'No, it is I who must apologise, Master Shakspere. The Arden murder is a crime that has preyed on my mind for many years. Take my description of it with my blessing. When you return, I will consider what can be done regarding Robert Cole.'

I could sense a mystery lying behind these words and was most intrigued, but decided it prudent not to pursue the matter further. I took my leave, and in my room that evening I read and re-read Stow's manuscript and then leant back in my panel-backed chair. I had all the information I needed. Now to write the play.

Nothing.

I pinched my lips together and scratched out a few more words of the opening I had already written where Thomas suspects Alice after she calls out Mosby's name in her sleep, and I tried to extend the scene when Alice gives Adam Fowle the pair of silver dice to present to Mosby as a sign to show that she wished to renew her affection for him. My quill came to a halt as I finished my first sentence. I scratched the back of my neck, then tapped my finger on the table in the hope that this would unleash a torrent of words. Still nothing. I took a fresh sheaf of paper, closed my eyes, took a deep breath and slowly exhaled as I opened them again. The blank sheet of paper was still there, taunting me to do better. I pounded my fist on the table, then toyed with sundry ideas for an hour or so, sketching out a few more hazy notions of how to get started. Nothing seemed to work.

Disappointed, I decided to visit John Stow again and return his manuscript, as I had now made full use of it. We chatted amicably for a while and then, once again, the conversation turned to more troublesome matters.

'I must apologise for my outburst the other day,' Stow said, taking a hard, obvious swallow, 'when you raised the question of perusing the papers I hold from Robert Cole. You and I shared confidences with each other on our views of the ruling classes and the tyranny that religious beliefs hold over the country, and after that part of our conversation I confess I cautioned myself that I had been more candid than was prudent with a newly made acquaintance. I have felt the cold hand of that tyranny before, when I have spoken openly of my distrust of authority. I take it you have heard the accusation made about me and the Spanish ambassador?'

I confessed I had not, and Stow told me the story. 'A pamphlet, written by the ambassador, had been published criticising Queen Elizabeth, and the authorities were searching for the accomplices who helped to circulate it. It is true that I had been lent two copies and made one for myself, but I never circulated any pamphlet publicly. Nevertheless, my interest in it, even as an antiquarian, attracted suspicion from the ecclesiastical authorities, and I was reported to them as having many dangerous and superstitious books in my possession.'

Stow said these last words with dripping disdain.

'My house was searched by Bishop Grindal, the Bishop of London, and his henchmen. An inventory was made of all the books in my home, especially those thought to be in defence of papistry, but I was able to satisfy my inter-rogators as to the soundness of my Protestantism.' He gave me a knowing smile before turning serious again. 'But the experience left me scarred. I vowed I would never incur the wrath of the authorities again.'

I responded by telling him about my dealings with Sir Thomas Lucy, how my insolence towards those in authority had landed me in the stocks and caused me to flee Stratford and leave my family behind.

There was a long pause before Stow spoke again. 'There is something I have not told you regarding the story of Robert Cole, and all that he uncovered about the murder. Your question on your last visit, asking to see such of his papers as I possess, sparked alarm in me that I was on the verge of being indiscreet. I told myself that when you returned my manuscript, I would take the measure of you again, to decide whether it was safe to say more, as this is intelligence that I have shared with no-one before. It is of the utmost sensitivity.'

Stow stood up and paced around the room. When he sat down, he leant forward and took my hands in his, dropping his voice to a whisper as he spoke.

'But knowing what I know, and believing beyond everything else that my purpose in life is to seek the truth and then speak it, is a burden that has burnt away at me these last twelve years. Can you give me a chance to reflect once more and be ready to visit me in my quarters tomorrow? I will send a boy in the morning to let you know if I have decided to meet. If not, I ask you to forget all that I have said to you, and let us never see each other again. Would you agree to this arrangement?'

I slept fitfully that night, wondering what possible revelations Cole had uncovered and why they were not included in what had already been published on the Arden murder. I rose early the next morning and waited to hear Stow's message. At nine of the clock, a small boy arrived, begging my pardon and asking me to visit Master Stow at my earliest convenience.

I headed off to Leadenhall Street again.

Chapter Sixteen
Alice ~ 1548

THE VICTORY over Sir Anthony transformed Thomas; he embraced his position as mayor and threw himself into a frenzy of activity. He had passion for the first time; passion for power and influence.

'I have promised the jurats that I can make Faversham a model town,' he told Tom and me after we had played dice together. 'But only if they gave me the power and authority to do so. To a man, they agreed. Now I have powers that no mayor in Faversham has ever had before me, and also the funds from the charter. The name of Thomas Arden will live forever in this town. Never again will I have to resort to demanding some coin here and there to make my fortune.'

I could not have cared less about my husband's boasting, but to my surprise, Tom egged him on to say more. 'A most fortunate set of events, if I may say so,' he said to Thomas, raising his glass. 'You seem to have the goodmen of the town in thrall. Please, tell me more of your plans. I am in awe at your accomplishments.'

I was uncomfortable that Tom felt the need to flatter my husband, just to keep disorder from creeping into our arrangement, especially when his blandishments were to do with matters of commerce, which I found stultifyingly boring. But that was the difference with men, I presumed.

They would not be engaged in a conversation about hats or fashions, just as politics and the changing tides of religion held no interest for ladies of good breeding.

'I am to choose twelve of the twenty-four common councillors and only they, plus the jurats and the mayor, will now be called to the wardmote to make laws and statutes,' Thomas explained. 'My good friend Thomas Dunkyn is to be appointed steward; he was mayor four years ago and will provide wise counsel on what path to take. I have awarded him a salary of five pounds a year for his efforts. Even with another five pounds a year for my mayor's salary, the eight pounds fee-farm paid to the King, and the six pounds to his steward, William Roper, there will still be funds a-plenty to carry out great works.' Thomas warmed to his discourse. 'I have grand schemes in hand. My first priorities will be a common carrier to deal with the town's dung problem, and paving the streets in the commercial district. If the owners of the properties on these streets do not pay their share of the cost of the exercise, the rent they receive from their tenants will be forfeited to the mayor's coffers.'

Tom listened attentively to every detail as my husband continued. 'Then there will be laws dealing with hogs and swine wandering loose in the town. Repairs to the courthouse. I tell you, Tom Mosby, within two years you will not recognise Faversham.'

'There will be talk of a knighthood, I am sure,' Tom replied. 'But all you have spoken of is for the good of the town. What about the good of Thomas Arden? Five pounds a year seems a low price for what you will achieve.'

Thomas gave a sly grin. 'You are a cynical one, Tom Mosby. The costs of these projects will be great indeed, but my powers of patronage are even greater. There is talk that William Marshall will be the mayor one day, and so I have granted him eight pounds four shillings and ninepence for repairing the streets at Cooksditch; that will keep him sweet so that he presents no challenge to me while I remain in the post. And dear Thomas Dunkyn has claimed fifteen pounds six shillings and fivepence for some repairs to the courthouse and clearing the dunghills. What a bargain, eh?'

Tom gasped. 'Fifteen pounds for shovelling shit? And you agreed to this?'

Thomas laughed. 'What can I say? Master Dunkyn is an honourable man and if he says that is what it will cost, I believe him. Maybe he shifts it with a silver spoon, I don't know. But we've talked enough on these matters, I can see Alice is bored by our conversation. Let me regale you another time.'

It was only when I was alone with Tom later that I understood the significance of what had been discussed.

'These sums your husband has described are vast, much more than Faversham can afford,' Tom told me. 'The town has a mountain of debt, the cost of obtaining the town charter was over thirty-five pounds, and before the charter Faversham's annual income was a shilling under twenty. Five pounds each for steward and mayor, fourteen pounds to the King and his steward, and almost twenty-four pounds to Dunkyn and Marshall? That adds up to forty-eight pounds of expenses, against twenty pounds of income. And then there are all the other costs, like buying stone and repairing roads. Thomas likes to play a game of dice, but he is gambling with the town's finances. If Faversham's income does not at least double in the next year, the town will be in dire financial straits indeed.'

I was much in admiration that my dear Tom, a tailor, had such a profound understanding of these issues. It proved that he had great ambition to advance himself, so that he too could one day sit alongside the goodmen of the town and debate these weighty matters. But what he said worried me. Thomas was ambitious, but he was also headstrong and foolhardy. I needed reassurance that all would be well.

'Can you explain this charter to me?' I asked Thomas the next day. 'I must confess, I did not understand the significance of this undertaking. But it seems that the future of the town is dependent on the framing of a single document. How can that be?'

Thomas patiently explained its importance. 'With the dissolution of Faversham's abbey, the town had to establish and legitimise its claim to the rights previously enjoyed by the abbot. But that had little impact on the town's income, which rose just over a pound a year. We needed more sources of funds, and that is where the charter comes in. The town now has the right to buy and sell land, receive income from the thrice-weekly market and the annual fayres, and take ownership of goods and chattels forfeited from felons, waifs and strays, all of which has made my new charter a momentous development in Faversham's history.'

'But does your plan make sense? I am but a woman, and my head was spinning with the numbers you discussed with Tom last night. But the expenses of the town are greater than her income. Is that not a bad thing?'

Thomas laughed. 'You have been spending too much time watching me in my counting house with my tally sticks. You display remarkable financial acumen for one of the fairer sex. Do not tell any of the jurats of your concerns; they are all caught up in the wave of euphoria that has greeted the announcement of my grand design.' His voice dropped to a whisper. 'But I fear you may be right. My ambition is to make Faversham the equal of London with her civic amenities, but we have none of the resources of that great city. Last year our revenue was four shillings less than our income, with the town twenty pounds in debt. And we owe the King fifteen pounds, the drivers and the carters four pounds, the stonemasons more than two pounds. There will have to be some pain to get ourselves out of this predicament. Fees and levies are to be applied to anyone purchasing property in the town and a new tax, a roll of streets, is to be introduced. The jurats have assigned me the right to jail any who refuse to pay what they owe.' He sighed. 'Which might make me unpopular, but there is no other way.'

Beneath Thomas's bluster I sensed his unease about the situation, and when I told Tom what he had said, he nodded sagely and confirmed that my husband was heading for choppy waters.

For the rest of that year of 1548 and all through '49, Thomas's projects continued unabated, and the town's debt became greater and greater. The roll-of-streets tax was finally announced at the end of 1549, to the general dismay of the town. Thomas stumbled home from a night's drinking at the Fleur de Lis with Dunkyn, and told me of the abuse and vitriol that been hurled at him. Tom and I were awake when he staggered in, and Tom went to fetch more wine to help cheer my husband's mood.

'The town of Faversham is a little town full of little people with closed minds,' Tom told my husband. 'Your plan is a great one, and future generations will thank you for it. Pay no heed to their protestations.'

'The cost is for all to suffer, even me,' Thomas lamented. 'They do not see that, the ungrateful fools.'

'You should stand up to their impudence. You are the mayor after all, and the charter you negotiated has already changed the town out of all recognition.'

'Changed its finances out of all recognition,' Thomas said, his words slurred. 'And not in the way that was expected. And I also have to pay from my own purse my share of all this expenditure.' He shook his head in despair. 'Do you know how much this roll-of-streets tax is going to cost me?'

'Then don't pay!' Tom said.

Thomas and I looked at him blankly.

'You have the power to punish those who fail to pay, do you not? Then that means you also have the power to decide who does pay. Exempt yourself and Dunkyn from the tax, say that such distasteful financial matters harm the dignity of the office of mayor and steward, and that you must be free to make decisions that are in the best interest of the town, without having to worry about the personal implications to yourself. Certainly, a few blowhards might object, but dismiss their concerns. You are the greatest mayor in Faversham's history. You should not have to involve yourself in such trifling matters as the payment of a roll-of-streets tax.'

'God-a-mercy, that is a grand plan,' Thomas exclaimed. 'I will draw up the papers now while the idea is fresh and head off to Dunkyn's to get his mark to make it official. Well done, Tom Mosby. You have earned your keep tonight.'

If there was outrage at the news that Thomas and Dunkyn would not pay the tax to fund the schemes that they themselves proposed, it was nothing compared to the fury that was unleashed when the new arrangements for the St Valentine's Fayre were announced. The fayre was the centrepiece of the town charter, the main source of new income for the town. By tradition, it ran for seven days from February 14th, and traders from all over Kent came to Faversham to ply their wares. The fayre had always been held partly in the town and partly in the abbey grounds, with the town and the abbey splitting the ground rents and profits according to the size of their share of the land used. But the abbey grounds were now owned by Thomas, and as mayor he had the authority to decide where the fayre should be held. He pronounced that it would be entirely on abbey grounds – thus, all the rent revenue from the fayre would come to him.

'It is plain for all to see that the charter confers upon the mayor the right to choose the fayre's location,' Thomas told me. 'And I would not be much of a man if I did not play that to my advantage. The abbey grounds are a fine place for the fayre, the land is well-drained and there is plenty of space for all who want to visit. Given time, the goodmen of the town will see that the new location will benefit them as much as me.'

But that was not how the townsfolk saw it. Coming so soon after he had exempted Dunkyn and himself from paying new taxes, for many it was the final straw. Richard Dryland, Lewis Marden, John Wrewke, the previous mayor – even William Marshall, with whom Thomas had tried so assiduously to keep in favour – all spoke out against him. I already had to endure many of the goodwives of Faversham shunning me because of Thomas's cruel ways with those less fortunate than himself. Now their menfolk also crossed the street when they saw me approaching. It was clear that my husband had gone too far, but was too proud a man to back down now.

I pleaded with him to curtail his grand projects, to be humbler in his dealing with others. But my pleas fell on deaf ears.

By the end of the summer, things had gone from bad to worse. In May 1550, William Marshall had, as expected, been elected mayor. But if Thomas thought that his payments to Marshall would sweeten his disposition towards him, he was mistaken. On November 21st, six months after Marshall took office, a special wardmote meeting was held. Only six jurats were in attendance, the minimum number required for a quorum, and all six were among Thomas's fiercest critics. Thomas and Dunkyn were not told of the meeting, nor were their few remaining allies, John Seth, John Dryland, Robert Colwell and Ralph Rogers. It was an ambush.

When Thomas was told by Dunkyn that the meeting had taken place, and what had been agreed, I saw the blood drain from his face. A clause had been added to the decree setting out the new tax to pay for Thomas's expenditure on town projects. Now, if any man should resist making the payment, Mayor William Marshall could call for a wardmote vote to have the recalcitrant debtor disenfranchised. If that man was a jurat, as were both Dunkyn and Thomas, they would be pulled from the bench and disenfranchised forever.

I asked Thomas what was meant by disenfranchisement, and he told me he would be in disgrace, cast out from Faversham society and shunned by any who had ever had dealings with him. It was the most severe punishment possible for a gentleman, even worse than going to jail, because the label was without limit of time. The Arden house would be like a lepers' colony in the centre of town. There were stories of goodmen of Rye, Exeter and Norwich having been disenfranchised in the past, but no-one in living memory had been dealt this most severe of punishments and humiliation in Faversham. And nowhere in England had such a punishment been handed down to a man who had been the town's mayor.

Thomas had to act, and quickly.

'Perhaps I have tried to make too many changes, too speedily,' he said to Dunkyn, as the two men sat in the parlour discussing what to do next, caring little that Tom and I could hear every word. 'I am forgetting that this is a town with no imagination as to what can be achieved if its leaders are bold enough. We have paid a high price for our daring schemes, both in terms of our standing in the town and now with these financial consequences. It is a bitter pill to swallow, but now it is perhaps prudent to appear humble. It pains me to say it, but we have no choice but to pay this loathsome tax.'

Dunkyn appeared to be on the point of agreeing, but to my surprise my Tom was the one who spoke next.

'That would be a great humiliation to bear, Master Arden,' he said. 'Many in this town who respect you as a great leader will think less of you if you capitulate to this outrageous threat. William Marshall's decree is a bluff – no town mayor in England has ever been disenfranchised, and none ever will be. Look how he managed to get this motion passed. A meeting called in secret, with barely a quorum and only those who think ill of you in attendance. For a motion of disenfranchisement to be valid, the full town council would require to meet, with all the jurats and the common councillors in attendance. Your reputation is still strong with many of the goodmen of this town. Stand up to William Marshall's impudence and your power and influence will be untarnished. Give in to it, and you will lose the respect of those who admire you.'

'You think I should reject this decree? That would be a bold move indeed.' Thomas's lips closed in a tight grimace.

Dunkyn looked at the floor and said nothing. The air crackled with tension as Tom pressed on.

'Do not even deign to announce the rejection of it yourself. Master Dunkyn here is a most eloquent speaker. Permit him to instruct the wardmote of your decision. Let him speak on your behalf, saying neither of you will pay the tax. Then let Marshall call his full council meeting if he dares, when all your supporters will be in attendance. You will win handsomely, and no-one in Faversham will ever dare cross you again.'

Dunkyn looked up. 'I would love to put that man in his place. But if things were to go against us, the consequences would be very grave indeed.'

'The Thomas Arden I know revels in taking risks,' Tom said, and as an afterthought added: 'And you too are a bold man when it comes to business affairs, Master Dunkyn. Demand a meeting with the jurats, tell them that you are standing firm against their demands and challenge them to do their worst. You will not regret it.'

Thomas smiled for the first time. 'What do you say, Dunkyn? Shall we give William Marshall the comeuppance he deserves?'

Dunkyn rubbed the back of his neck. 'If you feel you must, then I agree,' he said eventually.

Tom slapped them both on the back. 'Bravo,' he said, his voice strong and triumphant. 'You are great men indeed.'

Dunkyn visited again after his meeting with William Marshall to report that things had not gone well.

'Marshall called me stubborn and disobedient and has now drafted a disenfranchisement motion. It goes before the full council on December 22nd and we will not be allowed to attend or vote. I am worried, Thomas. Were this to go against us, we would be finished.'

Thomas looked worried too. The days dragged by, and I decided to confront my Tom about the wisdom of his advice not to pay the roll-of-streets tax. 'My husband is vain and self-important and you appealed to these flaws with your advice to him not to pay the tax. It is not too late. Could you not tell him you have had a change of heart? I fear for all of us when the vote is taken.'

'If the vote goes against Thomas, he is finished; but if he backs down now, it would be a humiliation for him. He granted many favours to the jurats and the councillors when mayor. It only needs half of them to remember his generosity and he will triumph.'

'But William Marshall was the chief beneficiary of his projects and it is he who is leading the charge against him,' I said. 'I am greatly troubled, Tom. We have so much to lose and so little to gain by this act of defiance. He is still my husband, after all. I should tell him of my concerns.'

'He is your husband in name only,' Tom said. 'He sits around drinking all day with Dunkyn; he is in no state to think clearly. There are only a few days to go until all this is over. If you wish to assist him, help get his affairs in order. Once this ordeal is behind us, we can all start thinking of what our future will be.'

I was heartened by Tom's words and spent the next few days assisting Thomas in whatever way I could. I organised his books of account and was shocked to see how much his income had dropped since scandal had enveloped him.

Perhaps Tom was right. Perhaps my husband needed to stand up to those who attacked him so that he could begin to rebuild his reputation once the vote was taken.

THOMAS AND DUNKYN SAT in the parlour on December 22nd, awaiting news of the council's decision. The hours passed slowly, and I told myself that the length of time it was taking was a good sign. If William Marshall had the votes in his pocket, it would have been over quickly. Then, at twelve noon exactly, there was a loud knocking at the door.

William Marshall stood there grim faced, with ten of the twelve jurats behind him. I knew at once what the decision had been.

Marshall read out the proclamation.

> *Thomas Arden, being a jurat of Faversham and sworn to maintain the franchises, liberties and freedoms of the said town, has, contrary to his oath, gone about and laboured by diverse ways and means to the uttermost of his power to infringe and undo the said franchises, liberties and freedoms. Therefore, the said Thomas Arden shall be deposed from the bench and no more be*

jurat of the said town. And from henceforth to be utterly
disenfranchised forever. Let this decree be entered into
the wardmote book, this 22nd December, 1550.

Before Thomas could reply, Marshall turned to Dunkyn
and read out his decree. If anything, it was even more
damning. The first passage was in most particulars identical
to that of the proclamation addressed to Thomas, but it went
on to state the following:

And also, for his stubborn and disobedient answers and
behaviour to the mayor and jurats sitting in council, the
mayor and jurats do violently pluck Thomas Dunkyn
from the bench and no more be jurat of the town of
Faversham. And that the said Thomas Dunkyn, for
these and other like causes, shall be disposed from the
bench and no more be a jurat of the same town. And
from henceforth to be utterly disenfranchised forever.
Let this decree be entered into the wardmote book, this
22nd December, 1550.

The men turned and left without another word.
Our world had been destroyed.

Chapter Seventeen
Will ~ 1591

I RETURNED TO Stow's house with some degree of trepidation. He tried to put me at ease by telling me he much admired the London playhouses, and planned to feature them in a survey of London he was working on as his next book. He said that he had heard many compliments about the play in which I was performing at the moment. This was *Dido, Queen of Carthage* by Kit Marlowe, and I played the parts of Ilioneus, a Greek slave, and Ganymede, the Trojan hero. My time on stage was so short that I could take little credit for the play's success, but I enjoyed Stow's praise nonetheless.

'I have been most attentive,' I told Stow, 'as to how the leader of our company, Richard Burbage, stages the ending where Dido burns to death by throwing herself on the funeral pyre she has built, after her lover Aeneas leaves her. I will have a similar ending in my Arden play, when Alice Arden meets her end in a blaze of torment. Seeing the audience's reaction to Dido being consumed by theatrical flames gives me hope that meeting her end in a similar way will bring Alice Arden's story to a most dramatic climax.'

I expected Stow to agree with me on this point and so was surprised to see his expression turn to one of anguish.

He pressed his fists against his cheeks, the usual fire in his eyes replaced by a watery dullness.

'It is cruel justice,' he said, 'that she will have to meet her fate, night after night, for time immemorial, rather than just on that fateful day on Canterbury Hill.'

My surprise turned to astonishment. 'Why do you have such sympathy for a vile murderess?' I asked him. 'Alice Arden was surely as evil a woman as ever walked on God's earth.'

'Perhaps you are right,' Stow replied. 'Come, let us talk of other matters.'

He ushered me into his study, a room more cramped than the one where he usually received visitors. He lifted some books off the only spare chair and bade me sit. Then he closed the door before sitting behind his desk. Our view of each other was blocked by the books piled between us, so those he also moved and placed on the floor.

These preliminaries over, he spoke again, but his voice had a resigned weariness to it. For the first time in all our conversations, he sounded like an old man.

'When we last met, I told you of my persecution by Bishop Grindal, who decried me as a suspicious person with many dangerous and superstitious books in my possession, when my only crime was to be a collector of scholarly works. You countered with your tale of Sir Thomas Lucy and how you were thrown in the stocks and narrowly escaped a whipping, on account of some impudent ditty you wrote about the man.'

He leant across the desk and grasped my forearm before speaking again. 'We are both men who have been victims of injustice and have seen the perils of upsetting those in authority. Tell me, Will, should that make us more passionate about pursuing truth and fighting wrongs? Or should we count our blessings, and never again venture to speak out about matters that could harm us? Speak honestly to me on this matter, and from the heart. I need to hear your words.' Stow fixed me with an intense stare.

To be honest, I was somewhat perplexed by the turn the conversation had taken, and struggled to find the words to respond. 'Truth and justice are indeed principles worth fighting for,' I replied, hesitantly. 'If one discovers an injustice has been committed, one must do everything in one's power to right it.'

Stow sighed. 'Well said. That is the principle by which I have lived my life. But there has been one exception, and that is to do with Alice Arden. The record of her trial portrays her as a person of the lowest moral standing, the daughter of a respectable family who succumbed to the temptations of the flesh with a lowly tailor and who flaunted her carnal desires for him in front of her husband, and ultimately the whole of Faversham.'

Stow drew himself up, as though summoning the courage to continue.

'But there is more to this tale than what is commonly known. Much, much more. And I have never spoken of it before this moment.'

My stomach churned with an uneasy expectation as I waited for him to continue.

'When I went to visit Robert Cole at his church, I thought he would be able to provide some small embellishments to what he had written, perhaps explain some points that were not clear. But when I met with him, he told me something of much greater significance.'

I nodded. To what, I did not know, but it seemed some action was required on my part for Stow to continue.

'His action in praying with Alice Arden on the eve of her execution was tolerated by the townsfolk, seen as the earnest naivety of an idealistic young priest. But a year later, the final Faversham participant in the murder was tried and sentenced to death. Cole decided that once again he should go and pray with the convicted man, and through his determination to do so became the sworn enemy of Cyriak Pettit, Member of Parliament for Winchelsea, one of the officials at the trial. Cole had to flee Faversham with his wife and family to escape mortal danger.'

'But why would Pettit object to Cole doing what he thought to be right?'

'Because this murderer was Sir Anthony Aucher's man, John Greene.' Stow paused for a moment, as if the conversation was using up every ounce of his energy. 'Both men – Aucher, who was Thomas Arden's fiercest business rival, and Greene, who had a long hatred of Thomas Arden after being cruelly cheated of land after one of Arden's property purchases – had reason to rejoice at Arden's death.'

I could hardly bring myself to ask the question that had been burning inside me as I had listened to Stow talk.

'Greene – what did he confess?'

'That Alice Arden was not the ringleader of the plan to murder her husband. That Sir Anthony Aucher, from one of the most respected families in Kent, had plotted to bring about Arden's downfall as mayor and have him disenfranchised.'

I felt my skin tingle as Stow continued. 'Not only that, Aucher goaded Greene on to have Arden murdered. And

Greene's accomplice was none other than Tom Mosby, Alice's paramour, who, far from being in lovestruck thrall with Alice Arden, was being paid coin by Aucher, via John Greene, to lie with her – first to find out the secrets of Thomas Arden's financial dealings so Aucher could thwart them; then to spur Arden on to make more and more reckless decisions to antagonise the people of Faversham; and, finally, to entice Alice to undertake the murder so the pair could be together.'

I gasped. 'Mosby was also Aucher's man? That defies belief. The man is beneath contempt.'

'A true scoundrel,' Stow agreed. 'Mosby had no plan to stay with Alice after the deed had been done. He would collect a reward from John Greene, put up by Sir Anthony Aucher, and then he and Greene would escape, leaving Alice to face retribution for the crime. So yes, she was party to the striking of the fatal blows. But it was Aucher who was truly responsible for Thomas Arden's untimely death.'

I could hardly breathe. I sagged into my chair as the impact of Stow's words overwhelmed me.

'But why did Greene not admit to this at his trial? Did he not want to see Aucher also hanged for his part in the murder?'

'He would have been a fool to do so. His end was to be brief, he was spared the torture meted out to Alice and Mosby because he was thought to be a minor player in the plot to kill Thomas Arden. Had he admitted that his role was the central one, controlling all the players at the behest of Sir Anthony Aucher, he would have suffered a similarly cruel method of execution as Alice and Mosby. He took his secret to the grave, with only Robert Cole knowing the true story. Aucher suspected that if Cole were to pray with Greene the night before his execution, Greene could tell Cole everything, so did all he could to prevent it. And when that failed, he charged a corrupt official, Cyriak Pettit, with having Cole either arrested on some false pretence or hounded out of town.

'Cole recorded a pamphlet in the Stationers' Register called *A Cruel Murder Done in Kent*, with a view to one day publishing an account of the murder, but in the end could not bring himself to do so without revealing Aucher's involvement. It was only forty years after the event that he unburdened his soul by revealing all to me. By then he was an old man, weighed down by the frailty of his years, and, as he knew of my reputation as a chronicler and pursuer of the truth, he entrusted to me the signed confession that he had obtained from John Greene on the eve of his execution. Cole died a few months after our meeting and I have kept it hidden all these years.'

Stow pressed something on the side of his study desk and a secret drawer sprang out from above the writing surface.

'Here it is,' he said. 'You are the first to read it since I placed it there, fourteen years ago.'

I glanced at the title.

The Confession of John Greene of Faversham, to Me, Robert Cole, on the Eve of his Execution, June 25th 1552, written in my hand and signed by the said John Greene.

I took it in my shaking hands and began to read.

*I leave on this paper my testimony regarding the
monstrous and wicked murder of Thomas Arden, late of
Abbey Gate, Faversham in Kent, that I did assist and
participate in yesteryear, on the xvth day of February
in the fourth year of the reign of Edward VIth, and
which I freely divulge to Robert Cole, a good man and
true, on this day, the xxvth day of June in the year of
our Lord 1552, as I await the dawn of the day of my
execution. May the Lord grant me the grace to confess
my sins on this matter and to be a trusted witness to
the events that led up to this crime, so all may know
the truth of what transpired and that I may beg
forgiveness for my sins and escape eternal damnation.*

I looked up at Stow. 'So these accounts by Alice and
Greene are how Cole came to know so much about the
Arden murder. Have the pages of Alice's confession also
survived?'

'Nothing Alice said was written down at the time. But
when Cole heard Greene's words, he knew that they had to
be recorded. He gave Greene his word that nothing would
be disclosed until after his execution, and that putting his
mark to this testament would stand him in good stead when
he stood before the Lord in judgment. But read on, damn
you. You need to know more.'

*I do confess that I harboured the sin of hatred for
Thomas Arden, as a result of his cheating me out of
land which had belonged to my family for generations,
which the said Thomas Arden pursued purely to satisfy
his cardinal sin of greed. I petitioned my master, Sir*

Anthony Aucher of Otterden in Kent, to deal with
Thomas Arden and take vengeance upon him for the
harm Thomas Arden had done to me, and also to his
own good name with the slanderous accusations that
Thomas Arden made to sway the jurats in his favour,
which do not bear repetition here.

'Do we know what these accusations are that Arden made? They seem to have caused great offence.'

Stow shrugged. 'I asked Cole that same question, but he could not recall the details, only that it was to do with some trifling matter, a property sale or the like, that had caused Arden to air Aucher's radical sympathies. But it is of little consequence, it is what follows that is truly shocking.'

I offered to strike Thomas Arden down, and indeed
had already made to do so before, on the day when
Arden deceived the town councillors so they found in
his favour, but my master had greater wisdom than
me and bade me stay my hand, for he had a plan of far
deeper cunning and guile.

He said, 'I will ruin Thomas Arden, and you, good
John Greene of Faversham, will help me do so when
the opportunity presents itself. Inform me of any
intelligence you receive about this charlatan, so I can
judge when and how we will strike.'

An evening of drinking with my friend and fellow
tailor Tom Mosby gave me such intelligence. Mosby's
tongue was loosened and he confessed to the cardinal
sin of lust, boasting that although Alice Arden was

*a lady of high breeding, she had the lusty desires of a
country wench, and when he lived near the estate of
her step-father, Sir Edward North, he could see she
had an eye for him. Mosby boasted that he then took
Alice's maidenhood; but, after the end of the dog days of
summer, she announced her betrothal to Thomas Arden
and their dalliances came to an end.*

I paused. 'He who is a braggart should fear derision, for it
will come to pass that every braggart shall be found an ass.
Mosby is beneath contempt for such boasting.'

Stow gave an ironic chuckle. 'You are finding out the true
worth of the man. But that is but a foretaste of his crime.'

I raised my eyebrows and continued.

*Mosby told me that his journey to Faversham to have
some sport with her again turned out to be a wasted
errand, as fickle Alice rebuffed his advances when he
approached her. But he discovered all was not well
in the Arden household. The marital bed was going
unused, and he judged that if he bided his time, Alice
would finally succumb to her carnal desires. I passed
this information on to my master, as a dutiful servant
should, and opined that if Mosby were to succeed
and confess publicly that he had bedded Alice Arden
with her husband's knowledge and approval, Arden
would become not just a cuckold but a wittol – to be
cuckolded is one thing to but to condone one's wife's
adultery is another altogether. Wittols are less than
men, as by demonstrating that they are unable to
exercise appropriate authority in their home, they can*

have no public standing or respect. Arden's position in Faversham society would be at an end.

Mosby was no besotted lover, I told my master, but a caddish rake, intent only on pursuing his carnal desires. If the price was right, he would have no hesitation in betraying Alice's trust and affection, and denouncing her as an adulteress and her husband a wittol.

I set the document down again.

'The swine. This was the man for whom Alice sacrificed her life, someone she thought loved her when all along he cared not a jot. His base morals can fall no lower.' I shook my head in disbelief.

'But they can, Will Shakspere, they can. You are about to find out just how low a man can stoop.'

I took a deep breath and continued.

But my master was not content for this to be the full extent of Arden's disgrace. He instructed me to involve Tom Mosby in our scheming, and to promise him a reward of fifty pounds for his trouble, so that Alice Arden would play a greater part in her husband's downfall. Mosby was not only to bed her, he was to manipulate her to gain intelligence to be used to plot against her husband. She would know the household accounts and whatever felonious activity Arden was party to.

Mosby was to get her to whisper these secrets into his ear, so that they could be passed on to my master and he could thwart all of Arden's plans. And Mosby was

to use every opportunity to goad Arden on to make
more and more corrupt and self-serving decisions that
would outrage the goodmen of Faversham so that they
would rise up against him. Mosby agreed with great
enthusiasm, Arden was brought down, and it was
fitting that it was Thomas Arden's sanctioning of the
depravity in his home that caused his downfall. Then
would Mosby make public that Arden was a wittol, to
his further disgrace and shame.

'Is this the lowness you spoke of?' I asked Stow. He
shook his head and there was a glint in his eye, as though
he was enjoying the discomfort he was putting me through.
I decided to read to the end before I spoke again.

I swear before God that I thought this was the limit of
the intrigue planned and that it should have been the
depth and extent of Thomas Arden's fall. But although
I will not speak ill of my master, it is well known that
he shows no mercy to his enemies and that his hatred
of those who cross him is insatiable. In February 1548,
Thomas Arden tricked the Privy Council into issuing a
judgment that my master pay twenty marks to Thomas
and Alice Arden, as long as one of them doth live, for
two inns that my master had purchased, in a dishonest
appendix to the contract legally and openly signed with
Thomas Arden. My master fell into a fury when he
heard this news, and said that if once a year twenty
marks had to leave his purse for the Ardens, it would
not be for long.

My master said there would be a hundred pounds for Mosby and two hundred for me if we were to use Alice to finish Arden off, and this would be best done when Arden was disgraced and his passing would go unmourned by the people of Faversham. Alice would have then reached her lowest point, when she would be most likely to agree to his killing.

When Arden was to be disenfranchised, I met with Mosby at the Fleur de Lis to deliver him his fifty-pound reward and said there was another hundred in it for him if he were to tell Alice he was ending his dalliance with her unless he had her hand in marriage, and to convince her that this could only be achieved by Arden's slaying. I told him that, if she failed to do the deed herself, he was to name me to Alice as an enemy of Thomas Arden who could be recruited as an accomplice, and who would provide the means and the method for the despatch.

With Arden gone, his passing unlamented, Mosby could marry Alice and lead the life of a country gentleman, if it was believed a stranger had committed the crime. If suspicion were to fall on Alice, he would flee and leave her to face retribution for the crime. I would be assisted by my master to flee to a distant part of the realm and start a new life with my two-hundred-pound reward.

My hatred of Thomas Arden blinded me to the evil of what I agreed to do and I freely confess I was party to his murder.

May God have mercy on my soul.

There followed the letters 'J', 'O' and 'N' written in a clumsy scrawl, followed by words in Cole's handwriting:

My mark, in my own hand, by me, John Greene.

I felt my stomach clench as I put down the sheaf of paper.

'An astonishing document. But now that Robert Cole has passed from this earth, why have you not made public this terrible truth? All involved in this dastardly conspiracy must surely no longer be with us, that is true, but these revelations must be made public.'

'I have thought long and hard on that question,' Stow replied. 'But the Aucher family still hold great sway in Kent and beyond. I take my obligations as a seeker of truth very seriously, but I fear being publicly hounded if I speak out. I am not a rich man. I cannot afford to offend those with deep pockets. They could ruin me. I cannot tell the story in my chronicles.'

He leant forward, his eyes glowing. 'But you can tell it in your play.'

I recoiled at that. 'You fear being ruined, but do not concern yourself that I might be? Is this honest John Stow who speaks to me?' I stood up and glared across the table.

Stow waved me to sit down. 'I do not say this to ruin you, but to help you write a great play. As I have said before, in my world words are either true or false, fact or fiction, right or wrong. You can be much more subtle. You can hint at the truth, tease the audience as to what they believe or don't believe, allow them to make up their own mind as to who is guilty and who is not. I am not asking you to stand up and accuse the late Sir Anthony Aucher of conspiracy to murder.

But were you to hint as much, your play would be the talk of the town. Then we can see what way the wind blows. If there is outrage and hostility at the merest suggestion of Aucher's involvement, then you say the play was an ill-judged fancy. But you will have still made your mark as a writer.'

Stow had begun his argument in a voice devoid of emotion, but now he warmed to his theme.

'If, on the other hand, the public's sympathies are with Alice, I can produce the Greene confession, the truth will finally be revealed and you will be the hero of the hour, the most talked about new man in all of London. Think what the play will be. The obsession of the rich and powerful Sir Anthony Aucher, striving to bring down Thomas Arden, a self-made man from Norwich whom Holinshed describes as the son of a beggar-woman. Alice Arden, a guileless maiden, seduced and manipulated by callous and cynical men, including Tom Mosby, the man she loved and by whom she thought her love returned. Robert Cole, an idealistic priest who, in doing God's work, uncovered the truth that haunted him for the rest of his days. This story could be the making of you.'

I stared down at the floor, then at the ceiling, everywhere except in Stow's direction.

'I could change Aucher's name, I suppose,' I said eventually. 'I plan to do the same with another character, Arden's friend and confidant, Thomas Dunkyn. That would surely mitigate the risk.' I cursed my impetuous tongue. It had got me into trouble before, now it was tempting me into foolishness again.

I resolved not to give Stow his answer until I had reflected further on all of this. Alone in my chambers that evening,

I lit a pipe and tried to work out where my destiny lay. This could be the missing element to writing a great play. The Aucher character could flit like a ghost in the background of all of the scenes when Greene was on stage, whispering ideas and encouragement, egging him on to see the deed through.

I nodded to myself, as though doing so would help me decide. But still I hesitated. The Cyriak Pettit incident, where Robert Cole had been persecuted on the basis of mere suspicion that he might be told evidence of Aucher's involvement by Greene, had shown me the lengths to which those protecting the establishment might go to keep the truth of the Arden murder secret. I thought of Edward Arden, his head on a spike on London Bridge. I thought of Sir Thomas Lucy. And I had sworn I would not place myself in danger again. But I would need a breakthrough, some bold act to bring me to the attention of the public. I would never achieve anything in this world without courage.

'Boldness be my friend,' I said out loud. 'Arm me with audacity from head to foot.'

I stared into the smoke-filled darkness, letting my mind drift and wander around the myriad of possibilities of how to tell the story.

In the small hours, I decided. I would base the story around Thomas Arden and his friend Thomas Dunkyn whom the innkeeper Adam Fowle had told me about. I would give Dunkyn another name – Franklin, say – for discretion and to protect an innocent bystander. The friendship would be a useful dramatic device, permitting me to write raw and honest conversations between the two men about the deep pain I imagined Arden must have felt over being cuckolded by Tom Mosby. Then, at the end, Franklin could address the audience directly, calling for truth and justice to prevail, never mentioning Aucher by name, but asking why a sworn enemy of Arden was never called for questioning on whether he had any part in the crime, when he had cause to wish Arden dead and his man was the only one of the Faversham conspirators to escape into the night after the deed was done.

I readied myself for the task. The chair on which I was sitting and the table in front of me were the only furniture in the room apart from my bed, and all that was on the table was a smoakie light fed with stinking tallow. Next to it I placed twenty-five sheaves of coarse, thick paper, six goose feathers, and a pen knife and ink horn that I had purchased with the rest of my savings from a scrivener's shop in Paternoster Row.

I sharpened the first quill and dipped it into the ink horn. This was it. For three years I had dreamed of this moment, when I would finally have the material for my first play, the time to write it and, most importantly, the inspiration as to what I was going to say. I started scratching quill to paper, nervous and hesitant, opening the play with Arden consumed by a melancholy that Franklin was unable to lift, even after he announced that letters patent from the King had arrived granting Arden the lands of Faversham Abbey. In only the second line, I mentioned these papers had been sent by the Duke of Somerset, Lord Protector to the boy king Edward VI. I liked that. The audience would know immediately they were witnessing a play set in modern times, rather than the usual diet of myths and fables. I could already imagine the gasps when they heard these words.

That thought caused a fury to explode inside me and I started writing so fast it was as if a demon had possessed me. My quill grated furiously as I wrote, my hand unable to keep up with the thoughts racing through my brain. I abandoned punctuation, leaving spaces between the words so that I could return and complete the draft at my leisure. Sometimes I omitted the name of the speaker in the rush to get on; it too could be filled in at a later stage. On and on I went, with scarcely a blot left on the paper, and I ached with frustration when I had to stop to sharpen my quill feather with the pen knife. I wrote until I could keep my eyes open no longer; then did the same the next night, and the one after that.

Armed with Holinshed's *Chronicles*, I could expand on the rough draft of the play I had written based on the information gleaned from the Faversham wardmote book. I split the scene set in Arden's house in two, placing one part at the beginning and one at the end of the play. Then I wrote the rest: two scenes with Arden travelling to and from London, following Holinshed's descriptions of the attempts to murder him there; and another where both Alice and Mosby come to regret their plan to murder Thomas, but are spurred on by the scheming Greene, his cunning and ruthless master Sir Anthony Aucher never far away to make sure that they do not soften their resolve.

And finally, the climax of the play – the second part of my original draft set in Arden's house; the murder itself. A frenzy of strangling and stabbing; the body hastily despatched; the culprits arrested, all save Greene and Mosby; each stating their remorse for their actions and pleading unsuccessfully for mercy.

By the end of the fourth day I had filled all twenty-five sheaves of paper, fifty lines on each side; in the left margin the speech-prefixes, in the right, the stage directions. I gave the last line to William Marshall, the new Faversham mayor – '*To speedy execution with them all!*' – and with that had Alice Arden dragged on stage and burned at the stake.

I drew a small fleuron underneath the text to signify the play was finished and stared at it in wonder.

I had written my first play. *Arden of Faversham*.

Chapter Eighteen
Alice ~ 1550

WITHIN MOMENTS of the mayor's men leaving, the recriminations started.

'I am ruined!' Dunkyn cried. He glared at Thomas. 'And it is all your fault.'

Thomas, in turn, rounded on Tom. 'This is your doing, Tom Mosby. I should have shown humility and begged forgiveness from the council and offered to pay the taxes in full. Now I am destroyed and humiliated, never able to show my face in society again. Not only have you stolen my wife, you have stolen my very existence.' He turned to me. 'Alice, this man has betrayed us. Have nothing more to do with him.'

Tom dropped to his knees. 'Forgive me, Master Arden. This punishment is brutal. No-one could have foreseen its severity. I am destroyed by this news as much as you are. If we are to be shunned by the town, we must stay strong and support each other.'

My heart had been racing since the jurats delivered their news and now uncontrollable flushes of heat came over me. It pained me to think it, but my husband was right: it was my Tom's unwise counsel that had got us into this mess. But I could not find it in myself to condemn the man I loved, and his selfless offer of support for Thomas showed that he was a man of principle.

'Tom is right,' I said to my husband. 'Now we need each other more than ever.'

'Be gone with you,' Thomas replied. 'I need time to think, time to reflect on this calamity.' He turned to Dunkyn. 'Come, good friend. We shall share a bottle together while we come to terms with our predicament.' Thomas slammed the door behind him as the two men left.

I could finally vent my frustration. 'Why did you tell Thomas not to pay the roll-of-streets tax?' I demanded. 'If only he had done so, then all would be well. Now we face disaster.'

'If he had given in once, then his enemies would have come after him again and again. It was not only refusing to pay the tax that has led to his downfall. Everything he has done since becoming mayor has made him enemies. His grandiose schemes, and making payments from the town's coffers to himself for the St Valentine's Fayre and to Dunkyn for the courthouse repairs. If you are honest, you will admit he has no real friends amongst the goodmen of the town, save for his familiarity with Dunkyn. When he needed supporters in his hour of need, there were none to be found.'

'But what will we do now, Tom? How will my husband win favour again? If he does not, my life will be in ruins.'

'Thomas lacks the grace to make amends for his follies,' Tom replied, speaking to the air rather than to me. 'You are right, he faces a life of wretchedness. You have to ask yourself if you want to share it with him.'

'You mean you and I leave Faversham together? But Thomas would never tolerate that, you said so yourself. And now more than ever, he needs me at his side. If I were to leave without his blessing, my jointure from my step-father would become his by law. We would be without a penny in the world.'

Tom stood straight and tall. 'Then there is only one thing left to do. Thomas Arden faces a life that is not worth living. You said so yourself. Send him to his Maker, free him from a life of despair and all that remains of his fortune will become yours. You would be free to marry again, keep your jointure, and we could start a new life together, a prosperous couple with the past behind us, and you with the Mosby name rather than the reviled Arden. There, I've said it. Arden must die and we must have a hand in the doing of it.'

I reeled in shock at Tom's words, my hand rushing to my mouth.

'Murder, Tom? Is that what you are suggesting?'

'It is,' Tom replied softly. 'What is the alternative? That I leave Faversham and find a new town to settle on my own? That you live a life alone with Thomas Arden, not only in a loveless marriage but shunned by all of Faversham? His fortune dwindling as the merchantmen of Kent have nothing to do with him? Is that what you want? Or a life with me, loving and loved, maybe even a family, in a new town, far away. Which would you prefer?'

For a fleeting moment I was tempted, but then I thought about committing the act, watching my husband die in front of me. Thomas had done me no harm, he was just unable to love me as I craved to be loved. True, he had allowed his pride and vanity to destroy his life and the lives of those around him. But were these such great sins that they should be punished by death? I could not bring myself to say so.

I buried my head in Tom's chest, but gave no reply other than my sobs.

Finally, I spoke. 'No, Tom, I cannot do this. I have no love for my husband, but I would rather end my own life than take his.' I nodded vigorously. 'Yes, that is what I must do. Life in Faversham with Thomas would be unbearable, yet he would never allow me to leave him. I will find a dagger and do the deed this moment.'

I went to push past Tom to reach the kitchen, but he grabbed hold of me, pinning my arms to my side. 'I will not allow it, Alice,' he said. 'I could not bear to see any harm come to you.' His voice softened. 'But if you cannot stomach the savagery of the act, then let him die quietly, peacefully. A death no more brutal than succumbing to a fatal illness.' He kissed me lightly on the lips. 'If I could conjure up such a fate for him, would you be party to that?' He gently released me from his grasp. I made no effort to run away.

I stood back from him, made a fist and bit into my knuckles. 'How could you contrive it, even if I was to agree? Thomas is hale and hearty and suffers no maladies.'

I hadn't said no. I saw Tom hesitate, weigh up his words.

'There is a painter in this town by the name of William Blackbourne. He is skilled in making potions from all sorts of exotic materials to prepare the coloured oils for his work.' His voice dropped almost to a whisper. 'I have heard that he is also skilled in making concoctions that have a more nefarious purpose. Poisons that can kill a man quickly, painlessly and leave no trace behind. Were you to procure such a potion from him, you could add it to Thomas's food and then leave it to do its work. You would spare Thomas a life of misery and we would finally be free to be together, to start a new life away from this scandal. What do you say, Alice? If he dies without agony, will you help me do the deed?'

'No, I cannot,' I replied. 'I cannot contemplate killing a man, especially if that man is my husband. What you describe is a perversion of all that is holy.'

'Then I must sever all ties with you and Thomas Arden,' Tom replied. 'I hear myself described as Arden's man, even though no such formal arrangement has ever been published. I will move my belongings out today, and stay at the Fleur de Lis until I can find a more permanent arrangement. But I fear that may have to be somewhere other than Faversham. No-one will want to employ a tailor so closely associated with the Arden name.'

'Do not leave me, Tom,' I said. 'I cannot bear to think of a life without you. You were not part of any of my husband's schemes; you have done nothing to turn the people of Faversham against you.'

'I will give it a month,' Tom replied. 'I cannot live on air and if I receive no custom in that time, then my mind will be made up. And even if I do stay, our time together has come to an end. As long as your husband is alive, we must never be together again.'

NOT ONLY DID I not see Tom for the next two weeks, I hardly saw my husband either. He spent most days at Dunkyn's house, even Christmas Day, which I spent in the joyless company of Cislye, Elisabeth and Michael. When he returned the next day, I could not contain my fury.

'You leave me abandoned and alone, after dragging my life into the gutter along with yours. And now you spend

Christmas with Thomas Dunkyn. A pair of drunken sots. Who is your wife? Him or me?'

Thomas was unsteady on his feet, and my words caused him to blanch.

'Leave me alone; do not say such words,' he said, waving my question away. His voice trembled, as it seemed to me with fear. 'It never mattered where I stayed when Mosby was here. Why should you care now?'

'Because now you are all I have,' I replied, and as I said the words, a dread came upon me. That was the truth.

Something in our exchange must truly have shocked Thomas out of his daze, because after that he spent every night at Abbey Gate. But we played no games in the evening, I never practised on the virginal. Our days were spent in endless misery, and every time I went for a walk around the town, I was met with hostility and made to feel unwelcome in every shop I entered. Thomas told me that the words of the disenfranchisements of Dunkyn and him had been recorded verbatim in the wardmote book. Our shame was a matter of public record and would live for eternity.

I could not survive this existence. I asked Michael to visit the Fleur de Lis and inform Tom that I needed to see him.

I had resolved that when we met, I would tell him of my agreement to his plan.

WE ARRANGED TO MEET at the Deadman's Stile on the Whitstable Road leading out of town, to avoid being seen or overheard. But I needed to feel his embrace, no matter what the risk. I pulled Tom towards me and held him tight, so tight it was hard to breathe. I felt no response from him and reluctantly released my grip. This was a meeting of accomplices, not lovers.

'How do we procure this thing from Blackbourne?' I asked him, my voice cool and matter-of-fact. 'And why do you assume he will agree to play a part in this subterfuge?'

'You ask him for poison, saying you have a problem with vermin. Tell him the creatures are wise to its taste and you will have to administer it subtly for it to have any effect. He might guess your true intention, but do not worry about him speaking out. Blackbourne has debts all over town. He will charge you dearly for this service and then he will be a part of this conspiracy. His silence will be guaranteed.'

'Should it not be you who makes this request of him? Would he talk to a woman about such things?'

Tom smiled, though there was no gaiety in his voice. 'A poisoner's best clients are the fairer sex. It is a method of despatch best suited to female wiles; men prefer more violent means. It will be you who has to administer the poison, so it is you who should receive instruction as to how to use it.'

My heartbeat was thrashing in my ears. It all sounded so simple the way Tom described it.

'Tell me where this painter resides,' I said, giving a curt nod. 'I will visit him on the morrow.'

WILLIAM BLACKBOURNE'S HOME WAS on the road to Davington, an unsavoury part of Faversham I rarely frequented. I headed down West Street to Stonebridge Pond, and found the cottage at the top of Davington Hill.

Blackbourne was sitting outside, supping a flagon of ale, even though the day had barely begun. He was around the same age as my Tom, but he had gone to seed, with a large belly and a florid complexion born, no doubt, from many a night's hard drinking. He was not the sort of person I would have chosen to risk with a matter of discretion, but I had no other choice. He greeted me with a tradesman's smile, sensing that there was some business to be done and that flattery was the way to achieve it.

'Come in, fair lady,' he said, beckoning me to his painting room, a chaotic jumble of brushes and jars. 'It is Mistress Arden, is it not? I pray it is your good self that you wish me to render in oils, though it will test all my skills to capture such radiant beauty. Please, take a seat and tell me what you desire.'

Being so easily recognised did nothing to settle my nerves. 'I regret it is not your skills as a painter that have caused me to seek you out, Master Blackbourne. These are difficult times for my husband and myself, and commissioning a portrait would be an indulgence we can ill afford.'

Disappointment flashed across the painter's face and I cursed my loose tongue. Why had I raised the issue of the scandal that now surrounded the Arden name? I needed to be more guarded in my dealings with this man.

I perched on the edge of a stool and forced myself to give a breezy smile.

'I have a problem with vermin and the vile creatures are evading the traps that have been set for them. I am told you have some powders I can use, so that they will meet a hasty end.'

Blackbourne's deep-set eyes glinted and he gave me a different look now, coolly assessing me.

'You are the wife of Thomas Arden, are you not? What a sad fate to have befallen such a great man.' He paused and allowed himself a small chuckle before continuing. 'And now you seek some poison, for your house is plagued with vermin? It seems there is no end to the Arden misfortune.'

He had guessed, I was sure of that. My indiscretion in mentioning Thomas's downfall had turned out to be a blessing. Now we could conclude the transaction without either of us saying anything incriminating.

'Our other misfortunes are no concern of yours. Can you prepare such a concoction to rid me of this loathsome problem?'

Blackbourne's look changed once more. He gave me the kind of lascivious stare reserved for women of ill repute rather than ladies of high standing. I blushed and looked away, so that he could not see how offended I was by his attentions.

'I think I have a better understanding of your problem now, Alice.' I bridled at his familiarity but did not respond. 'Yes, I do have such a concoction, ratsbane as it is known, but it is a deadly powder that should be handled with care.' He looked me in the eye, the faintest smirk playing across his face. 'Shall I deliver it safely into your husband's hands? That would be the wisest course of action, I think.'

'My husband is greatly distracted by the recent unfortunate turn of events,' I replied, fighting to keep my composure. 'He trusts me to do his dealings for him. And I do not want talk of our infestation to add to all the other harmful gossip surrounding us by you visiting our home. I trust I can be sure of your utmost silence and discretion?' I slipped a gold coin out from my handkerchief and handed it to him.

There was no going back now. A gold sovereign was far too great an amount for such a small purchase.

'Well, well, that is most generous,' Blackbourne replied. He gave me a look of steel. 'But a second coin would be more generous still.'

I blushed again. 'This is all I have at the moment. I will return with a second when the powder has done its business. Can you assist me, Master Blackbourne?' I said, allowing a sharper tone to enter my voice. 'And with some haste? I do not want to tarry here long. I am sure you understand.'

'Yes, of course, Alice.' Blackbourne squeezed past me and reached up for a glass flask on the top shelf behind me. His body pressed next to mine and lingered there a moment too long.

He uncorked the flask and deposited two spoons of a darkish powder in a small jar and pressed a cork down on it with all his force. As he returned the flask to the shelf, I shifted aside to avoid his touch again. When he handed me the jar, he had a business-like air about him.

'Now this is most important. Ratsbane has a pungent taste that will have to be disguised for it to be effective. Add it to porridge, but put it first into the bowl and then the oats and milk on top. Do not do it any other way.' He seemed to be enjoying the subterfuge. 'Rats are cunning creatures. They will not take the poison if it is served to them directly. Now let me bid you good day. I look forward to you visiting again with the second coin you have promised me.'

As we stepped outside, he glanced all around to check that no-one was about. He need not have bothered; this was the loneliest spot in all of Faversham.

'A secluded spot is a good place to be a painter,' he said to me. 'It is important not to be disturbed at work.'

I hurried home. If the poison had to be administered in porridge, that meant waiting until the morrow, but perhaps there was some value in the delay. My husband had said he would be riding to Canterbury to meet with Sir Thomas Cheyne, so the poison would do its work when he was on the road, far from any help.

I could not wait for the morrow to come, and yet I feared it. As Thomas and I supped in silence on cold chicken pie that night, I thought of life, and the taking of it, and how dismal it all was. Our last meal together.

I could not sleep when I retired, and it was only in the depths of night that I finally fell into a restless slumber. When I awoke, dreary winter sunshine had already entered the room. I jumped up quickly. I had not meant to sleep this late.

I arrived in the kitchen and saw that the porringer was full almost to the brim with oats and milk. I uttered a most unladylike oath that Elisabeth should have been so diligent. I had heard Thomas stir as I rushed to get dressed, and knew he would be joining us at any moment. I had to act. I could not face another day of delay, and Thomas's journey to Canterbury was the perfect opportunity to do the deed. If I mixed the powder into the porridge and stirred it vigorously, I told myself, then surely that would be the same as adding the porridge on top of it. As I heard Thomas start to descend the stairs, I tipped the ratsbane into the porringer and mixed it in with a ferocity that would have seemed most alarming to any onlooker.

Thomas ambled in and grunted a greeting. I had let some of the porridge spill onto the table and wiped it up with a cloth. As I went to wash the cloth, I got some of the porridge on my fingers; without thinking, I moved my hand to my face to lick it off and only realised what I was doing when my finger was but an inch from my lips. Shaken, I managed to compose myself and turned to Thomas.

'Your porridge is ready, dear husband. Take your fill – it will stand you in good stead on your journey.'

Thomas walked past me to the open door and shouted, 'Michael! Saddle the mare.'

Michael appeared at once. 'Will I be accompanying you today, master?'

Thomas gave a dismissive wave and a look of thinly disguised delight crossed Michael's face. He had been growing closer to Cislye, and Thomas's absence on a long journey to Canterbury would allow them plenty of time to be together.

I focused on the matter at hand. 'Why do you not eat, Thomas? Your porridge grows cold.'

Thomas was still standing in the doorway.

'Be sure to tighten the girth,' he said. 'She has a way of breathing in at the first try.'

'Your porridge, Thomas,' I said again, trying to keep the agitation out of my voice. 'Leave Michael to saddle up. He knows the mare as well as you do.'

I added some milk and butter to the bowl.

Thomas finally sat down and took up a spoon. He scooped up a measure of the porridge without so much as a glance in my direction, and it finally passed his lips. Before I could take a breath, he spat it out and it landed on the rushes on the floor.

'By cock and pie, that milk has turned! Elisabeth, did you not check the milk for sourness before filling the porringer?' He took a gulp of water to wash around his mouth, then spat again. 'Fools. I am surrounded by fools. Why is it so difficult to make a simple bowl of porridge?'

'There is nothing I can do to please you,' I replied, trying to sound as if my pride was wounded.

Elisabeth burst into tears. 'The milk is fresh, I can assure you,' she said to Thomas. 'Let me see what is the issue.' She picked up a spoon and went to taste it.

'No!' I said, rather too forcefully. Thomas and Elisabeth both turned to look at me. I settled myself and scolded Elisabeth. 'If your master says it is not wholesome, then that should be the end of the matter. Bring him some bread and cheese. I will pour away the milk and this foul dish. My husband needs no further delay.'

With shaking hands I cleaned out the porringer myself, trying not to make it too obvious that I was assiduously removing all traces of the contents, before returning it to its place in the buttery. Elisabeth prepared some bread and cheese, choking back her tears at being the object of Thomas's anger.

Just as Thomas was preparing to ride off, there was another development. Dunkyn arrived to speak to him. They went off to his counting room and I knew what they would be discussing: their precarious financial position and how they could make new contacts in London to counter it. After a twenty-minute conversation, they emerged and Dunkyn said his farewell. Thomas put on his cloak and made ready to leave.

As he was about to climb into the saddle, he fell to the ground, vomiting profusely.

'Are you ill, Master Thomas?' said Michael, a trifle unnecessarily. He turned to the maid. 'Elisabeth, quick. Fetch a bowl.' Thomas retched again and I glanced at the vomit. It was too fresh to have done its work. Devastated by the turn of events, I too was sick – sick with fear that my attempt had failed; worse, that it could now be discovered.

Thomas continued to purge the poison for another five minutes and then lay down, so weak he could hardly move. 'Michael, ride and tell Sir Thomas Cheyne I have taken ill and am delayed,' he said weakly.

Then he turned to me. 'Alice, you seem less stricken. When you are recovered, demand some significant compensation from our fishmonger. Our supper last night must have had some pestilence in it, there can be no other explanation. I have a good mind to visit the fellow myself and flog him until he begs for mercy. I have never had a sickness like this before.' He retched again, but nothing passed his lips. 'Thank the Lord. The worst is behind me.'

I had failed.

I TOLD TOM THE news that evening when we met as arranged at the Deadman's Stile, and he tried hard to disguise his anger at my foolishness.

'You are certain he suspected nothing? Even after tasting sour milk in his porridge, he believed he was felled by the fish from the night before?'

I nodded. 'He was too ill to visit the fishmonger himself and have him flogged, which was just as well as the fellow would have vehemently protested his innocence. I nursed Thomas for the rest of the day, and he seemed quite appreciative of my attentions. But we have had a narrow escape. Let us banish this foolish idea from our minds once and for all.'

To my astonishment, Tom did not agree.

'We have put events in motion; we should see them to the end. Let us enlist an accomplice to help us achieve our goal. The tailor, John Greene, hates Thomas Arden with a vengeance for stealing his land. When I visited with him the other day to trade some cloths, he told me he must soon travel to London to attend to some business for his master, Sir Anthony Aucher. He could arrange to travel there at the time of Thomas Arden's next visit, and find some local assassin to do the deed. I'd wager there are many London villains who would slit a man's throat for little compensation.' Tom paused, his eyes fixed on the sky. 'Your carelessness with the porringer might turn to our advantage. A murder in London, even better in the lawless lands of Rainham Down between the Gravesend ferry and Faversham, would be seen as the common consequence of travelling to London without an armed attendant. Your husband travels only with Michael Saunderson, to save himself the cost of a bodyguard. Let his penny-pinching be his undoing.'

It was a bold plan, but it had, as it seemed to me, a potentially fatal flaw.

'Are you sure that John Greene hates Thomas with such a passion that he would arrange for his murder? And where would the coin come from to pay this assassin? If I took sufficient funds from the household accounts, my husband would notice and I would not have answers to his questions. It is too great a risk.'

Tom gave an enigmatic smile. 'I know John Greene and how he feels about Thomas Arden. He would not hesitate to be part of a plan to despatch him – he is a sworn enemy. And it would please his master, Sir Anthony, to hear of Thomas's demise. And as for the coin, I have ten pounds, my life savings. I will gladly forfeit this for us to have a life together. I have to return some garments to Master Greene on the morrow. Let me broach the subject with him then, with all discretion and delicacy. If I sense he is willing, I will tell him more. When is Thomas next planning to travel to London?'

'Around three weeks from now, at the end of January. Surely all could not be made ready by then?'

'I believe it could,' said Tom. But I was not convinced. His plan seemed sound enough, but he had thought of it in an instant, when in a rage over my mishandling of the ratsbane. And I knew nothing of this John Greene, except that he hated my husband and had threatened both of us when he visited our house. I could not trust my fate to a plan so hastily conceived and in the hands of a man I did not know.

'Let us reflect on this some more,' I said to Tom. 'We should not rush so momentous a decision.'

Tom looked me in the eye and spoke very evenly. 'We have agreed to the killing of Thomas Arden; we now need to find the means. John Greene has spoken to me passionately and at length about his hatred for Thomas Arden. He will agree in a heartbeat to being part of the plan. Three weeks is time a-plenty to prepare. Let us not miss this one chance.'

And so, I gave him my blessing. I felt uncomfortable at bringing a stranger into our confidence, but I was greatly moved that Tom would sacrifice his lifelong savings, just to be with me. And although I had never spoken to Greene since that fateful day when he turned up at our home armed with a cudgel, it seemed my Tom was better acquainted with him than I had realised. John Greene was obviously a man who could keep a secret.

THE NEXT DAY, TOM returned from his meeting to tell me that Greene had not only agreed to be involved, he had shown great enthusiasm for the plan and wanted if possible to expedite it. With that in mind, he had said that Tom and I should meet with him that evening in his cottage, safe from prying eyes.

It had not occurred to me that I was to become so directly involved with the man who would be charged to despatch my husband, but when I thought about it, it made some sense. The poison plan had failed due to a lack of planning. I had panicked when I saw the porringer was full and I should have bided my time and added the ratsbane on another day. With this second attempt, we would leave nothing to chance; there would be no spontaneous acts that could endanger the enterprise. I knew my husband's travel plans and arrangements in London better than anyone. I had to be party to the discussions on the scheme.

Greene lived on the edge of the Nagden marshes to the north of Faversham, which meant I did not have to pass through the town to get to his cottage. Tom was already there when I arrived, but I still flinched when I saw the man I had last encountered with a raised cudgel.

Greene was quick to put me at my ease.

'I bear you no ill will, Mistress Arden,' he said. 'It was unfortunate that you had to witness my rage at your husband's treachery in cheating me out of land that rightfully belonged to my family, but that is in the past. We are bonded together in our desire to see the end of Thomas Arden. Let us now do what is right, and have him pay the price for his malevolence.'

'He is so evil beloved that no man would inquire after his death,' I replied. 'So. My husband plans to visit London in the next week or two, to see if there is any future in engaging with London grocers to rekindle his fortunes. Tom has suggested that this would present the best opportunity to strike him down.'

'Aye, in the streets of London or even better on Rainham Down. Do you know the details of his plans? Does he intend to travel alone?'

'His custom is to take his manservant, Michael Saunderson,' I replied.

Greene shot a glance at Tom and my heart raced.

'No! Michael is a good man and true; he must not come to any harm as a result of this enterprise. If he has to suffer for this plan to succeed, I want no part in it.'

'I have met this Saunderson fellow before,' said Greene. 'He was the one who defended Thomas Arden, was he not, when I visited your home? Had he not restrained me that day, I might have finished off your husband there and then in my fury.'

'And you would have been hanging from the gallows by St Anne's Cross the next day,' Tom said. 'Michael was only doing what would be expected of a manservant, and his first thought was to protect Alice. He is no enemy of ours; I count him almost as family. He wishes to wed my sister, Cislye, and she is much enamoured by the idea. Alice is right. There must be no chance of his being harmed in the event that, as a loyal servant, he attempted to thwart our plans.'

'He has shown courage before. If he stands in our assassin's way, he would have to be cut down,' Greene said. His grim expression signalled that he would not be persuaded otherwise.

'Then he must be party to our plans,' said Tom. 'I have spoken to him about Thomas Arden when we have been alone. Arden has placed many obstacles in the way of Cislye and Michael announcing their betrothal, purely out of a selfish belief that they would leave his service and he would be inconvenienced by having to find new servants. Michael is too honourable a man to strike the blow himself, but he can be convinced to stand aside to allow another to do it. Let us take him into our confidence. Cislye and Elisabeth also. It is the only way this plan can be sure to succeed.'

'John Greene, Blackbourne the painter and now Michael, Cislye and Elisabeth?' I cried. 'It is too many. The more that know, the greater the risk we will be found out.'

'Cislye is my sister,' Tom replied. 'She would not see her brother hanged. Elisabeth neither. Were Michael to tell, my sister would never forgive him. They may not hate Thomas Arden as much as we do, but Cislye and Michael would be advantaged by his demise, able to freely marry and to receive a dowry from the Arden coffers if they waited until you and

I were wed. Elisabeth is little more than a child; she will do her mother's bidding. Yes, it is a risk, but the greater risk is that Michael gets in the way of the murder, and my sister loses the man she loves. If we want to do right by them, they need to be involved.'

'Then you must persuade them, not I,' I said. 'I have had enough of these dealings. I will report on my husband's plans for London, nothing more. Who is involved and how it will be done are matters in which I will have no further part.'

'I will speak first to Cislye and Elisabeth, then to Michael,' Tom replied. 'And give the nod when they have joined us in our scheme.' He turned to Greene. 'Make plans to travel to London. You will follow Arden's steps and look to find someone to take him off.'

'Only when this fellow Saunderson is on board,' said Greene. 'He bested me once at Arden's house; I have no wish to have to fight with him again. I will take George Bradshaw, the goldsmith, with me on the trip. He is known as an honest man and can vouch for my whereabouts if I am questioned about Arden's fate.'

'Zounds!' I cried. 'Not another conspirator!'

The two men looked shocked at my language and I blushed.

'Do not worry, Mistress Arden,' Greene replied. 'Bradshaw is a man of the highest reputation for trust and honesty, as is required in his profession. He will know nothing of these endeavours. He will be a paid companion to ensure my safety through the lawless lands west of Buckland, and will be my alibi if any suspicion falls upon me.' He laughed as he turned to Tom. 'I would watch this one, Tom Mosby. She has the airs of a lady, but she curses like a sailor.'

Feeling much embarrassed, I took no further part in the discussion as the final plans were laid. Tom moved back into Abbey Gate from the Fleur de Lis, so that he would stay fully informed of my husband's plans. Thomas did not object; indeed, he seemed to welcome a respite from the hostility and resentment he encountered every day on the streets of Faversham. The townsfolk were out to see him ruined, no-one would do business with him and the tenants of his properties were being offered bribes to end their leases. It mattered not whether they could do this legally – any tenant who requested a leet court ruling to void their agreement found it automatically granted.

When I waved my husband off on his trip to London three weeks later, I wondered if the next time I saw him, it would be his cold and lifeless body.

I prayed for that to be the case.

Chapter Nineteen
Will ~ 1591

THE LAST WORDS I wrote in *Arden of Faversham* were some of the first to be spoken: Mosby's in Act I, Scene I when he asks Arden whether land he purchased belonged to John Greene.

'*Greene, one of Sir Anthony Ager's men,*' I made sure to remind the audience.

Arden's reply, '*As for the lands, Mosby, they are mine. By letters patents from His Majesty,*' set up the conflict, right from the start of the play, that would lead to the battle with Aucher and his downfall.

Full of excitement and trepidation, I took the play along to the Curtain to show Burbage, Pope and Kemp. The three men placed the manuscript on a table in front of them and started reading. Burbage was the fastest reader and when he came to the end of a page, he would move it slightly, then wait for a nod from the other two before turning to the next sheaf. I scrutinised their faces as they read, looking for any clue as to what they were thinking. I had their attention at least.

When they had finished, Burbage spoke first.

'It is a marvel,' he said, breaking out into a wide grin. 'A work of great accomplishment made even greater by being your first play. The passion and deceit of Alice, the greed and callousness of Thomas, the cunning and scheming of Mosby – this tale has everything.' His voice dropped to a theatrical whisper. 'And lurking in the background, like some malevolent puppet-master, the true villain. Will Shakspere, you are destined for great things.'

I breathed again, giddy with relief. I glanced at Pope for confirmation of his approval and he had the back of a finger between his teeth, his brow furrowed in concentration. Burbage followed my glance and turned to Pope.

'Look, Thomas, see how he writes. These murderers are not demons, they are real people with real emotions.' He turned the document back to its opening pages and started to list its virtues. 'Alice's hesitancy about going ahead with the act. Mosby's disgust with the vile life he is leading, sharing his bed with another man's wife: *How long shall I live in this Hell of grief? Convey me from the presence of that strumpet. 'Tis fearful sleeping in a serpent's bed.* This is a style of writing that could only have come from the pen of a precocious new talent, unconstrained by notions of what should and should not be done. Nothing that Kydd or Marlowe has written has bettered these words. Permit me to play Mosby on stage, so that I may hear the applause ring out as I speak these lines to the audience.'

Pope still had not said a word since he had finished reading.

Burbage frowned. 'What ails you, man? Do you not see we have a rising star in our midst?'

Pope finally spoke, shaking his head as he took the manuscript out of Burbage's hand.

'This is folly. Will, you risk a charge of *scandalum magnatum*, writing something to the injury of a person of nobility.'

The phrase was all too familiar from my dealings with Sir Thomas Lucy.

Pope looked hard at me. 'Ager is Sir Anthony Aucher, is he not?' he said. 'Who has been in his grave for thirty years, but the Aucher family still have great influence in the land. They will not take kindly to the talk your play will generate.'

'Let them do their worst,' I replied. 'Their protestations will only bring more to see the performance. I have used discretion – as you have seen, his name is Sir Anthony Ager, not Aucher, in the play. I will perform the part myself so that none of our fellow actors have to risk the Auchers' wrath.'

Kemp had been silent throughout these exchanges. Now he leant forward and gave a too-quick smile. 'I admire your optimism, Will Shakspere. But, in any case, we cannot perform the play on the London stage without it being approved by the Master of the Revels. We will need to perform it to him in his offices.'

I had no knowledge of this and looked over to Burbage for guidance.

Burbage laid his hand on my shoulder. 'Kemp speaks the truth, Will. Anything to be performed in public has first to be played in front of Edmund Tilney, the Master of the Revels, and then entered into the Stationers' Register in St Paul's, as has been the practice this past thirty years. The Master of the Revels' approval is to assure the authorities of the absence of seditious or immoral material, and the Stationers' Register protects you from unscrupulous companies who might be tempted to reprint and perform your plays without permission.'

Burbage turned to Pope and Kemp.

'Let this be how we resolve our conundrum. I will arrange for the four of us to perform the play in the Revels' Office and we will see how the Master responds. This ghost called Ager is a shadowy figure. It may well be that its presence does not cause any consternation, as it is not clear whether we are meant to believe it is real or imaginary. If the Master of the Revels agrees, we can discuss any changes that will have to be made before it is performed.'

Burbage turned his attention to me. 'You have written a bold, I might say audacious play, Will. There are a few passages that will have to be revised where they show an inexperienced hand, but we can talk of these anon. First, I will make the necessary arrangements with the Revels' Office.'

Pope's caution did not dampen my enthusiasm, and I decided to return to the Bell Savage Inn to see if Thomas Watson was there, so I could inform him that his help in telling me about Holinshed's *Chronicles* had allowed me to complete my first play. I headed off to Ludgate Hill, clutching my precious manuscript under my arm.

When I arrived at the inn, Watson hailed me as a long-lost friend and smiled when he saw the sheaves of paper under my arm. He was in the company of another man, who he introduced to me as Robert Greene, one of the University Wits that Watson had told me about at our first meeting.

'Master Shakspere is a glover from Stratford, who has moved to London to be an actor,' he told Greene. 'Now he is here to surprise us, I wager. Will, is that a manuscript I see tucked under your arm?'

I confirmed that it was indeed my first play I was holding, and thanked him for his assistance.

'Well, Greene,' Watson said to his companion, a twinkle in his eye. 'Not only is this fellow from the provinces now one of Lord Strange's Men, it seems he will soon have his first play performed on the London stage. I'm right, am I not, Will?' He slapped me on my back and moved his face to within a few inches of Greene's. 'Why, this fellow had not had so much as a pamphlet published in his name and now has written a play, as if that were no more difficult than stitching a pair of gloves.'

Greene flashed a cold smile. 'A play by a Stratford glover, eh? That will indeed be a new experience for the London stage. What stories will you tell? The art of tanning, perhaps? How to skin a squirrel? Perhaps describing some peculiar northern custom to entertain us? Speak, Will Shakspere. I am all ears.'

I ignored the barbs. 'My play is *Arden of Faversham*, the story of the murder of Thomas Arden, as reported in Holinshed's *Chronicles*, updated for a modern audience. It has an ending similar to *Dido of Carthage*, which has proved most popular with London audiences.'

'The murder of Arden?' Greene crossed his arms in front of him, shaking his head. 'That was but forty years ago, was it not? And a most distasteful tale, if I remember correctly. A wife and her servants striking down a respected gentleman. So, you have not written a play based on Ovid's *Metamorphoses* or any other of the Greek essayists?' He shook his head in haughty disdain. 'A story from forty years ago is like repeating the gossip of an Essex fishwife. No, no, my boy. Plays should be about the great events told in epic sagas passed down through the centuries. They endure forever, just as society should endure, and their re-telling today is no threat to stability and order. Go away and write another.'

I was so furious that my impetuous tongue took on a life of its own. Before I could stop myself, I blurted out the secret at the heart of the play.

'Perhaps,' I said, 'we should have plays that tell stories from today's world. There is an account of the murder in Holinshed's *Chronicles* that I discovered due to Thomas Watson's good counsel, but that does not tell the full story. There was a sinister nobleman who had a hand in these events. My play will be the first to reveal the truth about the murder.'

As soon as I said the words, I regretted them.

'Will,' Watson said, his voice now devoid of the jollity of a few moments ago. 'I have read *Chronicles*. Arden was Sir Edward North's man, was he not? And he was Sir Thomas Cheyne's man, too? Are you damning these great men with your accusations?'

I realised the trouble I was getting myself into. 'They are mentioned by Holinshed, that is true. In my play, I give Sir Edward North the name of Clifford, so that his son, Roger, second Baron North, is not embarrassed by his father's connection to Thomas Arden. Sir Thomas Cheyne has but a small part in the play, and is treated with the utmost respect. I make no suggestion that either man had any hand in the murder.'

'But there is one who did?' Greene was getting agitated now. 'Speak, man. Tell us who you are accusing.'

I confessed to part of the truth. 'I have a restless spectre, an evil ghost, who flits about in the background doing mischief to bring Arden down. That is all that I meant by telling the full story. Alice Arden could not have imagined such a heinous crime on her own.'

'You see?' Greene turned to Watson. 'This is why our plays should only be based on the classics. This upstart crow from Stratford expects the Cheyne and North families to sit through a performance of this sordid tale, enduring the ridicule of the crowd. Even to have William Cheyne see his father played on the stage by one of Lord Strange's Men. What will you have him do, Shakspere? Dance a jig? I tell you, sir, it will be a sorry sight that I have no intention of attending.'

'I do not share those concerns,' Watson said. He turned to me. 'But Will, if I may speak frankly, I am more worried by this truth that you speak of. The mischievous demon. Is he only a figment of your imagination, or was there some real person in your mind when you wrote him?' Watson put his arm around me and led me out of the inn. 'Come outside so we may speak more freely.'

Standing in the inn's archway, I took Watson into my confidence, but again only partly, telling him about the confession heard by the priest Robert Cole that implicated Sir Anthony Aucher, but not revealing that it had been John Stow who had told me of its existence, or that the document of the confession was in his possession.

Watson made no secret of his concern. 'Will, I must tell you this is a foolhardy venture of yours, to even hint that a member of one of the great families of Kent is mixed up in one of the most notorious murders of our times. You saw Greene's reaction, and although his words may be driven, frankly, by spite and malice, there will be others who share his view that a playhouse is a place of entertainment, not a forum for stoking controversy. I would think very carefully before you decide to perform such a provocative play.'

Chastened by his words, I hurried off to see John Stow to tell him of these concerns.

'There is only one thing to do,' he said to me. 'When you meet with Edmund Tilney, the Master of the Revels, do not hide the fact that your ghost is based on a real person. But tell Tilney that this is a fancy, nothing more, based on your fertile imagination that Arden's sworn enemy, Sir Anthony Aucher, could easily be considered as being involved because his man was one of the murderers. This way we can keep the confession Robert Cole obtained a secret, so that the authorities do not go searching for it and there can still be a time one day in the future when the truth can be revealed. Make me a copy of your play that I can store in the secret compartment with my Cole papers, as insurance against the play being destroyed there and then in the Revels Office.'

I went back to my lodgings and began scribbling out a copy of the play. When it was done, I hurried back to Stow's residence, with a glance over my shoulder every few yards in case one of the Master of the Revels' men were about to come behind me and fell me with a halberd.

The next day, when I arrived at the Curtain, Burbage told me that the meeting had been set for two days hence, and that the four of us should rehearse the play that day and the next, so that we would be ready to perform. Kemp and Pope joined us, and before we began, I told the three of them my plan to admit to the fact that the ghost was based on a real person.

Burbage did not agree. 'You are being too cautious, Will. Why risk censure when there is no need to do so? The plays that are banned are those that contain politically volatile material like *The Book of Sir Thomas More*, which dealt with a topic that could cause riots on the street. Your play contains no more than a gentle hint that a long-dead nobleman was connected to a murder. He was not even there when the fateful blow was struck. If Tilney does not spot any controversy, why tell him about it?'

Pope was on my side. 'The Aucher family has grown in importance in the last forty years; they are not to be trifled with. I am in agreement with Will. The Master of the Revels has the authority to imprison and torture anyone who performs subversive material. Let us not take any risk.'

Kemp nodded his agreement and that settled the matter.

I SPENT THE NEXT two days in a state of apprehension. I could not believe that my play could be in jeopardy, but it was worrying that two men had separately expressed their concerns. The four of us arrived at St John's Gate in Clerkenwell in good time for our appointment and waited to be summoned.

The Revels' Office had previously been a priory, and its great hall was where plays were performed to be vetted. The rest of the building consisted of a wardrobe and other separate rooms where tailors, embroiderers, property makers, painters, wire-drawers and carpenters worked, producing what was needed for a play to go ahead once approval had been given, all these activities under the Master's watchful eye. The frenetic activity gave me optimism that this was a place that wanted plays to go ahead, not ban them, and

Tilney did not seem the ogre I expected him to be – he was much younger and welcomed us most courteously. After being introduced as the author by Burbage, I began by explaining the significance of the Ager ghost. Tilney's smile disappeared and then, as we started the reading, I knew from his grim face that all was lost.

He gave his pronouncement as soon as we had taken a bow after the last line was spoken. The play was banned, and a new version would only be tolerated if I wrote a soliloquy at the end emphasising that sole blame for the murder lay at the feet of Alice Arden, and that she alone was responsible for initiating and planning it.

I was devastated, but the consequences could have been much worse.

'When hearing this scurrilous tract I have taken into account your youth and inexperience,' Tilney told me, 'and the fact that you confessed to revealing the true story without waiting for the wardens to discover your sedition. When I asked who this Will Shakspere was, who was to appear before me today, I was told you were the son of a provincial glover, an immature upstart who has fanciful ideas to write for the London stage, but who lacks the classical education required to tell the great stories from bygone ages. That has saved you from greater punishment. Had a writer like Kydd or Marlowe penned such a play, I would have considered it a deliberate affront to the dignity of our nobles and an attempt to provoke unrest and disorder. But you are not a writer of their standing and experience, so I will graciously excuse your behaviour as youthful impetuosity, the unformed writings of one who does not know better. Learn this lesson well, Will Shakspere. If you misbehave again, you will not find me so understanding.'

My whole body quaked and trembled. Not only had Tilney's admonition been terrifying in itself – everything I had worked for, dreamed about, had come crashing down. My mind was spinning as I tried to take in his words, to make sense of them. My limbs felt too heavy to move, but somehow I managed to drag myself out of his office. Despite my distress, I could not help but take a crumb of comfort from the irony of the Master of the Revels' words. His dismissive description of me could only have come from Robert Greene, and the vitriol of Greene's words had spared me from greater punishment. I wished to flee, to be left alone, but Burbage insisted we head off to the Curtain to discuss what to do next. In a daze, I went along.

Burbage shook his head as he opened our discussion.

'That was a disaster, but a salvageable one,' he said to the three of us. 'Will, how long will it take you to make the changes the Master of the Revels demands?'

'I cannot change a word,' I replied. 'The Ager ghost is central to the play I have written, it was the driving force behind the creativity you all said you admired. Without it, the play is worthless, a hollow shell. I cannot do what I have been ordered to do.'

'Then the play is dead,' Burbage replied. 'Are you sure of your decision, Will? You have taken three years to write a play. Do you have another to replace it with? I cannot believe you are of sound mind to be taking this position.'

'Art has been tongue-tied by authority this loathsome day,' I said. 'If my plays have to be castrated to be performed, then I fear I may indeed not write another. I cannot change the words to please some narrow-minded official. Leave me be. My heart is as full of sorrow as the seas are of sand.'

The three men looked at each other in disbelief, then Burbage put a friendly arm on my shoulder.

'Go and ponder on this some more, Will. You do not have to decide today.'

'God save you and prosper you, sir, and thank you for your kindness,' I replied. I hurriedly made my departure as I hardly trusted the tears behind my eyes not to reveal themselves.

I headed back to my lodgings, gathered up all the papers strewn around the room and, along with my manuscript of *Arden of Faversham*, threw everything into my fire grate. With one spark of my flint, I watched my dreams go up in smoke.

I had indeed learned my lesson. If I needed a reminder of the folly of upsetting those in authority, as I had done years before with Sir Thomas Lucy, I had just received it.

My writing days were over. It was time to return to Stratford.

Chapter Twenty
Alice ~ 1551

TIME HAD PASSED slowly since Thomas and Michael left for London. Every day, almost every hour, I would look down Abbey Street, waiting for Michael's return. Would Thomas's dead body be with him? I could not bear the thought I would have to look at it, witness the result of the foul deed to which I had been party. How would I know how to behave, how best to play the part of the distraught widow whose life had been destroyed? An uncontrollable twitch started to play out below one eye, and I began muttering to myself, slurred nonsense phrases that drew looks of alarm from Elisabeth. When I was sure she would not notice, I would creep down to the cellar and open one of Thomas's bottles of wine. It did nothing but blacken my mood.

But it was the nights that were the worst. I would lie awake, unable to sleep, imagining the events that would be unfolding in London. I would hear an owl hoot, or a dog bark, and would wonder if that was the moment my husband had met his end. The waiting was unbearable, and I rued the day I had agreed to this diabolical scheme. But it was too late now to have regrets. I had to be strong. Soon this would all be over.

I was tending the vegetable garden when I heard Thomas's greeting.

'Good morrow, Alice! I have made good time from the Gravesend ferry. Will you tell Elisabeth to make haste and prepare some victuals for Michael and me? We have ridden hard.'

I felt my legs weaken beneath me, and it was only by steadying myself with the hoe that I avoided falling to the ground. I looked at my husband for indications of his state of mind, dreading what expression I would see. Anguish after the attempt on his life? Suspicion that I had been responsible? Relief that he had made it home safely? Nothing. Just that vague, bland expression that he always wore. My gaze darted to Michael Saunderson riding along behind him. His expression was one of studied indifference. But the torment blazing in his eyes gave away his true feelings.

I wanted to escape, to run away and hide, but with all the self-control I could muster, I forced myself to speak in a calm, controlled voice.

'Thomas. What an unexpected surprise. You should have sent word of your arrival. How was your journey? Have you found a London saviour to address our misfortunes?'

Thomas made to reply, but at that moment Elisabeth stepped out of the house. When she saw my husband, alive and well, the stupid girl let out a scream and bolted inside, sobbing. Thomas frowned as he looked at me.

'What on earth is the matter with her? She looks as though she has seen a ghost.'

'Only a vain girl, caught looking in a ragged state by her master,' I managed, and attempted a carefree laugh. 'Let me go to her at once and tell her not to be so dramatic. I will have her prepare a plate of cold meats for you weary travellers.'

I went inside. Elisabeth was rocking back and forth on a kitchen stool, moaning, her arms wrapped tightly around her chest.

'Stop this at once, Elisabeth,' I hissed. 'I have no idea what has transpired in London, but Master Arden seems unperturbed by the experience. Until we find out from Michael what has happened, we must act as if we expected nothing untoward to have occurred. Run and tell Tom and Cislye that my husband has returned unharmed, so they do not make the same exhibition of themselves that you have done.'

I tried to cut a few slices from a hock of salted ham, but my trembling hands made a mess of my attempt. When I returned to the two men, they had dismounted and Michael was leading the horses away.

'So how was your journey, and your stay in London? Uneventful?' My voice squeaked as I said this last word.

'Uneventful, but successful,' Thomas replied. 'I met with two grocers, a Master Prune and a Master Cole, who are looking to have an agent in Kent to supply them with fruit and vegetables. They will come to Faversham in a few days to discuss matters further. We will not make a fortune selling onions, but it is the beginning of something new. Hopefully, it will lead to better things.'

'Wonderful. And all was good otherwise while you were there? I hear that London is becoming a most unruly city.'

Thomas sighed. 'Saunderson was as jumpy as a scalded kitten the entire trip. Honestly, I do not know why I entrust my safety to that fellow. He was scared of his own shadow. Had we come across any reprobates, I'm not sure he would have been of any use. Maybe I should take Tom Mosby with me next time, eh? He looks like he could handle himself in a fracas.'

'Well, you are home safely, that's all that matters,' I replied.

Just then Tom appeared, his face as white as death itself.

'Ah, Tom,' I said. 'We were just speaking of you. My husband has returned from London, safe and sound.' Then quickly: 'Let us help Michael unpack the travelling sacks.'

I was relieved to see that he had the self-control not to display any emotion.

As soon as we were out of earshot, Tom grabbed Michael by the collar.

'You fool!' he exclaimed. 'How could you have failed in so simple a task? And where is John Greene? He has some explaining to do.'

'He was successful in securing an assassin,' Michael replied. 'Too successful, if you ask me. Greene followed behind us, out of Arden's sight, and recruited a masterless man, one Black Will, who my companion Bradshaw had known when a soldier in Boulogne. We met Black Will at the junction of the roads to Leeds and Gravesend, and when Arden and I continued on to Gravesend, Greene followed the ruffian on the Leeds road and made the promise of a ten-pound reward. Then Greene and Black Will followed us to London to do the deed in St Paul's.'

Tom was unable to contain his rage. 'And his attempt was thwarted? By whom? And was Arden aware? Speak, man!'

The colour rose in Michael's cheeks. 'Black Will is the most murderous devil ever to walk God's earth, and I wanted no part of his venture while I stayed at the same rooms as my master, lest he despatch me also, by accident or design. He was to take Arden's life in London, at the parsonage in

Cornhill where Master Arden stays when he is visiting the city. Greene was to point Arden out to Black Will when he went for his evening walk around St Paul's, but there were too many on the streets for the assassin to have the opportunity to strike. Your husband had instructed me to walk with him, and Greene foolishly told me that Black Will had said that if he found the two of us alone, he would have struck me down also so there would be no witness to the crime and it had taken much persuasion to have him agree to desist from that action. On hearing this, I was of course in fear of my life, and said I would play no part in assisting any further attempts to strike again. Black Will followed us from London, his intention being to ambush Arden on the way back to Faversham. But at every opportunity, Greene told me later, someone would pass along the road as the assassin was about to strike. He could not have killed Arden without the risk of being felled himself. And had he been captured and caught, we would all have been done for.'

'But Thomas was unaware?' I asked, my heart in my mouth. 'He knew nothing of any of these attempts?'

'He suspected naught,' Michael replied. 'That is the one small mercy of this whole sorry episode.'

'Then the opportunity is lost, again,' I said. 'And we will not have such good prospects a third time. Ten pounds to that assassin would have been money well spent, there are none of his type in these parts.' I tugged at my hair. 'I dare not try the ratsbane again. Curse our misfortune!'

'Black Will has not departed,' Michael said. 'Greene managed to have a few words with me while Master Arden was distracted talking to some travellers on the road to Gravesend. He told me about the failed attempts on our journey to Faversham and that he had left Black Will at the coldharbour on the Ospringe Road while he returned to his master, Sir Anthony Aucher, to give him news of the errands he was sent to run in London. Once his audience with Sir Anthony is over, he is to meet us on the Nagden marshes to take stock of the situation. Whatever we decide, we will have to act quickly. Black Will's presence in the coldharbour will surely create some fear and consternation amongst his fellow travellers. He must be seen as a passing vagrant. If he were to spend a second night, it would cause too much suspicion. Let us meet on the marshes this eve and hear what Greene has to say.'

I returned to my husband and listened attentively as Thomas described his time in London. It seemed indeed that he suspected nothing. He gave no indication that he was ever aware that his life had been in danger; indeed, he was most animated about the prospect of doing business with the London grocers, who would be visiting Faversham for the St Valentine's Fayre.

I needed an excuse for being absent in the evening.

'Begging your pardon, Thomas, but in my excitement at your arrival, I forgot to mention a social engagement I had arranged. Goodwife Norwell has graciously allowed me to visit this eve, perhaps a first step in being welcomed back to Faversham society. But a wife's place is by her husband when he has returned from an arduous journey. Shall I send Elisabeth with a message that I will be unable to attend?'

I crossed my fingers behind my back.

'Goodwife Norwell, you say? I did not think the Norwells cared that much about us. We scarcely associated with them when I was mayor; it seems strange that they would welcome you now.'

This was true. I had chosen her for my alibi precisely because they were the Faversham family Thomas was least likely to encounter around town, as they led a reclusive existence on Flood Lane, near Stonebridge Pond.

He smiled. 'Visit them and charm them, dear wife. It may be that your feminine wiles will be as useful in our rehabilitation as my business ventures. Take Michael with you and be back before dark. That part of town is a wild place at night.'

Thomas's concern for my wellbeing touched me and, for a brief moment, I considered abandoning my part in bringing about his end. But I was being foolish. With so many now involved in the plot, and a hired assassin on hand, things had already gone too far to be stopped.

WHEN MICHAEL AND I arrived at the marshes, Tom saw us and called out for us to join him at the secluded spot he had found. We waited for John Greene to arrive, and after twenty minutes we saw him hurrying along the bank of Faversham Creek. He joined us and wasted no time in expanding on events in London and the journey back to Faversham that Michael had previously described.

'Let us not spend time assigning blame,' Tom said, when Greene had finished. 'Black Will has to be on his way from the coldharbour, or he will be arrested as a vagrant. He will have already attracted attention by his presence there. If he were to strike Thomas Arden now, suspicion would fall on such a hideous creature being in our midst, and we would run the risk of his being tracked down and interrogated. We must let him go on his way, then bide our time until Arden visits London again. You follow him and recruit another assassin from the rough streets of Cheapside. How long that will be, we cannot tell.'

Saunderson's face turned ashen. 'I will not go through that ordeal again. I want no part in any London plan. And if my master insists on me accompanying him on his next London venture, I will inform him the moment I fear his life is in danger, as mine will be too. That chance is gone, Master Greene. You have to accept it.'

Greene had other ideas. 'We need not be so hasty. My master, Sir Anthony Aucher, entrusts me with the key to his storehouse in Preston-next-Faversham, less than a mile from Abbey Street. Black Will can stay there, and if he keeps hidden, no alarm will be raised. The St Valentine's Fayre will soon be upon us, and many strangers will be in town. Black Will can strike then, and it will look to all that Arden has been robbed and killed by a passing stranger. With all the crowds, Black Will can easily slip away and never be seen again.'

Tom shook his head. 'If he is the brute you say he is, how are we to keep his presence hidden? We do not have his like in Faversham. Were he to be seen on the streets, he would be detained by the authorities and who knows what tales he might tell.'

I too could not face defeat, now that we had come so far.

'If the deed has to be done in Faversham, then this Black Will is the one to do it,' I said, a new-found conviction in my voice. 'Let Black Will stay in the storehouse until there is a chance for him to strike without suspicion. My husband plans to entertain some business contacts on the second night of the fayre, February 15th, so we already know his whereabouts that night – and that is the day the town will be most crowded. Let us plan for the murder to be that eve, after his visitors leave, and let them observe an evening of husband and wife relaxed in the company of guests before a cruel blow is struck by an unknown person.'

'That is too long to wait,' Tom replied, shaking his head. 'Black Will is sure to be discovered.'

The solution was obvious to me, but it took all my nerve to say it. I turned to Greene.

'You say Black Will can be safely hidden in Sir Anthony's storehouse and there is no chance of discovery?' He nodded. 'Then I will take meat and drink to him until the St Valentine's Fayre. Black Will does not have to venture outside, and someone of his ilk will be well-practised at laying low.'

Michael was shocked. 'You risk your life and honour consorting with that sort. Let me supply him. Although I fear him more than the devil himself, he will not strike me down for bringing him his daily sustenance.'

I summoned up my courage to resist Michael's offer. 'It is easier for me to do this; my husband would think it strange to see you in the kitchen. If Black Will so much as lays a finger on me, you can dismiss him and we can abort the plan.'

Michael looked at Tom and Greene, then at me.

'You have courage, Mistress Alice. Never fear, I will be on hand to deal with this fellow, if needs be.'

'And we will be too,' Greene added, nodding to Tom. 'If he is any trouble, it may take all three of us to deal with him.' He shuddered. 'I will be glad to see the back of that brute.'

I REGRETTED MY BOLDNESS the following day as I stood outside the Aucher storehouse, trying to gather my strength to go inside and greet the man who had struck fear into all who met him. Greene had informed Black Will of the arrangement, and now Greene, Tom and Michael lurked in the shadows next to the storehouse, out of sight but within earshot if I called out. As I stood there, holding a haunch of salt ham, a piece of cheese and loaf of bread, I feared I was about to come face to face with the devil himself.

I knocked and entered and saw a body stir in the window-less gloom. Black Will stood up and remained motionless, which was some small comfort as he was indeed a fearsome creature. His hair was matted and tangled, with filthy bits of lint and old food trapped in his unruly beard. Even from ten paces away, his rank odour hit me with such force that I flinched. I placed the ham and cheese at my feet, not daring to step forward.

'I am Alice Arden, and I have been tasked with bringing you food during your short stay here,' I said, trying to keep the tremble out of my voice. 'I will visit again on the morrow. Is there anything I should fetch you?'

'The wife.' Black Will replied, saying each word slowly, looking at me with undisguised lust. 'And a pretty one too. Who would have thought that one so fair would be party to deeds so foul? Who is your husband to be despatched in favour of, pray tell? Greene? Surely not that poltroon, Saunderson? Or do both take your fancy? You look like a lass who enjoys a good stabbing.' He made some lewd movements with his pelvis and burst into a rasping laugh.

I ignored his obscene behaviour. 'I would remind you to watch your tongue, Black Will. The circumstances of this terrible affair are no concern of yours. Do the deed you have been commissioned for, and then be on your way. If I have to endure such insults again, you will starve rather than receive another visit.'

My words were bold, but inside my heart was beating close to exploding. To my horror, I feared my bladder would release itself at any moment. I turned to leave.

'God save and prosper you, sir.'

He did not respond to my farewell. 'Tell John Greene that he has to have my reward prepared for the second night of the St Valentine's Fayre,' Black Will said. 'For I depart then with my coin, Arden or no Arden. I will not stay cooped up in this cage a moment longer.' He chuckled. 'We make a pretty pair, Alice Arden. For all your airs and graces, you are not that much different from me. Forgive my rough ways. And bring me some wine tomorrow. The beer in this storehouse is not fit for piss.'

I hurried back home. Two more days of this. Two days of Elisabeth separating out food for me to take to Black Will without arousing Thomas's suspicions. Two days of going to the storehouse, entering and leaving without being seen. And worst of all, two days of looking my husband in the eye, knowing that his hours on this earth were numbered. It was almost too much to bear.

It fell to Tom to make the final arrangements for the deed itself. Black Will would hide in a closet in the parlour, where Thomas, Tom and myself would retire after the grocers had finished their business with Thomas, and left. Tom would entice my husband into a game of backgammon, to which he was greatly partial. Then, when Tom judged the moment to be right, he would give Black Will the cue to strike. Thomas would be finished off there and then, and the two men would meet with Greene, who would give Black Will his reward and see him on his way. I was charged with disposing of the body with Michael and Cislye, and Elisabeth was to stay behind and clean up any mess. I pushed away the doubts and misgivings I had when Thomas was in London. It was a simple plan, but a good one. Now all I had to do was wait.

WHEN THE DAY FINALLY arrived, the weather was fitting for so dark a deed. Heavy clouds hung in the air and icy cold blasts of wind came in from the coast. I told myself this was a good thing – there would be fewer people about late at night and it would be easier to move the body without being seen. A few moments after Thomas left for town, Black Will and Tom appeared. They had obviously been waiting in hiding until they saw him depart. It was a shock to see the monster next to my beloved Tom, but I was pleased to notice he had availed himself of the soap I had left for him when I made my last visit that morning, and had rubbed himself down with a linen cloth. At least the worry that his stench would give him away was now greatly diminished.

We made Black Will as comfortable as possible in the closet, then went to make the final preparations for the meal. With everything ready, we waited for Thomas's return. Tom put his arm around me; then this turned into an embrace and we were kissing passionately. Reluctantly, I broke away. My husband would be arriving at any moment, and I wanted no chance of any discord at his seeing us in intimacy. I gave a rueful smile. There would be boundless time for that for years to come.

When Thomas arrived he was in a foul mood.

'Blast this weather and blast Prune and Cole,' he said, in place of a greeting. 'A messenger sent news that the ferry to Gravesend was delayed because of the weather and they will arrive late for supper. Damn their hides! I am famished, but dare not eat for spoiling my appetite for when they arrive. It is an important conference we have this evening, and it would be discourteous not to wait for them.'

He took off his coat and boots and put on his gown and house slippers.

My mind was whirling. What did this mean for our plan? Was Black Will to stay cooped up in the closet for hours yet? Would that not greatly increase the risk of his discovery? I glanced at Tom in panic. He also had a wide-eyed look that betrayed his inner turmoil.

I almost didn't hear Thomas's next words, I was so distracted.

'Let us at least gain some benefit from the situation. Mosby, what say you to a game of backgammon? I see the board is set in the parlour. Alice, bring us some wine. You can observe, and learn how the game should be played.'

Tom and I avoided looking at each other as I went into the parlour in a daze. It was as if my husband had joined the conspiracy to bring about his own end. Too late, I realised he had entered the room first and would choose which seat to take. If he were to face the closet, we would be done for, as he would catch sight of Black Will when he made his move, and have more chance to defend himself and cry for help. The same realisation had dawned on Tom, and I observed him trying to push past my husband to be first to sit. But his path was blocked, and only if he had behaved in so ill-mannered a way as to raise suspicion would he have been able to choose to sit facing the closet. I held my breath as Thomas made his choice. With a puff of his cheeks, he sat facing away from where Black Will was hiding. Tom collapsed onto the other stool.

Thomas won the toss of the dice to determine who played first and then rolled a double six.

'By Jove, this is my lucky night.'

Tom and I smiled weakly. I stood to the side, struck dumb by what was unfolding in front of me.

Tom also threw a double six.

'These dice are not true,' he said. 'Either that or fortune smiles on both of us tonight.'

I marvelled at Tom's calmness as my husband threw again, and then the turn came back to Tom. He threw and cried, 'Now may I take you, sir, if I will!'

The cue for Black Will.

Thomas uttered what were to be his last words. 'Take me?' he said, as he studied the board in confusion. 'Which way?'

I was expecting Black Will to burst out of the closet and kill Thomas in a frenzy, but instead, the closet door gently swung open and he crept with an astonishing cat-like grace across the room, clutching a napkin. It was only in the last second that Thomas became aware of someone behind him, but as he went to turn his head, Black Will threw the napkin around my husband's neck and pulled the two ends together. Thomas vainly tried to wrench his hands away, at the same time kicking wildly as he was pulled back off his stool and

Black Will pinned him to the ground. I stared, transfixed, and then looked away, not able to watch Thomas's helplessness as Black Will drew the napkin tighter and tighter. Apart from the crash of the stool falling over, not a sound had escaped the room to betray the events unfolding within it.

I sensed movement. Tom had brought along his huge tailor's pressing-iron, which he had placed in the corner of the room, and fourteen pounds of cast iron smashed into my husband's skull. Black Will released his grip and Thomas gave a faint groan. The brute pulled out a dagger from his belt and with one quick movement sliced across Thomas's neck. Blood flew everywhere as I recoiled against the far wall, my hands covering my face in horror.

'Did anyone hear?' I heard Tom asking.

I opened my eyes. My husband lay on the floor, motionless, his eyes a glassy stare. A man who had never harmed me, never laid a finger on me, whose trust I had betrayed. A sob escaped my lips, but I caught myself and forced my emotions back under control.

'None could have heard. Let us move him quickly. Someone could arrive at any moment.'

Tom glanced outside. 'The night is still too young; many revellers are abroad. It is dangerous to move him now.' He looked around. 'The cellar. Let us set him there and bring him out of the house in the dead of night. Come, Black Will. Help me with this and you can be gone. Alice, you fetch Elisabeth. You must deal with the disarray that has been caused so that no suspicion is aroused.'

'Not before I have finished the job,' said Black Will as he pulled off Thomas's rings and emptied his purse.

'For God's sake, man, leave him alone,' said Tom. 'Haven't you done enough?'

'It would be a peculiar tale for a stranger to set about a wealthy merchant and not profit from his actions,' Black Will replied. 'And if I benefit from helping make this deception, it is of no concern of yours.'

The two men carried the body over to the cellar door and dragged it down the stairs.

'The deed is done,' Black Will said, a note of satisfaction in his voice. 'Come, man, we must be off. Leave these womenfolk to clear up this mess.'

Tom came over to embrace me, but I froze as he touched me.

'I will return as soon as I have despatched this fellow into John Greene's care. When it is quiet, we will move the body and then I will take a room at the Fleur de Lis tonight. I should not be here when Arden's body is found.' He released his grip on me, stepped back and looked me in the eye. 'The worst is behind us now, Alice. We have to be strong for a few hours more, then our new life begins.'

As soon as the two men left, I called for Elisabeth, Cislye and Michael, who had been sheltering upstairs. They stepped into the parlour, their faces pictures of dread. Elisabeth was whimpering uncontrollably, while Michael looked as though he would be sick at any moment. Only Cislye looked strong, though she held her stomach as if pained.

'The deed is done. Now we must be quick and address this disarray before our visitors arrive. Elisabeth, fetch fresh rushes and spread them on the floor. Cislye, bring some hot water and let us scrub out this blood. Michael, come with me to the cellar. I need to check all is in order there.'

'Is that where…?' Cislye said, looking away from me.

I nodded. 'Elisabeth, stop that wailing. Were someone to hear, it would be the end for us. Burn these spoiled rushes and fetch new ones.'

I followed Michael down the steps to the cellar. He lit a candle, and I gasped at what I saw. Thomas's body was lying on its side, the incriminating dagger beside him where it had been thrown.

I went over to have a closer look.

'Fools!' I cried. 'They should have wrapped him in blankets to soak up the blood. Now we have twice the work to do.' I pulled myself together. 'No matter. Michael, bring some blankets to soak up what is here, and place others underneath …' I struggled to say Thomas's name.

A sudden draught caused the candle to flutter and the light danced around the room.

'He moved!' I cried. My senses deserted me and I picked up the dagger and stabbed the body, five, six, seven times. I was in a frenzy, unable to stop.

Michael grabbed my arm and twisted the dagger from my grasp. 'It was the shadow playing over his face, nothing more,' he said, hauling me away. 'Now you have your own gown to deal with. Go and change, I will deal with things here. What matters now is that you are presentable when the visitors arrive. Leave now and attend to yourself.'

I meekly accepted orders from my servant and hurried up the stairs, dressing myself in a fresh gown to help me carry off the dreadful subterfuge that was approaching. By the time I returned, the house had an appearance of normality.

'All is prepared, as best it can be,' said Michael. 'But the blood has seeped deeply into the floor and it will not survive inspection if the new rushes are moved. There is no time to sand; we will have to hope that we have the hours through the night to finish this task.'

'I wish Tom would return,' I said. 'What is keeping him? Black Will should be long gone by now.'

At this, there was a rap at the door. 'They are here!' I cried. 'Quick, spread the rushes. Michael, answer the door.'

I almost fainted with relief when I saw it was Tom. 'Where have you been?' I said. 'There is much to do here and the London grocers will arrive at any moment. Has Black Will fled?'

'Yes, and John Greene has ridden off to take shelter in the grounds of Aucher's house in Otterden. The fool. His sudden disappearance is bound to arouse suspicion, but he could not be dissuaded.'

'We have more pressing matters to deal with now,' I said. 'How busy are the streets? Is it safe to move the body from the cellar?'

'Not yet. It can wait until after the visitors from London leave. Is everything prepared for their arrival?'

I glanced around. 'All that is possible.' I looked over to Elisabeth and Cislye. 'Busy yourself in the kitchen, clean the cloths, burn those that cannot be saved. We must begin the charade that this has been a most uneventful evening.'

By the time the grocers Prune and Cole arrived, I had composed myself well enough to play the part of the serene hostess.

'I know not where Master Arden is,' I told them. 'We will not tarry for him, come ye and sit down, for he will not be long.'

We started our supper, but after an hour of polite conversation the two grocers looked at each other with concern.

'I have no wish to alarm you, Mistress Arden,' Prune said, 'but it is peculiar that your husband is so delayed. He was most insistent at meeting with Cole and myself during our brief visit to Faversham, and with the St Valentine's Fayre upon us, there are many unruly elements in the town tonight. Do you not think it prudent we alert the magistrate to his disappearance?'

'I do marvel why he is so long delayed,' I replied, as coolly as I could manage. 'Well, he will come anon, I am sure. He had some dealings to attend to regarding his sponsor, Sir Thomas Cheyne, and set off to visit him at his home on the Isle of Sheppey. He must have found the return ferry delayed, as was yours. It is a busy time for the town today. Let us not bother the authorities until we are sure there is an issue to attend to.'

'As you wish,' replied Cole. 'But in any case, Master Prune and I should soon be departing for the Fleur de Lis. It is a most foul night to be walking late and the landlord is sure to have a full house. It is best we arrive before he thinks to release our rooms to any other travellers who may be stranded in Faversham tonight.'

'That might be for the best,' I agreed, perhaps a little too eagerly. 'I am sure Thomas will be most distraught to have missed your visit. Cislye's brother, Tom, is also staying at the Fleur de Lis tonight. Hopefully, he can bring you news of Thomas's safe arrival. Be sure to tell Adam Fowle to save a bed for him.'

The two grocers made their farewells and we began the business of moving the body. Finally, we had some good fortune. It was indeed such a wild night that the streets were empty of any revellers. Tom and Michael hauled the body up from the cellar and then the rest of us helped drag it into the meadow of Almery Croft behind the house. A few flecks of snow betrayed the fact that a storm was coming and, by the time we had finished our grim task, the snow was falling heavily. Tom departed for the Fleur de Lis and Cislye, Elisabeth, Michael and I returned to the house. No-one said anything as we shook off the snow when we arrived in the hallway.

Now all we had to do was keep our nerve and wait for the corpse to be discovered. Then this ordeal would all be over.

Chapter Twenty-one
Will ~ 1592

I SAID MY GOODBYES to Burbage, Kemp and Pope and headed back to Stratford to tell Anne I had failed. I had squandered my savings on a book for research and laboured with paper and quill for more hours than I cared to admit, only to have my words banned by the authorities. The creative spirit had been sucked out of me; the fear of censorship would now hang over every word I wrote and any new play would be lifeless as a result. The salary of a jobbing actor in London was no more than that of a glover in Stratford, and I had risen as high as my acting talents would allow. It was time to face reality and go back to my previous life.

I walked the whole way, not just to save money, but to be alone with my thoughts. On the last stop of my journey, I stayed two nights at the Anchor in Chipping Norton, where I drank from cock crow to sunset for the first time in my life. I rose early the next morning, my head foggy and my spirits in the very dregs, to walk the last twenty miles to Stratford. I crested a hill and crossed the Fosse Way, the great Roman road to Leicester, finally walking over the Clopton Bridge and along Bridge Street before turning right into Henley Street.

Home.

My arrival was greeted with joyous surprise. Susanna was nine now, with the awkward shyness of a girl beginning to leave childhood behind, and she greeted my arrival by crouching down and hiding behind Anne's legs. Judith and Hamnet were six, no longer babes, and tumbled madly with delight when they saw me, giggling with joy as I spun them around the room. Mother and Father smiled benignly, ever the limit of their displays of affection. And Anne. Well, Anne was the one whose emotions were the most difficult to fathom. There was a sparkle in her eye, but no elation in her demeanour; she could see past the forced jollity of my arrival and sensed the deep sadness in my heart.

I told my family a few inconsequential details of my journey; then my sister Joan and my brothers Gilbert, Richard and young Edmund heard of my arrival and joined us. I regaled them all with stories of my London life, leaving them open-jawed with my descriptions of busy streets and jostling crowds, fine palaces and grand churches. They had heard of these places from my previous visits home, but they were always hungry to hear more. Anne, for the most part, kept silent, sending me glances of concern whenever she caught my eye. We would have a lot to talk about when the excitement had abated.

We finally had our chance when we retired to my parents' bedroom, having been offered the family home's best bed for the first night of my return. We enjoyed each other's passion for over an hour, and, as we lay side by side afterwards, I turned and lit a candle. I needed to see Anne's face when I told her my real news.

'I am coming home to live with you and the children again,' I told her. 'My dreams are over. I see now how selfish and foolish I have been, believing that a grammar school boy from Stratford could hope to survive and flourish in London society. I worked from dawn to dusk, Anne, just to provide the least a husband should for his family. And in the end, it was all for nothing. Standing at the end of a row of actors after a performance, never seeing my work being performed on stage. The life of a glover is all that I should reach for.'

Anne frowned and rubbed an eye with her finger.

'I thought things were going well,' she said. 'When William Greenway came and gave me your news after his last visit to London, he told me you had made the acquaintance of a great man called Stow, that you were on stage at a playhouse every night, and that you had almost completed your first play. What has happened to bring you so low?'

'My play was banned by the Master of the Revels because it would offend a great Kent family. My years in London have all been for nothing. I cannot face starting again.'

Anne leant over and gave me a kiss. 'What were the particulars of the issue? Why would the Kent family be so upset?'

I shrugged. 'It was the story of a murder, and I received some intelligence that a recent ancestor of the family was secretly involved in it. The Master of the Revels said it could only be performed if I removed all reference to that scandal from the text.'

Anne sat up straight. 'That is all? The Master of the Revels did not ban the play, only asked you to change it? Surely that would not be so difficult?' Her eyes narrowed and she shifted a little away from me.

'Then it would not be the play I wanted to write,' I replied. 'The guilt of the nobleman is central to the plot and allows me to right a great wrong done to a reckless young woman over forty years ago. The play would be greatly diminished if I had to make the changes demanded.'

'But would it still be performed, even if it were, as you say, greatly diminished?'

Anne's questions were making me uncomfortable.

'In a manner, yes,' I said. 'My master at Lord Strange's Men, Richard Burbage, asked me to make the changes. But I said I could not.'

'And how much would you be paid, had you done so?' The edge to Anne's voice was growing sharper with each question.

'Six pounds. But that is not the point, Anne. The play would then be solely about an evil woman who had committed the most terrible crime imaginable, rather than the story of someone cruelly taken advantage of, while the real culprit went unpunished. The play would have had its heart ripped out of it.'

Anne was bolt upright now with her hands on her hips. 'You have forsaken six pounds to uphold the honour of a woman you have never met from over forty years ago? This is what we get for our children hardly seeing their father for four years and me enduring ridicule that I have a husband enjoying the fleshpots of London while I toil away in Stratford?' The candlelight made her glare seem all the more intense. 'Pick up your quill and make the changes the Master of the Revels demands. I tell you, if I knew how to put pen to paper I would do so myself to please him.' She almost hissed these last words.

'I cannot, Anne. John Stow trusted me to tell the story of the Kent nobleman and I cannot disappoint him.'

'Then tell John Stow to come up to Stratford and bring food for our table,' she said. 'Good night, Will Shakspere. We will talk of this on the morrow.'

And with that, she blew out the candle and slumped back down onto the pillow, her back towards me. I stared into the darkness for a few moments and then put my arm around her. She pushed it away.

WHEN I AWOKE THE next morning, I lay still and stared at the ceiling for a few moments, recalling all that Anne had said. My stomach twisted as I realised she was right. Glovers from Stratford did not have the luxury to indulge their emotions at the expense of monetary reward.

I nudged Anne awake. 'You were right last night, dear wife. My pride has blinded me to the most judicious action I should take. John Stow has the only copy of my play; I will return to London and retrieve it from him, make the changes the Master of the Revels demands. And then I will put London behind me and return home for good. But grant me one small comfort. I will not put the name of Will Shakspere to something I am not proud to call my own. Let me publish it with no name of the author given.'

'Will it still be worth six pounds, if your name is not on it?'

I nodded.

'Then do what you must, husband,' she said, shaking her head in evident bemusement. 'But don't return without the six pounds.'

We spent some time in bed together to banish any bad feeling from the night before, then went down to join Father and Mother at the eating table.

'My stay will be shorter than I hoped,' I told them. 'I have to return to London to deal with some pressing matters, but I hope they will be most lucrative. I should be back before the next quarter day with a sizable purse from my efforts, and to return to the gloving trade. My adventures in London are almost at an end.'

I was expecting this news to be well received, but instead Father looked at Mother and they shifted uneasily.

'This is most unexpected, Will,' Father said eventually. 'Your mother and I both thought that you had set your mind to living your life in London, and to visit us when your busy time allows. You have returned to Stratford no more than a handful of times these last four years. As you know, I have been schooling your brother, Richard, in the art of glove-making. He has now served his apprenticeship and I have promised him he will inherit the family business. I told you this would be so when you first departed for London. I cannot go back on my word.'

Father paused for a second as a thought occurred to him. 'But what about my other business, Will? There is a living to be made in wool trading and I have not made as much of it as I should have, and the thought of travelling back and forth from Warwickshire to Faversham in Kent, the town for export, wearies my heart. Most of England's finest wool is exported from Kent. There is good money to be had, selling our county's fleeces to the Hanseatic merchants from Holland. You have a wanderlust about you. Is that not a business you could pursue?'

'I know Faversham well. Too well,' I said.

'So you are already well-placed to make business contacts there? Even better.'

I said nothing in reply. So, that was my choice. Spend time away from my family as one of Lord Strange's Men in London, or spend time away driving wool wagons between Stratford and, of all places, Faversham, spending the night at the Fleur de Lis and forever being reminded of the Arden murder. I clenched my fists as I thought of these options. I had only myself to blame for the position in which I found myself. I could not have expected the world to wait for me as I tried to make my fortune on the London stage.

I sat down with Anne to discuss my options.

'These six pounds you will be paid,' she said. 'Will that be the same for another play?'

I nodded.

'Then how long do these things take to write and how many of them can you do?'

I tried to explain that it was not like making a pair of gloves, that such questions were impossible to answer, and in any case, my fear of censorship again meant I could not face trying to write another play. But she just looked at me, waiting.

'Kit Marlowe,' I said hesitantly, 'is the greatest writer of our age, and he has produced six plays in the last seven years. His rival, Thomas Kydd, has written two in the last two years. But when I write, I write quickly. If you force me to answer, I say I could do two plays this year, and maybe two each year after, until inspiration deserts me. Perhaps six in total, to match Marlowe. But these numbers mean nothing, if my plays are banned again. I cannot promise anything.'

'And your father cannot promise that customers will still buy his gloves next month,' Anne retorted. 'So, twelve pounds a year, on top of what you receive as an actor. Have I understood that correctly?'

'Six pounds a play from the company who first perform it, more if it is well received. But then if others want to stage the play later, they will make me a payment for the right to do so.'

Anne looked astonished. 'They will pay for these words on paper, even though you have no part in their performance? I cannot believe such a thing is possible.'

I assured her that it was, and the payment could be a pound, maybe more. Anne got out her tallying sticks, shaking her head in disbelief. She could barely scratch her name, and could recognise only a few written words, but she understood the language of numbers better than any man. When she had finished, she put down the sticks and gave me a stern look which melted into a grin.

'Will, go write your plays. If what you tell me is true, you will make more coin with this nonsense than you ever will trading wool. It pains me to say it, but there is more for you in London than there ever will be in Stratford.'

I gave a half-hearted nod in agreement. 'And I will follow the advice I was given by a man called Robert Greene, but chose to ignore. From this day forth, I will never write another play set in modern times. My plays will be based on the great sagas, the historical events of our ancestors. Fantasies of the past and history from hundreds of years ago have less chance of causing offence than the stories of today.'

REINVIGORATED BY ANNE'S GOOD sense, I headed back to London a few days later and met with John Stow to retrieve his copy of my play and tell him of my plans to rewrite it in line with the Master of the Revels' demands. He resigned himself to that and confirmed what I had thought; that it could have been much worse. Robert Greene's criticism of my character had inadvertently worked in my favour.

Then I headed off to the Curtain to tell Burbage of my decision. He welcomed me back into the company as by good fortune they had not yet chosen another actor to replace me. The next rehearsal was in two days, I was told. I was back with Lord Strange's Men again.

In the meantime, I headed over to the Bell Savage Inn to find Thomas Watson. I had departed for Stratford suddenly, and so had not told him of the result of the meeting with the Master of the Revels. It would only be polite to do so, but I prayed that Robert Greene would not be drinking with him. Suffering his scorn at my censorship would be more than I could bear.

Watson was there on his own, and he greeted me with his own news. In the year since we had first met, he had written three plays and had them performed in the inn yards by some of the minor London companies. A fourth was to play in the Bell Savage Inn in the coming weeks. I expressed my admiration at his efforts, but he shrugged off my praise, telling me they were mere trifles, not worthy of comparison to the works of Marlowe and Kydd. I sensed a false modesty and resolved to see one of these plays as soon as I had the chance.

'Your success has put me to shame,' I told him. 'Not only have I written only one play to your four; it pains me to say it, but Robert Greene's words came true. It was rejected by the Master of the Revels because of the scandal it would cause, and I have been ordered to rewrite it, removing all references to the Kent nobleman at the centre of the plot. I decided I could not bring myself to do so, and returned to my home town in Stratford, intending to abandon my dreams of becoming a writer. When my wife heard I had turned my back on six pounds, I was despatched back to London to make the changes and collect the coin.' I laughed with little mirth. 'But the thought of making these changes pains me greatly. I do not know if I can bring myself to do so.'

'Then let us do it together,' Watson replied. 'I told you I have no experience of being on the stage, and I fear my plays expose my lack of understanding of how a play should be performed. Allow me to make the changes demanded of you, and you can explain to me how you decide what directions are given to the actors in the performance of them. What do you reckon, Will? How many words do you need to lose?'

'A few hundred, at the most,' I replied. 'The nobleman is a ghost. Although he is often on the stage, he says very little. But I cannot take advantage of your kind offer, Master Watson. You would have to be rewarded for your efforts and I do not want to face the wrath of my wife for sharing the coin for the play with another, simply because I am too sensitive a flower to make the changes myself. My wife is a tiger wrapped in a woman's hide.'

Watson burst out laughing. 'Do not worry on that account. Being blooded in the art of stagecraft is payment enough. Go fetch your manuscript. We can begin this day.'

WITH WATSON'S HELP, IT took but a few days to make the changes to *Arden of Faversham*. Feeling both excitement and anxiety, I submitted it for approval. Two days later, it was returned with the Master of the Revels' seal attached. In its new form, the play could be staged.

Richard Burbage put me in touch with Edward White, the publisher, telling me that he was the best man to protect my interests and have my play recorded in the Stationers' Register. The play would be licensed by John Aylmer, the Bishop of London, as every published work had to be accredited by someone approved by the authorities, and then it would be entered in the Register. All this would cost me seven shillings, but it meant that no company could perform the play without paying my publisher for approval.

It was a bittersweet moment when I saw it finally entered into the Stationers' Register, the title officially recorded as *The Tragedy of Arden of Faversham and Black Will*. I did permit myself that one small indulgence with that addition to the title. Black Will might have been the name of the assassin hired to carry out the killing on Thomas Arden, but it was also a secret alias for the author of the play. My mood was black indeed, and, with the inclusion of an accomplice of the assassin in the play called Shakebag, there were clues a-plenty that Black Will Shakebag was a name close to that of the anonymous author of the play.

Burbage was delighted that the play had finally been approved, but his elation turned to dismay when I told him I did not want to be recognised as the author. I could not be dissuaded, and we agreed that it would be first performed by Lord Strange's Men, and then he would hawk it to another company once the audience numbers started to dwindle. In return for him swearing an oath not to reveal me as the author, I made a solemn pledge to produce another play before we left for our summer tour.

I took no part in the rehearsals to make sure the rest of the company would not realise I was the author, but I could not resist the temptation to stand in the crowd and watch the first public performance. It felt quite unreal hearing the words I had written being spoken aloud on stage. I silently mouthed every line, and when there was an audience reaction, a gasp or a burst of laughter, my skin crawled with excitement. I wanted to shout out to those around me that these were my words they were hearing, but prudence made me curb my tongue. I was in ecstasy, transported to some rapturous dream world. Any last remaining thoughts that I would return to Stratford as a wool trader fled from my mind as I savoured the moment.

Then came the shameful, unforgivable epilogue. Thomas Pope as Franklin, Thomas's friend, strode to the front of the stage and turned to address the audience in stentorian tones:

> *'Thus, have you seen the truth of Arden's death.*
> *Gentlemen, we hope you'll pardon this naked tragedy,*
> *Wherein no filed points are foisted in*
> *To make it gracious to the ear or eye;*
> *For simple truth is gracious enough,*
> *And needs no other points of glosing stuff.'*

In a heartbeat, euphoria turned to despair. My stomach heaved at hearing the words Watson had written being cheered by the crowd, as they celebrated Alice's guilt and downfall, believing the lie that Alice Arden was both the initiator and planner of the murder. No-one seemed to find it odd that Franklin had made such a strong declaration that no-one else was involved, when there was now no hint of this anywhere in the play.

I would never attend another performance, and was relieved when the run finished and Burbage was able to sell the play on to Pembroke's Men to perform at the Boar's Head Inn in Whitechapel, a mile east of the Curtain. And when I saw that its name was being commonly shortened back to *Arden of Faversham*, I cared not a jot that my hint of it also being the tragedy of 'Black Will Shakebag' had been lost. The play was now in the past for me. I could say farewell to Thomas Arden.

Who the author of the play was seemed to be of little interest to the crowds attending. Richard Burbage, John Stow, Thomas Pope and Will Kemp knew, but they were sworn to secrecy and were honourable men. I was sure it would be an open secret amongst Watson and the other University Wits, but only Robert Greene was a notorious gossip and scandal-monger, and he would never spread a rumour that might improve the standing of the man he described as an 'upstart crow'.

I now had to write my second play, and needed to choose the subject. I had learnt my lesson. This time my words would be spoken by kings who had been dead for a century or more, or were from lands far away, with distant battles providing no sensitive associations with the politics of today. But I did not have a story already prepared for me, as I had with the Arden murder.

I was toying with the idea of writing with Thomas Watson again, when I heard the terrible news that he was dead, struck down at the age of thirty-seven. His funeral was a sombre affair, with many of London's finest writers in attendance. I had my first glimpse of Kit Marlowe and Thomas Kydd, but did not have the courage to introduce myself.

Instead, it was Thomas Nashe who introduced himself to me. Of all the University Wits, he was the one of similar age, and I remembered Watson's description of him as one who had borne himself beyond the promise of his age. His name appeared on the title page of *Dido, Queen of Carthage*, along with Kit Marlowe, which was published in 1589 when I was still a call-boy, so he was already held in high regard.

After we shared our sadness at Watson's early death, he took me to one side and said he had something he wanted to discuss.

'I have a fancy to write a new play, *Henry VI*, the tale of King Henry's wife and her lover, the Earl of Suffolk, plotting against him. Not dissimilar to Alice and Mosby plotting against Thomas Arden in *The Tragedy of Arden of Faversham and Black Will*, for which Thomas Watson, God rest his soul, had told me you were responsible. He spoke highly of you.'

He saw my alarm and hastened to reassure me. 'Do not worry, I know you do not want it known you are the author, but Thomas and I shared the deepest confidences. He would have told no-one else of your involvement, I am confident of that. I purchased a copy of the play from Edward White for sixpence and was most impressed by your skills. Would you like for us to write *Henry VI* together?'

He meant well and I was flattered, but I hesitated to return to a similar story to the one that had caused me so much pain. Still, Nashe insisted, telling me that the quickest way to write a play was to base it on one you have done before, and the success of *Arden of Faversham* meant that wives and paramours plotting against husbands was now much in fashion.

In the end, I found the writing cathartic, as if I were exorcising the Arden demons from my soul. And I was learning from a master. Thomas Nashe taught me a great deal about the craft of play writing, and I was ashamed of my arrogance for thinking I had a God-given talent that would allow me to pen plays of quality without having served any form of apprenticeship. But even more than that, it felt that with his proposition that we work together in scripting the play, I was finally being recognised as a true writer.

I gave Greenway the six pounds to pass on to Anne, and asked him to tell her I was staying in London as I had already started my next play. There was much about Henry VI in Holinshed's *Chronicles*, and Nashe and I were able to finish it in only four weeks. We took the play to Burbage to see if it could be performed by Lord Strange's Men and he readily agreed, and our recital in front of the Master of the Revels met with no opposition. We performed the play over the summer, and I was finally recognised as the author of a play and of the lines I recited on stage, taking the part of Jack Cade, the Kent rebel who marched on London to overthrow the King. This took up most of Act IV until I met my end in an orchard in Chapel Cross, deep in Sussex.

Now I could send Anne half of the second six pounds, along with another pound from Pembroke's Men for performing *Arden of Faversham* and my usual pound a month from my acting wages; all within less than two months of my return to London. I smiled as I imagined her reaction.

Then another plague. All the playhouses were ordered to be closed again, and Richard Burbage announced that he was assembling a touring company under the patronage of Henry Herbert, second Earl of Pembury. I was chosen to be a member of the troupe and it was with some relief that we headed north out of plague-ridden London to begin our tour. We played Stratford in July and it was a joyous occasion. Even Father was impressed that my writing skills had resulted in being paid so much, so soon.

After that, I spent my evenings writing two new plays about Henry VI, one set before the first play, the second after, so I would not need any new reference books to educate myself about the history of my subject. I started with the earlier play, opening the story with the Duke of Bedford leading the English army against the French, and being told that Henry V was dead and Henry VI was the new boy king. And Holinshed's *Chronicles* told me that the messenger was none other than Sir William Lucy of Charlecote Park, the great-great grandfather of Sir Thomas Lucy.

I poised my quill over the paper, savouring the power that a writer has over his characters, able to make them do anything, be anything. But Sir William Lucy was not going to be a scarecrow or an ass, like his great-great grandson. I was fulsome in my praise of Sir Thomas Lucy's ancestor, describing him as a nobleman known for his wisdom, intelligence, and unwavering loyalty to the crown, the personification of duty and honour. I wanted to make sure there was nothing Sir Thomas could object to. Such irony. My first play would have offended a noble family who had done me no wrong; my third would incur the pleasure of one who had pained me.

We performed the two new *Henry* plays on tour and had them printed in London, so that those who enjoyed them could read the words in their homes while the playhouses remained closed. I did the same with my next play, *Richard*

III, making sure he was characterised as a despot so as not to offend Queen Elizabeth, making full use of the revisions I had made to Thomas Lodge's *The True Tragedy of Richard III* when I rewrote his play for one fewer player, six years earlier. Then some lighter fare, the comedies *Two Gentlemen of Verona* and *The Comedy of Errors*.

By the time the playhouses reopened and we returned to London to perform again as Lord Strange's Men, my reputation as a writer of plays had grown and the ravages of the plague meant that frankly there were fewer other writers still around. I did not mourn Robert Greene's passing a few weeks after Thomas Watson, but when Thomas Kydd died the following year, and then Kit Marlowe was stabbed to death, there was only John Lyly, Thomas Lodge and George Peele still alive, along with Thomas Nashe and myself, who had plays performed on stage. It meant that Burbage was always asking me when I would have the next play for Lord Strange's Men.

Anne and my family could now live a comfortable life thanks to my writing, and I could also provide for my parents' every need. And when all the playhouses and inn yards of London were fully reopened, and three of my plays were playing in London at once, I was able to entrust Greenway with a twenty-pound fortune to take to Stratford.

THEN A NEW OPPORTUNITY presented itself. It began sadly, with the death of our patron Lord Strange. Once our period of grieving was over, I was summoned to a meeting of the two Burbages, James and Richard, to discuss our new circumstances. They had very ambitious plans.

'Our new patron will be Lord Hunsdon, the Lord Chamberlain,' James Burbage told me. 'A great nobleman and courtier who seeks to bring order to the confusion of playing companies starting up, now that the threat of plague has lifted. He will be the patron of our company, to be called the Lord Chamberlain's Men, led by Richard here and performing at my two playhouses in Shoreditch. Hunsdon's son-in-law, Charles Howard, the Lord High Admiral, will be the patron of the Lord Admiral's Men, to be led by Ned Alleyn, and they will perform at Philip Henslowe's playhouse at the Rose. Both companies outside the city walls, one north of the river, one south. The Lord Chamberlain wants me to hire only the best players for his grand design and perform only the best plays. I will have half of the box office takings to pay for my playhouses, the other half will go to the Lord Chamberlain's company, led by Richard here.' His son bowed his head in acknowledgement. 'There will be eight sharers in the company, each of whom will put up fifty pounds and then be eligible for a one-eighth share of the income from performances, after the jobbing performers and the writer of the play have been paid. I will be inviting Thomas Pope and Will Kemp to be sharers along with Richard, and I would like to make the same offer to you. What say you, Will? You will not be a hired man any more, but a partner. Are you ready for such a responsibility?'

'I am honoured and flattered,' I replied. 'But I fear this has come too soon for me. My circumstances have only recently improved and I have a wife and family to care for in Stratford. It pains me to say so, but I do not have fifty pounds to take advantage of your offer.'

Richard glanced at his father, who gave a quick nod. 'We thought this might be the case,' Richard said. 'Your rise in fortune has been great, but also very rapid. But when Ned Alleyn joins the Lord Admiral's Men, he will take Marlowe's plays with him. We need dramas of that quality to compete. Pledge that the Lord Chamberlain's Men will be the sole producers of your plays, that only we will be allowed to perform them first, and you can become a sharer without having to pay your fee – and you will still be paid six pounds for every new play. You will be free to have it performed elsewhere when it comes time for us to move on and you have written another to replace it. That will keep your quill busy.' Richard grabbed my arm to catch me as I near fainted. 'Careful, I do not want to see damage to my investment. What will be your first play for the Lord Chamberlain's Men?'

It was *Titus Andronicus,* and its blood and gore took the London stage by storm. And with this move, my star was fully established in the London firmament. I was now sharing in the profits of the biggest and most successful company of actors in London. I wrote fast, four plays a year, and when, in 1595, *Romeo and Juliet* and *A Midsummer Night's Dream* opened at the Theatre in quick succession, it was with no false modesty that I admitted to being regarded as the finest writer of plays in the land.

I moved into more comfortable lodgings in Bishopsgate, purchasing a sturdier table for my notes, a chest for my growing library of reference books and a sloping box to place them on while writing; but otherwise not spending on any other furnishings or decorations. I learnt fencing at the school of Roco Bonetti in Blackfriars, useful both for my performances on stage and my security, now that I was well-known about town. And I also took care to develop an image for myself in keeping with my new stature. There was nothing I could do about my large forehead and prematurely balding pate, but I developed a more flamboyant personal style, taking to wearing a gold earring in my left ear.

But there was nothing extravagant or scandalous about my lifestyle. I remained entirely focused on my writing, rather than accepting the constant invitations to carouse and take part in revelries with my fellow members of Lord Chamberlain's Men. Whenever rehearsals and business affairs allowed, usually late at night and in early morning by flickering candlelight, I would write, chewing sage leaves as I did so to keep my mind sharp and fertile. It led to my gaining a reputation as a drab, dull man, but I didn't care. I would write my plays, earn my coin, and one day, when my pen no longer flowed, I would return to Stratford and live out the rest of my life as I had promised Anne, wealthy and content.

Everything was perfect.

Chapter Twenty-two
Alice ~ 1551

I T WAS MICHAEL who made me aware how foolhardy was my claim that Thomas must have been detained when visiting Sir Thomas Cheyne on the Isle of Sheppey.

'When they arrive at the Fleur de Lis, the London grocers will repeat your story as to why they did not meet with Master Arden,' Michael said. 'Sir Thomas will likely be questioned when the body is discovered, and he will state that there was no cause for Thomas Arden to visit him that day. Many will claim that your story was an invention, and suspicion will fall upon you. You need to raise the alarm now, claim you have just recalled that his errand was in town, with whom you know not, and ask for a hue and cry to be raised to ascertain his whereabouts.' He bit his lip. 'You need to act, Mistress Alice. It is already much longer than a worried wife would wait before raising the alarm about her missing husband.'

'I promised Tom that I would wait until the morrow,' I protested. 'If there is to be a change of plan, I must consult him first. Send for him to join us from the Fleur de Lis.'

Michael shook his head in frustration. 'The inn will be shuttered for the night, and the only way to have the landlord open the doors would be to raise the alarm. And why would a worried wife need to consult with Tom Mosby? You must act now, Mistress Alice. Our lives depend on it.'

Reluctantly, I told Michael to go forth, raise the hue and cry and entreat others to assist. But it was early, too early, for the manhunt to begin. My only hope was that the filthy weather and the low esteem in which Thomas was now held would discourage many from venturing far to search through this godless night.

But that was not the case. Dunkyn was the first to arrive, having heard the commotion. I had never seen a man so bereft as he screamed and wailed that Thomas must be found. When the mayor, William Marshall, arrived to ascertain the details of Thomas's disappearance, I realised I had to match Dunkyn in my despair.

'I have waited too long in raising the alarm,' I said to Marshall, sobbing and weeping as I spoke. 'You have all treated him so badly and I did not want Thomas to be beholden to you over a wife's flight of fancy that he may have come to harm. But now night is upon us, and I fear Thomas may be in great jeopardy. He may have walked by the creek, slipped and fallen in. With such loathsome weather, he would not be able to save himself. Help me find him, I beg of you.'

'The town is asleep, Mistress Alice,' Marshall replied. 'If there is a search to be done, it can wait until the morrow. There is little chance of success in this inky darkness, and to venture to the river in these conditions would place other lives at risk. If your husband fell in during daylight and has not returned, he will be already drowned. We shall begin at first light.'

I tried to hide my relief that my hopes for a delay in the search were being fulfilled, but Dunkyn's incessant wailing made me feel I should lament some more.

'No woman,' I cried, 'ever had such neighbours as I. You care not a whit for the safety of my husband, you wish only to be back warm and dry in your beds tonight. Shame on all of you.'

To my horror, my words had some effect.

'Then we will limit our search to the town and leave the river until the morrow, when it will be safe to venture there,' Marshall said, scowling at my insistence. 'There you have it, Mistress Arden. Your husband may have fallen from favour, but he is still a Christian soul and I will not shirk from my responsibilities to offer such help as I am able. Call your maid servant to comfort you, and wait for news.' He turned to Michael. 'You, man – come with me. We will begin the search in the abbey grounds.'

As the door slammed behind them, Cislye, Elisabeth and I stared at each other in despair.

'They will surely find him, Mistress Alice,' Elisabeth said, breathless with fear. 'What are we to do? I do not want to die.'

I tried to compose myself. 'No-one will be punished if we remain calm. Let us busy ourselves in the parlour, scratching as much blood out of the floor boards as we can. If we apply ourselves, we surely must have a chance of evading suspicion.'

But that hope lasted only a few minutes. There was a knocking at the door, so loud, violent and insistent that the lock would have been broken with a few more blows. I opened the door myself, such was my fear at what I would discover. There was Mayor Marshall, Thomas's slipper in his hand, a few blood-soaked rushes sticking to the sole.

'We have found your husband, Alice Arden. Dead. And a few paces from your back door. Dressed in his house gown and slippers, with blood-soaked rushes stuck to his clothes and feet.' He pushed past me into the house and looked around. 'That means he had *not* been abroad in the town on business. He was carried there by persons unknown from this house, and the footsteps in the snow confirm it.' I looked past him and saw there was indeed an inch of snow blanketing the ground.

There was a grim twist to Marshall's mouth as he spoke again. 'Come, men, let us search this house. We will find where this foul deed was done.'

I could do nothing and it took only a few moments for the parlour rushes to be pulled aside, revealing our half-completed attempts to conceal the murder. There was no possible pretence I could offer that I had not known of the events that had unfolded. The bloody dagger was discovered, then the blood-stained rag used to clean it. So determined were we to deal with the stained floorboards, they had completely escaped our attention.

'What say you to this, Mistress Arden?' Marshall demanded.

I was undone, denial useless.

'Oh, the blood of God help, for this blood have I shed.'

Dunkyn leapt across the room and put his hands around my neck. 'You shameless whore! You have murdered the greatest and most noble man to walk the streets of Faversham.' His eyes blazed as he tightened his grip. I felt as if my own were about to explode out of my head and I tried vainly to pull his hands away.

It took two strong men to drag Dunkyn away from me and I folded over, spluttering and gasping as I fought for air.

'Bide your time, Master Dunkyn,' Marshall said. 'The retribution to this woman will be great indeed. For now, we need her alive, to discover all there is to know about the murder that has been committed here tonight.'

'Only lies and deceit will spill out of her mouth,' said Dunkyn. 'But I tell you what I know to be true. Tom Mosby will have had a hand in this, just as he has had his filthy way with Alice Arden in this house every night, while poor Thomas slept alone in his bed. If Mosby is not to be found here, no doubt he will be at the Fleur de Lis. Despatch your men to catch him; you will be sure to find blood on his hands.'

Marshall nodded to the men who had dragged Dunkyn off me, and they hurried away. Even in this darkest moment, it threw me into even greater despair. If Tom had heard of my undoing, he might have had a chance to flee before his guilt was suspected. Now he had no chance. I wept for him more than I wept for myself.

The remaining men procured some rope, and Michael, Cislye, Elisabeth and my hands were tied behind our backs and we were roughly pushed out of the house and taken to the town jail in Middle Row, a few hundred paces away. Michael was locked in one cell, Cislye, Elisabeth and I in another. Cislye and I were silent, unable to comprehend what had happened, but Elisabeth could not stop her crying.

'Promise they will have mercy on me, Mistress Arden. This was all your doing. I never wanted to be part of this. Tell them I am innocent.'

'I promise,' I said. 'You are but a girl, you will come to no harm.'

A jailer overheard and gave a cruel laugh. 'Girl or no girl, she will roast in Hell,' he said gleefully. 'But not before she has roasted here first.'

Elisabeth started screaming again, her cries so deafening that they pierced my ears. There was a commotion, and Tom was dragged in and thrown into the cell with Michael.

'This one's the greatest fool of all of them,' the man who had brought him said to the prison guard. 'Asleep at the Fleur de Lis, with Arden's blood on his purse and hose. All that cunny he had with Mistress Arden must have softened his brain.' He looked over at me. 'What a witch this one is, to cast such a spell on men.'

I spent the night praying, asking God for forgiveness, asking for a miracle that I might be spared. Elisabeth wailed and sobbed all night, begging to be released. Even had I wanted to sleep, it would have been impossible. At first light, I was taken from the jail to a room in the Guildhall to be interrogated. Four of the town's jurats were there; I recognised Richard Dryland and Lewis Marden, but did not know the others. Marshall led the questioning, starting off with demanding I name all who were involved.

I told them everything. The pact to murder my husband I had made with Tom Mosby, and that we shared a bed together; the attempt on Thomas's life with the ratsbane, Blackbourne supplying the poison; involving Cislye and Elisabeth as accomplices to the murder; what I had been told of the events in London with Michael, Greene and Black Will. I did for a moment toy with trying to plead for Elisabeth, but I knew I would soon be facing my Maker and if I had any chance of redemption, I must confess all of my sins and name all the other sinners. As I was led away from the room, there was a look of grim satisfaction on my inquisitors' faces. My cell door was opened to toss me back inside and I saw Tom Mosby being dragged out, next to be interrogated.

The trial was arranged for the day after next for the five of us. I spent the time lying in a crumpled heap in the corner of the cell. Elisabeth had finally exhausted herself with her tears, and Cislye laid her daughter's head in her lap and gently stroked her hair, hour after hour. I envied the two women their intimacy. There was no word from Mother, and I received no visits from any of the goodwives of Faversham. Cislye and Elisabeth at least had each other. I had no-one.

WHEN THE MORNING OF the trial arrived, I was permitted to wash and have a change of clothing. When I looked in the mirror, I was shocked by my appearance: grey and gaunt, dark circles under my eyes, grey strands appearing in my red hair, a bald patch on the crown of my head. I tried to look my best, for what reason I could not find the answer. As we were led from the jail, Cislye, Elisabeth and I in one set of chains, Michael and Tom in another, each of us stared in front of us in sullen dejection. I stole a single glance at Tom. One of his eyes was blackened, and he had a rude bruise on his cheek. What I would have given to be allowed into his cell with him, to help tend his injuries, ease his suffering. To tell him I loved him.

The trial was to be held in the Guildhall, which had been set up with a chair where the mayor would sit, and on each side of it were benches where the jurats already sat, looking down on a table and chair where the town clerk would record proceedings. The steward, who would be the lawyer for the prosecution, was engaging the clerk in earnest conversation. The rest of the hall was filled with row after row of pews, every seat occupied; the whole of Faversham seemed to have turned out. A few enterprising countrywomen were walking up and down the aisles with trays around their necks, selling sweetbreads and apples, which were being eagerly devoured. It looked more like a circus than a solemn legal gathering.

Everyone was facing away from us, so it was a few moments before the first cry went up that the prisoners had arrived. The screams of abuse were overwhelming: 'Quean!' 'Strumpet!' 'Magdalen!' screeched at me from all corners. Four guards stepped forward, two on either side of us, and they crossed the long shafts of their halberds to provide us with a passage through the mob. A chunk of bread hit the side of my face, then a stone struck the axe blade of one of the halberds. A guard uncrossed his weapon and waved it menacingly at the culprit. The town clerk picked up the Faversham moot horn that was lying on the table and placed it to his lips. The deep-pitched call resonated around the room. The horn was only blown on the most serious of occasions, so it succeeded in quietening the crowd.

The front bench had been kept unoccupied, and it was there that the five of us sat, the four guards with their upright halberds sitting between each of us. An expectant hush descended on the hall and we all awaited the arrival of the mayor, who would judge us. I glanced around to see if Mother and Sir Edward North had attended, but they were nowhere to be seen. I did spot Sir Thomas Cheyne, sitting next to Sir Anthony Aucher in uncomfortable silence; I presumed they were there because Thomas was Cheyne's man, Sir Anthony because his man Greene had been one of my accomplices. It had been ten years since I had last seen Sir Anthony, at that Abbey Gate housewarming party that I thought would herald the start of a wonderful life in Faversham. And this was how that dream ended. Sir Anthony caught my eye, gave me a smug smile and nodded. Shocked, I turned away.

The mayor entered, and the clerk blew the moot horn again and read out a proclamation.

> 'This court of special sessions in the town of Faversham,
> in the county of Kent, in the month of February, in the
> fourth year of the reign of our blessed King Edward
> VI, and under the guidance of God, does now begin
> and makes the following indictment of murder of one
> Thomas Arden, gentleman, former mayor of Faversham
> and lately a member of the township council of jurats,
> on the night of the fifteenth of February, in his own
> parlour, the said crime being the heinous work of the
> following accused: to wit, Mistress Alice Arden, wife
> of the said Thomas Arden; the fornicator, Thomas
> Mosby, tailor; one Cislye Pounder, sister of Tom Mosby;
> Michael Saunderson and Elisabeth Stafford, servants
> of Thomas Arden.'

He paused.

*John Greene, tailor, the masterless man, Black Will,
and William Blackbourne, painter, are to be tried in
their absence.'*

William Marshall stood up, dressed in the very same scarlet mayoral robes that Thomas had once worn, and read out a second declaration.

*'Let me assert before you all the ancient rights and
privileges of the town of Faversham as it has found
favour in the eyes of kings and queens since time
immemorable, that the town councillors have the right
and privilege to hold general sessions and to hold a
court leet over any inhabitant of Faversham accused of
any crime, so that they are to be judged by their own
people and no outsiders, with full power over life and
death.'*

A chill ran through me. Any decision taken today would be final. I had entertained the vain hope that, even at this late hour, my mother would plead with Sir Edward North to use his contacts in the Privy Council to spare me. Now, even if such an unlikely event were to occur, the mayor was making it clear that, under Faversham's ancient rights, no such appeal would be tolerated.

The mayor proceeded with his speech.

*'In remembrance of the commandments which God has
graciously given to the Kings of England to set down
for our good guidance, the accused are charged with
breaking the sixth commandment, "Thou shalt not kill",*

*and Alice Arden and Thomas Mosby are furthermore
charged with breaking the seventh commandment,
"Thou shalt not commit adultery." And, if any as
who be present aided, abetted, or comforted those
that committed a murder, they shall also be principal
murderers in the eyes of the law, as well as those who
performed the deed, though they strike never a stroke
therein, for the law draws the stroke of the murderer
to be the stroke of them all that be present and do assist
him, as according to the law of the fourth year of Henry
VII. Furthermore, Alice Arden, Elisabeth Stafford and
Michael Saunderson, if any servant has killed his or her
master, or any wife her husband, the crime is not only
murder, it is also petty treason, which will be punished
over and above the crime of murder. Stand, all of you,
and state how you plead.'*

'Alice Arden, how do you plead?'

I held myself tight, curling my hands into tight fists. I
looked at the mayor, trying to see from his face whether
there was any hope of clemency. I thought of the many gay
evenings I had spent with him and his wife. Surely these
fond memories would weigh on his mind when reaching his
verdict, or at least passing sentence? I had been silent for five
seconds now, and with each passing moment, the murmur
of the crowd behind me grew louder and louder. I had to
speak. Plead guilty, stand tall and proud, admit what I had
done? Plead innocence, betray my love for Tom and debase
myself by begging to be let free?

Marshall's face turned to anger and he spoke again.

'Alice Arden, how do you plead?'

'Guilty.'

The hall erupted into uproar and the four guards stood and turned towards the crowd, pointing the spike at the top of their halberds towards them. This had no effect, so one guard stepped forward and struck the nearest man with the shaft. This subdued the crowd, and Tom's name was called next. My heart leapt as I heard him speak the same.

'Guilty.'

I did not hear the words of the others. I became conscious of the iron manacles on my wrists, and absurdly examined them to see if I could slip them off. Already the skin below them was chafed raw.

I would spend my final days chained like a dog, denied any dignity, receiving no comfort.

Chapter Twenty-three
Will ~ 1596

I T WAS IN the summer of 1596 that the damned plague struck again. All the playhouses in London were closed, and Richard Burbage hurriedly put together a provincial tour to get us out of the city. For this tour, we would be known not as the Lord Chamberlain's Men, but as Lord Hunsdon's Men. The Lord Chamberlain, Henry Carey, had died, and his son, George Carey, second Lord Hunsdon, had not yet been confirmed as his replacement, so we had to use simply his name in the meantime. The plan was to head to Kent, so that we could quickly return when deaths fell below thirty a day, the number the authorities had decreed would allow the playhouses to be reopened. And that meant travelling back to Faversham.

Burbage and I departed the day after the rest of the troupe, travelling by barge all the way from London to Faversham to make a grand entrance at the quay. The town had changed out of all recognition in the years since I last visited, the population doubled. The boys that had been hired when the rest of the troupe had arrived had done a good job of nailing up handbills and, as we proceeded into town, a large crowd lined the streets cheering our arrival. I was most gratified to hear shouts of, 'Shakspere!' *'Two Gentlemen of Verona!'* and gave many waves of acknowledgement.

'There will be a good crowd here on the morrow,' Richard Burbage said, giving his own wave. 'And they have come to see Will Shakspere, by the sound of it.'

I blushed with embarrassment, thrilled that my reputation had travelled ahead of me, no doubt from performances of my plays by previous troupes to visit the town.

'Settle yourself well at the inn, lads,' Burbage said. 'We may be here for a few days more if the crowds insist on seeing all of Will's plays.'

Everyone was much cheered by this pronouncement. Faversham ale had lost none of its potency over the years.

The Faversham boys were standing to attention outside the Bear Inn when we reached the town marketplace, and Burbage slipped them some coin for their efforts with the handbills, and arranged for them to guard the props during our stay and to be available to collect the money at the gate for the performance the following afternoon.

'One penny to stand in the yard, three pennies to sit,' he told them. 'And if I catch any of you winking at someone known to you and letting them in *gratis*, I will be sure to tan your hide.' He glanced up at the ominous clouds gathering overhead. 'Now get busy with that tarpaulin to cloak the props. It looks like a storm is coming in tonight.'

The Fleur de Lis was still there, and the new landlord seemed to thrive on the notoriety that *Arden of Faversham* had contributed to his business, and regaled us with a story that the play had only come about because his predecessor had disclosed to a passing player a description of the events. Will Kemp and I exchanged amused glances, but kept our lips sealed. Arden's house was now a famous local site, with the owner charging a ha'penny for a tour, including the wasteland spot where Arden's body was discovered, where the grass still did not grow. As I wandered around, recalling the places I had mentioned in my play, I felt an eerie presence, as if Thomas's ghost was following me everywhere I went, waiting to punish me for failing to expose the truth about Sir Anthony Aucher. I was in a subdued mood that evening, and even the excitement of bear baiting at the Bear Inn failed to lift my spirits. I would be glad to be moving to Canterbury, the highlight of our Kent tour, once our stay in Faversham had come to an end.

A storm did pass through in the night and when I awoke, the air was clear and crisp, pierced by bright sunlight, the heavens refreshed by the tempest's fury. I was invigorated, having stayed up to the witching hour writing my latest play, *King John*. I was pleased with my efforts, writing all in verse for the first time, and the character of Faulconbridge the Bastard seemed so real to me that I half-expected to meet him on the walk to the rehearsal. In short, it was a perfect morning. There was nothing about that particular Thursday to indicate that something was going to happen to transform my life forever. Nothing to suggest that, within the hour, I would be a changed person, about to begin an entirely different life. I was about to walk through a door, a door that would divide my life into before that day and after, a door that would slam behind me, preventing me from ever returning to who I once had been.

The first harbinger of this change was my astonishment and elation on seeing William Greenway, my neighbour from Stratford, ride into town, his horse at such a gallop that it caused consternation to those he rode past. But elation turned to apprehension when I saw the look on his face when he spied me. No joyous greeting, just a grim determination in his eyes. He jumped off his horse and we hurried towards each other.

'Your son Hamnet is gravely ill, Will. He had been poorly for some time, but Anne did not want to trouble you with worry, and kept it to herself. But when his condition worsened, she bade me ride to London to seek you out. In Stratford, we had known nothing of the plague in the city, and when your landlady told me that you had just left and were to be in Faversham on Lammas Day, I made speedy my departure to reach you, although I dreaded the moment of our meeting. Forgive me for bringing such terrible news.'

I dropped to my knees, and a wave of guilt came over me. Guilt that I had not shared more of my son's childhood. Guilt that I had not been more of a husband and father to my family. Guilt that I was using this latest closure of the London playhouses not as an opportunity to return to the bosom of my family, but to seek out more fame, adulation and riches in the English shires. I had to hate someone for this news. Not Anne, who would have done her best in caring for our son. Not Greenway, who was only the messenger. No, the only person I could hate was myself, for my selfishness and indifference to those who loved me.

I told Burbage, and he assembled the troupe to tell them that I would be departing for Stratford forthwith. That afternoon's performance would still go ahead; they would find a way to organise the play with one fewer actor and would send word to London to despatch a replacement for me. I was grateful for his support; in my Queen's Men days the performance would have gone ahead as planned, and the player denied a chance to leave. I saddled up a horse and headed off with Greenway on the long ride to Stratford.

The journey gave me plenty of time for contemplation. Why, of all places, did I have to be in Faversham when I heard the news? This was surely the ghost of Thomas Arden's doing. I pushed such fanciful notions out of my head, helped by frequent gallops which meant we covered the three-day ride to Stratford in only two. As I crossed the Clopton Bridge to enter into the town, I steeled myself for what lay ahead.

I STOOD AT HAMNET's bedside for eight days, listening to every gasp and groan he made, willing his next breath to show the first sign of recovery. But to no avail. On August 11th, Hamnet breathed his last. My son was gone, and, in accordance with the teachings of the Protestant faith at his funeral, it would only be on the day of the resurrection that I would meet him again. There were no ghosts, the minister told me – the dead are dead and Catholics are wasting their time saying mass, chanting prayers or giving alms to hasten the soul's passage to Heaven. I didn't believe him. Although I could not feel any presence from my son, Thomas Arden's spirit still haunted me. My visit to Faversham had stirred Arden's restless soul, and Hamnet's death was the result.

I did not tell anyone of these fears, but instead began to question the futility of my life in London. I had achieved fame, fortune and adulation beyond my wildest dreams, but to what purpose? I had all the material goods I ever wanted, enough gold coin to live comfortably for the rest of my life. But with Hamnet's death, I came to realise that life was the only thing that could never be bought, its loss the one thing that could never be replaced. That evening, with the rituals of the funeral behind us, I sat down to discuss the future with Anne.

'Hamnet was eleven years old, Anne. Eleven. And how many days in these years did I spend with him, watching him grow up, seeing him blossom and reach the cusp of manhood? From now on, I will spend more time in Stratford, to rebuild our family life that has been so cruelly shattered. Let me try to compensate for some of the years I have lost.'

Anne agreed. 'We said that if you ever reached Marlowe's tally of six plays, you would have earned enough to make our life in Stratford comfortable. How many plays have you written now, Will?'

'Fourteen. You are right, Anne. It is time to return home.'

That night, I wrote a few words to try to comfort my soul.

> *Grief fills the room up of my absent child,*
> *Lies in his bed, walks up and down with me,*
> *Puts on his pretty looks, repeats his words,*
> *Remembers me of all his gracious parts,*
> *Stuffs out his vacant garments with his form;*
> *Then, have I reason to be fond of grief?*
> *Fare you well: had you such a loss as I,*
> *I could give better comfort than you do.*
> *I will not keep this form upon my head,*
> *When there is such disorder in my wit.*
> *O Lord! My boy, my fair son!*
> *My life, my joy, my food, my all the world!*

They were the words I had needed for Constance's soliloquy in act three of King John, and I let my grief guide my quill as I poured my anguish on to the page. Then I put away my writing paraphernalia and began to rebuild my life in Stratford; purchasing New Place, on the corner of Chapel Lane and Chapel Street, the most substantial property in the town. I journeyed to London only when required to address some business matter with Richard Burbage, as I was still a sharer in the Lord Chamberlain's company. The rest of the time, I tried to be a good father to Susanna and Judith, a good son to my parents, and, above all, a good husband to Anne.

I occupied my time by restoring New Place to its former glory, and by endeavouring to raise the status of the name of Shakspere in the town. I paid twenty pounds to England's Garter Principal King of Arms, William Dethick, and his West England deputy, William Camden, to secure for my father a Shakspere coat of arms, which would be passed down to his descendants in perpetuity, and with it the title of gentleman, which I would also be allowed to style myself on his death. And, because it had always rankled that my mother's branch of the Arden family had withered away to nothing, I petitioned the Kings of Arms to combine the Shakspere coat of arms with the Arden one, which would allow me to one day call myself William Arden, gent., if I so wished. I had letters patent drafted and, in a moment of conceit, had the arms of the illustrious Park Hall Ardens drawn as the ones to be impaled with the Shakspere ones. The diligent Kings of Arms spotted my deception, and changed the drawing to a sketch of Mother's less-renowned Wilmcote Ardens, to give Father the right to that coat of arms, graciously believing my story that it was a clerical error, a momentary lapse of concentration.

I also tried to buy back my mother's Arden inheritance, with which poverty had forced her to part, but I could not persuade the new owners to sell. Instead, I purchased thirty acres of land on the edge of the Forest of Arden. I told Anne my thoughts of styling myself 'William Arden, gent.' on my father's death, and she smiled kindly on the idea. Perhaps then, the ghost of Thomas Arden would be satisfied.

The improvements to New Place kept me busy after Hamnet's death, and I had scarcely given any thought to the Lord Chamberlain's Men in that time. When they did come back to my attention, it was with sad news indeed. James Burbage, the man who had opened the first playhouse in London, and who had been kind to me ever since my first day in the city, was dead. I wondered how the Lord Chamberlain's Men would survive his passing, and whether Richard would now take over the running of the Theatre and the Curtain in addition to being their main actor. I hurried down to London to find out more.

Richard and I consoled each other in our grief and, once I returned from paying my respects at his father's grave, we met again to discuss the practical matters of how the Lord Chamberlain's Men would survive and even prosper, now that our great leader was gone.

Somewhat tentatively, Richard asked me about my plans. The last six months had been the most time I had ever been away from the city of London, and the longest I had gone without writing a play.

'Do you have a new work in mind?' he asked. 'Everywhere I go, I am pressed to answer when a new Will Shakspere play is to be performed.'

I shook my head. 'If the crowd are waiting for a new Shakspere play, it will be a long wait,' I replied. 'Hamnet's death reminded me that there are more important things in life than being on the stage. I travelled to London to pay my respects to your father, but now I will return to Stratford and my family. I have bought a fine dwelling in the town, but it had fallen into disrepair, and requires much of my attention.'

I gave a half-smile of apology before continuing.

'With the death of my only son, and Anne being forty-three years of age, the Shakspere name will no doubt die out on my passing. I had petitioned for a coat of arms to be granted to my father before Hamnet took ill, and when I was told it was to be granted, I incorporated my mother's name, Arden, into the letters patent. William Arden is the name I will have taken when we next meet, to be forever known as the saviour of the Forest of Arden. If the name of Shakspere is to wither and die on my passing, at least the name of Arden will not. This way, my fortune will be put to good use.'

Burbage could not hide his dismay. 'Will, a madness has descended upon you. What possesses you to care so much for the Arden name?'

'I owe it to my mother to restore the good name of her family. The Arden name has suffered many cruel blows in recent years. Edward Arden of the Park Hall Ardens was unjustly executed for plotting against Queen Elizabeth, and I have never forgotten the heads on the spikes at Southwark when I first came to London. And, as you know, there have been other cruel injustices done to the Arden name that haunt me also. Glorifying that once-proud name will bring me much comfort in my autumn years.'

'Will, it is not the Arden name you should be seeking to glorify, but the name of Shakspere. And you can do that with your plays. Will Shakspere is famous in London. You would lose everything by calling yourself Will Arden.'

'Plays are like the seeds of a dandelion clock, one gust and they are gone. Who wrote many of the great plays of the past? Their names are forgotten, in many cases the plays themselves are lost. But the Forest of Arden, that will endure forever.'

Burbage could not be persuaded. 'Will, you do yourself a disservice. We live in a modern world, and Edward White has published many copies of your plays; they are to be found in all corners of the land. *Romeo and Juliet*, *Midsummer Night's Dream*, *Julius Caesar*, these and many others will be performed long after your passing. Why, some may even still be performed when the grandchildren of your daughters are old enough to attend them. God has given you a talent, Will, a talent that is second to none. Use that to have people cherish your memory. Pick up your quill again and write a play. Then another and another. Let these be your legacy.'

I sighed. 'Your words may be true, dear Richard. But the muse has deserted me. I have not started a new play since Hamnet died. Even if I believed in your bold ideas, I do not now possess the means to follow them.'

Burbage offered me further encouragement. 'You have suffered a terrible tragedy, Will. No father wants to bury their son, and it has taken its toll on you. If you have this obsession with the name Arden, use it to write your next play. Have some hero be called Arden, or have the setting of the play be called the Forest of Arden and make it a mythical paradise, a Garden of Eden transported here on earth. And write a comedy, a fantasy, something to lift you out of your despondency, not some dark and depressive tale which will further foul your mood. You will not regret it.'

Burbage's words stirred something inside me, and I decided to follow his advice. But rather than do my writing late at night in a lonely garret in London, I wrote during the day in Stratford, making a room in New Place my study, and put quill to paper in sunshine, surrounded by my loving family. The result was *As You Like It*, a play that I did set in an earthly paradise called the Forest of Arden, where a young couple seek true romance in an enchanted forest and where love was found on every tree. Thomas Arden's ghost must have been pleased, for the words started to flow freely again. Within two months, the play was ready, and I headed down to London to hand the finished script to Richard Burbage. He flicked through the pages, nodding at some, laughing at others. When he finished, he looked me squarely in the eye.

'Good, Will,' he said, grinning from ear to ear. 'Now go and write another.'

IT HAD BEEN SEVERAL years since I had last been in touch with John Stow and I sent him a cryptic message, telling him that the name of Arden would finally be in a Shakspere play and inviting him to the opening performance. As I stood in the wings watching the play unfold, I saw him with the groundlings, not sitting in the cushioned seat I had arranged. I had never seen a man so distempered with anger, and I realised at once that my joke had backfired. As soon as the play was finished, he pushed through the crowds and left before I could approach him.

I visited him the next day, and took a copy of his magnificent *A Survey of London* with me to have him sign it. It had touched me dearly when I read it. Many still regarded actors as vagabonds, playhouses as places of ill repute, of no higher standing than whorehouses and opium dens. Stow had elevated our standing, describing us as providing respectable entertainment, singling out Burbage's playhouse, the Theatre, with a specific mention in his book, and saying nothing about Philip Henslowe's Rose. I hoped that expressing my gratitude for his generosity of spirit would go at least some way to make amends for any offence I had caused by inviting him to see *As You Like It*.

Stow did tell me that he had felt misled by my invitation to come and see an Arden play, considering it a mischievous prank which dishonoured the memory of the Arden murder.

'I had been elated that you would finally tell the truth about Alice Arden,' he told me, 'and instead I found myself watching some nonsense about a mythical paradise where young couples cavort and women go to free themselves from the oppression of men. I am a serious man, Will Shakspere. Women having freedom from the oppression of men? I will not waste my time with such fantasies.'

'An indulgence on my part, no more,' I replied. 'Merely to honour my mother's name.'

'Times have changed. And now you are famous and a favourite of the Queen. If you were to admit you were the author of the original *Arden of Faversham*, none could stop you from publishing it.'

I could not be convinced. 'What about *Isle of Dogs?* That was a satire about Henry Brooke, Baron Cobham. Not only was the play banned and all copies destroyed, but its authors, Thomas Nashe and Ben Jonson, were punished. They repeated the foolhardy ways of my own youth. I learnt not to offend the high and mighty when I crossed Sir Thomas Lucy. And when I tried to expose Sir Anthony Aucher with the Arden play, it nearly caused me financial ruin. I must say no, dear John.'

We parted on bad terms, and it pained me to see an old friend, one who had given me such strong support, disappointed by my cowardice.

Burbage's encouragement to start writing again had had the desired effect, and I sat in my study in Stratford and wrote play after play. *Troilus and Cressida, Twelfth Night,* and *All's Well That Ends Well* followed each other in quick succession. And it amused me to find that I had a new rival, young Ben Jonson, whose *Isle of Dogs* play had been banned. He was matching me with his productivity, and it was not long before we had a chance to meet. When I found he was the step-son of a bricklayer, and had served his bricklaying apprenticeship before becoming an actor, I immediately warmed to him and promised him my support, offering to make a now rare appearance on stage to act in his play, *Every Man in his Humour.*

Jonson and I became close friends and, although he was only eight years younger than me, I felt like a father figure to him. And he taught me a little about myself. When I asked him one day about the unusual spelling of his surname, he told me it was because it was easier to represent in Greek. I recovered from my surprise that a bricklayer should be aware of such concerns, chiding myself for developing the prejudices that had been shown me all these years ago. But when Jonson and I criticised each other, it was with affection and mutual respect, not envy and malice. Although he could occasionally be a little ponderous, I enjoyed my time with him more than any other man in London.

And having a young rival made me want to write better and better plays, and I was under a lot of pressure from Burbage to have a good one for our next production. In 1597, he had hatched an audacious plan to relocate the Theatre, timber by timber, to a new site for our playhouse in Southwark, south of the Thames and easily accessible by wherry across the river from Bankside, so patrons would no longer have to walk through the lawless fields of Shoreditch. It was to be called the Globe, and would have capacity for three thousand people, a thousand more than the Theatre, and I was one of five members of the company who owned half the shares of the playhouse between us, with Richard Burbage owning the other half. He told me that we needed my best-ever play for the opening night, and I headed off to the St Paul's booksellers to see what I could find to inspire me. In a dusky corner of Andrew Wise's dwelling at the Sign of the Angel in Paternoster Row, I found a chronicle in Latin, *The History of the Danes*, published in the year 1200. I flicked through the various chapters until I came to *The Tale of Amleth*, the story of a rightful prince displaced by his conniving uncle. I had my play. And, with a trick of the letters, I could shift the letter 'h' from the end of Amleth's name to the beginning. Then we would have Hamlet, the other spelling of my son's name. *The Tale of Hamlet* would be the Globe's opening play. Constance's soliloquy in *King John* had been the closest I had ever come to writing a eulogy for my son, but now he would be memorialised at last.

It became my most personal play. Once I had fully translated the Latin text, I realised that the story was of a ghost, telling Hamlet that he, the ghost, had been murdered by Hamlet's uncle, who had evaded detection. Hamlet vowed to avenge the ghost's murder by feigning madness. A chill went down my spine. Had Thomas Arden's ghost come back to taunt me one last time? No matter, I told myself. If I needed to go mad to write the play, at least there would be method in it. By the time I finished, I was emotionally drained, but ecstatic at producing my best work to date.

It was a play I would call simply *Hamlet*.

Chapter Twenty-four

Alice ～ 1551

ALL OF THE guilty pleas having been made, William Marshall walked along the two jurat benches, each man nodding to the words he spoke to them. I turned to look at the crowd again: a sea of faces, each in a paroxysm of rage. All except one. At the end of one of the middle rows, a young man was staring at me, his expression not of rage, but of concern. It affected me more than all the vitriol surrounding me. He seemed troubled, almost as if he cared for me. Who could he be? I was sure I had never seen him before.

The mayor sat on the abbot chair and the four guards thumped their halberds on the floor. The crowd fell silent. Tension hung in the air.

'The accused prisoners, standing before the court, are all adjudged guilty for this most foul deed, the murder of Master Thomas Arden, gent., and for the debased morals that led to this cowardly act. And now this Court will pronounce sentence on the felons all. The accused, having been tried and condemned, are now adjudged to die in diverse places by diverse means, to act as foul examples to all men, lest others be tempted to transgress God's Holy Law. The accused Alice Arden is found guilty of petty treason and is to be burned on Canterbury Hill.'

A huge cheer went up. Burned? As a child I was told that was the cruellest of deaths, reserved only for witches and those who were heretics. Burned? Surely someone would have pity on me? Did I have a friend who could slip me some ratsbane before the evil day? The truth came like a punch in my stomach. I did not.

When the cheer subsided, Marshall continued.

'Tom Mosby and Cislye Pounder, you are found guilty of murder and you will be hanged in Smithfield in London.'

A groan went through the crowd at having been denied a local execution.

'Michael Saunderson and Elisabeth Stafford, as servants of Thomas Arden, you are found guilty of petty treason. Michael Saunderson, you will be drawn and hanged in chains, Elisabeth Stafford you will be burned at the stake, both within the boundaries of Faversham.'

A cheer to equal mine, as two gruesome deaths could be had without the inconvenience of a day's ride to Canterbury. Marshall didn't wait for silence before he started speaking again, shouting over the noise of the crowd.

'The other accused who have yet to be brought to justice, namely, John Greene, tailor; William Blackbourne, painter; the masterless man known as Black Will – these men are hereby adjudged guilty in their absence, their sentences to be meted out when they are apprehended.'

With the sentences handed out, Marshall stood up to signal proceedings were at a close. He delivered his final words to us.

'May God have mercy on your souls.'

I admired the cunning of the sentences. Executions in London as a warning to the inhabitants of that great city, and to ensure word of the punishments travelled the length and breadth of the country. Two put to death in Faversham, to satisfy the blood lust of the locals. And I would meet my death in Canterbury, so a great show could be organised for gawkers to travel from all over Kent to witness my end. We were pulled to our feet and led out of the Guildhall, the journey painfully slow as Elisabeth could not be persuaded to rise from the floor and had to be dragged along in the chains holding us together. Every mouth screamed abuse, every fist was shaken in our faces. Except for that one young man. His features were composed, and, as I passed him, he made the sign of the cross to me. I nodded my gratitude.

I still could not take in what had happened, and, as I sat in my cell in the prison next to the Guildhall that night, I rocked back and forth, wondering again and again how it had come to this, and how we all could be so foolish as to be caught so easily. My only solace was that Elisabeth had been taken away and locked in the dungeon under the Guildhall, so the jailers would not be disturbed by her wailing. I should have felt pity for her, but my heart was empty. I could not even feel pity for myself.

There was the jangling of keys and I looked up as my cell door was unlocked. What further torture was I to be subjected to? To my surprise, it was the stranger who had been watching me so intently in the courtroom. He introduced himself as Robert Cole, and told me he was a priest who had been living in the town this last year. I expressed my surprise, as Clement Norton was the priest of our church, and I was unaware that there was another man of God in our midst.

'Reverend Norton is a good man and true, but he has joined in the outrage against you and your fellow conspirators,' Cole told me. 'He has said that your sins are so great, it would be blasphemy for any priest to visit you.' He sighed. 'I would like to believe that deep in his heart he knows this to be wrong, but he fears for his safety were he to pray with you.'

I could not bring myself to believe how much I was despised by the townsfolk. I was certain that no-one – not my family, not those I once counted as friends in Faversham – would come to visit me during my last few days before being taken to Canterbury. To know that I had been rejected by God only added to my torment.

'If it is as you say, then I am doomed to eternal damnation,' I said, lowering my head. 'I am abandoned by all in my time of need.' I straightened myself up. 'If this be so, then I will go to my end with dignity. That is all that is left for me.'

'Brave words, Alice Arden,' Cole replied. 'But fear not, I will pray with you. The crime you have committed is wicked beyond measure, but it is for God to pass judgment on your sins.'

I could not believe that I had been granted this small grain of compassion and my thanks for his kindness stumbled out.

'Make clean your heart, and tell me all that transpired that led you to commit these mortal sins,' Cole commanded me. 'Spare no detail, no matter how painful it is to speak of. Then, in God's court in Heaven, you can plead more virtuously for His mercy in the afterlife, and not suffer the pangs of Hell and the damnation of eternity. It is your only chance of redemption.'

I took him through the whole sordid tale. The only bitterness I allowed myself to show was to remonstrate that John

Greene had played Tom Mosby and me for fools. His hatred of Thomas Arden had been assuaged by my husband's killing but, unlike the rest of us, he had put careful plans in place to avoid being apprehended afterwards. I was surprised that he had the means and opportunity to disappear so successfully, and did wonder if his master, Sir Anthony Aucher, had played some part in aiding his flight, but I kept that conjecture to myself. I could not believe that a man from such a noble family could have had any part in this wickedness.

As he was making ready to leave, I asked him more about his own situation.

'I have to earn my keep by doing honest hard labour for any who require it,' Cole replied. 'For the truth is, I have no parish because my views are at odds with the conservative beliefs that are most prevalent in Kent. I am a freewiller. I believe that grace is given freely by God, without entitlement or merit. Reverend Norton believes that rich men can buy their way into Heaven by making generous donations to the church, and dissuades me at every turn from saying otherwise. Were it not for my family, I would not have stayed long in this town when I found how much hostility I would face. The Bishop of Rochester, John Ponet, has counselled me to bide my time, that change is in the air and more radical views may soon find favour again, but I am not a patient man. If I am not granted a parish soon, then I will head off to London, to do what I can to save souls there.'

I blinked in astonishment. 'But if your situation in Faversham is so precarious, what do you have to gain by helping me?' I asked. 'Surely all will be of the same mind as Reverend Norton, that I am beyond redemption and should not be indulged with any act of kindness or compassion? Is that not the truth?'

'The truth indeed,' replied Cole. 'But a man of God does not choose which battles he will fight and which he will not, what sinner he will comfort and whom he will ignore. I have to do God's work, no matter what revulsion I feel. Make no mistake, Alice Arden, I find no justification for your actions in what you have told me. Thomas Arden may not have been a loving husband to you, but that does not excuse your crimes. I will attend to your spiritual needs, because my calling tells me I must do so. But do not think I condone your behaviour in any way.'

I blushed with shame.

I ATE THIN PORRIDGE twice a day, as I sat in my prison cell waiting for the date of my execution. I received no other visitors and, when it came time to move me to Canterbury, I was flung into a locked wagon in the dead of night, so that my departure would go unheralded and no commotion would ensue. I was taken to the dungeon in the city's castle, where I would spend the last two days before my execution. The drip, drip, drip of moisture down the dungeon walls felt like a clock ticking down the last few hours of my life. I lay there shaking and shuddering, jumping at any sudden sound. I wanted to plead with the guards to save my life, to look the other way and help me escape, but I kept strong and did not demean myself. That was all I had left, I kept telling myself. My dignity.

Robert Cole came to see me on the eve of my execution as promised. He told me he had written an account of the murder, which he had lodged with Edward White, a London publisher, so that my story could be told and no other woman would be tempted to go down the path I had taken. The other reason he had travelled to London, he told me, was to seek out a parish. As he had expected, even the little succour and support he had given me had led to much vitriol from the people of Faversham, and rocks had been flung at him in the street and his family threatened. I was in awe at the bravery and selflessness of a man who would put himself in danger and be so much reviled, simply for doing God's work.

I told Cole that I knew what I had done was evil, and that my execution would be just punishment for my sins, but that I hoped I would meet my death with grace and that it would be over quickly. The priest averted his eyes as he held my hands in his to bestow upon me a final blessing. He told me he would be present when I met my end, and would be accompanied by John Ponet, who was attending as an esteemed observer from the church. Cole said he would try to persuade Bishop Ponet to say a prayer on my behalf, and it gave me great comfort that a man so powerful as he might speak to God about me, giving me some small hope of salvation, to escape the fires of eternal damnation. Then the guards called for Cole to leave and, as the cell door slammed shut, I closed my eyes to try to find some peace in my last hours on earth.

But that proved to be impossible. A large crowd gathered outside my cell, all riotously drunk, screaming abuse at me through the bars. I curled into a ball and covered my ears to block out the terrible things shouted. Surely, it would stop soon; the jailers would not permit such disorder to go on for too long. But what was happening made no sense. A crowd would not be allowed into the jail on the eve of an execution, unless it had been sanctioned by a magistrate. But why would a judge allow such an unruly occurrence? The jeers got louder, the crowd grew bigger, the noise turned from shouts of anger and hatred to an evil cackling. Then a huge cheer went up, and I heard the jangling of keys over the guffaws and laughs of the mob. I uncurled a little and saw the men jostling for position, each trying to be first in line behind my cell door. Their eyes were crazed, frenzied, but the one at the front had a look of triumph. He was a mountain of a man, who by his own brute strength had pushed himself to the front of the mob. The cell door opened and he stepped inside, to shouts of encouragement from the others. Was I to be despatched here and now, not waiting until the morrow? If so, I was ready.

He came over and leered at me, and ripped my dress from my body. Only then did I know what was about to happen.

Behind him, the others were making ready.

Chapter Twenty-five
Will ~ 1605

THERE WAS ONE last chapter to the Arden story, when I had a final meeting with John Stow as he was nearing the end of his life. The preceding years had not been happy ones between us; we never met again after our acrimonious discussion about revisiting *Arden of Faversham* and, when Stow's next edition of *A Survey of London* was published, all mentions of London playhouses were removed from the text, an act of petty vengeance that hurt me deeply. But now I heard that Stow was ill, so I had no hesitation in paying him a visit.

I was shocked at his circumstances. John Stow had never been a rich man, but now he was living in poverty, relying on the charity of those who held him in deep respect to save him from destitution. We talked for a while about everything, everybody; anything but the Arden murder. Finally, Stow raised the subject that had caused such division between us.

'I am reaching the end of my life, Will, growing old as the world does. My body is fading away, just as the memories of Alice Arden have faded. One day, not long from now, her name will evoke no sense of outrage, no claim that she is evil personified, no certainty that she deserved every blow laid against her. That is my dilemma. Do I finally publish the full account of her crime so that the world will one day reconsider its view of the murder of Thomas Arden, or should Alice Arden's soul be left in peace, to find some comfort in anonymity?'

I spoke in a soothing tone. 'John, you are an old man. Do not burden yourself with these troubles any longer.'

Stow ignored me and continued. 'I have tried twice now to use your plays to tell the truth about the murder, and the part played by Sir Anthony Aucher. I see now that was foolish and cowardly of me. If I want the story to be told, then I should be the one to tell it. My printer tells me that the copies of my *Annales of England* have almost sold out, and a new edition is to be printed next month. I have written a foreword for this new edition, stating that in my revised *Summarie of Englyshe Chronicles* to follow, I will include more historical events than the previous one. That is where I will tell the real story of Alice Arden. It will be too late for any consequences. My death is nigh, and in any case, what would they do to an old man of eighty years? I am one of the oldest men in London.'

'You have many years left yet,' I assured him. 'But do not think that death will allow you to cheat Sir Anthony's supporters of their revenge. Your legacy is a great one, and I know many noble men plan to make sure it is cherished forever. But if your name becomes a byword for scandal and malicious gossip, then that eternal fame is put in jeopardy. Do not risk all you have achieved in your lifetime for this one lost cause.'

Stow shook his head. 'My mind is made up, Will. Here, allow me to show you what I will do.' He produced his original manuscript detailing the Arden murder, *The History of a Moste Horrible Murder Commytyd at Fevershame in Kente.*

'This is the account I wrote many years ago, describing the Arden murder, which I lent to you, and which Holinshed used for his description of events.' He reached behind his desk and turned the carving to reveal the hidden compartment he had shown me so many years before. He removed the document inside.

'And this is Robert Cole's transcript of John Greene's confession that I showed you once before, where he names Sir Anthony Aucher as the mastermind behind the plot. I am going to rewrite *The History of a Moste Horrible Murder Commytyd at Fevershame in Kente* to include all these details, and publish it in my expanded *Summarie*. The truth will finally be told.'

He grabbed my arm, using all his strength to hold it in a vice-like grip. 'Will, when I am gone, arrange this for me. Protect the Greene confession so that it can be made public, and arrange to have its contents secretly printed as a pamphlet and distributed across the city when my new *Summarie of Englyshe Chronicles* is published with the Aucher story in it. There are many anonymously printed pamphlets disseminated this way, and their authors are rarely identified. Grant me this last wish.'

I looked at him in pity. 'What is it, John, that troubles you so much about this murder? Why have you spent forty years fighting to have the story told? Alice Arden was a murderess, of that there is no doubt, and she gave her account of the crime freely and without torture. She deserved to die, as did her other conspirators. Yes, Sir Anthony Aucher remained free and was buried an innocent man. But why this obsession? Why does Alice Arden deserve saving after all this time? A self-confessed killer.'

Stow lifted himself out of his chair, and then stood for a moment, exhausted by the effort. He shuffled over to a bookshelf, lifted a book and brought it back to me. I glanced at the cover: *A Short Treatise of Political Power*, by John Ponet. I knew the name; he had been Bishop of Rochester at the time of the Arden murder, and I had heard of the book, but I could not see the connection between something Ponet had written in exile on the source and limits of political power, and the Arden murder. Stow opened it at a bookmark and fixed his gaze on me.

'Do you remember in my description of Alice's execution, I described not only that Robert Cole had given me an account of the murder and attended Alice's execution, but also that there was another esteemed observer there on the day?'

He paused to recover his breath, and I searched my mind to recall the words. 'As you say this, yes, I remember it from your manuscript. Written in Latin, was it not?'

Stow nodded.

'So, who was the second man?'

'The same John Ponet. As Bishop of Rochester, he was Coles's superior and accompanied him to the execution after Cole had prayed with Alice the night before.' Stow laid the book down before continuing. 'In his book, *A Short Treatise of Political Power*, published in 1556, he told the story of how, in 595 AD, a German king, Cacanus, killed an Italian duke and besieged his city. The duke's widow, Romilda, saw Cacanus and fell in love with him, her husband's murderer. She begged Cacanus to bed her, so she could enjoy the sick thrill of fornicating with a man she should despise. Cacanus did so out of expediency, to avoid her rallying her husband's troops against him, even though he felt nothing but contempt for her. But Cacanus vowed that Romilda would pay for her callous lechery.'

He paused again to regain his strength, and I must admit, I thought his mind had gone feeble, recounting this thousand-year-old tale from a distant land that had nothing to do with the Arden murder.

'And this was the punishment Cacanus meted out. It disgusts me so much, I cannot say it aloud. Here, read for yourself.'

He handed me the book, and I read the paragraph at which he was pointing. I wished I had not.

> In the next morning, Cacanus leaveth his chamber
> and left the gates open free to every man; and (as some
> did to the wicked woman in Faversham in Kent that
> not long since killed her husband) he gave every man
> liberty that would want to offer his devotion into her
> corporal body. So at length when he thought her tired
> and her insatiable lust somewhat staunched (for like
> it would never have been fully gutted), he caused her
> to be thrust on a stake naked, so that she should be an
> example to others.

I closed the book in horror. There was silence in the room before Stow finally spoke again.

'You see? Ponet was describing an act of barbarism committed a thousand years ago when people were savages, but in the process tells us that Alice Arden was subjected to the same brutal judicially approved rape the night before her execution. Something that could only have happened if those in authority opened the gates of Canterbury jail and sanctioned that any man who so desired could also satisfy his lust. Ponet was in Canterbury for Alice's execution, we know that from Cole. As a senior bishop, he would be told what had transpired in the jail the night before; he may even have been party to the decision. This atrocity happened to Alice Arden, Will. In our land, in our time. That is why I have fought to have the truth told about the murder. Yes, Alice played her part. But no woman should suffer thus, no matter how evil the crime. Especially when the real instigator of the crime went unpunished.'

Now, I realised. It was not the ghost of Thomas Arden I had felt that day I visited Faversham, it was the ghost of Alice Arden. Alice was the one who needed to be avenged for the dark deeds of fifty years ago.

I had no choice.

'This is a terrible tale you have told me, John. These men's actions bring shame on all of us. I see now that Alice Arden needs to be avenged. Once your new *Summarie of Englyshe Chronicles* is published, I will do as you wish, whatever the consequences.'

THE NEW EDITION OF Stow's *Annals of England* was published on March 26th, 1605, and, true to his word, there was Stow's declaration that an expanded *Summarie of Englyshe Chronicles* would follow shortly. The wheels had been put into motion to expose Sir Anthony Aucher. But events came to a head much sooner than I anticipated. On April 5th, ten days after the new edition of *Annals of England* was published, John Stow died.

I needed Richard Burbage's help in fulfilling Stow's last request, as only he would know where I could find a printer who would produce the pamphlet in such secrecy that there was no danger of being caught. I finally told him that it was John Stow I had sought out when trying to write *Arden of Faversham*. I told him of the kind help and support that he had given me, and of how I had spurned him not once, but twice, in his attempt to use my writing and then my fame to tell the truth about Alice Arden. And how finally, in his dying days, he had asked me to publish anonymously the secret papers he had kept in a hidden drawer in the desk in his study, proving the case that Alice Arden was wrongly accused of being the sole instigator of the plot to murder her husband.

And so,' I concluded, 'I feel obligated to honour his final dying wish, to have these papers published. I could surely do that, without harm to myself. What say you, Richard?'

Burbage blew a noisy breath. 'Will, why make such a stir? The murder was more than fifty years ago, and with every year it fades from memory. I think you would do yourself great harm to be associated with this. With the old queen dead, we have now been granted the honour of being named the King's Men, and there is talk of King James granting you a knighthood. John Stow was a great man, but his mind had become addled with age. It must be so, for no rational man would risk so much to achieve so little. You are much more sensible on these matters. Forget Alice Arden.'

But I could not fail my old friend a third time. I promised Burbage I would sleep on this matter before taking it further, but my mind was made up. Whatever the risk, I would grant Stow his last wish.

The next day, I headed off to Stow's house to retrieve the papers. I arrived to find his widow, Elisabeth, distraught.

'It is Master Will Shakspere, is it not?' she said to me when I was shown into her presence. 'My husband has spoken of you many times, and it is so inopportune that we should finally meet at such a terrible time. Please excuse my demeanour, but I am beside myself with anguish. My husband is not yet in his grave and already his study has been desecrated, his desk vandalised and his papers stolen. Who could be so cruel as to have done such a thing?'

I took in these words with a sickening dread.

'Shocking news, Mistress Stow. Can I see the disorder of which you speak?'

She led me to the study and my worst fears were realised. The secret drawer had been prised open, its contents emptied. Everything else was untouched, but for a few papers strewn around the room.

'Pray tell me, what has been taken?' I asked her. But I already knew the answer.

'Pages from John's only manuscript of his new *Summarie of Englyshe Chronicles*,' she replied. 'The last thing he was working on before he died. And whatever was in that secret drawer. How could anyone be so heartless?'

I made my departure as soon as was seemly, and in a fury headed off to confront Richard Burbage, cursing my stupidity at revealing my knowledge of the desk's secret compartment to him.

Of course, he denied everything. 'I tell you, Will, I had no part in this despicable act and the distress it has caused to Elisabeth Stow. Let us inform the city wardens of this crime. They may still track down the guilty men and retrieve what is lost.'

'Do not take me for a fool, Burbage,' I replied, glaring at him. 'I know this is your doing, to save the reputation of our company if I became immersed in scandal. No doubt you have already destroyed all that you have taken. Well, no matter. I know the truth. I will rewrite *Arden of Faversham* and announce that I am the author, and we will give it a gala performance. I will not betray the trust that John Stow placed in me.'

I could barely contain my anger as Burbage tried to persuade me otherwise. His arguments struck me, blow by blow. I was the only one now alive who knew the whole truth. There was not a single piece of evidence still in existence that backed up my claim. The current Anthony Aucher was a powerful man, and would have me arrested if I dared to perform the play. And the Globe would be closed for allowing me to do so.

I refused to listen. I owed it to John Stow. I owed it to Alice Arden.

It was Ben Jonson who finally convinced me to desist.

'I was a young actor with the Admiral's Men in 1597,' he reminded me. 'And was much enamoured by Thomas Nashe's flair for courting controversy and mocking people. He entreated me to write *The Isle of Dogs* with him: me the son of a bricklayer, he a great writer who had already written a play with Kit Marlowe. I was flattered. *The Isle of Dogs* was an amusing piece, poking fun at Henry Brooke, Baron Cobham, but the Privy Council were not amused. I was thrown in Marshalsea Prison, and tortured for my impudence. The charges that you wish to lay at the feet of a nobleman in your play are much more serious than the ones I made. I urge you, Will, let cool heads prevail. Find some other way to repay your debt to John Stow.'

Eventually, I saw the sense in his words. John Stow had died penniless, but he deserved to be remembered. I visited Elisabeth Stow again, and asked if she would consider allowing a memorial to be produced in his honour, which I would be happy to arrange as long as no mention was made of my patronage, as I did not want my involvement to over-shadow the great man. She graciously agreed and secured approval from St Andrew Undershaft, the church next to Stow's home, that it should be the memorial's location. I commissioned the greatest sculptor in the land, Nicholas Johnson, to produce a sculpture of Stow, insisting that he be sitting at his desk, writing his lost *Summarie of Englyshe Chronicles* – a fitting tribute to his final wishes.

It was my duty to produce the words for an inscription that would be carved above him, something that would endure forever, to remind the world of his quest for truth. In the end I chose not my own words, but an epigram by Pliny the Younger: *Aut scribenda agere, aut legenda scribere;* 'Either do things worth writing, or write things worth reading.' It summed up the man perfectly.

I visited the church to see the memorial when it was put in place and was most struck by it, a fine likeness carved in Derbyshire marble and alabaster. I contacted Nicholas Johnson again, and asked him to produce a similar likeness for my own memorial, which I would sit for and he would carve while I was still alive, so I could have some small chance of being remembered after I was gone. I was pleased with the final result. I was seated in exactly the same pose as Stow, as if we were brothers. I hoped that paid my debt to him.

All of these events had me thinking of my own mortality, and when I went back to writing plays, I returned to Holinshed's *Chronicles* for inspiration. The results were *King Lear* and *Macbeth*. *King Lear* was about an aged monarch, dividing his kingdom between his daughters, as I will have to do one day with my own estate. And *Macbeth* brought home to me again that for all my efforts to secure a Shakspere coat of arms and commission a monument in Stratford, the loss of my only son meant that the Shakspere name would end and be soon forgotten after my death. *'Upon my head they placed a fruitless crown, and put a barren sceptre in my grip,'* I had Macbeth say. The same could be said of me.

I wrote a number of plays in the years that followed, visiting London less often. When I did, I stayed with a Huguenot family in Silver Street, well away from the play-houses. After *The Tempest* was performed in 1610, I rarely visited the city again, but when I did, I always made a point of seeing Ben Jonson, and it was with him I shared my fears that all I had achieved would one day be for nothing.

'Thomas Watson was the first of the University Wits to welcome me in London,' I told him. 'He was a great writer, who is now all but forgotten and none of his plays survive. We collaborated on my *Henry VI,* but now only my name is remembered. The public is a fickle mistress, it is you and your *Bartholomew Fayre* they talk of now, and I fade into the shadows with every passing day. But good luck to you, Ben Jonson. You are my worthy successor.'

'You are wrong, Will, your plays will live forever.'

I hoped he was right. And also, that one day some scrap of paper would be found, that someone would come along, to tell the truth of the Arden murder.

That one day, the true story of Alice Arden would be written.

CHRONOLOGY OF RECORDED
HISTORICAL EVENTS

1537 Thomas Arden marries Alice Brigandine and becomes Sir Edward North's man.

1540 Thomas moves to Faversham, becomes customs collector and also becomes Sir Thomas Cheyne's man.

1541 Thomas starts buying land from the dissolution of the monasteries.

1542 John Greene buys his freedom and becomes Anthony Aucher's man.

1543 Thomas is elected one of Faversham's twenty-four common councillors. He cheats Greene out of his family's land.

1544 Thomas is offered a fee of twenty pounds to secure a new charter of incorporation for Faversham. He sells land to Anthony Aucher for a fixed fee and twenty marks a year for life.

1547 Anthony Aucher is knighted.

1548 Thomas becomes Faversham's mayor.

1549 Aucher meets a representative of the Privy Council. He finally starts paying the twenty marks a year from his property purchase to Thomas and Alice.

1550 Thomas moves the St Valentine's Fayre to the abbey ground he owns. He and Thomas Dunkyn are disenfranchised.

1551 Thomas Arden is murdered. Alice, Tom Mosby, Michael Saunderson, Cislye Pounder and Elisabeth Stafford are executed.

1552 Greene is executed. Robert Cole flees Faversham in fear of his life. Black Will is arrested and burned on a scaffold. William Blackbourne is arrested and hung in chains until he dies of starvation.

1556 Bishop Ponet publishes *A Short Treatise of Political Power*. Aucher is disgraced because of financial irregularities. He is forced to pay back £4,500 to the crown and has to resign as Keeper of the Jewel House.

1558 Cole becomes rector of St Mary le Bow church in London. Aucher dies.

1564 William Shakespeare is born.

1569 John Stow's house is searched by Bishop Grindal.

1573 Stow acquires publisher Reginald Wolfe's books.

1574 Stow writes *The History of a Moste Horrible Murder Commytyd at Fevershame in Kente*.

1576 Cole dies.

1587 John Towne of the Queen's Men kills William Knell in Thame, near Stratford. The second edition of Holinshed's *Chronicles* is published, describing the Arden murder.

1591 Lord Strange's troupe visits Faversham. Later that year, *Arden of Faversham* is performed by Pembroke's Men.

1592 *Arden of Faversham* is entered into the Stationers' Company Register. *Henry VI* is performed and

Shakespeare becomes famous. London playhouses are closed because of the plague.

1594 The playhouses reopen. Shakespeare joins the Lord Chamberlain's Men.

1596 Shakespeare visits Faversham. Ten days later, his son, Hamnet, dies.

1597 Shakespeare buys New Place in Stratford-upon-Avon.

1599 The Globe opens. The Shakespeare family are granted a coat of arms.

1605 Stow's final edition of *Annals of England* is published. He dies eight days later.

1611 Shakespeare retires.

THANK YOU

Thank you for reading *Arden*. If you enjoyed the story, you might also be interested in my previous novel, *The Maids of Biddenden,* the imagined biography of real-life 12th-century conjoined twins born to a wealthy family from the village of Biddenden in Kent. My other novels, *Love's Long Road*, *Silent Money* and *A Friend in Deed,* are psychological thrillers. The first two are crime thrillers set in 1970s Glasgow, the third is a political thriller set in 2020s London.

If you have any questions or comments on *Arden*, I'd love to hear from you. My email address is gdharper@gdharper.com and you can follow me on Instagram: @gdharperauthor.

Best wishes,
GD Harper

ACKNOWLEDGEMENTS

My thanks go to the experts who have provided me with assistance in the writing of this novel and the authors of my source material.

Insights into the Arden murder and transcripts of related historical documents: *Thomas Arden In Faversham: The Man Behind the Myth* by Patricia Hyde. This book is dedicated to her memory.

Insights into *Arden of Faversham:* Professor Catherine Richardson's foreword to the 2022 Arden Shakespeare edition of *Arden of Faversham,* edited by Professor Richardson. The Arden Shakespeare have been publishing scholarly editions of Shakespeare's works since 1899, just one of the many Arden connections to Shakespeare that survive to the present day. I am also deeply indebted to Professor Richardson for being so generous with her time and helping me with corrections and suggestions for improvements to the draft manuscript. However, any errors and omissions that remain are solely my responsibility.

Details of James Burbage's playhouses: Heather Knight, an archaeologist who specialises in the archaeology of London's sixteenth and seventeenth century playhouses, and who led the excavation on the sites of the Theatre and the Curtain playhouses. Once again, any errors and omissions that remain are solely my responsibility.

Procedure and pronouncements of the Thomas Arden murder trial: *Feversham* by Dianne Davidson.

Information on Sir Anthony Aucher: 'Anthony Aucher – Entrepreneur and Creative Accountant', *The Dover Historian*.

Information on William Shakespeare's life and work: *Shakespeare The Biography* by Peter Ackroyd; *Shakespeare: An Ungentle Life* by Katherine Duncan-Jones; *Will in the World* by Stephen Greenblatt; *1599: A Year in the Life of William Shakespeare* by James Shapiro.

Information about life in 16th-century England: *How to be a Tudor* by Ruth Goodman; *The Time Traveller's Guide to Elizabethan England* by Ian Mortimer; *Shakespeare's London* by Stephen Porter.

Description of the London plague and the charnel house scene: *The Wonderfull Yeare* by Thomas Decker, a playwright for the Admiral's Men.

I would like to record my gratitude to Faversham Town Council, who gave me unfettered access to the Faversham wardmote book during the writing of this novel and generously allowed me to use their images of the Faversham charter and moot horn.

Thanks also to Elena Kravchenko for her support and encouragement, and to Leigh Allison, Clare Hatherill and Marquise for their feedback on the first draft of this novel. Thanks too to my editing and production team: editors Debi Alper and Michael Faulkner, proofreader Alison Jack, typesetter Michael Campbell at MC Writing Services, cover designer Stefan Proudfoot at Spiffing Publishing, and mapmaker Robyn Kinsman-Blake.

And, finally, thanks as always to Agnes, for her loving support and her patience in having to put up with me writing this book.

THE STORY OF *ARDEN*

I visited Canterbury in October 2021, as part of the research for my previous novel, *The Maids of Biddenden*, wanting to follow the route that Mary and Eliza took when they first visited the city. I came across the Chaucer Bookshop on the Watling Street Roman road to London, which, although I did not know it then, started at the bookshop, went northwest through Faversham and on to London where it passed Robert Cole's church, and also St Paul's Cathedral, near where Shakespeare would have purchased his copy of Holinshed's *Chronicles*, to end along the boundary of the northern edge of the Forest of Arden, finishing at the forest's northwest corner, like a physical strand tying all elements of the book together.

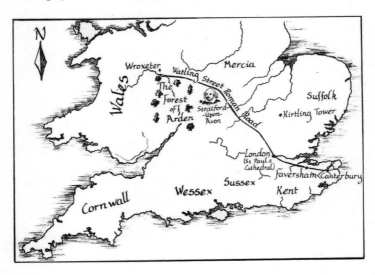

On a whim, I popped into the bookshop for a look. Perusing the Kent History shelves looking for more information on the medieval conjoined twins known as the Biddenden Maids, I came across Patricia Hyde's *Thomas Arden: The Man Behind the Myth*, the first full-scale study of the Faversham mayor. I had been looking for a topic for my next historical novel, and so purchased it, and later also tracked down *The Early Town Books of Faversham c. 1251 to 1581*, the Faversham wardmote books which Patricia Hyde and Duncan Harrington had transcribed. These two books provided me with a treasure trove of information and transcripts, and, as I read them, I began to have my suspicions that Sir Anthony Aucher had some involvement in Thomas Arden's murder.

A two-year search of historical documents of the time followed, and I am indebted to the Doddington Parochial Library in Faversham, the British Library and the Stationers' Company for allowing me generous access to many of the original documents and manuscripts quoted in this book.

With the exception of the Aucher conspiracy, the details of the Arden murder follow the descriptions in Holinshed's second edition of *Chronicles of England, Scotland and Ireland*, published in 1587, and John Stow's manuscript, *The History of a Moste Horrible Murder Commytyd at Fevershame in Kente*. Robert Cole's account of the trial is unfortunately lost and, as I said in the introduction to the novel, John Greene's confession is fiction, a literary device I used to bring the Aucher conspiracy to life.

Holinshed starts his account by describing Thomas and Alice.

There dwelt at Faversham in the county of Kent a
gentleman called Master Arden; a decent gentleman,
and of a comely personage. This Master Arden married
a well-favoured young gentlewoman who was Sir
Edward North's wife's daughter; young, tall and well-
favoured of shape and countenance.

Kirtling Tower, where Alice first met Tom Mosby and
Thomas Arden, dates from 1219. Sir Edward rebuilt the
castle in the 1540s using the funds from Alice's mother's
Mirfyn estate. Its beautiful gardens are occasionally open
to the public.

Stow picks up the story with his description of the
Widow Cook incident, when Alice has her first concerns
about Thomas's ruthless business style. He writes:

This field Arden had taken by extortion from Cook's
widow and given her nothing for it, for which she did
not only shed many a tear, but also cursed the same
Arden to his face continually and in every place where
she was praying that a vengeance and plague might
light upon him and that all the world might wonder
over him, and could never be otherwise persuaded till
God had suffered him to come to his end.

Stow also first mentions Anthony Aucher when describing
the property dispute with John Greene, when he writes as
follows:

One Greene of Faversham, who was one of Sir
Anthony Aucher's servants, and Master Arden had

*extorted a piece of ground from him on the back side
of the abbey, and there had been blows passed between
them and great threatenings.*

The Faversham Borough Records also bring Aucher into
the story in 1544:

*This is the agreement made in the halimote court held
at Faversham between Anthony Aucher and Thomas
Arden and his wife Alice regarding two properties,
one called the George and the other called the Garret.
Thomas and Alice Arden have recognised the aforesaid
properties to belong to Anthony Aucher. And for this
agreement Anthony Aucher has given the same Thomas
and Alice Arden twenty-three pounds six shillings and
eight pence of silver.*

It was four years later, on February 8th 1548, that the Privy
Council wrote a letter to Thomas Arden, by then the mayor
of Faversham, saying as follows:

*The Privy Council orders the sending to the Lords one
Ashehurst, to answer to the things objected to him in the
letter of Sir Anthony Aucher of the 5th of this present
month.*

And then in the *List of Deeds of Master Arden's Evidences
Searched, Faversham Borough Records* contained in the Harley
Manuscript Collection in the British Library, the property
deal between Aucher and Arden is further described as
containing this clause:

Master Aucher will deed to Master Arden and his wife twenty marks by year for term of these lives and longer liver.

When Thomas became mayor in 1548, it was duly noted in the wardmote book of that year:

Thomas Arden, chief controller of the king's majesty custom here was chosen mayor the 26th day of March 1548, in the second year of the reign of Edward VI, God king of England, France and Ireland, defender of the faith.

His ambitious but extravagant plans to improve the town are well documented, giving a fascinating glimpse of everyday life in the sixteenth century and what mattered to the people of the town. Here are some examples:

Statutes for Making Laws Within the Towne of Faversham. In the 2nd year of Edward VI by the true hand of Thomas Arden, then mayor.

An Act for paving West Street, Preston Street and Key Lane in the town of Faversham.

The Mayor ordered, from henceforth forever, that the street called West Street shall be paved both sides from West Broke Cross to the tenement of Goody Princhett in East Street.

An Act for hogs and swine

And furthermore, it is ordered by the said mayor that if
any hogs and swine do go abroad in any street within
the town of Faversham not having the proper mark of
the owner, then that owner shall lose and forfeit to him
or them that will impound them. And if any owners
of such hogs and swine happen to be obstinate and not
pay the said forfeit, then upon complaint to the mayor,
the mayor will make speedy order that it be paid. And
upon refusal of the payment thereof, the mayor will
have full power and authority to commit such offenders
to jail, there to remain until the said complaint be fully
answered and paid.

The charter of King Henry VIII was granted to the town
of Faversham in 1546, negotiated by Thomas Arden and
signed by him, and contains this clause:

ALSO henceforth a fayre or fayres every year forever
on the feast of St Valentine to endure for seven days and
held in such convenient place within the said town of
Faversham as the mayor shall assign by proclamation
where the fayre be held.

Stow then reveals in his manuscript how Arden used this
to his own advantage:

The fayre was to be kept partly in the town and partly
in the abbey, but Arden for his own lucre had in this
present year brought it to be wholly kept within the
abbey ground which he had purchased, so that all the

gains came to him and none to the townspeople, for
which deed he had many a curse.

The implied explanation in the novel for Thomas's lack of desire for Alice, that he was gay and in a loving homosexual relationship with Thomas Dunkyn, hiding this in plain sight both from the Faversham community and from Alice and Mosby, was speculation on my part. Had anyone suspected or discovered this, Thomas would have been imprisoned and it would have been a much easier way for his enemies to bring him down.

Dunkyn is named Franklin in the play *Arden of Faversham*, and there is this exchange in Arden's London lodgings between Arden and Franklin in Act I, Scene IV, with Arden's manservant, Michael Saunderson in attendance:

Arden: What o'clock is't, sirrah?

Michael: Almost ten.

Arden: See, how runs away the weary time! Come, Master Franklin, shall we go to bed?

Franklin: I pray you go before; I'll follow you.

Michael and Arden then leave and Franklin delivers a soliloquy to the audience before Michael returns and speaks to Franklin:

Michael: My master would desire you to come to bed.

Franklin: Is he himself already in bed?

Michael: He is, and fain would have the light away.

It is fair to say that a modern audience's interpretation of this scene would have been somewhat different to that of an audience in Shakespeare's time.

Arden decided to make his will just under two months before he was killed, and it is unclear how much Alice had a hand in this decision. It was recorded in the wardmote book and is remarkable for the fact that Thomas left a provision for a sermon to be given in perpetuity praising his good name. He signed it two days before he and Dunkyn were disenfranchised, showing that, even at that late stage, he had no idea the trouble he was in.

Master Thomas Arden's Will
The 20th of December 1550

This is the last Will of me Thomas Arden made the day and year abovesaid. First, I stand bound to Sir Edward North in a thousand marks sterling to make my wife a jointure of £40 a year for life and I will that Alice shall have first my house wherein I dwell, the tenement adjoining my cartgate, with the gardens, dovehouse and stable belonging to the same.

And also that the mayor, jurats and commonality of Faversham shall cause yearly in Faversham church for ever upon the day of my burial, a solemn ceremony to be made by the preacher of Christchurch in Canterbury or some other learned man, to be paid £5 for reciting in his sermon my good name, so other goodmen may be provoked to give the like.

And of this my last will, I order and make Alice my said wife to be my executor and Sir Edward North to be my overseer, and for this I give him my best horse.

By me, Thomas Arden in my own hand

Two days later, Arden and Dunkyn were disenfranchised and fifty-five days after that, Thomas Arden was murdered, with both events recorded in the Faversham wardmote book.

Regarding the details of the murder, the first attempt to kill Thomas is described by Holinshed, giving some of the reported dialogue between Thomas and Alice used in the novel:

There was a painter dwelling in Faversham who had skill of poisons. Alice demanded of him whether he had such a skill and he denied not, but that he had indeed. 'That can I do,' said he, and forthwith made her such a one, and willed her to put it into the bottom of a porringer and then after to pour milk on it; which circumstances she did wrongly, putting the milk in first, and afterwards the poison.

Now Master Arden, proposing that day to ride to Canterbury, his wife brought him his breakfast, which was wont to be milk and butter. He, having received a spoonful or two of the milk, misliked the taste and colour thereof, and said to his wife, 'Mistress Alice, what milk have you given me here?' Wherewithall she said, 'There is nothing I can do to please you.' Then Master Arden fell into extreme purging upwards and downwards, and so escaped for that time.

Holinshed then brings Greene back into the picture, naming Anthony Aucher and showing him yet again on the periphery of the crime:

> *Alice Arden fell in acquaintance with one Greene of Faversham, from which Greene Master Arden had wrested a piece of ground on the backside of the Abbey of Faversham. Therefore she, knowing that Greene hated her husband began to practise with him how to make him away, and concluded that if he could get any that would kill him, he should have £10 for a reward. This Greene, having doings for his master, Sir Anthony Aucher, had occasion to go up to London for his master, and desired one Bradshaw, a goldsmith of Faversham that was his neighbour, to accompany him to Gravesend and he would content him for his pains. This Bradshaw, being an honest man, was content and rode with him.*
>
> *In London, Arden being ready to go home, it was agreed that Black Will should kill him on Rainham Down. Master Arden rode on, and ere came at the place where Black Will be lay in wait for him, but there overtook some diverse gentlemen of his acquaintance, who kept him company, so that Black Will missed here his purpose. After that, Master Arden was come home unharmed.*

The location of the Aucher storehouse is revealed by Stow, in his manuscript, when he writes as follows:

> *Then Black Will was lying in Preston where he was kept all that while in a storehouse of Sir Anthony*

Aucher and came Mistress Arden to see him and
brought and sent him meat many times.

When it came to the murder itself, Holinshed spared no
gory details, again giving us the reported dialogue used in
the act itself as Mosby and Thomas played backgammon:

When they came into the parlour, Mosby sat down on
the bench, having his face toward the place where Black
Will hid. In their play, Mosby said thus (which seemed
to be the watch-word for Black Will's coming forth):
'Now may I take you, sir, if I will.'

'Take me?' quoth Master Arden. 'Which way?' With
that, Black Will stepped forth and cast a towel about
his neck, so to stop his breath and strangle him. Then
Mosby, having at his girdle a pressing-iron of fourteen
pounds weight, struck Arden on the head with the
same, so that he fell down and gave a great groan,
insomuch that they thought he had been killed.

Alice and Mosby bare Arden away, and as they were
about to lay him down, the pangs of death coming on
him, he gave a great groan and stretched himself. Black
Will gave him a great gash in the face and so killed him
out of hand, laid him along, took the money out of his
purse and the rings from his fingers.

Then two Londoners came to supper, the one named
Prune and the other Cole, that were grocers, which,
before the murder was committed, were bidden to
supper. When they came Alice said, 'I marvel where
Master Arden is. We will not tarry for him, come ye

and sit down, for he will not be long. He will come anon, I am sure. In the meanwhile, shall we play a game at the tables?'

But the Londoners said they must go to the Fleur de Lis or else they should be shut out at doors, and so, taking their leave, departed. When they were gone, the dead body was carried out to lay in a field next to the churchyard joining to Arden's garden wall, through the which he went to the church.

Holinshed's description of the discovery of the murder gives us yet more dialogue from the crime:

Being now very late, Alice sent forth servants to make enquiry for Arden in different places, namely where in the town where he was wont to be, but all who made answer said that they could tell nothing of him. Then she began to make an outcry, and said, 'No woman had such neighbours as I have,' and herewith wept, insomuch that her neighbours came in and found her making great lamentation, pretending to worry what was become of her husband. Whereupon the mayor and others came to make search for him.

The mayor, going about the fayre in this search, at length came to the ground where Arden lay, and said, 'Stay, for methink I see one lie here.' Looking and beholding the body, they found that it was Master Arden's dead body there, thoroughly dead. Viewing diligently the manner of his body and wounds, they found rushes sticking in his slippers, and, marking further, espied certain footsteps, by reason of the snow, betwixt the place where he lay and the garden door, so it appeared plainly that he was brought along that way from the house through the garden and so into the field where he lay.

The mayor, and his company that were with him, went into the house, and examined Alice of the matter. Alice herself, beholding her husband's blood said, 'Oh, the blood of God help, for this blood have I shed.'

Then were they all attached and committed to prison, and the mayor with others went presently to the Fleur de Lis where they found Mosby in bed. And, as they came towards him, they espied his hose and purse stained with some of Master Arden's blood, and, when he asked what they meant by their coming, they said, 'See, here ye may understand wherefore by these tokens,' showing him the blood on his hose and purse. Then he confessed the deed, and so he and all the other that had conspired the murder were apprehended and laid in prison, except Greene, Black Will, and Blackbourne the painter, who had fled.

The final part of Holinshed's account describes the punishments meted out to the perpetrators:

As for the bloody criminals, they were executed in several places; Michael, Mr Arden's man, was hanged in chains at Faversham, and one of the maid servants was burned there, most bitterly lamenting her condition, and loudly exclaiming against her

mistress who had brought her to that deplorable end,
for which she would never forgive her. Mosby and his
sister were hanged in Smithfield, in London. As for
Mrs Arden, she was burned at Canterbury. Greene
was apprehended a year later; tried, condemned, and
hanged in chains in the highway between Ospringe
and Boughton, over against Faversham; Black Will
was burned on a scaffold at Flushing, in Zeeland.

This brings Holinshed's account to an end.

Alice's gang rape in prison I believe to be a real historical event, and the reason it has never featured in any account of the Arden murder is that the John Ponet book is completely unrelated to the events in Faversham, and it was only by reading Professor Lena Cowen Orlin's chapter on the Alice Arden rapes in her book, *Private Matters in Post-Reformation England*, that I discovered the reference. To me, it is a very credible piece of evidence that the rape occurred, as Ponet was in the right place at the right time and had the authority to know what was going on, and his chilling, almost dismissive, description of it as an aside adds to the credibility that he was describing a true event. He was very much a man of his time with the attitudes that go with that, which is why he didn't express outrage or sympathy towards Alice. Judicially approved rape of women prisoners, particularly those about to be executed, is suspected of having gone on at this time, but it was never officially sanctioned or recorded, which is why this is one of the rare examples of there being specific evidence for it. On March 23rd 1551, nine days after Alice's execution, Ponet was appointed Bishop of Winchester.

When Holinshed's account of the murder was published it caused a sensation, ensuring that the murder's notoriety was still very much alive in Shakespeare's time, forty years later. Sir Anthony Aucher was never investigated for his part in the Arden murder, but he was later accused of fraud and corruption and was forced to pay back some £4,500 to the crown in misappropriated funds. In 1556, his accounts as Keeper of the Jewel House were audited; he resigned the office and narrowly avoided imprisonment. Although primarily an administrator rather than a military man, he ended his days as Marshal of Calais, and died from wounds received when the French captured the town in January 1558. He is buried in St Mary's Church in Bishopbourne, Kent.

Alice's *ménage à trois* with Thomas and Mosby is described with unusual frankness by Holinshed, when he writes in his Chronicles:

> *Alice Arden contracted an unlawful familiarity with*
> *one Mosby, a black swarthy fellow. It happened by*
> *some means or other that they fell out, but she being*
> *desirous of a reconciliation, and to have her former*
> *familiarity with him, sent him a pair of silver dice*
> *by the hands of one Adam Fowle, living at the Fleur*
> *de Lis in Faversham, as a present. And after Mosby*
> *obtained such favour at her hands, he lay with her,*
> *abusing her body. And although (as it was said) Master*
> *Arden perceived right well their mutual familiarity, he*
> *was contented to wink at her filthy disorder, and both*
> *permitted and also invited Mosby very often to be in*
> *his house.*

Shakespeare explored Alice's feelings about the relationship with Mosby in her opening soliloquy in *Arden of Faversham*, Act I, Scene I, where she says:

> *Sweet Mosby is the man that hath my heart:*
> *And he usurps it, having nought but this,*
> *That I am tied to him by marriage.*
> *Love is a god, and marriage is but words;*
> *And therefore Mosby's title is the best.*
> *Tush! whether it be or no, he shall be mine.*

The silver dice Adam Fowle gave to Mosby on Alice's behalf almost proved to be Fowle's undoing, as, after the culprits were uncovered, Holinshed tells us this:

> *Adam Fowle was brought into trouble about this*
> *unhappy affair; he was carried up to London with*
> *his legs tied under a horse's belly, and committed to*
> *Marshalsea Prison. The chief grounds for this was*
> *Mosby's saying that if it had not been for Adam Fowle,*
> *he would not have been brought into trouble; but when*
> *the matter was thoroughly searched into, and Mosby*
> *had cleared Fowle of any manner of privity to the*
> *murder, Fowle was at length discharged.*

The description of Alice Arden being burned at the stake comes from an account in the Newgate Calendar, which in turn was based on eye-witness testimony. It took two hours for Alice's execution to be completed, as opposed to one hour for Elisabeth Stafford, suggesting that Alice's burning was deliberately extended to prolong her suffering.

John Foxe, in the 1563 edition of his *Acts and Monuments*, describes the persecution that Cole faced in Faversham after the Arden trial. His narrow escape from being murdered by Cyriak Pettit gives us some insight to the character of this brave and principled man.

> *The happy escape of Robert Cole, minister now of Bow in London, from the hands of Master Pettit, justice in Kent, being his mortal enemy, and one that sought his life. Who meeting him by chance, not far from Faversham in a lane so narrow that one of them must need to touch the other, yet so overcame the danger, that he was past and gone before the judge did know it was him, and so the said Cole escaped.*

> *And in speaking of such a person, I cannot but say something to his justly deserved commendation. In so dangerous a time, setting all things apart, not only his goods, ease and liberty, but also neglecting his own body and life, Robert Cole seemeth to me to be a sincere and faithful minister, worthy of honour in the church of Christ.*

Regarding the authorship of *Arden of Faversham*, Shakespeare scholars have used various techniques of statistical linguistic analysis to search systematically for plays that share particular groupings of words, for example pairings of words that occur within five words of each other. In the *Oxford Handbook of Tudor Drama*, published in 2012, Macdonald P. Jackson states that, of the 143 plays surviving from the period 1580–1600, twenty-eight share four or more phrases or significant word-pairings with scenes from *Arden of Faversham*. Seventeen of these twenty-eight plays are by Shakespeare, and all the ones that top the list are his early plays, making it highly likely that a young William Shakespeare was involved. In 2020, after five years of research, Professor Gary Taylor published a paper in the *Review of English Studies* which proved there was 'strong and consistent evidence' that Thomas Watson collaborated on the writing of *Arden of Faversham*. *The Guardian* newspaper reported these findings at the time, and the article can be found online.

All the plays of Thomas Watson are now lost. Although it is thought that he only wrote plays for a short time towards the end of his life, he must have been quite prolific, as his employer, William Cornwallis, commented that 'twenty fictions and knaves in a play was his daily practice and living'. The author, Francis Meres, wrote in 1598 that 'he was the best for tragedy', in a book that included the first reviews of Shakespeare's early plays. Watson died in 1592, shortly after *Arden of Faversham* was first performed by Pembroke's Men.

John Stow's *Survey of London* is still in print, and he is commemorated by a statue in the City of London. As narrated in the novel, he is shown sitting at his desk, writing with a quill pen, and the quill is replaced every few years in a ceremony to honour Stow's memory. Sir George Buck, English antiquarian, wrote around 1560:

> *Honest John Stow, who could not flatter and speak dishonestly, and who was a man very diligent and much inquisitive to uncover all things concerning the affairs or words or persons of princes. A good antiquary and diligent searcher of knowledge.*

I hope I've reflected that description of his character.

Bishop Grindal's letter to the Privy Council on 24th February, 1569 clearly shows the religious intolerance and suspicion of the time when he writes, after searching Stow's library:

John Stow hath a great sort of foolish books of old print and also a great sort of old written English chronicles, and also old fantastical popish books printed with many written in old English in parchment, all which we have been permitted to take inventory of. His books declare him to be a great favourer of papistry.

This was the traumatic experience that Stow gives Will as his reason for not publishing the truth about the Arden murder when he first discovered it.

There is no evidence that Shakespeare was involved in the commissioning of Stow's memorial statue or writing the inscription above it, but Stow's statue does bear a striking similarity to the figure of Shakespeare in his own memorial at Stratford-upon-Avon. Both statues are now thought to be the work of the same sculptor, Nicholas Johnson, with the Stratford monument believed to be commissioned by Shakespeare himself during his lifetime.

Robert Cole's church, St Mary le Bow, is still standing, but the original church burnt down in the Great Fire of London and all records of Cole's time there were lost.

Regarding Shakespeare's early days in Stratford, there is no contemporary record of the Thomas Lucy deer-poaching story having taken place, and many historians believe it not to be true, as there were no deer kept in Charlecote Park until after Shakespeare's death. Having said that, it does appear, on separate occasions, in later accounts of Shakespeare's life, such as in rough manuscript notes of a Gloucestershire clergyman, Richard Davies, who wrote in 1688:

> *Shakespeare was much given to all unluckiness in stealing venison and rabbits, particularly from Sir Thomas Lucy who at last made him fly his native county to his great advancement.*

The Shakespearean scholar, Samuel Schoenbaum, points out the Lucy family had been granted the rights to have a 'free warren' on their land by Henry VIII, allowing them to kill game such as rabbits, pheasants and deer in a stipulated area, and it might be this game that Shakespeare was accused of poaching.

The story is given further credence in the preface to *The Works of William Shakespeare*, Rowe (editor), Volume 1, 1709, where Rowe writes:

> *He had, by a misfortune common enough to young fellows, fallen into a frequent practice of poaching, more than once robbing a park that belonged to Sir Thomas Lucy of Charlecote, near Stratford. For this he was prosecuted by that gentleman, as he thought somewhat too severely; and in order to revenge that ill usage, he made a ballad upon him. It is said to have been very bitter, that it redoubled the prosecution against him to such a degree that he was obliged to leave his business and family in Warwickshire for some time, and shelter himself in London.*

The actual text of the Sir Thomas Lucy poem that I quote in the novel, which got Shakespeare into so much trouble, is thought by many to be a Victorian invention.

As to whether he left Stratford as a member of an acting troupe, again there is no documentary evidence that Shakespeare joined the Queen's Men when they visited Stratford. However, the timing and logistics all seem to fit. John Towne did kill William Knell in a drunken brawl in Thame, a few miles away, and the troupe would therefore have had an urgent need to find a new player. A report by the coroner of Thame in Oxfordshire, from June 13th, 1587 stated:

> *John Towne, late of Shoreditch, was in the White Hound in Thame when William Knell came, and had in his right hand a sword and jumped upon John Towne, intending to kill him. Towne, in fear to save his life, drew his sword of iron (price five shillings) and held it in his right hand and thrust it into the neck of William Knell and made a mortal wound three inches deep and one inch wide.*

Will's decision to leave Stratford any other way would have been both a momentous and a difficult one, as the Vagrancy Act made it illegal for an unattached man to travel outside of his home town. The act specifically excluded companies of players properly authorised by lords from being considered vagabonds, which is why they were given names like the Earl of Leicester's Men, Lord Strange's Men, etc. Unless he had established trading connections with another part of the country, there would have been almost no other way for Will to leave Stratford suddenly.

Perhaps the most compelling evidence that Will joined the Queen's Men to leave Stratford is that their repertoire consisted of *The Troublesome Reign of King John*, *The True Tragedy of Richard III*, *The Famous Victories of Henry the Fifth* and *King Leir*, all plays that Shakespeare would later write versions of under his own name. The similarities in text between his plays and the ones performed by the Queen's Men show he must have been familiar with them. The fact that he joined a troupe that had plays that needed to be rewritten for one fewer actor and, somewhat unusually, had a playwright in the shape of Dick Tarlton as one of its members to show Will the basics of playwriting, provides an explanation as to how a young Will Shakespeare, with no previous theatrical experience, could have learnt how to write a play.

The Theatre was located in Shoreditch in 1917 and the remains of it were found in 2008, with trial excavations in 2011 revealing the foundations of the Curtain 200 metres to the south. At the time of writing, the results of both excavations, led by the theatre archaeologist, Heather Knight, are being analysed. Now the excavation has finished, there are plans to open a Museum of Shakespeare on the site of the Curtain, bringing to life the story of a playhouse where Shakespeare learnt his craft.

Shakespeare's time in London before becoming famous occurred during his so-called 'lost years', when historians can find no documentary evidence of his activities in either Stratford or London, although the visit of Lord Strange's Men to Faversham in 1592 is documented in the Faversham wardmote book. The entry by the publisher Edward White in the Stationers' Register for the *Arden* play gives no clue as to the author of the play:

> *Edward White: Entered for his copy under the hands of the Lord Bishop of London and the wardens. The Tragedy of Arden of Faversham and Black Will. April 3 1592. Six pence a copy.*
>
> *Wardens: G. Allen, H. Conneway*

On the left of the entry are an asterisk and the initials 'G.S.', which were made by the 18th-century Shakespeare expert George Steevens, who marked entries in the Register he thought were works of Shakespeare, showing there was speculation that Shakespeare was the author of the play over 250 years ago.

There is similarly no indication of who the author was of the mysterious *A Cruel Murder Done in Kent*, also registered by Edward White.

> *Edward White: Received of Edward White for his license to imprint A Cruel Murder Done in Kent. Four pence a copy.*
>
> *Wardens: J. Gonneld, R. Watkins*

The story of 'Shakespeare's Boys' is a charming anecdote. It first appeared in print in 1753, 137 years after Shakespeare's death, in *The Lives of the Poets of Great Britain and Ireland*, written by Robert Shiels, who declared that when Shakespeare came to London, his first expedient was to wait at the door of the playhouse, and hold the horses of those that had no servants, that they might be ready again after the performance. Shiels wrote as follows:

In this office he became so conspicuous for his care and readiness, that in a short time every man, as he alighted, called for William Shakespeare, and scarcely any other waiter was trusted with a horse, while William Shakespeare could be had. This was the first dawn of better fortune. Shakespeare, finding more horses put into his hand than he could hold, hired boys to wait under his inspection, who, when William Shakespeare was summoned, were immediately to present themselves, 'I am Shakespeare's Boy, Sir.' In time Shakespeare found higher employment; but as long as the practice of riding to the playhouse continued, the waiters that held the horses retained the appellation of Shakespeare's Boys.

The provenance of the story dates back to Sir William Davenant, born in 1606, who was closely associated as a playwright with Shakespeare's former colleagues in the King's Men, the name that Shakespeare's company, the Lord Chamberlain's Men, took on when King James came to the throne, so Davenant comes across as a credible source. However, Shiels admits that Davenant told the story to a Mr Betterton, who communicated it to a Mr Rowe, who in turn told it to a Mr Pope. Mr Pope then told it to a Dr Newton, who told it to a gentleman that Shiels does not name, who then passed the story on to him to find its way into print. It may be, to coin a phrase, a tale that grew in the telling.

I have cited Peter Ackroyd and Ian Mortimer's books in the acknowledgements, but I must also make special mention of their research into the forensic analysis of the pen strokes on the few pages of Shakespeare's handwritten manuscripts that have survived, which I used to describe Shakespeare's frenetic writing style. John Hemings and Henry Condell provide an almost contemporaneous description of this in their introduction to the *First Folio* in 1623, when they write:

> *His mind and hand went together: And what he thought, he uttered with that easiness, that we have scarce received from him a blot in his papers.*

Ben Jonson also states the following in *Discoveries Made upon Men and Matter* in 1640, although it's not completely clear it's Shakespeare he's writing about:

> *When he hath set himself to writing, he would join night and day and press upon himself without release, not minding if he fainted.*

Not everyone was so enamoured. Robert Greene wrote in *Greene's Groats-Worth of Wit*:

> *There is now an upstart crow, beautified with our feathers, who supposes he is as well able to bombast out a blank verse as the best of us: and being a jack of all trades and master of none, he is, in his own conceit, the only Shake-scene in the country.*

This is very much in keeping with the character described in the novel. A rebuttal came from Will Kemp, who both praised Shakespeare and criticised Greene when he wrote:

> *Few of the 'University Wits' pen plays well, they smell too much of that writer Ovid, and that writer Metamorphoses, and talk too much of Proserpina and Jupiter. Why, here's our fellow Shakespeare, who puts them all down.*

Insights into Shakespeare's personality came from the cleric John Aubrey, in a 1679 manuscript where he has this to say:

> *The more to be admired is that he was not a company keeper, he lived in Shoreditch and would not be debauched, & if invited to, claimed gout and he was in pain.*

He also described Shakespeare, with remarkable prescience, in *Brief Lives*, 1680, thus:

> *Mr William Shakespeare was born at Stratford-upon-Avon in the County of Warwick. This William, being inclined naturally to poetry and acting, came to London: and was an actor at one of the playhouses, and did exceedingly well.*

> *He began early to make essays at dramatic poetry, which at that time was very low; and his plays took well. He was a handsome, well-shaped man: very good company, and of a very ready and pleasant smooth wit.*

Ben Jonson and he did gather humours of men daily where ever they came. He was wont to say that he never blotted out a line in his life. Said Ben Johnson, 'I wish he had blotted out a thousand.'

His comedies will remain as long as the English tongue is understood, for he handles well the ways of mankind. Now our present writers reflect so much on particular persons, that in twenty years hence they will not be understood.

Finally, we know that Shakespeare was in Faversham a few days before the death of his son, Hamnet, because of an entry in the Faversham wardmote book on August 2nd, 1596:

Paid to my Lord Hunsdon's players on Lammas Day, August 1st ... 16 Shillings.

Lord Hunsdon's Men was the name given to the company Shakespeare was a member of at that time, rather than the Lord Chamberlain's Men as they were more commonly referred to.

The bawdy poems that Shakespeare recites in the Greyhound in Stratford are based on the very sexually explicit poetry of Thomas Nashe. If you are not easily shocked, you can find more examples of these online. Nashe is widely believed to have collaborated with Shakespeare on the writing of the Henry VI plays, which Samuel Schoenbaum believes were the first plays Shakespeare wrote under his own name.

Stow did include a mention of the London playhouses in his 1598 *A Survey of London*, specifically mentioning the

Theatre, where Shakespeare performed, giving a veneer of respectability to what many of the time regarded as a debauched pursuit:

Sports and Pastimes of Old Times used in this City. In late time, there hath been played comedies, tragedies, interludes and histories, both true and feigned; for the acting whereof in public places, as the Theatre, have been erected.

However, later editions had this section deleted, causing me to speculate that Shakespeare did something to offend him.

Stow also wrote in the foreword to his 1605 edition of his *Annales of England*:

If God permit me life to publish or leave to posterity a far larger volume of my Summarie of Englyshe Chronicles, long since by me laboured, then, good reader, I desire thee to take heed of these old hidden histories and records which I have painfully (to my great cost and charges) brought to light.

However, Stow died before finishing this larger volume, so we will never know what were the 'old hidden histories and records' he desired the reader to take heed of, nor what he meant by the 'pain, great cost and charges' he said he would have to endure to have them published.

Stow's *Chronicles* was completed by Edmond Howes after Stow's death and published in 1615. On my last visit to the Doddington Parochial Library in Faversham to consult the wardmote book, when I finished I looked around at the many other old leather-bound books in the library. They didn't seem to be arranged in any sort of order, and the titles weren't written on the spines, so I had no idea what they were.

I picked one up at random, and to my astonishment I found it was the 1615 edition of Stow's *Chronicles*, a find made even more remarkable by the fact that there is no specific connection between the *Chronicles* and Faversham. I was able to take a photograph of the two books together, the wardmote book from the 1550s and Stow's *Chronicles* from 1615: the book that started off my story of Shakespeare writing *Arden of Faversham*, and the one that finished it, both over 400 years old.

Ben Jonson did fulfil his promise to Shakespeare that his plays would not be forgotten, writing the preface to the first edition of the *First Folio*, the printing of thirty-six of Shakespeare's plays, without which many of them would have been lost forever, just as Thomas Watson's have been. The *First Folio* was entered into the Stationers' Register on November 8 1623, 400 years ago to the day as I type these words.

The Fleur de Lis pub was behind the Ship Inn on Market Place at the time of the murder, but now is the name of the museum south of the marketplace in Preston Street. Arden House at 80 Abbey Street is privately owned, and, on a walking tour of Faversham in the summer of 2023, I had the chance to play the part of Black Will in a street performance of the murder scene in *Arden of Faversham* in Abbey Street, outside Thomas Arden's house where the actual murder took place. It remains a fond, if slightly surreal, moment in the writing of this book.

The Charters and Magna Carta Exhibition at the Faversham Visitor Information Centre has on display the town charter negotiated by Thomas Arden and signed by him, as well as the town's moot horn, which would have been blown to signify the start of the trial of Alice Arden and her accomplices. A facsimile of the page of the wardmote book, showing the date and payment made to the Hunsdon Men, the theatre troupe that Shakespeare was a part of when they visited Faversham, is also occasionally on display in the Fleur de Lis Museum in Preston Street.

The community physic garden that Alice visits is located in Abbey Place, around the corner from the Arden house, the same location as in the novel. For the last twenty-five years it has been providing companionship, therapeutic activities, training and skill building for people with mental health issues and those who are socially isolated.

The map of London showing the places mentioned in the novel is historically accurate, as is the Faversham one, except that I have speculated on the location of the homes of John Greene, William Blackbourne and the Norwell family, as well as the 17th-century physic garden and the Ospringe Road coldharbour.

The Arden murder has not only been made into a play, but also an opera, musical, ballet, puppet show, murder ballad, children's book, a contemporary play, *Ardy Fafirsin,* and even a previous novel, *Feversham* by Diane Davidson. There are many events each year in Faversham commemorating the murder and also Shakespeare's visits to the town. The Arden Theatre in Faversham is a thriving centre for the arts, and Shepard Neame, Britain's oldest brewery, continues Faversham's fine tradition of brewing excellent ales. The centre of the town is still very much as it was in Alice Arden's and Shakespeare's time; the market celebrated its 1000-year anniversary in May 2024 and claims to be the oldest street market in Kent. The distinctive timber pillars at the base of the town's Guildhall are what remain of the building's open arcade at the time of Shakespeare's visit. Then it was a market hall, with the old Guildhall where Shakespeare would have performed and where Alice's trial took place being in nearby Court Street.

Finally, I should stress again that I wrote this book as a work of fiction, nothing more, and although I have tried throughout the story to accurately reflect the historical facts, it should not be seen as a scholarly exploration of the Arden murder, nor the early life of Shakespeare. However, were the premise of this novel to be true, it would mean that Shakespeare's experience of having his first play banned led him to never writing another contemporary drama, so we have the historical, fantasy and comedy plays that we know today as a result.

GD Harper

www.gdharper.com